THE
GOLDEN
MISTRESS

BASIL BEYEA

Simon and Schuster
New York

DESIGNED BY IRVING PERKINS
MANUFACTURED IN THE UNITED STATES OF AMERICA

1 2 3 4 5 6 7 8 9 10

LIBRARY OF CONGRESS CATALOGING IN PUBLICATION DATA

BEYEA, BASIL.
THE GOLDEN MISTRESS.
I. JUMEL, ELIZA (BOWEN) 1775?–1865—FICTION.
I. TITLE.
PZ4.B5733GO [PS3552.E87] 813'.5'4 74-34589
ISBN 0-671-21995-2

To David Peter Birkett, M.D.,
with affection and respect

and

To the Memory of A. Flemish Macliesh (1911–1973)
—poet, novelist and dear friend

PART ONE

CHAPTER I

WHEN Joshua Burr rented the old gaol house in Providence, Rhode Island, to Margaret Fairchild, he asked no questions. He pocketed the silver quickly, thankful that he had been paid twenty-four dollars in hard money instead of the fourteen hundred Continental paper dollars he had expected.

He did not wonder how a freed slave like Margaret should happen to have such a sum so readily available, and in silver too, because her former owner had been Major Fairchild—that wealthy and, in his view, insane old man who had set free all his slaves in October of 1781 when the news came that Cornwallis had surrendered at Yorktown. Such madness, which some people called devotion to the principles of democracy, might well have included generous cash settlements on his favorite slaves, and Margaret looked to be the kind of thrifty, hard-working woman who would know the value of money and how to hold on to it.

It did not occur to Joshua to ask her what she had been doing in Newport during her four years of freedom since the Revolution. Such questions seemed foolish when the feel of silver against his palm gave him assurance that the old gaol, with its crumbling walls and dank interior, would at last bring him some revenue.

It was hardly a place where Joshua himself would want to live, and until now nobody else had wanted to live there, either. Freed slaves were no doubt less particular.

But Margaret Fairchild had no intention of making her home in the old gaol. For her, it offered certain geographical and architectural advantages as a place of business. It was near enough to the waterfront to be easily accessible to her customers, and yet far enough from Market Square and the center of town so that it would not attract undue attention. The arrangement of its rooms

9

was ideal for her purposes. At the rear of the building, the four cells that had once housed prisoners awaiting their appearance before the Town Council would serve admirably as quarters for her girls. The cells were small, but there was room enough for a cot in each one, and Margaret saw no need for any further furnishings, except possibly a curtain covering each doorway so that her customers could be entertained in privacy.

The large entrance room, where prisoners had once been charged with their infractions of the law, could now become a place where men would await pleasure instead of punishment. And while they waited, Margaret saw no reason why they could not be served rum—at an additional charge, of course.

And so, before Joshua Burr's slightly astonished eyes, the old gaol became the latest and most prosperous disorderly house in Providence. To an outraged citizenry, Joshua shrugged his shoulders innocently. The Fairchild woman had paid a year's rent in silver, her appearance had been highly respectable even for a Negress, and he had assumed she would live there quietly and alone. So far as he was concerned, a house of this sort at least had the virtue of keeping women of low repute off the streets.

The townspeople did not agree. Although the existence of such a place was no more unusual to them than it was to the citizens of any port town in the thirteen coastal states, this one violated their sense of the fitness of things. That these particular disorderly goings on were taking place in their old gaol, which had been built to curb wrongdoing, not encourage it, was a flagrant affront to the town's whole moral structure. And so, on a warm evening in July, they took action.

Business had been exceptionally good in the old gaol that day. *The Golden Plover,* with a full cargo of molasses from the West Indies, had docked that afternoon in the Providence River. The port was already lined with ships, and the streets swarmed with sailors in search of pleasure. By nightfall, many of them had found their way to the old gaol. In various stages of drunkenness, they crowded into the large entrance room and waited their turn to visit the women in the cells at the rear of the building. They sat in whatever broken-down chairs were available. They sprawled full-length on the floor. They passed the time in drinking and in telling long-winded, bumbling stories of their achievements, both heroic and amatory. They lied and they argued. Some slept.

Margaret Fairchild sat primly in a straight-backed chair near the entrance. Deaf to the noise that filled the room, she gave all her attention to the red sweater that she was knitting. Only when a new customer appeared at the door did she raise her eyes and become part of her surroundings. Then, setting the sweater aside for the moment, she prepared to bargain. Solemn and dignified, she quoted prices and received payment, sometimes in silver or paper currency, often in barter. A bottle of Madeira or West Indies rum, or a bolt of calico or silk, could be worth more than money.

Margaret did not think of her profession as disreputable. It seemed in her own eyes as much a necessity as Mr. Weeden's bakery down on Mill Street and therefore just as respectable. She neither looked nor behaved like a bawd. Her matronly figure was always neatly dressed, her crisp black hair tidily covered by a clean kerchief knotted at the back of her head. She did not drink, use foul language, or carouse with her customers.

She had learned that aloofness and a quiet firmness of voice could usually control the brawling and violence that she feared above all things. Quarrelsome customers were calmly shown the door with the suggestion that they settle their differences outside.

She did not even mingle with the men to the extent of serving them drinks. In a far corner of the room, there was a battered oaken table on which there were bottles of rum, a random assortment of grimy pewter mugs and chipped glasses, and a cracked earthenware pitcher of water. Underneath the table two small girls sat on the floor and quietly played with their cornhusk dolls.

Like Margaret, they seemed oblivious to the uproar that swirled around them. Only the banging of a pewter mug on the stone floor had the power to intrude on their world of make-believe. Then, like small trained dogs responding to a whistle, they would abruptly leave their play and come to attention. The younger one, who was about ten, would trot dutifully over to the thirsty customer to get his mug, while her sister took up a position at the side of the table, a bottle of rum in hand.

When the mug had been refilled, the younger child would carry it back to the customer, holding it carefully with both hands. As she offered it to him, she would curtsy with great solemnity, while her face lighted up in a smile that was astonishingly warm and intimate. Dimples made an unexpected appearance, her eyes twinkled, and the effect on the most unsociable customer was usually immediate.

"You're a bonny lass," he might say. "What's your name?"

The reply was always gravely proud. "Miss Eliza Bowen. But you can call me Betsy." The faint underlining of the *you* with its implied compliment usually elicited a penny, and sometimes more than one. The more the better, since the pennies had to be shared with her sister, Polly.

If no pennies at all were forthcoming, Betsy would stand there, unmoving, and the smile would be turned on again, more radiant than before, the dimples deeper. The large, lustrous eyes that were of a strange violet color would fix themselves with unwavering intensity on the eyes of the ungenerous drinker. Then she would toss her head gently but with spirit, so that the mass of red-gold curls bounced back from her forehead.

"Sir," she would say softly, "bean't you forgettin' something?"

Sometimes the response to her coquetry was more ardent than she had counted on, and a large hairy hand would reach out and squeeze one of her plump little buttocks. When this happened, she would step swiftly backward with a dancer's grace, and still smiling, still dimpling, she would say in measured tones, "Sir, now you owes me a sixpence!"

If there were other men in the room when this happened, Betsy knew exactly what would follow, and like an actress she would wait for the roar of laughter and approval. With an assured and knowing smile, she would wait while the men forced the pinch-fisted sailor to pay up.

There were times when the situation would turn ugly, and a man might fumble in her skirts in an attempt to get fuller value for his pennies. Then, she had learned that she could not be sure that the others would come to her rescue. They might even urge the attacker on.

When that happened, she knew that Margaret Fairchild, anxious to avoid trouble at all costs, would not even look up from her knitting. There was only one thing to do and that was to scream just as loudly as she could, "Black Bets! Black Bets! Help me!"

Almost immediately a mammoth black female figure would appear in the doorway that led to the cells. Sometimes half-dressed, sometimes mother-naked, Black Bets would stand there menacingly, her huge ebony body with its great pendulous breasts glistening with sweat in the candlelight. In her ham of a right hand there was the reassuring shine of the knife that she kept close to her for occasions like this.

The angry roar that would suddenly rise in that soft throat was that of a tigress defending its young, and it was more terrifying than the weapon she carried. "Take your dirty hand offen that chile or I cuts your rotten doodle right outen you and nails it over the door for good luck!"

No customer, however big and blustering, however drunk, had ever dared to put Black Bets to the test. On the streets of the port she might be jeered at, sometimes even stoned so that she had to run for cover, followed by cries of "Nigger bitch! Nigger whore-bitch!" ringing in her ears. But here, in this damp, evil-smelling old gaol, she was an almighty dusky empress, more powerful than Margaret herself. She made her own laws and enforced them with a bread knife.

Only when Betsy had been released by her attacker would Black Bets lower her weapon. Then she would look fiercely at the suddenly sheepish faces of the men in the room, and shaking her left fist at them, she would say, "Now you bums listen at me and listen good! These here is Phebe Bowen's young 'uns, and there ain't nobody a-goin' to tetch 'em till they *ready!* So keep your hands off and ask the Lawd for patience. You's all gettin' to pleasure yourselves just as soon as may be."

Then, with a final brandishing of the knife by way of farewell, she would add, " 'Cause iffen you don't, you won't have no use for womans ever again in your life!"

After Black Bets had left, the room would be unnaturally quiet. But not for long. The rum soon warmed in the men again, and the glow of anticipated pleasure made them talkative and expansive. When a sailor would stumble blindly from one of the cells, still buttoning his trousers, one of the waiting men would sometimes stop him before he left and ask, "Who was you with?"

13

Then the sailor might mumble the name of the woman he had left: Phebe, or Debbie, or Esther, or Black Bets herself. But the regular patrons had grown to know the women well in the seven months that the old gaol had carried on its flourishing business.

Most popular, because she was white, pretty and still young, was Phebe Bowen, the mother of Betsy and Polly. Next in demand was Esther, a shy and gentle mulatto girl of eighteen. Then there was Debbie, white but almost forty, a favorite with the men who liked their women boisterous, foul-tongued, and athletically amorous. And last, there was Black Bets, whose velvet-skinned dark flesh could enfold a man like a mother, who could be pliant and yielding when she was not goaded to anger by violence.

But on this midsummer evening there was no violence. Margaret knitted quietly in her chair by the door. Betsy and Polly played with their dolls under the table when they were not serving rum to the customers. The men, mostly sailors from the ships in port, paid, waited, and after perfunctory visits to the women in the cells, left.

Suddenly, the door burst open, and a boy of fourteen ran into the room, sweating and out of breath from running. He looked about him wildly and then came to an embarrassed halt as the eyes of the men turned toward him curiously.

Polly scrambled out from under the table and went over to him. "Get out of here, John Thomas!" she said. "Mama told you never to come to this place, and you know it!"

"But they're comin' here!" the boy shouted. "They got torches and axes! They're goin' to burn the place down and kill everybody!"

A sea captain who sat near the door took his pipe from his mouth and spat. "What you talkin' about, boy? Who's got torches and axes?"

"Everybody! Why, the whole town is comin' up here, and they're good and mad too! Sam Allen roused 'em up and said the tents of wickedness has got to be pulled down!"

The room had become quiet, and in the silence, shouting voices from the direction of the river could be heard. As the voices grew louder, the men looked at one another uneasily and stirred in their chairs. Finally some got up and went over to Margaret, who had abandoned her knitting and stood tense and listening at the door.

A young sailor faced her belligerently. "We got to get out of here, nigger woman. Give us back our money and our barter."

Margaret did not argue with him. She knew what was going to happen. It had already happened to her last year in Newport. And so, as the men began lining up before her, she amiably returned whatever payments they had made. At least the money and barter goods would not fall into the greedy hands of Bobby Brown, the town sergeant.

The sea captain was the last to leave, pausing in the open doorway and looking toward the river. He could see the flaring torches that were moving slowly up Towne Street. The voices were louder now, chanting in an angry chorus. He looked back into the room at the three children who stood huddled near the table. Their faces were white and terror-stricken.

"I'd better get your ma," he said, and went through the doorway that led to the cells.

The women waited. Dressed now, they sat in the chairs left vacant by their customers. They would have fled along with them, but they had no place to go. Like Margaret, they had all been taken into custody before, but this was the first time that they had been threatened with violence, and they were apprehensive.

Phebe Bowen sat in a chair with her children gathered around her. She was outwardly calm, her doll-like Irish face set in a fixedly cheerful expression, the corners of her small mouth turned up in a stiff smile that was meant to be reassuring.

"Betsy," she said, "be a good girl and get Mama a mug of rum." Then she turned to her son. Her face assumed a look of maternal sternness that seemed alien to the round softness of its pale features. "John Thomas, I want for you to get out of this place real quick. Go out the back door."

"I ain't goin' to leave you, Mama," said the boy, struggling to keep the fear out of his voice. He stood with his legs thrust apart in a stance of defiance, his chest puffed out like a small pigeon's.

Phebe turned her eyes quickly away from him, fearful that she might cry. Her voice became harsh as she said, "You got no business here, boy. I can look out for meself and the girls. I want for you to leave—you hear me?"

15

The boy shook his head. "I ain't goin' to."

Betsy returned with a full mug of rum. She carried it carefully in both hands as though it were something precious. It was a kind of medicine that always made her mother feel better, and she knew that her mother needed it now.

"Thanks, lovey," Phebe said, taking a great gulp. She blew out her breath and shivered, then turned again to John Thomas and said mildly, "You still workin' as 'prentice to Asa Hopkins, son?"

"Yes, ma'am."

"Is he good to you?"

"Yes, ma'am."

"Well, now, if you want to stay with him, you better not get caught in this place. We'll all be put in the lockup."

John Thomas seemed relieved. "You won't be killed or hurted?"

Phebe's laughter sounded almost genuine. "Why, son, they never *kills* women like us. The menfolk will soon be wantin' our company again—even the highborn gentlemen. So they don't kill us. They just puts us away in gaol, savin' us for a rainy day!" She giggled at her feeble joke and gave John Thomas a playful push.

"But, Mama, I don't want to leave you—"

Phebe interrupted him angrily. "Don't be a dunce! If you stay, you'll lose your work with Asa Hopkins and turn into a no-good bastid like your father was! So get out!"

The sound of the mob was louder now, but the boy still made no move to leave. Phebe got up from her chair and strode to the fireplace. She seized the poker in her hand and waved it threateningly at him.

"Now, you git!" she screamed. "Out the back door and over to Olney Lane, and don't you stop runnin' till you're home!"

John Thomas, who had learned to respect his mother's temper, gave up arguing and fled. After he had gone, Phebe tossed the poker into the fireplace and went back to her chair. She sighed, sat down, and took another pull at the mug of rum. Abruptly then, she doubled up and began to cry. It was a hard, convulsive crying that sounded not too different from laughter.

Betsy and Polly laced their arms over her back and tried to comfort her. Betsy leaned toward her and kissed her ear.

"Mama," she said, "we don't mind goin' to gaol, long as we be

16

with you. But why don't we all run away—just like John Thomas?"

Phebe looked at the child's calm, earnest face, and her soggy eyes lighted with amusement. "Betsy, lovey, don't nothin' scare you?"

"Oh, I'm scared right enough. Only why don't we get out of here and run?"

"Because we ain't got no place to run to. Now don't you fret yourself. They won't be hurtin' us, not when they see you and Polly—me own pretty ones. Ain't that so, Bets?"

Black Bets smiled reassuringly at the girls. "Now why in the sweet Jesus' name will they be hurtin' you when they got my ole black hide to whup? They likes to whup black skins."

"I won't let em!" cried Betsy, making a fist. "I'll spit right in their faces!"

Black Bets laughed and hugged Betsy to her. "Ole Bets don't mind a whuppin'. Ole hide gettin' tough now. It don't hurt much no more."

When the mob reached the door, the men became ominously silent, as though awaiting a heavenly signal to begin their work of avenging the Lord. The women in the room sat stiffly expectant in their chairs, their eyes downcast, their shoulders hunched forward in resignation.

Then, in the silence, the clear, reedlike voice of Sam Allen rang out. "Open up! Open up in the name of Almighty God!"

Suddenly, there was the shattering sound of splintered wood as an ax crashed into the solid oak door. Phebe got up and moved toward it. She waited, and the ax drove into the door again. Quickly, then, she drew back the bolt, swung the door open, and stepped back.

Sam Allen stood there in the flickering light from the torches. He was a tall, lean man of about forty. His face, with its high forehead and prominent cheekbones, had a gaunt, ascetic look that the intense blue eyes gazing out remotely somehow accentuated. But there was nothing ascetic about his mouth. The red fullness of his sensual lips contrasted sharply with the pale, tight-drawn skin of his face.

Phebe stared at him ingenuously, as though she were a virtuous housewife rudely awakened from sleep. "What is it you want?" she asked.

Sam Allen, momentarily taken off guard by her calmly respectable manner, found himself speechless. The other men crowded up behind him, their eyes thirsty for scenes of orgy and licentious riot. What they saw were five tired women, poorly dressed but clean, and two little girls with angelic faces.

Sam breathed deeply, as though to rekindle his inner fires of moral indignation. In the low, intoning voice of a preacher, he said, "This is a house of sin and wantonness—"

" 'Tis the old gaol," said Phebe simply.

"It is in truth a gaol, ma'am—a gaol for the souls of depraved women such as you. It is a canker on the face of our town, and God wills that we cut it out before it spreads!" He turned to one of the men behind him. "Sergeant! Arrest these unfortunate women!"

Bobby Brown, the town sergeant, strutted into the room, his buttocks reared out pompously behind him. When the women rose as if in greeting, he came to a clumsy halt, his jauntiness gone, and looked at them sheepishly. Bobby Brown had lain with all of them, and now his beady eyes lingered nostalgically on the buxom figure of Debbie, who with hands on hips and feet apart was returning his stare. In a mocking, contemptuous voice, she said, "Hello, Bobby Brown. Ain't seen *you* in two weeks. Did your thing fall off?"

The sergeant's blow caught her full on the jaw, and she went sprawling to the stone floor. Suddenly, Betsy was beside him. With all the strength she could muster, she kicked him hard on the left shin. When he stooped in pain, she spat in his face. Enraged, he sought to grab her, but she ran from him.

All at once, the crowd surged into the room, furious and violent. They grappled with the women and dragged them, fighting and shrieking, out into the night. Betsy and Polly froze in terror as two men seized their mother and shoved her toward the door. Then, like wild creatures whose nest has been attacked, they began to scream.

As Sam Allen looked at the howling children his face softened. Swiftly, he crossed the room and drew them protectively toward him. "Innocent children of God in the house of Satan," he muttered.

"Yes, sir," said Betsy. She looked up at him plaintively. "Oh, please don't let them hurt my mama!"

Sam was touched by the appeal in her small, upturned face. "Your mother will be dealt with justly and fairly," he said.

"She won't be hurted?"

"The men are rough, child, but they will not harm her."

His voice was reassuring and kindly, and Betsy seized his hand in hers and leaned her small body against his leg. Sam moved away uneasily and looked down at her with suspicious eyes.

"And have you been corrupted by the men, my child?" he asked.

The word was new to her. "Corrupted?"

Sam stumbled for words. "Have they—have they taken you to bed?"

"Oh, you mean was we fucked?" she said. "Oh, no, sir. Black Bets took care of us. She said we wasn't ready yet."

The casual bluntness of her words, spoken so innocently in her childish treble, rendered Sam momentarily speechless.

"At least," he said finally, "it is only your tongue that has become tainted. God is indeed merciful."

"Yes, sir. But there ain't nothin' wrong with my tongue, sir." She stuck it out at him to prove that it was indeed sound and healthy.

Meanwhile, the men had begun their work of demolishing the decrepit and rotting old building. The noise of their axes was earsplitting. Sam took both girls by the hand and moved toward the door. Polly, stunned and frightened by the din, went willingly, but Betsy planted her bare feet on the stone floor and balked.

"Where are you takin' us?" she shouted.

"To a place where you will be safe. They aim to burn this building down. Come along, now!"

Betsy still refused to move. "Are you takin' us to our mother?"

"No. Your mother is going to gaol."

"Then I want to go to gaol, too," she said.

Sam looked at the pathetically defiant little figure in exasperation. Then, without further words, he swooped her up in his arms and carried her, kicking and biting, out the door. Polly followed, skittish and wary as a terrified cat.

The sudden darkness outside seemed to have a quieting effect on Betsy. She gave up protesting, sighed, and finally leaned her head against Sam's bony chest.

Circling his neck with one of her arms, she said, "Please, sir, I hope you won't try to do it to us. Black Bets says—"

Sam put his hand across her mouth. "I know what Black Bets says, my child. No harm will come to you, so be quiet now."

He could feel her arm tightening around his neck, her dirty, tousled hair brushing lightly against his face. All at once he felt overwhelmed with pity and a great sadness. In silence, as he stumbled through the darkness with the child in his arms, he began to pray. He asked God to cleanse and protect this young soul, this lily he had found growing on a dunghill.

Betsy snuggled herself more closely against him. "You're what my mama calls a kind gentleman," she murmured.

"I am a Christian," said Sam.

"What's that?" asked Betsy.

"Hush!" he said, because he did not know how to answer her. It had never occurred to him that anyone, however young, might not know what a Christian was. He did not know how to talk to children, anyway. He had none of his own, and the children of his friends and neighbors were certainly not like this child. They were clean and properly dressed. They were meek in manner, obedient, and very polite. And they did not use obscene words and ask what a Christian was.

For that matter, he had never carried a child in his arms before. It made him feel strangely tender and somehow ill at ease. And yet, it was pleasant, and he felt that the Lord would approve of what he was doing. Indeed, as he found himself thinking that the Lord had sent him forth this evening not only to uproot evil but to rescue the fallen, he was filled with warmth and benevolence toward all human creatures. He held Betsy more closely to him, his fingers closing over her small grimy hand.

Betsy raised her head and brushed the lobe of Sam's ear with her lips—the careless, spontaneous kiss of a child answering love with love. And Sam's eyes filled with sudden and altogether unexpected tears.

CHAPTER 2

T HE late-afternoon sun of a hot July day poured through the high windows of the State House. The doors that faced toward the Great Salt Cove had been left open, but the air hung quiet and sultry over Towne Street, and no breeze came west from the port to relieve the stifling heat of the large room where the Town Council sat in session.

Sam Allen sat alone on a long wooden bench and quietly watched the proceedings. During the two days that had passed since the night he had delivered Phebe's children to the workhouse, he had been haunted by Betsy's tear-stained, angry face. He still heard her cry of desolation when she realized that he was leaving her there and not taking her with him. Unreasonably, he felt that he had somehow betrayed her. It was in vain that he told himself that she was just another one of those unfortunate children who grew like weeds in the North End, that he was powerless to help her except by remembering her in his prayers.

But that was not altogether true. He could, of course, arrange with the Town Council to have her bound out to him, take her into his household, and eventually even adopt her. However, this seemed altogether too great a responsibility to assume merely because he was touched by the plight of an unhappy child.

And then, the night before, his duty had been made plain to him while he slept. He had dreamed that he was sitting in the sparsely furnished one-room building that had served as the Baptist meetinghouse in the years before the new and splendid church had been built on Towne Street. His father was standing by the lectern at the far end of the room, pausing, as Sam had seen him do times without number, to gather force before launching into his sermon.

No congregation filled the roughhewn pews. Sam was alone, and his father talked to him directly. His voice, stern and commanding, carried that tone of utter conviction that Sam knew so well. It brooked no argument. Only once in his life had Sam dared to lift his own voice in opposition—on that terrible and historic day when he had announced that he could not and would not continue with his education for the ministry. His father had stormed and raged, but Sam had clung stubbornly to his decision. He told his father that he wanted to sail the sea in ships because it was what he loved. Moreover, he felt that he was unworthy of the ministry because of an incorrigibly sinful nature.

His father, until the day he had quietly and unexpectedly died some fifteen years later, had never become reconciled to Sam's wicked abandonment of man's highest profession, and he never let Sam forget it. With his dying breath he had prayed that his son would sell the ship that he had only recently managed to buy and take up again the holy path on which his feet had been set.

Even then, Sam had not changed his mind, but he lived with a sense of guilt and sinfulness from which he was never entirely free, even when God saw fit to let him prosper as a shipowner engaged in trade. He might have been even more successful if he had permitted his ships to engage in the slave trade that was still making shipowners the richest men in New England. But Sam's father had called the triangle of slaves, molasses, and rum a wicked and barbarous business, and Sam, as a concession to his memory, would not allow his ships to take part in it.

And now, as he sat here on a hard bench in the old meetinghouse, his father had come back from the dead to counsel and guide him.

"Am I my brother's keeper?" the old man thundered at him. "My son, my son! Of all the questions that man has asked his God, surely it is the most heartless and shameful!"

Sam, alone among the empty pews, listened with bowed head as his father continued.

"Now, hear me and heed my word, my son! Take up this miserable child as though she were thine own! Redeem her soul for the greater glory of God! Then, at last, will I know that you have not given yourself completely to Mammon, and you may begin to atone for your willful abandonment of a life as one of the Lord's anointed!"

On this hot afternoon in the State House, it seemed to Sam that the dream was now repeating itself in reality. Again, he found himself sitting on a hard bench in a large room, alone and listening. It gave him an odd feeling of reliving an event that had already happened, and this served somehow to strengthen his belief that his father had indeed counseled him from beyond the grave.

But now the voice he was hearing was not his father's. It belonged to the Town Council's clerk, who for almost two hours had been droning forth his monotonous catalogue of human misbehavior, interrupted from time to time by the Council's judgments and penalties, issued mechanically, like responses to a dismal litany.

When the complaint against Margaret Fairchild was finally brought up for consideration, Sam looked studiously at the five women prisoners who were led before the raised platform where the Council sat in judgment. Their heads were bowed, he thought, not so much in repentance as in exhaustion. They were disheveled and dirty after two days in gaol, and as the clerk began to read, they waited, sweating and uneasy: Black Bets, sagging like a huge sack of spilling grain; Debbie, her feet planted apart in a last gesture of defiance; Esther, shifting the weight of her thin young body nervously from one foot to the other; and Phebe, pale and unsubstantial as a ghost, hands clasped before her, eyes downcast, like a small girl being scolded for her naughtiness.

Only Margaret Fairchild seemed unconcerned. Neither the heat nor the charges against her seemed to oppress her. She had dressed neatly for her appearance before the law and now turned blankly impassive eyes toward her accusers. Even the mention of her name had no visible effect on the placid features of her broad face.

"Said Margaret Bowler, alias Margaret Fairchild," the singsong voice of the clerk intoned, "being brought before the Council for examination respecting the place of her last lawful settlement, saith that she was the servant of Major Fairchild, who verbally gave her her freedom in 1781; that she has since lived and kept house in Newport; that she hired the old gaol house of Mr. Joshua Burr on January seventh of this year of our Lord and paid him twenty-four dollars in silver in rent for one year."

The clerk took a deep breath and went on. "When the house was pulled down by the mob on Monday night last, there were with her, lodging in the house, Phebe Bowen, alias Kelly, and her two daughters, Polly, aged twelve, and Betsy, aged ten; and another white woman called Debbie, believed to be of Taunton; a Negro woman known only as Black Bets and belonging to Sandwich; and a mulatto girl of about eighteen called Esther, late of Smithfield. Said Margaret Bowler, alias Margaret Fairchild, did keep and maintain from January of this year until Monday night last a disorderly house frequented by sailors and disreputable men of this town."

Colonel Amos Atwell, head of the Council, stirred from his dozing and opened his acute blue eyes. "Not men of this town, sir. We do not harbor disreputable men. Amend the wording to 'disreputable men of other parts.' Proceed."

The other councilmen stirred in their chairs, nodding unenthusiastic assent to the correction. In the brief quiet that followed, they sniffed, cleared their throats, and suppressed yawns. Aware that the hearings were almost over, they sat up expectantly, happy at the prospect of escaping from the stifling room and the sight of the bedraggled, ill-smelling women who stood before them.

Sam Allen listened with nervous impatience while disposition of the case was made. Margaret was to be conveniently shipped back to Newport; Debbie to be returned immediately to Taunton, accompanied by Phebe, who seemed to have no known residence except Providence; Esther to her home in Smithfield, where her natural mother, being white, might lead her to a more moral way of life; and Black Bets back to Sandwich.

To the councilmen's disappointment, the meeting did not immediately adjourn. Colonel Atwell turned to them and said, "The children of Phebe Bowen, alias Kelly, are lodged in the workhouse, in which place they will remain unless suitable accommodation can be found for them with a reputable family."

Sam Allen leaned forward intently as Colonel Atwell continued.

"God grant that they may still be innocent of their mother's sinful activities and that they may in God's future be guided by virtuous tutelage toward a path of rectitude and salvation."

As Phebe raised her head slowly her eyes met those of the Colonel. Tears began to trickle down her pale cheeks and her hands twisted against each other convulsively. When she spoke, her voice was a hoarse and shaking whisper.

24

"If it please you, sir—you ain't takin' me daughters away for good and all, are you?"

Colonel Atwell looked at the frail figure not unkindly, but his voice was coldly judgmental. "The Council finds you an unfit mother, and most especially for daughters now approaching an age of—ah—sinful possibilities."

Phebe's body stiffened in anger. Her voice rang shrilly in the room. "You think I'd be puttin' me own daughters to work as whores? Not if I was starvin' and dyin'! I make a livin' how I can with men what follows the sea. Call me a whore if you've a mind to. But me daughters, sir—they will be ladies, great rich ladies, not a poor slut like me!" She paused, and her voice now became soft and pleading. "Please, sir, I beg you—don't take 'em away from me!"

She began to cry bitterly. The Colonel looked at her with Christian pity, while the other councilmen shifted in their chairs and averted their eyes from the hysterically sobbing woman. A display of such unrestrained emotion made them uncomfortable. Somehow, it seemed not quite decent.

Black Bets moved quickly to Phebe and enfolding her in her arms pressed Phebe's contorted wet face against her bosom and patted her on the shoulder. Her eyes blazed furiously in the direction of the Colonel, as though to shame him.

At last, when Phebe's sobs had subsided, the Colonel spoke. "I am sure, Mrs. Bowen, that your intentions are of the best, but the company you habitually keep is not. You have appeared before this Council in the past, and for the same offenses against the public morality. I will not condemn you, for I am mindful of our Lord's charity to the woman Magdalene. What the Council does is for the good of your daughters, to separate them from the rude company of coarse and licentious men, the inevitable partners of your—ah—business enterprise."

Colonel Atwell rose from his seat authoritatively and looked at the other members of the Council. "If there be no further business—"

"Colonel Atwell—if it please you, sir!" Sam had risen quickly from his seat and now stood before the platform, his lithe, tall body drawn to full military attention.

25

"Sam Allen," said the Colonel, "is there something you wish to tell the Council?"

Sam's gaze moved nervously along the row of councilmen, who were looking at him with a mixture of curiosity and annoyance.

"Good sirs, I have talked with Nathaniel Thompson, the overseer of the poor. Mrs. Allen and I wish to take into our custody the younger daughter of this unfortunate woman. God has not seen fit to grant us a child of our own, and we would welcome the child Betsy in our home, there to teach and instruct her in Christian ways."

Colonel Atwell nodded approvingly. "And the other child? You will take her, too?"

"Alas, not," said Sam. "But my friend and neighbor Henry Wyatt will undertake the care of the child Polly."

The Colonel turned again toward Phebe, who was looking at Sam with a fixed and suspicious stare of appraisal.

"Mrs. Bowen, you may put your fears to rest. Your daughters will be well cared for—well fed, well dressed, well reared—"

Sam turned his penetrating blue eyes toward her, and said, after a pause, "They will be well loved, ma'am. Mr. Wyatt has only sons and will welcome a daughter in his household. And I—" Sam looked down in embarrassment. "And I—I have no children at all. Betsy will receive whatever love I—that is, Mrs. Allen and I—have to offer."

That, Phebe thought to herself, might not be much. To her, Sam looked like a preacher, with his thin, pale face and his austere air of a Baptist or a Congregationalist. Phebe distrusted all preachers, and as for Baptists and Congregationalists, experience had taught her that they could be more wanton in bed than a sailor in port after four months at sea.

But Phebe said nothing. She shrugged her shoulders, sighed, and accepted the inevitable, thankful that at least her children would not spend their childhood in the workhouse picking oakum.

CHAPTER 3

L YDIA Allen was a thin, nervous woman whose face habitually wore a sweet expression of pain endlessly but bravely endured for the greater glory of God. Like a pale household wraith, she went about her chores in the Allen house on Benefit Street, sweeping, scouring, and polishing from early morning until late afternoon on all days except the Sabbath, when, like Jehovah, she rested.

She was helped by Nellie Forman, a strapping, homely, and mindless drudge who could manage the tasks that were too strenuous for Lydia's own frail, middle-aged body. But she did all the cooking herself. The food she prepared though wholesome was altogether tasteless—boiled, usually, in pots of a scrupulous cleanliness. No spice or herb, not even pepper, sullied the purity of the dishes she placed before her husband. It was well known that such condiments served only to inflame the passions. Salt, since it had Biblical sanction, was permitted.

At four in the afternoon Lydia retired to the sterile sanctuary of her white bedroom. Until Sam returned from his shipping office near the wharves at India Point, she dozed serenely on her hard narrow bed and relived in chaste dreams scenes from her placid and uneventful childhood. Mama and Papa, long dead of a plague that had swept through the town in the summer of her eleventh year, lived once again, and life was happy and good.

For Lydia, a life that was happy and good was like existence aboard a sailing ship that lay in becalmed waters, where no winds came to ruffle the placid monotony of things, where no movement took place in any direction. Consequently, the early years of her marriage, before Sam had learned to control his passions, had made her acutely miserable.

The approach of nightfall had filled her with a daily dread of that moment when she and Sam would lie down in their four-poster bed to sleep. Then, no matter what the season, Sam might turn toward her and move his hands lustfully over her small breasts that grew taut with fear instead of pleasure. It could happen on warm midsummer eves as well as during the long, cold nights of deep winter, and in spring, oh, always in spring.

So far as she was concerned, Adam's sin had been exclusively Adam's own and remained a sin, even when sanctified by marriage vows. Certainly, she could not imagine how Eve had ever been tempted to commit a transgression that was so thoroughly unenjoyable, that took place in an orgy of sweat and frantic, undignified squirmings.

She was thankful when Sam at long last had finally conquered the temptations of the flesh—a victory greatly assisted by her own strategic retreat to a room of her own. But this action brought with it a feeling of sinfulness on her own part. On certain nights, a phrase from the Scriptures would echo accusingly in her ears: the Lord's admonition to be fruitful and multiply. Finally, tormented and unable to sleep, she would rise from the coolness of her virginal bed and go to Sam's room. She would lie down at his side and wait, silently and sacrificially offering her body to him in the interests of populating God's earth.

Afterward, sobbing and feverish, she would return to her room and fall to her knees in prayer, saying, "For your sake, dear God, I have endured these indignities upon my body." She felt ravished and violated, as indeed she had been. Sam, for the moment released from his enforced continence by God's and Lydia's consent, would become for a few mad-struck moments a tiger consuming its prey, voracious and insatiable.

The next morning, Lydia would not appear at breakfast, nor at several meals following. While Nellie continued with the cleaning and scrubbing, Lydia lay on her bed, weeping and ill. In the evenings during her convalescence, she would be visited by Sam, slow-moving, penitent, in a deep melancholy. Eventually, his soothing apologies would restore her to health.

Then, the waiting for God's miracle of newly created life would begin. There would be hopes, even prayers that their mutual sin might be crowned with fruitfulness. But life had never stirred in

Lydia's unreceptive womb. As year succeeded year, it became evident that she was barren, that after all, God had not chosen her to perpetuate His creation. Lydia's relief at being released from this disagreeable duty to make shuddering pilgrimages to Sam's room at midnight was immense.

Sam had been equally relieved. Presented with the clear impossibility of having children, it was no longer necessary for him to go through the tortures of self-loathing that followed the lust that ravaged him whenever Lydia obeyed God's orders to be fruitful and suddenly appeared at the door of his bedroom.

He was finally able to achieve, during his waking hours, at least, complete control over the demands of his flesh. He worked hard, ate sparingly, and devoted his leisure hours to religious contemplation. He labored to redeem not only himself but the pitiable sinners he saw around him. As time went on, the tranquil blue of his eyes took on a burning intensity, and people said that Sam Allen no longer looked at you, he looked through you.

Sam's dreams, unlike Lydia's, were not of happy childhood things. Although they might begin innocently enough, they magically and perversely changed from a placid daylight scene into a sudden night of licentiousness during which he possessed women of all kinds and of all ages.

Sometimes it might be the Reverend Arnold's prim but buxom wife, whom he would find inexplicably lying asleep on a haystack at noon. And then, all at once, it would be night, and he would leap upon her, stripping her of bodice and petticoats until she lay naked and quivering beneath him, her head tilted backward in sensual abandon, her legs spread wide, while her outstretched arms pulled him toward her feverish, panting body.

Once it was a swart and foul-smelling Narragansett Indian squaw whom he saw from horseback as she was picking blueberries at the side of the road. The abrupt darkness fell, and he dismounted. Seizing her violently and throwing her to the ground, he tore aside her grimy buckskins and hurled himself astride her with as little ceremony as a rooster mounting a hen in the chicken yard.

Sometimes the women were exotic creatures out of the Bible itself: a glittering Sheba, her half-nude body bejeweled and glowing as she lay waiting for him on a couch strewn with flowers; or an adolescent but very nubile Salome, swathed in diaphanous veils of soft and mysterious colors, glided slowly toward him and into his arms, until he could feel her firm, fresh-budded breasts straining against his chest.

But the women were never Lydia, and the feeling of sinfulness that would engulf him at his abrupt awakening from these dreams was heightened by the knowledge that he had committed adultery in fantasy if not in fact. Then, as he became aware of the cold sliminess of the sheet near his belly, disgust would rise in him like a smothering tide and he would pray aloud for deliverance from his attachment to the flesh.

Always, he dreaded going back to sleep again because he knew that new dreams would come to him, such fearsome nightmares that they would more than expiate the lusts so recently indulged in. The moment he lost consciousness, he would find himself transported to hell itself, and there, surrounded on all sides by flaring pits of burning pitch and smoking brimstone, he was condemned to be a prisoner for all eternity.

Devils with hideous grinning faces would seize his naked body in their clawed and hairy hands, pin him on his back to the molten earth beneath him, and then, with red-hot knives, slowly proceed to emasculate him. The pain was so excruciating that he screamed aloud in agony.

Then Lydia herself would make a belated appearance. Dressed in the flowing white robes of a ministering angel, she would gather up his mutilated, charred body in her spindly arms and cradle his head against her thin, flat breasts.

The sound of his own convulsive crying would mercifully awaken him at last. Sweating and with wildly beating heart, he would lie back in his bed, thankful to find himself delivered from the vision of hell that the Lord had sent him as punishment. But the sense of sin persisted, a stain that could never be entirely removed, no matter how much he prayed, no matter how earnestly he sought purity and virtue.

On mornings after such dreams, he rose from his bed like a man in a trance, the taper he carried as he went downstairs shaking in his clenched hand. At breakfast he was pale and distracted and ate without appetite. Only toward the end of the meal was he able to raise his eyes to Lydia's and attempt conversation.

It was on such a morning, after a night of wild dreaming, that he told Lydia of his plan to take Betsy into their household. He made the announcement tersely and without preamble.

"Lydia," he said quietly, "we are to have a child."

She looked up at him in quick apprehension. "A child?" she repeated. The prospect of a renewal of their attempts at conception filled her with a cold dread.

"I have arranged with Nate Thompson, the overseer of the poor, for us to undertake the care of an unfortunate child."

Lydia sighed in relief. Her hand went nervously to the lace cap on her head and tidied it as though it had been awry. "A child?" she said again. "We are to have a—a baby in the house?"

"Not a baby. She is ten." Sam paused and cleared his throat. "God has not seen fit to bless our union with offspring. But there are children—here in our village—who need Christian parents. It is meet that we offer ourselves to answer this call, thus bringing the Lord's blessings to His less fortunate children."

"Yes, Sam," said Lydia, bowing her head in assent, though she did not really believe that they should be doing anything of the sort. At last, she looked up and asked, "What is the child's name?"

"Betsy. Betsy Bowen. She is the daughter of one of the women who were—living in the old gaol when it was torn down on Monday."

Lydia drew in her breath sharply. "Oh! One of those—those— But, Sam, do you not fear that she will bring sinfulness to our household?"

"Perhaps. But she is a child, and with God's help, we can wash her clean of impurity. It is a duty that lies clearly in our path. Do you not see it so, Lydia?"

Lydia nodded uncertainly. "Yes. I see that it is our duty, Sam, but—"

Sam abruptly slid his chair away from the table and rose. "There is no need for further discussion, ma'am. I shall bring the child at four this afternoon. She will sleep in the small bedroom next to mine. See that Nellie prepares it for her."

He left the room quickly, and Lydia stared helplessly after him, trying to adjust herself to his unexpected announcement. Her gaze, glassy with anxiety, fixed itself unseeingly on the soiled breakfast dishes.

31

A child, she thought. Whatever would she do with a child? She knew nothing about children and their care. More than that, she hated the thought of having some wild creature running about the house, upsetting things, making noise, dirtying her immaculate floors. She found herself violently resenting this imminent invasion of her orderly world, and by the sinfully begotten offspring of a harlot, at that.

She knew better than to question one of Sam's decisions, especially when it rose from a moral or religious conviction. And so she tried to resign herself to the reality of becoming, at this late date, a mother, comforting herself with the thought that at least the child was not an infant, perpetually squalling, soiling itself, and puking down its bib. And it was a girl—a child whose nakedness would not offend her eyes.

CHAPTER 4

A T five o'clock that afternoon Betsy Bowen had the first bath of her life in the Allen kitchen. She sat in an oaken tub bound with shining copper hoops, while Nellie Forman, perspiring and breathing hard, poured warm water over her and scrubbed her with a soapy brush.

Two days in the workhouse had left Betsy even dirtier than usual, her face smudged, her curly hair matted with grime. Lydia had taken one look at her, stifled a genteel cry of horror, and called at once for Nellie to prepare a bath. She had anticipated some objections from Betsy, but there were none. The novelty of the experience filled the child with wonder and even excitement, although she yelled in rage whenever Nellie wielded the brush too strenuously or got soap in her eyes.

The sun of late afternoon shone through the open kitchen window, throwing a shaft of brilliant yellow light on Betsy as she stood up wet and dripping in the tub. It burnished the glistening red-gold of her hair and glowed along the petal-like softness of her fair skin.

Lydia, sitting primly in a chair near the open hearth, looked at Betsy curiously, as though she were an odd but beautiful seashell found on some unknown beach. It is a pretty child, she thought, not what one would expect in a strumpet's daughter. She looked— and something vaguely tender stirred in Lydia's memory—like an oversized doll, or even, in spite of her evil origin, a rosy-faced angel.

Betsy stared back at Lydia, not only with curiosity, but with frank and suspicious appraisal in her eyes. Sam had told her that Lydia was to be her new mother, and so she surveyed the woman thoroughly, comparing her to Phebe. But she could find no likeness whatever. This woman, so pale and white, so completely lacking in animation and spirit, did not even seem altogether real. Why didn't she talk? Did her face ever smile? Why did she just sit there, so silent and unmoving?

Finally, Betsy craned her neck forward like an inquisitive chicken and turned her eyes full on Lydia—those strangely colored eyes of violet-blue. "What's your name, ma'am?" she asked loudly.

Lydia started, like someone suddenly awakened. Swallowing nervously, she said, "Lydia—Lydia Allen. But you may call me—Mother, if you wish."

"But you're not my mother," said Betsy flatly.

"No, child." Lydia sought frantically for something to say. "You may call me—Aunt—Aunt Lydia, if you've a mind to."

"But you ain't my aunt neither," said Betsy.

"No, but—but maybe you could pretend."

This idea had a magical effect on Betsy. The corners of her small mouth turned up winsomely in a smile of extraordinary charm. Then she began to chant Lydia's name rhythmically, splashing her feet in the water by way of accent.

"Aunt-ie Lyd-ya—Aunt-ie Lyd-ya—"

"Here now!" said Nellie. "That's enough of that! Out you get and I'll dry you orf."

Betsy leaped out of the tub gaily, spattering water all over the shining planks of the kitchen floor as she grabbed the toweling out of Nellie's hands. "I can dry meself," she said, and began to chant again. "Auntie Lyd-ya! Aunt-ie Lyd-ya! Liddy, Liddy—la, la, Liddy!" Then the chant became melodic, and in a piping, childish treble she sang, "Oh, Liddy was a sailor's lass—she liked the boys to pat her arse—"

Lydia's mouth dropped open in shock. "Hush, child!" she cried. "Where—where did you ever learn a song like that?"

"From Mama," said Betsy. Puzzled by Lydia's reaction, she added by way of explanation, "Only the name is Lily, not Liddy. I changed it. That's only the beginning." She started singing again. "She allus took 'em to her bed—and when they—"

Lydia rose quickly from her chair and clapped her hand over Betsy's mouth. " 'Tis a sinful song, child. You will not sing it again in this house!"

Betsy looked at her in surprise, and then, humming the rest of the song, continued to dry herself. "Don't you never sing, Aunt Liddy?"

"No, child, not even in church."

"I heared people singing songs in church once."

"Methodists!" snorted Lydia. "They are ungodly people. In the First Baptist Church our joy comes of the spirit. We do not need to sing, except for the psalms, of course."

"That's too bad," said Betsy. "I like to sing. So does Mama. Sometimes we sing together."

Lydia leaned toward her intently. "It is best that you forget your mother, my child."

This idea seemed silly to Betsy. "Now how could I ever do that?" she asked.

"You must try."

"Why?"

Lydia paused, trying to think of an answer. "Because," she said finally, "your mother is not a good woman."

Betsy pondered this. "Well," she said, "I don't know if she's good or not, but I like her better than *you*. I like Sam better than you, too. Where is he?"

"Your—uncle went back to his shipping office to work. He will be home soon. Now put on the fine new clothes he bought you."

Lydia picked up the underclothing gingerly and held it out to her. "You do know how to dress yourself, don't you?"

Betsy nodded and began putting on the muslin garments. The dress of homespun, simple and unadorned, made her eyes light up with pleasure and she crowed delightedly, "Oh, it's so clean and pretty." Impulsively, she ran to Lydia and threw her arms around her waist, hugging her to her. "Oh, thank you, Auntie Liddy!"

Lydia stiffened at the unexpected show of affection. She patted Betsy on the head awkwardly, and then, stepping backward in embarrassment, she said, "Are you hungry?"

Betsy jumped in the air with enthusiasm. "Damme, that I am! Like Mama says, 'I'm so hungry I could eat the leg off the lamb of God'!"

Lydia's arms rose in the air, her eyes cast heavenward to ask the Lord's forgiveness for such blasphemous words.

When Sam returned home, he found Betsy and Nellie seated at the kitchen table, where Betsy was receiving her first lesson in the use of a spoon. Lydia had fled to the downstairs sitting room, where she lay on a sofa in a state that bordered on shock. The sight of Betsy scooping up food in her hands and cramming it into her mouth had been the final, nauseating touch to the series of jolts she had suffered that afternoon.

Whimpering tearfully, she told Sam that she could not undertake Betsy's care. "You must take her back to the workhouse at once, Sam. She is little better than a wild animal!"

"She is one of God's children," said Sam quietly.

Lydia sat bolt upright on the sofa. "One of God's children! More likely one of Satan's! She has the filthy, blaspheming tongue of a witch-child, and she will bring us nothing but trouble!" She sank back on the sofa.

Sam patted her hand gently. "We must have patience, dear Lydia. How would the child not be, as you say, an animal? What could she possess of virtue and godliness when she has never known either? We have been chosen by the Lord to throw His light on this darkness, and we cannot fail Him."

Lydia said nothing, but continued to whimper, while Sam stroked her hand. At last, she raised her head and said with a firmness born of desperation, "I cannot! And that's an end on it!"

Sam's tenderness vanished. He stood up and looked down at her in sudden contempt. "Stop your sniveling!" he said harshly. "The child stays! And you had best pray for the courage not merely to endure her presence but to fulfill your proper duties as a Christian mother. Now get up at once and prepare the child for bed!"

Lydia lay very still. Since tears would not accomplish her purpose, she stopped crying. In a faint, meekly obedient voice she said, "Very well, Samuel. I shall try, truly I shall. But—but I am not well tonight." She reached out an imploring hand toward him. "Cannot Nellie put the child to bed? My head aches, I am weak and dizzy, in truth, I am ill—"

"In that event, ma'am," said Sam, "retire to your bedroom and sleep. But tomorrow I shall expect you to assume your duties without further complaint."

After Sam had left, Lydia remained motionless on the sofa. She stared at her mother's oil portrait that hung over the mantelpiece. "Oh, Mama, what shall I do?" she asked plaintively of the image that looked straight through her with its piercing ice-blue eyes.

Then it was as though her mother's voice spoke to her, the thin, pale lips in the austere face pronouncing the precise words of advice that she did not wish to hear. "Do as your husband says," the dry, reedy voice said. "Pray! For prayer is our only help in time of tribulation."

And so Lydia prayed, but not for the courage to undertake the burden that Sam had placed upon her. She prayed that Betsy, in some swift and miraculous way, would be removed from her home, so that peace could once again reign.

It was Sam, not Nellie, who put Betsy to bed on her first night in the Allen home. He led her upstairs, one of her hands in one of his, while in the other hand he carried a new nightdress.

Betsy, who had never lived in a house that had stairs, marveled at the long flight of shining steps that led to still another new world above the kitchen. Halfway up, she stumbled and fell in her eagerness to reach the top, and so Sam picked her up and carried her in his arms the rest of the way.

As he entered the small bedroom that was to be hers, she squirmed, anxious to get down and explore it. While he watched in quiet amusement, she trotted about the room like an inquisitive puppy sniffing out its new quarters. First, she studied all the furnishings with alert and serious eyes. Then she sat herself down on the bed, bounced up and down, and peered underneath it. She pulled out the chamber pot and admired it. She went to the washstand and stroked the smooth lines of the gleaming earthenware water pitcher. She pulled open all the drawers of the small pine chest and then slammed them all shut. She got down on her hands and knees and caressed the hooked rug, then rubbed her cheek against it. At last, she got to her feet and ran to him. She turned a radiant face up to him and threw her arms around his bony legs.

37

Sam moved away slightly and disentangled her arms from his legs. His face, as it regarded her, was serious and unsmiling, but a new and tender expression had for the moment replaced the remote look that so often gave him the appearance of indifference.

"This is your room, Betsy. Do you like it?"

"Oh, it is the prettiest, cleanest room I ever did see!"

"Then see that you keep it neat and tidy." As she nodded enthusiastically, he said, "Well, it is time now for you to go to sleep. Put on your nightdress." He held it out to her.

"Go to sleep?" she said in surprise. "But it's still daylight. It's too early to go to bed, Sam."

"You will please to call me Uncle, my child. And you will go to bed—now. It is a proper time for children to sleep. You have learned many bad habits of living, Betsy. We are going to change them. I expect you to be both obedient and dutiful."

Betsy listened in awe. She had never been told what to do by a male voice before. Its calm authority was very different from Phebe's sea-gull cry. She liked it, and so she gave him a shy smile and said demurely, "Yes, Uncle." She took off her clothes quickly, flinging the garments to the floor, and stood suddenly naked before him.

He turned his eyes away in haste and said, "Pick up your clothing and place it neatly on the chair. Then get into your nightdress so that I can tuck you into bed."

But she stood there in front of him without moving, naked and obstinate. "It's too hot to wear a nightdress," she said.

"You will wear it anyway."

She still made no move to obey. In an attempt to distract him, she seized one of her small nipples between her thumb and forefinger. "Know what this is?" she asked. "It looks like a mosquiter bite, but Mama says it's a titty, and someday it will get big and round like hers and fill up with milk and—"

Sam cuffed her hard on the head. Her face screwed up in astonishment for a second before she began to cry, which she did almost silently, the tears moving slowly down her cheeks.

Her hurt, puzzled look filled Sam with quick shame, and he said, "I am sorry, Betsy. But you must not say words like that and make an immodest display of your body."

"Why is 'titty' a bad word?" she wanted to know.

"Never mind. Don't say it." He paused awkwardly, wondering himself why it was a bad word. He held out the nightdress to her. "Here. Put it on at once."

Frowning, Betsy did as she was told. She got into bed, rubbed the back of her hand over her eyes to dry them, and then looked at Sam, smiling timidly.

"You must say your prayers before getting into bed, lass," said Sam, and his voice was softer now.

"I don't know any prayers."

"Then I will teach you one. Come, kneel down next to me and fold your hands like this."

She scrambled down beside him and folded her hands.

"Now," he said, "repeat these words after me. Almighty God, look down in mercy on thy humble servant, Betsy, unworthy and sinful . . ."

She repeated the strange words after him, mimicking the solemn tone of his voice. She wanted to please him, but even more, she did not want another cuff on the head.

At last, the praying over, she leaped back into the bed, snuggling down between the clean-smelling linen sheets, and Sam turned to leave.

"Good night, Betsy. God keep thee and protect thy soul till morning."

"Amen," said Betsy dutifully. As Sam nodded his approval, she said, "My Mama always kisses me good night. Ain't you goin' to?"

Sam paused uncertainly. Then he moved to the bed and stiffly planted a perfunctory kiss on her forehead.

Betsy smiled up at him. "Mama kisses me on the mouth. Like this." She pulled his head toward her and gave him a wet, childish kiss, full on the lips.

Sam jerked his face away from hers abruptly, rubbing his hand across his mouth, as though to erase all trace of her caress. Then, without a word, he left the room.

CHAPTER 5

O F all the strange things that Betsy discovered in the new world she had entered, the strangest was the clock. She had known, of course, that clocks existed, but her mother had never owned one, and so Betsy did not even know how to tell time.

From the moment that Sam taught her, she found the clock fascinating. It stood, tall and majestic, in the hallway, ticking away the minutes with monotonous resolution, sounding the hours and half-hours with authority. With a clock like that, there could be no arguing.

It told you what time to rise in the morning, when to eat, and the hour for going to bed. And she knew that all night long, even while she slept, it continued with its never-varying ticktock and its periodic striking, because once, awaking in the middle of the night, she had crept downstairs to find out if it was still going. When she found that it was, she was both pleased and terrified.

Betsy decided that it was neither Sam nor Lydia who ruled life in the Allen house. It was the clock. And sometimes, while she was saying her prayers, she thought that the clock might even be God Himself and she prayed to it earnestly.

When its hands pointed to certain hours, food magically appeared on the table, food that was apparently in inexhaustible supply, because she could eat as much of it as she pleased. During her life with Phebe, when there had been no clock, eating had been a hit-or-miss thing. She ate when she felt like it—providing the food was there. During periods when the port was idle and Phebe's visitors were few, she had often been painfully hungry. She remembered nights when supper had consisted of a raw turnip, munched noisily in the dark.

All that was changed now. The hands of the clock said "Eat!"

and she ate. They said "Bedtime!" and she went to bed. And there, in the darkness of her little room, it was strangely quiet. There were no loud male voices in the next room, no hoarse whisperings, no grunts and cries.

At first the silence made her feel lonely and afraid. But soon she learned to listen for other, less violent, sounds—the sighing of the wind in the branches of the pine tree outside her window, the talk of katydids in the summer night, and the jaunty chirping of crickets.

If she woke up during the night, there was the reassuring voice of the bellman making his rounds, and it comforted her. Even he told her what time it was. "One o'clock and fair winds," he would sing out, and she would drop off to sleep again immediately. And if he should cry, "Five o'clock and storm a-comin'!" she would snuggle down cosily in her bed, happy that she would be safe and protected when the rain came pounding against the house, and thunder rumbled, and lightning flickered threateningly at the window.

She learned not only the special significance of the hours of the day, but the days of the week as well, with their set and specified chores. She liked Sunday the best, not because—as Sam and Lydia believed—she was beginning to love the Lord, but because Sunday was an exciting break in an otherwise humdrum week.

Preparations for the Sabbath began on Saturday night with the weekly bath, which Betsy thoroughly enjoyed. Although Nellie told her that she must be clean because she was going to church to meet God the next day, it was not cleanliness that delighted her. It was the feel of the warm water on her body, and the pleasant drowsiness that came later, after she had been tucked into bed for the night.

The next morning, in the flurry of activity that seized the household, her elation reached a climax. The intoxicating smells that rose from the kitchen as Nellie started cooking the Sunday dinner threw her into a mouth-watering fever of anticipation. Then the bustling ritual of dressing up for God sent her into a whirl of excitement and frantic primping.

Long before it was time to leave for the new Baptist Church on Towne Street she was ready and waiting, starched and resplendent in the dress reserved for "holy walking." It was a simple dress of plain white broadcloth, but it had a starched ruffle on it that filled her with pride.

The walk up Benefit Street to the meetinghouse always seemed far too short to her. Mincing along sedately between Sam and Lydia and trailed by Nellie, she stared in wonderment at everything and everybody—the handsome houses that lined the street, and the people who came out of them and moved so gravely and serenely toward the church that was said to be the most magnificent in all New England, with its ornamented portico and its towering steeple.

She had never even imagined that a world like this existed, where all the houses were neatly made of brick or stone or freshly painted wood, where there were no ramshackle old buildings with sagging roofs and rotting timbers, no huts that had walls of dried mud.

It was a world where people were always clean and trimly dressed, where nobody ever got drunk or swore or brawled, where on the Sabbath, they were especially quiet and dignified, greeting one another wordlessly, with solemn inclinations of the head. Though they might sometimes look at her with a flicker of curiosity in their eyes, they did not smile in greeting. And so, she did not smile either but lifted her small, uptilted nose a trifle higher in the air and walked along more elegantly than ever.

She became particularly disdainful whenever she saw her sister, Polly, because Polly had snubbed her. It had happened on the first Sunday Betsy had gone holy walking. As she had rounded the corner of Benefit Street and started down the hill to the church entrance, she had caught sight of Polly, escorted on all sides by members of the Wyatt family. Henry Wyatt and his wife were at the head of the family procession, Polly came next, flanked by two of the Wyatt boys, while still another Wyatt son, the eldest, brought up the rear.

Betsy had smiled, waved gaily, and called out to Polly, who had then turned a blank stare in her direction, as though she had never seen Betsy before. Resplendent in a dress with two ruffles and a pale-pink satin bow, Polly had turned her head away and looked straight ahead.

Betsy's surprise changed to hurt, and then swiftly to fury, and she stamped her small feet angrily as she marched along between

Sam and Lydia. Her eyes continued to follow Polly, and there was envy in them, not only because her sister was wearing a dress that was prettier than hers, but because she was almost completely encircled by males.

She resolved never to speak to Polly again, and the following Sunday, she had returned stare for stare and then had opened her mouth convulsively as though taken with an overpowering nausea that compelled her to turn her head away to avoid vomiting.

When the walk to the church came to an end and she would finally find herself stuffed into the Allen pew between Sam and Lydia, the church service itself was always a dreary and anticlimactic disappointment. All the pleasure of the bustling preparations and of the holy walking itself dissolved instantly at the sound of the Reverend Arnold's voice leading his congregation in prayer.

The prayer might last as long as half an hour, but she did not mind too much because while everyone's head was bowed, she was free to raise her eyes to the boy's pew in the right-hand gallery above her and watch the Wyatt boys. The two younger ones, about her own age, looked as though they might be fun to play games with, in spite of their scrubbed and solemn faces. When the tithingman who kept the boys in order was not looking, they sometimes made faces at her, and she delightedly stuck out her tongue at them in reply.

The oldest boy was different. He looked at her, but he never made faces. There was a strangely quiet air about him, and his eyes held a queer, faraway look. He puzzled her, and she stared at him often. She even ventured smiling at him, but he never smiled back.

When the praying was over at last, the psalm singing would begin. The congregation rose with a great clattering of the hinged seats as they flapped up. Betsy had looked forward to the prospect of psalm singing, but this was unlike any music she had ever heard. Her mother's lilting Irish voice had given her a sense of melody that made her detest the tedious wailing and toneless chanting that filled the church continuously for half an hour at a time. Finally, she made no attempt to sing at all and fidgeted back and forth from one foot to the other, looking forward to the moment when she could sit down on the hard seat again.

The Reverend Arnold's interminable sermon seemed to her like a continuation of the psalm singing—a song that consisted of only one deep bass note, held endlessly and forever, without color or variation. At the Reverend Arnold's opening words, a tithingman turned the handsome brassbound hourglass at the side of the pulpit, and Betsy gave forth an audible sigh because she had learned that the sand moved with an unbelievable slowness, and the glass would be turned once again before the service was over.

Whenever she grew restless and began to squirm against the hard bench, she would feel Sam's hand on her shoulder, its stern pressure commanding her to be quiet. If she dozed, the hand silently gave her a smart cuff on the head to awaken her. Then, wincing with pain, she would straighten up and turn her eyes again toward the Reverend Arnold.

Sometimes she stole a look at Sam out of the corner of her eye. Usually, he was staring straight ahead, as though unaware that she was even there. If he did happen to look at her, she immediately made her face assume a dutiful, contrite expression. She was rewarded by a brief nod of approval, and now and then his eyes might become for a few seconds alive and penetrating while they held her own. This response always made her glow with happiness, and she would seek out his long, bony hand and squeeze it. But it never gave back any answering pressure.

Since she could neither sleep during the sermon nor divert herself by looking at the Wyatt boys in the gallery without Sam's awareness, she learned to pass the time in daydreaming, which she could do with her eyes wide open.

Sometimes she would imagine herself to be the very rich and pampered child of a family that owned the biggest and most beautiful house on Benefit Street. She wore dresses of such stunning and beribboned loveliness and variety that she was adored at sight by everyone who looked at her. She ate interminably from dishes of silver and gold that were heaped with sweetmeats, fancy cakes, and tarts.

Polly, dressed in rags, begged her for one of her dresses, for a taste of the delicacies with which she gorged herself. She refused, with an imperious toss of her splendid curls, and promptly ordered the servants to take Polly back to the workhouse where she belonged.

Then she would give orders that her mother be released from gaol so that she could come live with her. She showered Phebe with gifts of all kinds: shimmering gowns of silk and satin; rings and necklaces of rubies and diamonds and pearls; innumerable bottles of rum; and wines that glowed with all the colors of the rainbow—crimson, sparkling white, and gold. There was even a mysterious blue wine that came in a ship from some faraway land—a magical potion that gave happiness forever to whoever drank it.

Together, she and Phebe drank the blue wine. They feasted and laughed, and when it was time for sleep, they retired to a softly shining golden bedroom. In an enormous feather bed with satin sheets and all hung about with crimson damask, she slept blissfully in her mother's arms.

For Betsy, sitting in the Allen pew, eyes misted with glory, the time passed quickly. She did not even hear the droning of the Reverend Arnold until he neared the end of his sermon. Then there was a point when his voice would grow loud and booming, and the sudden change would bring her out of her daydreams with a jolt.

The Reverend Arnold seemed to have become unaccountably angry. A great rage shook him, and he bellowed. The quiet air of the church quivered with excitement as he began castigating his flock for their sins without number. He called them names in tones of thunder. He threatened them with all the fires of hell and eternal damnation.

He made Betsy remember one of her mother's friends, a ship's captain who, when gloriously drunk, hurled imprecations about him like thunderbolts, cursing all women, all men, and the very God who had made him.

She waited patiently for the day when the Reverend Arnold, pushed to the limits of his endurance by the monstrous behavior of his unregenerate flock, would suddenly pick up the heavy Bible from the lectern and hurl it at them. She could almost hear the thud of the huge book as it landed on some wrongdoer's head. She could see the embattled sinners as they scrambled up the aisles screaming "Every man for himself!"

And there might be some sinners who would stand their ground and fight back, aiming their psalmbooks at the altar, firing them straight at the Reverend Arnold's bald head. The musty air of the meetinghouse would be alive with flying objects.

45

Betsy never gave up hoping that some fine Sunday that day would arrive. Her heart was heavy with disappointment when the service reached its quiet and uneventful conclusion, but then, as she moved out of the pew and up the aisle with the rest of the congregation, she would think cheerfully, Maybe next Sunday.

Outside the meetinghouse, the church members gathered in small groups, exchanging greetings and discreet, casually disguised bits of gossip. It always surprised Betsy that they should be so calm and apparently happy after the Reverend Arnold's scorching tirade of name-calling and dreadful predictions. They were not in the least frightened. On the contrary, they were more friendly and at ease than during the solemn walk to church. It was as though they had been naughty, gone to the Reverend Arnold to be scolded, and now, having received their punishment, felt relieved and all ready to be naughty again.

Betsy dreaded this time of sociability outside the church. She was stared at quite openly, so that she had the feeling that somehow she did not belong there. As the eyes of the townspeople surveyed her, she became acutely uncomfortable, looked at the ground, and dug the toe of her shoe into the cracks of the brick walk. Whether their eyes regarded her with curiosity or with pity, she recognized that the eyes were never friendly, sometimes even suspicious and openly hostile.

Covertly, she watched the other children greeting one another with shy smiles and polite handclasps. They talked in low tones, as though they shared some secret that she knew nothing about. But what she minded the most was that they completely ignored her. She felt the way she had felt when she had had the measles—separated from her brother and sister, alone and unwanted. It did not make her more cheerful to note that Polly, surrounded as she was by all those Wyatt boys, was accepted and approved by everyone.

And so she was relieved when the gathering at last broke up and it was time to walk back to the Allen house. Her spirits would begin to rise as she thought of the Sunday dinner that was waiting.

It might not be served on plates of gold like the sweetmeats of her daydreams, but Nellie's roast chicken with gravy was still the most delicious food she had ever tasted in all of her ten years. And she was allowed as much of it as she pleased.

CHAPTER 6

T HE Sundays came and went, the Reverend Arnold never threw the Bible at his flock, and Betsy became bored by the monotonous routine of her new way of life. Lydia was teaching her how to sew, how to knit, how to card wool and spin. With the exception of sewing, Betsy hated all of it, and Lydia, despairing of such an inattentive and unwilling pupil, set her to doing more menial tasks, such as emptying chamber pots and scouring the pewter.

Except for the Saturday-night bath and going to church on Sunday, the only events that Betsy could look forward to were breakfast, dinner and supper—and the few moments with Sam at prayer time before she went to sleep. Time passed slowly and drearily, and the clock became a tyrant instead of a source of fascination.

She missed the gay companionship of her mother, who had played games with her and had told her stories. Lydia and Nellie didn't know any games, they had no stories to tell, and so Betsy spent whatever leisure she had in moping restlessly about the house and yard in a desperate search for diversion.

She thought about running away, but she could think of no place to run to. Sam had told her that her mother had gone away, was somewhere in Massachusetts, and would never be allowed to come back to Providence again because she was not a desirable citizen. Betsy was not sure what a desirable citizen was and she had trouble even pronouncing Massachusetts, which sounded as though it must be on the other side of the world, in some faraway country where all undesirable citizens lived.

During the hot days of August, rebellion began to simmer in her, like a hurricane slowly gathering force. On an afternoon in early September the storm broke, explosively and without warning.

She had been sitting listlessly in a ladder-back chair in the freshly scrubbed kitchen. She was alone, because Lydia had retired to her bedroom for her afternoon nap, and Nellie had gone to Market Square. The only sound that broke the silence of the quiet house was the slow, monotonous bubbling of a pot of fish stew set on a trivet in the fireplace.

With her chin in her hand, she listened to the tiresome gurgle with mounting irritation, swinging her legs back and forth nervously and staring at the pot of stew as though it were an enemy. A sudden fury possessed her, and she ran to the fireplace. Grabbing a cloth in her hand, she yanked at the pot until she had pulled it off the trivet. Then she tipped it over, and a torrent of stew streamed over the hearth. Breathless and perspiring, she stood looking down at the mess with a satisfied smile.

The thud of the pot awakened Lydia, and in a few moments Betsy heard her hurried footsteps on the stairs. Betsy had no desire to run and hide. The prospect of seeing Lydia's horror-stricken face filled her with malicious glee.

Lydia did not disappoint her. At the sight of the milky lake of fish and potatoes spreading from the hearth to the gleaming pine boards of the floor she screamed, not just once but again and again. Her eyes darted to Betsy in angry disbelief. She seized her by the arm and shrieked, "What have you done, you child of Satan?"

Betsy jerked away from her, folded her arms, and looked up with a defiant grin. "I upset the pot, that's what I done."

"But how could you do a thing like that?"

"I just pulled it off the trivet and tipped it over."

Lydia struck out at her with her open hand. Betsy side-stepped the blow, laughed wildly, and yelled, "Don't you hit *me*, you ole bitch!" She ran out the door and down the brick walk toward the street with Lydia in pursuit.

Just then Sam came through the gate and looked at both of them in astonishment. As Betsy tried to run past him, he grabbed her by the shoulder and pushed her up the walk ahead of him toward the house. She kicked at him and thrashed about like an animal caught in a trap. When he slapped her on the face, she snatched his hand with both her own and sank her teeth into it.

48

Sam, howling with pain, furiously picked her up and carried her into the house. He dragged her upstairs to his bedroom and spanked her on her bare buttocks until she screamed for mercy. Then he took her back to the kitchen and ordered her to clean up the mess. When this had been done, he sent her to bed without supper.

Just before dark, he went to her room to make sure that she said her prayers and asked God's forgiveness for being wicked. Together, they beseeched God to make her strong against all future blandishments of the Devil.

As he was about to leave, Betsy looked up at him plaintively and said, "Ain't you goin' to kiss me good night, Uncle?"

"No," he said coldly. "Bad children are not deserving of love."

"I'm sorry I bit you," she said softly. "I promise never to do it again."

His anger had left him by now, and he had to make an effort to look stern and disapproving. And then, as he looked down at her small, heart-shaped face, so angelic and innocent now, he felt a surge of tenderness that he could not control. Impulsively, he leaned over and kissed her on the forehead.

Betsy lay back contentedly and rested her head on the pillow. Sighing, her eyes shining with sudden tears, she gave him a smile of pure sunlight.

When Sam came downstairs, Lydia was waiting for him. She stood tensely at the side of the kitchen hearth, her hands folded resolutely across her waist. "We must talk about the child," she said.

"What is there to talk about? She has misbehaved. She has been punished. It happens to all children." Sam shrugged and moved away, as though there was nothing more to be said.

"Wait, Sam! I can be patient no longer! The child must leave this house!" Her voice had risen to a note of near hysteria, and he looked at her in faint astonishment.

"The child stays," he said mildly, but the authority in his voice left no room for questioning. Lydia crumpled, lifted her apron to her face, and began to cry into it convulsively.

He waited silently for the fit of weeping to pass and then said, his voice gentle, "I know it is not easy, Lydia. Perhaps if you could spend more time with her—"

"Spend time with her! I have no time! What with scrubbing and washing clothes and—"

He interrupted the too familiar recital of all the many duties she performed by saying, "She needs to be kept busy, pleasantly occupied."

Lydia seized upon the idea. "Very well! Tomorrow I shall provide her with more work! It is truly said that Satan finds things for idle hands to do. I shall set her more difficult chores, perhaps—"

The vengeful note in her voice made Sam look at her with concern. "Betsy is only a child, Lydia. See that you do not set her tasks that will strain her constitution."

Lydia looked at her husband impatiently. "Her constitution," she said, "is of iron." As she saw that he was about to protest, she hurriedly added, "Of course, she will perform only those tasks appropriate to a child of her age."

Sam looked thoughtful. "All in all, Lydia, I think she has done well, better than I had hoped for, in fact, considering her previous mode of life."

Lydia gave a ladylike snort of contempt. "Well, her mode of *speech* has not greatly improved! She called me a dreadful name."

" 'Tis to be expected."

"And she fights like a wild creature. How is your hand?"

"The wound is small. It is nothing."

Lydia became indignant. "Nothing! She has bitten, in very truth, the hand that feeds her! Do you call that nothing? Why must you everlastingly defend this child in her wickedness?"

"I do not defend her," said Sam quietly. "And as for wickedness, the Scriptures tell us that it can be cast out only by Christian love—a virtue that you might cultivate more devotedly, my dear."

Though Sam's voice was even, his words stung Lydia, kindling a resentment that she was careful to conceal. There was no trace of irony in her voice as she replied, "We cannot all be so godly as you, Sam. I shall pray the Lord for greater patience."

Sam nodded approvingly, and Lydia quietly vowed to herself that she would also renew her prayers for deliverance from this unhappy burden that he had placed on her poor shoulders, shoulders already bowed down by suffering that he did not truly appreciate because she endured it in such brave silence.

As the weeks of early autumn passed, the Lord did not see fit to answer any of the prayers that came from the Allen household. He did not free Lydia of her burden, nor did he give Betsy enough strength to withstand temptation. Satan made regular and successful visits to the house on Benefit Street. He inspired Betsy to new and more monstrous acts of willful sinfulness, sometimes right in the midst of the very chores that were intended to keep her idle hands busy and free of iniquity.

One morning, as she was carrying a full chamber pot downstairs for emptying, she hurled it instead at the mantel in the front parlor, where it smashed to pieces, strewing its unsavory contents all over the fireplace and even spattering the oil portrait of Lydia's mother. It was the portrait, in fact, that had been Betsy's target, but her aim was poor.

On another occasion, Satan suggested to her that all the neatly made beds abovestairs were ripe for desecration. On a wild rampage she tore the sheets and blankets from the beds and threw them out of the windows, much to the surprise of passers-by on Benefit Street.

The punishments for these acts of outrage became increasingly severe. Sam finally provided himself with a birch rod, and soon the chastening process had taken on the established aspects of a ritual. Whenever Betsy misbehaved, Nellie's strong arms hauled her upstairs, by the hair if necessary, and locked her in the closet in Sam's room, and there, in the stifling darkness, she waited until Sam returned home.

At last, she would hear the slow, deliberate tread of his feet on the stairs, then his footsteps coming into the room. She would hold her breath until that frightening moment when the closet door was flung open and Sam stood suddenly revealed before her—like Jehovah, rod in hand. Blinking at the sudden light as she cowered in terror on the floor of the closet, she awaited his order to come out and take off her dress. At last, naked and shivering before him, she would be seized roughly by the shoulder and her body would be bent face down over the seat of a chair.

Sam towered over her with the birch rod upraised and his arm bared to the elbow. Then he would address her in a voice quite unlike his own—low, intense, with a throaty rumble that made her think of thunder.

"Thy sinfulness must be punished in this world as well as the next, Betsy," he intoned. "I pray God that this rod of righteousness may help thee to conquer future temptation."

The birch rod whipped through the air, burned and stung across her bare, trembling buttocks, and she would scream with pain. Then it was as though her cry inflamed him with even greater vengefulness. His eyes became bright and hard, his breath whistled through his clenched teeth, his face became so swollen with blood that a vein in his temple throbbed.

Her screams, sharp and piercing, cut through the quiet of the house. Lydia, hearing them, would drop to her knees in the kitchen, covering her ears with her hands and praying loudly for mercy on Betsy's evil soul.

The whippings never lasted for long. Within a few moments, Sam's hands would fall to his sides, as though he were suddenly sickened and ashamed. His body would sag, the rod falling from his hand and clattering to the floor. A remorseful gentleness would engulf him as he knelt by Betsy's side, tenderly lifting her from the chair and taking her in his lap. She would fling herself against his chest, crying hysterically, and then his arms would enfold her so tightly that she could hardly breathe.

His hands would move soothingly, caressingly over her soft, naked body. Her sobs would quiet, and she would begin to feel strangely happy and joyous. It was a moment that she waited for, a moment whose pleasure almost wiped out the memory of pain.

At last, he would help her put on her clothes, and then they would kneel side by side and pray that she would not be tempted to sinfulness ever again.

But in spite of all their prayers, Betsy's tantrums of rebellion continued, not so regularly as before, perhaps, but often enough to disturb Sam deeply. Each whipping left him increasingly troubled and shaken, and dimly he began to sense that the giving of punishment, like sin itself, can sometimes become an agreeable habit.

He prayed earnestly for a way out of his dilemma, and one afternoon, as he worked over a long and complicated shipping manifest, his prayers were answered. God granted him a revelation.

"How," the voice of God asked him, "can Betsy's soul be saved when she cannot even read the Scriptures?"

That night he persuaded Lydia to forgo her afternoon nap in order to teach Betsy to read the Bible. Inasmuch as this was a most godly undertaking, Lydia could hardly refuse to take part in it. And so at four o'clock the next afternoon she opened the door to the front parlor and sat Betsy down at a table beside her with an open Bible between them.

Lydia's own education had been sparse, and her spelling, Sam often said, left much to be desired. But she could at least read tolerably well, and with a sigh of resignation she began her new duties as schoolmistress.

Within the next few days she discovered, to her great surprise, that Betsy was an eager pupil, quick-witted and curious. The response awakened in her an enthusiasm as unfamiliar as it was unforeseen. As time went by, she found herself looking forward to each day's lesson and taking both pleasure and pride in Betsy's progress. The child's struggles with the long and difficult words of the Old Testament prompted her to search for the old primer that she herself had used as a girl.

Betsy loved the dog-eared book on sight and took it to bed with her every night, but the lessons in reading, to Lydia's great despair, had little effect on her pupil's habits of speech. Betsy still talked freely about the more private parts of her body and their functions and used the coarse words that were the only ones she knew. Worse still, her conversation was spiced with blaspheming oaths and interjections that she had heard sailors use.

Her mouth was washed with strong soap again and again. She was given periods of penance when she was not allowed to talk at all, sometimes for a whole day. Her mouth was burned with a hot mustard plaster so that her lips became blistered and sore.

And yet, for a long while, she clung obstinately to the forbidden words, perhaps in memory of the mother who had used them and who was no longer there. In time, however, the words began to disappear, popping out only unintentionally, and sometimes under the most inappropriate circumstances.

Once, when she was confined to her bed with cramps and

53

nausea, the Reverend Arnold came to call, in the hope that a session of earnest prayer would restore her to health. Lydia ushered him into Betsy's bedroom and he sat down sociably on the end of her bed.

"And what is troubling thee, my little lass?" he asked kindly.

" 'Tis the bellyache," said Betsy, "and it hurts me bad."

"A great pity, a great pity," said the Reverend Arnold in the honeyed tone he always used with the sick. "But the dear Lord sends us pain that we may be humble before Him."

"The Lord," said Betsy, "ain't got nothin' to do with it, sir. It's me guts. I bean't able to shit for two days."

The suddenly frozen expressions on the faces of Lydia and the clergyman told her that a bad word had slipped out again, and she quickly added, without much conviction, "Oh, I am wicked!" and clapped her hand across her mouth. Instant repentance, she had learned, often saved the day if Lydia was the only witness to her sinfulness. But it had no effect on Sam.

Although he now reserved the birch rod for only her more spectacular sinnings, he seized upon her every transgression, no matter how minor, as an occasion for bodily punishment of some kind, and he was particularly concerned about the purity of her speech.

There was the Sunday afternoon when Mrs. Peckham, who lived around the corner on George Street, came to call. She seemed charmed by Betsy. Clucking and cooing, she sat her upon her knee and fondled the soft ringlets of her hair.

"Such a pretty little girl," she babbled. "And kept so clean and tidy, too," she said with an approving glance at Lydia, who flushed with pleasure, while Sam nodded proud agreement.

Mrs. Peckham hugged Betsy enthusiastically to her fast-breathing bosom, which smelled of lavender blossom. Her eyes misted sentimentally as she said, "So fast does time pass that before we know it our Betsy will be a young woman grown, beautiful and blooming, ready to be taken in marriage by some fine young lad of the town!"

Betsy looked into Mrs. Peckham's cowlike eyes in astonishment. "Oh, no, ma'am," she said earnestly. "I ain't hardly old enough for marrying yet. Black Bets told me I didn't dast fuck too soon or I'd bleed me to death."

After a thoroughly shocked and unsettled Mrs. Peckham had made a hasty departure, never to return again, Sam led Betsy upstairs to his bedroom. He repeated his now familiar lecture on the use of foul words.

"Such words," he said, "fill the mouth with putrefaction, causing the teeth to rot and the breath to turn vile and noxious! The very smell of Satan steams from the lips!"

Though Betsy did not understand all the words, she nodded her head up and down so rapidly that it made her dizzy. She always hoped that such enthusiastic agreement might take away the necessity for punishment, but it never did.

"Stand before me," said Sam, "that I may cleanse thy mouth of evil!"

Trembling and white-faced, she approached him and waited for the blow to fall. His open palm smote her full across the mouth. She did not cry out, but continued to stand there, her head bowed, tears streaming down her cheeks. She waited in silence for the comforting sequel to violence, anticipating his quick movement toward her, the arms that encircled her so possessively, the heat of his lips planted on her own.

The flood of pleasure that warmed her then was brief but precious. Too soon it was time for them to kneel and pray together. Then they walked downstairs, hand in hand, strangely happy.

They sat down to supper in silence, Betsy in a chair close to Sam. During the saying of grace Lydia watched them covertly. She felt alone and separate, and as the meal continued, her feeling of isolation became more intense. Sam gave his attention wholly to the child, correcting her table manners, urging her to eat when she dawdled over her food.

Whenever Lydia made a bid for attention, Sam glanced at her and made as brief a response as he could without altogether ignoring her. She tried to conquer the jealousy that rose up in her. It was an emotion she had never felt before, and she did not know how to deal with it. As Sam began to spend more and more of his free time with Betsy, the feeling became continuous and persistent.

He had decided to give Betsy lessons in writing every night after supper. These hours of the early evening, when Nellie had left for the day and Lydia could be alone with her husband, had always been a time of quiet companionship that she had looked forward to. While she washed the dishes and scrubbed the pots, Sam cleaned the fireplace, taking away the ashes and setting the logs for a new fire. Then, with their chores completed, they sat down at the shining kitchen table and talked.

Like a child, she would recount at length all the troubles of her day, and he would give her words of comfort and encouragement, sprinkled with bits of praise. They would make household plans—repairs that needed doing, the purchase of a new piece of furniture or a needed article of clothing. Once a month they went over their expenditures in an account book that Lydia kept. She took great pride in the neatness and accuracy of her figures and glowed whenever Sam complimented her.

Now, except for the monthly accounting, these evening hours were no longer hers. They belonged to Betsy, and Lydia sat alone in her immaculate kitchen, reading her Bible and trying desperately to overcome the jealousy that burned in her. She no longer thought of Betsy as merely a burden, but as someone to be hated and feared.

She envied the child her prettiness, her glowing good health, her high spirits—assets that she herself had never had, even as a child. She resented Betsy's assured and even bold approach to other people. In her own mind, she condemned this as an unseemly forwardness, but it was a quality that she secretly admired.

And yet, she could not conceal from herself the true nature of her feelings, and she looked upon them as wicked. The Bible was quite explicit about the sins of envy and jealousy, and so Lydia prayed that the Lord would free her of them.

She made an honest effort to love her enemy, and during the reading lessons in the afternoon, she sometimes pressed Betsy's hand affectionately or patted her on the shoulder when she had done well. Betsy reacted to such gestures with surprise, and although she was friendly, she remained somehow remote and inaccessible, sensing perhaps that these demonstrations of affection were not completely genuine.

Lydia interpreted Betsy's aloofness and indifference as a sign that she might indeed be a witch-child. Witches were known to be cold and unfeeling. How could they be otherwise, when their souls were wholly given to the Devil? Though Sam might scoff at her whenever she talked of witchcraft, she knew that it existed.

When she had been a young girl, her mother had read aloud to her from Cotton Mather's *Wonders of the Invisible World,* and it had never entered her mind to question the justice and truth of the Salem trials. As a grown woman, she had seen with her own eyes manifestations of witchcraft right here in Providence, but in view of the popular feeling against a belief in witches, she thought it better not to talk about the subject, and especially not to Sam.

As her suspicions that Betsy was bound over to Satan became stronger, her envy of the child miraculously disappeared, and she took this as a sign from heaven that she was justified in her belief. It soon became possible for her to pray sincerely and openly for Betsy's destruction, instead of taking herself to task for the sin of jealousy. It seemed to her suddenly absurd that she had been jealous of a child who was endowed with evil powers—and who had cast a spell over Sam himself.

Lydia began to see herself as an agent of the Lord, chosen expressly to save Sam from the bondage into which, all unknowing, he had fallen. She heard the voice of the Lord telling her that it was her duty to crush Sam's attachment to the child as quickly as possible, before it was too late.

On a chilly gray day in early November, her belief received a final confirmation, and whatever doubts she may have had vanished completely. Late in the afternoon of that day, a kitten squeezed itself through the gate and into the front yard. Its tail held high, it walked slowly and deliberately up the brick walk toward the house. It was coal-black.

Lydia watched from her bedroom window, holding her breath in fear and fascination. She saw Betsy, who was sitting on the grass, searching for a four-leaf clover, look up. Lydia heard her squeal in delight when she saw the kitten, which started moving toward her immediately.

Betsy picked it up and cradled it in her arms, as though it were a doll. When it mewed loudly, Betsy, ecstatic at the sound of its voice, talked back to it.

"Oh, kitty, kitty, kitty," she said. "You'll be my very own kitty, and I'll call you Blackie."

Lydia turned away from the window, trembling all over. She nodded her head affirmatively several times and clamped her lips together in a hard, determined straight line. Now, at last, she knew.

In spite of Lydia's vehement and almost hysterical objections, Sam gave his permission for Betsy to keep the kitten as a pet. It would be a good thing, in any case, he argued, to have a cat about the house to control the mice that got into their food supplies. But his real reason was not a practical one at all. He had been unable to resist the pleading look in Betsy's eyes as she begged him to let her keep the kitten.

Lydia knew that it was useless to object any further. It was obvious to her now that Sam was under a spell and no longer had a will of his own. So while she watched Betsy playing with the kitten, talking to it, feeding it milk from a saucer, she decided that it must be killed. She foresaw that Betsy, with a familiar to aid her, would have powers far beyond the reach of prayer, and she did not intend to let this happen if it was in her power to prevent it.

And so, the next morning, after a night of sleeplessness, Lydia acted. While Betsy was upstairs helping Nellie with the dusting, Lydia drew a bucket of water from the well and poured it into a slop pail. Then, returning to the kitchen, she put on one of Sam's rawhide work gloves. Her heart was beating wildly, and she clenched her teeth, as though to strengthen her resolve.

The kitten was placidly lapping milk from a saucer near the fireplace. At Lydia's swift and silent approach, it looked up curiously, then backed away, its soft fur standing on end, its jeweled green eyes opened wide. It suddenly spat, and Lydia snatched it up vindictively, running out the door with it clutched in her gloved hand.

The kitten gave a short and piteous scream just before Lydia plunged it deep into the pail of water. As she felt it squirming desperately in her hand and saw it flailing its tiny legs helplessly in the water, she had a second of remorse. She shuddered and then gritted her teeth in renewed determination. She prayed aloud that the Lord would give her courage to do what must be done.

The kitten's struggles became less violent, then ceased altogether. At last, Lydia pulled it from the water, staring in horror at the lifeless form, its fur wet and matted against its body so that it seemed no larger than a small rat. With a shiver, she dropped it to the ground and ran back into the kitchen.

She was still sitting in a chair, trying to regain her composure, when Betsy came downstairs and started looking for the kitten. For a few moments, she watched Betsy in silence. Then, in a quavering voice, she said, "It's no use for you to look for your familiar."

Betsy looked at her in puzzlement and said, "I was looking for Blackie, my kitten."

"It is dead."

Betsy laughed, but a frown was gathering about her eyes. "How can it be dead? It was here just a while ago lapping milk."

"It is dead because I killed it!" screamed Lydia, as she sprang suddenly from her chair. She seized Betsy roughly by the arm and pulled the dress away from her neck. There was a small red welt there, where a mosquito had bitten her during the night.

"Just as I thought!" said Lydia triumphantly. "The wounds on the familiar always come out on the witch's own body!"

Betsy stared at her in bewilderment, too dazed even to speak, and Lydia, her voice high-pitched in hysteria, cried, "And don't stand there putting the evil eye on me!" She swooped toward the hearth and grabbed the small shovel used for ashes. Thrusting it toward Betsy, she commanded, "Take this and bury the wretched creature of Satan in the garden! And see to it that you put a stone on top of it so that it can't come back!"

Betsy, still completely mystified by Lydia's strange words and actions, mechanically took the shovel in her hand and went out into the yard. When she saw the wet, almost unrecognizable body of the kitten, she screamed in quick horror.

"Oh, my kitty!" she cried. "My poor little Blackie." She knelt down and tenderly touched the motionless kitten. "Wake up! Wake up! Please wake up!" she pleaded. When it did not stir, she drew her hand away and stood up. Her face was contorted as though she were going to cry, but instead, a sudden hot fury possessed her. She picked up the shovel and ran back to the kitchen.

She threw herself at Lydia with all the force in her small body,

59

and then with a wild swing of the shovel struck her hard on the leg. "I'll kill you, I'll kill you, just like you killed Blackie!" she screamed.

The blow caught Lydia on the kneecap, and she doubled up with pain. A righteous wrath rose up in her, and for the first time in her placid, pallid life, she wanted to fight, to hurt, to give pain for pain. Seizing Betsy by the hair, she swung her around in front of her.

"I'll beat you black and bloody! Child of Satan!" she screeched.

She twisted the shovel out of Betsy's hand, knocked her to the floor, and began beating her with a violence that she did not even try to control. Betsy, deprived of her weapon and thoroughly frightened by the crazed look in Lydia's eyes, ran out into the yard. She got halfway down the brick walk before Lydia caught up with her and hurled her to the ground again.

Lydia's skirt and petticoats billowed out in the stiff breeze that was blowing from the river. As they ballooned up to her face, she tried to pull them down, but Betsy seized the moment to tackle her feet and succeeded in toppling her over so that she went down like a ship in full sail.

Betsy jumped on top of her and wrenched the shovel from her hand. Then, with knees planted against Lydia's flat chest, she spat in her face. "Dirty bitch dog!" she yelled. "I ain't goin' to live here no more! I'll run away and find my mama!"

As Lydia struggled to get up, Betsy banged her head with the shovel, and Lydia fell back. "And my mama will get her sailor boys to tear the clothes offen your dirty bottom and hang you bare-arse to the yardarm!"

In a final spurt of fury, she crashed the shovel down on Lydia's head again. The blow fell squarely on Lydia's skull, and her mouth fell open in an unuttered cry of pain. She lay quite still.

Betsy looked down at her in surprise. She got up, and Lydia still did not move. She studied her curiously for a moment and then said, "You're dead now, just like Blackie, and I'm glad!"

She looked back to where the kitten lay, then went over to it, picked it up, and cradled it in her arms. As she walked down the brick walk toward the street, she at last began to cry. Then she brushed aside the tears that streaked down her dirty face, lifted her head, and resolutely started down Benefit Street.

When she reached the meetinghouse, she saw two boys playing in the road and went over to them. They pretended to ignore her until they saw the dead kitten in her arms. They gaped at her curiously.

"Which way is Massachusetts?" she asked.

The boys looked at each other and laughed. One of them came over to her and poked the kitten with his finger, and she drew away from him.

"Leave her be," she said. "She's dead."

The boy said, "And I s'pose you're goin' to Massachusetts for to bury her." He laughed raucously, as though he had made a joke.

"No. I'm goin' to look for my mama there."

"Well, if you're goin' to walk it, it'll take you all year."

"I don't care," said Betsy. "Which way is it?"

The boy jerked his thumb over his shoulder. "North—up past the Old North Buryin' Ground."

The other boy said, "And you better bury your cat there, before it stinks!"

Both boys roared with laughter. Betsy made a face at them and turned away. With their jeers following her, she turned down Old Gaol Lane toward Towne Street. She did not care how far away Massachusetts was. She was going there. She quickened her pace until she was almost running.

By noon she had reached Charles Street, where the Moshassuck River ran along the side of the road. In spite of the coolness of the autumn day, she was hot from walking so fast, and she was getting tired and hungry. She set the kitten down and leaned against a gatepost to rest. A very fat woman waddled out of the house beyond the gate, a retinue of dogs and cats trailing after her. Betsy looked at her with sudden interest. The woman returned her stare and then waved her hand in a friendly way.

Betsy was encouraged to call out, "Have you got something to eat, ma'am? I'm hungry."

The fat woman moved slowly in the direction of the gate with the rocking motion of a plump, inquisitive goose, until she had finally arrived in front of Betsy.

"If you're hungry, why don't you go home and eat, then?"

"I can't," said Betsy solemnly. "I'm on my way to Massachusetts."

"Massachusetts! You figger on walkin' to Massachusetts? That's a long way off, lass."

"I don't care. It's where my mother is, and it's where I'm going."

"What's your mother's name?"

"Phebe. They put her in the gaol, and now she's in Massachusetts."

"Phebe Bowen?"

Betsy nodded. "You know her?"

"Yes." The woman paused and looked at Betsy with a new interest. "Maybe you better come inside with me. I'll give you some johnnycake and tea."

Betsy smiled, nodding eagerly. She bent down to pick up the kitten and said, "Oh, thank you, ma'am."

The woman looked at her curiously. "What are you carryin' that around for? It's dead."

"I know," said Betsy. "It's Blackie. I love her even if she's dead. Please, can I bring her with me?"

The woman shrugged and opened the gate.

Betsy, seated on a stool before the fireplace, was stuffing her mouth full of soggy johnnycake, which she washed down with gulps of hot tea from a pewter mug. Now and then, she paused and studied the fat woman out of the corner of her eye.

She decided that the woman was even bigger than Black Bets, but her face, instead of being black, was very pink, and her eyes were very blue—even bluer than her mother's. She looked straight at you, without blinking, the way an owl does. Betsy liked her, even if she did look sort of strange.

When she had eaten as much as she could, she looked up and smiled politely. "Thank you," she said. "It tasted good. What's your name, ma'am?"

The woman's voice was deep, almost like a man's. "My name is Freelove Ballou but people call me Mother Ballou."

"You mean *everybody* calls you Mother? Why is that?"

"I guess it's because— Well, I help babies get born into the world."

Betsy stared at Mother Ballou in fascination. "How?"

Mother Ballou scratched her tangled gray hair. "I'm what they call a midwife. I help the mamas when they're givin' birth." She paused, and then, turning her head so that her owl's eyes were full upon Betsy, she said, "Matter of fact, child, you was born right here in this house."

Betsy's eyes opened wide. "I was?" As Mother Ballou nodded in a rather pleased way, Betsy said, "I don't remember it. I guess I was too little."

With her hunger satisfied, Betsy began to feel cheerful and talkative. She told Mother Ballou about how she had gone to live with the Allens, ending with a vivid and gory description of her fight with Lydia.

"And so I killed her," she concluded. "D'you think they'll hang me if they catch me?"

For the first time, Mother Ballou smiled. Two of her upper front teeth were missing. "I don't think so, lass. You probably didn't kill her. You just knocked her into a faint." She paused and then added, "I think it's best that you go back."

"No! I won't! I'm going to Massachusetts! But first I'm going to bury Blackie in the Old North Burying Ground."

Mother Ballou argued gently, finally persuading Betsy that the trip to Massachusetts was far too long to make on foot, even for a grownup.

Betsy sighed resignedly and looked thoughtful. "Do you think maybe I could stay here with you?"

"But I haven't any room for a little girl. It's best that I take you back to Sam Allen."

Betsy nodded assent, though she had no intention of returning to the Allens. "Can't we wait till after supper?" she pleaded. "Sam will be home then, and he won't let Aunt Liddy hurt me. Anyway, I'm too tired to walk now."

And so Mother Ballou let her go to sleep in the dilapidated wing chair near the fireplace and did not waken her until it was time for supper.

It was after dark when they set out for the Allen house. Betsy had refused Mother Ballou's offer to bury the kitten in her garden and insisted on carrying it with her. Though it was stiff and cold

63

now, its fur had dried and become fluffy again. Betsy was sure that if she hugged it to her closely, it would come back to life.

They walked in silence along the dark street. A rain so light that it was almost mist had begun to fall, and it had grown colder. Betsy pulled the shawl that Mother Ballou had given her more tightly around her.

In the darkness ahead of her, she seemed to see the figure of Lydia, vindictive and threatening. It lay in wait for her, ready to pounce. The maddened eyes in the furiously contorted face gleamed at her from the shadows. No matter which way she turned her head, the eyes seemed to follow her, burningly alive and piercing.

In a sudden and desperate terror, she wrenched her hand free of Mother Ballou's and ran back up Charles Street. She ran until she was out of breath, until she could no longer hear Mother Ballou's shrill cries commanding her to come back.

When Sam had come home, he had found Lydia prostrate on the kitchen floor, with Nellie splashing her with cold water from the well. He could get no coherent story of what had happened from either of them. Lydia moaned so continuously that she could not speak, and Nellie, in a tongue-tied hysteria, jabbered a confused story of witches and murder by the Devil's own, interrupting herself with reiterated predictions that Lydia was breathing her last. Sam refused her offer to fetch the minister, and after reassuring her that Lydia was not dying, he sent her home.

He had carried Lydia upstairs to her bedroom, put a cold compress on her head, and forced half a glass of rum between her unwilling lips. Gradually, her moaning had diminished, and she had drifted off into a troubled sleep. He had sat himself down in a ladder-back chair at the side of her bed to watch over her.

Lydia slept for more than an hour. When she awakened, she seemed calm and fully conscious, and so Sam asked her what had happened. In the whimpering tone that her voice took on in all moments of injury, real or fancied, she said, "Go away and leave me to my misery."

"But where is Betsy?" he asked.

"Gone," she whispered. "I don't want to talk about her." She turned her face away from him, burying her head in the pillow.

Sam stood up impatiently. "If she's run away, then I must go look for her and bring her home."

Lydia sat up suddenly in bed, rigid, her fists clenched in front of her. "No! No! No!" she screamed. "I'll not have her back in this house! Let her find her slut of a mother and stay with her! I'll not have her here!"

"But her mother's in Massachusetts, as you well know, Lydia."

"I don't care where she is! Let her rot in hell for all of me!" She paused for breath, and then, her eyes narrowing, she added, "A witch-child should have no trouble in getting to Massachusetts. By this time, she has no doubt rubbed herself with the juice of belladonna berries and is already there!"

Sam seized her by the arm angrily. "You are talking nonsense, Lydia—and wicked nonsense at that! I'll hear no more of it!"

Lydia shook herself free from him, crying, "You *will* hear more of it, Sam Allen—if you are not already so bewitched that you cannot see the truth! Betsy's heart is bound over to Satan, and I have proof of it!"

"Very well," he said, as though humoring a child, "what proof have you?"

Lydia sighed hopelessly. "What use will it be for me to tell you, when you don't even believe that witches exist?"

"You are wrong, Lydia. I think that witches may indeed be among us, but the injustices of Salem taught us that we must have great care in naming them unless there be good cause. The act for reversal of attainder became law many years ago, and we must abide by it. But law or no law, I have seen no signs of witchcraft in Betsy."

"No signs! What signs do you wait for? As though her evil behavior and her obscene tongue were not enough, did you not witness yesterday, along with me, the arrival of her familiar?"

Sam looked at her in surprise. "Surely, Lydia, you don't believe that a stray kitten—"

"Stray kitten, indeed! Black as the night from whence it came, its green eyes glowing with malice! From my bedroom window I watched it walk straight to the child, not timidly like an ordinary kitten, but with bold assurance. And why not? Satan had found his minion, and they recognized each other at once! And later on, in the kitchen, you yourself heard the child calling him by name— *Blackie*—"

Sam interrupted her impatiently. "And why should she not call the kitten Blackie, since that was its natural color? If this is all your proof—"

"Oh, there is more! Today, after I had drowned the evil creature—"

Sam looked at her incredulously. "You *drowned* her kitten?"

"Certainly! You may be sure it was no kitten; it was Satan himself, come to help her! It was my duty to destroy it. I wish you could have seen the child when she found out that her conspirator had been killed. She was possessed by the fury of a dozen demons!"

"I have no doubt of it," said Sam, all anger gone from his voice. It was touched now with sadness, as much for Lydia as for the death of the innocent kitten that Betsy had loved. He listened while Lydia rambled on, giving further documentation of Betsy's guilt with enthusiastic assurance now that she thought he had at last become sympathetic—free, perhaps, of the spell he had been under.

"And there were other things, too, that I had never remarked before. When the child cries, her eyes remain dry!" Her voice, triumphant in this announcement, now took on an ominous tone. "It is known that a witch has no tears, Sam. And when I tore aside her dress to see if the wounds on the body of the familiar had appeared on the witch's body, as is usual, there before my eyes was the final proof! I saw a great red mark on the back of her neck in *exactly* the spot where I had seized the kitten when I killed it and—"

"Don't tell me any more, Lydia," said Sam, brushing his hand across his eyes as though to erase the picture of Lydia's violence. "I have no doubt that your intentions were of the best, but you have done a wicked, cruel thing. I am not surprised that Betsy attacked you as she did. In her eyes—as in mine—you had murdered an innocent creature, and she sought vengeance."

Lydia looked at him coldly. "If that is your view of things, Sam Allen, it is clear that you are still under her spell."

Sam had reached the end of his patience, and now his voice rose in sudden anger. "I am under no spell, woman, so have done with your outlandish talk! You are as daft and unreasonable as the judges at Salem. You condemn without proof and—"

"And the crying without tears, and the mark on her body—they are not proof enough for you?"

"I have seen the child cry many times during punishment—and never without tears!"

"And the mark on the body—what was that?"

"I do not know. It might have been many things. But the child is no witch, and the sooner you leave off your mad fancies, the better!"

As he moved toward the door, Lydia stopped him with a cry. "Where are you going?"

"To search for Betsy. She should not be exposed to the elements on a night like this."

Lydia ran after him, seizing his hands in hers and trying to pull him back into the room.

"Get back into bed, Lydia! You are ill in mind as well as body, and it would be well if you prayed the Lord to return you to health with all possible speed."

"You are set on bringing the child back here, then?"

"I am. And you may as well accept it with good grace now as later!"

He started down the stairs, and she followed him, clenching the mahogany balustrade with both hands and screaming, "You'll rue this day, Sam Allen, mark what I say! You've entered a pact with Satan along with the child, and one day, when it's too late, you'll know it! Yes, Sam Allen, I'll pray—but it will be for *your* soul, not mine!"

Suddenly, there was a loud rapping of the brass knocker on the front door. Lydia raised her head in terror, as though the Devil himself were arriving to claim his own. From the top of the stairs, she watched breathlessly while Sam opened the door and admitted Mother Ballou.

Lydia drew back, her hand pressed against her breast to quiet the quick beating of her heart. There was a look of horror on her face as she ran back into her bedroom and with trembling fingers bolted the door behind her.

For a long time she had recognized that Mother Ballou, with her midwife's herbs and simples and her reputation for miraculous cures, was the most powerful witch in Providence.

The Old North Burying Ground bore no resemblance to the neat and well-kept graveyards within the town limits. The early settlers had long since taken up every foot of available space, and the spot had been abandoned and left untended for half a century or more.

Some people believed that Roger Williams himself slept here, somewhere among the toppled, sprawling headstones with their inscriptions eroded by time and crusted over with lichen and moss so as to be mostly illegible. But if the founder of the city did indeed rest here, his peace was undisturbed, for the Old North Burying Ground was now a jungle of vines and brambles, and the denseness of the undergrowth did not invite exploration.

If it had been summer, Sam might have been faced with an almost impenetrable wilderness, but it was late autumn, and the trees and bushes were bare of their leaves. If Betsy was here, as Mother Ballou believed her to be, it would not be too difficult to find her.

Sam lighted his pitch torch and plunged into the tangle of dead vegetation. He called Betsy's name again and again, pausing every few moments to wait for an answer because the cracking of dead twigs and branches underfoot echoed so noisily that he could not have heard an answering cry. As he held the torch aloft, straining his eyes into the darkness, he moved slowly forward in the flickering light.

He did not have far to go. During a pause he heard a sound that was like the whimpering of a wounded animal. He moved toward it and then, in a burst of light from his torch, he saw her. She lay curled up, wet and shivering, at the foot of a buttonwood tree, the dead kitten still clutched in her arms.

She did not move when he approached. And as he leaned down toward her, she looked at him with wide-staring eyes, as though she did not recognize him. Her face was smudged with dirt and dried blood from bramble scratches.

Sam jabbed the end of the torch into the ground and knelt down at her side. He pulled the shawl around her more tightly and tied it. Gently, he tried to take the kitten from her arms.

Thrusting a small fist at him Betsy came to sudden life. "No! Don't take her away!"

He gave a nod of reassurance as he sat down and lifted her onto his lap. As his arms went around her, a quick joy flooded him at the knowledge that she was alive and safe. He kissed her forehead and hugged her to him in silence. She began to sob convulsively, her head pressed hard against his chest.

When at last he spoke, his voice was so soft that it was barely audible. "There, there, child. Hush now. No harm will come to you. And you will not be punished—I promise."

Later, in silence, they buried the kitten, placing it in a hollow between the roots of the tree and covering it with leaves. Sam had never said a prayer for a kitten before, but he said one now. He asked that God watch over its soul, if it should perchance have one, and that He forgive the mortal who had so misguidedly brought its short life to so painful an ending.

Then, rising from his knees and stubbing out the torch on the wet earth, he took Betsy up in his arms and carried her home.

CHAPTER 7

L YDIA was used to accepting a defeat at Sam's hands with humble acquiescence, adding each one almost pleasurably to her long list of grievances and sufferings. But she did not resign herself to the defeat she experienced when Sam brought Betsy back home. Although she remained outwardly compliant and submissive, in her heart she declared war. For once, she could be sure that the Lord was on her side because the enemy was the Devil himself, incarnate in the body of a child.

Utterly convinced that Betsy had thrown an enchantment over Sam, now she became fearful that she might be ensnared herself. And so, while Betsy lay ill and feverish in bed for the two weeks that followed her running away, Lydia refused to enter her room. She sent Nellie upstairs with a tray of food at mealtimes, and it was Nellie who took care of all the sickbed chores. Lydia would not even wash Betsy's dishes for fear of contamination.

Her fear was contagious, and one evening Nellie announced to Sam that she could no longer risk exposure to a witch-child. Sam became furious at this new consequence of Lydia's superstitious beliefs. Before Nellie left to go home, he brought Lydia downstairs into the kitchen and angrily confronted the two women.

"There has been enough ungodly talk in this house!" he said. "I will have no more of it! Now, hear me, both of you! A child lies ill upstairs, and as master of this house, I order that she be taken care of properly and nursed back to health!" Turning violently to Nellie, he thrust his face toward hers earnestly. "Your mistress has given herself over to daft fancies that are both wicked and sinful! There is no need for you to believe them, too."

Nellie, intimidated by his angry tone, retreated a step and looked at him sheepishly. "I didn't mean no harm, Mr. Allen. But mayhap the child *is* a witch, like the mistress says. Mayhap she has powers—"

"If she has such powers, Nellie," said Sam, "then why should she fall sick, coughing and feverish?"

Impressed, Nellie nodded her head. " 'Tis true, sir. Witches never be sick, what with their magic herbs blessed by Satan." She looked at Lydia, as though in expectation of a counterargument, but Lydia said nothing.

Sam looked at Nellie, his eyes calm and persuasive. "Do you not think I am a godly man, Nellie?"

"Oh, yes, sir."

"Then you can believe me when I say that there is no witchcraft in this house. There is only an ailing child needing love and attention. And if your mistress insists on neglecting her, it is all the more worthy that you, as a good Christian woman of sound common sense, minister to the child's needs."

Nellie was pleased and flattered to learn that she possessed virtues that Lydia apparently did not. Nodding her head approvingly, her face flushed with pleasure, she murmured, "Thank you, sir. I will do my best for the child."

And so Nellie, stolid and undemonstrative by nature, did make an effort to follow Sam's request for "love and attention." Though she had no affection for Betsy, nor indeed for anyone, she lingered in the room for a few moments after delivering a tray of food and did her best to be more sociable.

Betsy was grateful for this sudden show of friendliness. While the fever had raged in her, she had spent most of the time sleeping, but when at last she had begun to recover, time hung heavy on her hands, and she counted the hours until Sam would return at night and sit by her bedside.

She welcomed Nellie's visits, trying to find ways of detaining her. She tried to teach her how to play cat's cradle with a piece of string, a game that she had learned from her mother. But Nellie's fat and roughened fingers were clumsy, and the movements were far too intricate for her dull wits to grasp. For moments at a time she would stare at the string on Betsy's delicate hands and then try to follow Betsy's instructions. Again and again, she plucked jerkily at the wrong strings and reduced the whole thing to a knotted tangle—to her own bewilderment and Betsy's despair.

Although Nellie could not play cat's cradle, her attempts at nursing were more successful and within a week Betsy was well enough to get out of bed. Sam issued firm orders excusing her from all household chores until she had regained her strength.

But he resumed her lessons immediately. Inasmuch as Lydia remained adamant in her decision to have as little contact with Betsy as possible, Sam now taught her to read as well as to write.

Betsy was delighted by the new arrangement. Her feelings toward Lydia had moved from indifference to fear and hatred. Whenever she looked at Lydia's face now, she saw it as it had been on that terrible day. No matter how placid and immobile it might be in reality, she saw it fixed in an expression of murderous hate, and the words "I'll beat you black and bloody!" still echoed in her ears. During those rare moments when they were alone together, she was watchful and suspicious, and Lydia did not look at her directly for fear of exposure to the evil eye that witches were said to possess.

Betsy herself was not even sure what a witch was, but it was clear to her that it was something definitely, however mysteriously, bad. And it was not just one of those bad words that somebody called you in anger. She was consumed with curiosity about it, and one evening, in the midst of her reading lesson, she stopped abruptly in the middle of a sentence and stared across the table at Sam.

"Well, go on," said Sam. "You know that next word."

"Am I a witch?" she blurted out.

"Certainly not. Continue reading."

"But what *is* a witch?" she persisted. "Aunt Liddy says I'm one, and I want to know what it is."

"Your Aunt Liddy has strange thoughts. Pay her no mind."

Betsy brought her hand down angrily on the open primer. "But I want to know! Tell me!"

Sam sighed. "I suppose you will give me no rest till I do. Very well, then. But I want you to promise that after I have told you, you will put it out of your mind and not think about it again."

"I promise," she said solemnly.

Sam paused, trying to find words that would be clear and yet not frightening. "Well, child, it is believed that some people, mostly females, make a pact with Satan—"

"What's a pact?"

"They sell their souls to him."

"For how much?"

"Not for money, child—for power—power to do whatever they please—by magic."

"Oh, I'd like that!" said Betsy, clapping her hands together in delight.

"Hush! That's wicked talk, child. No doubt we would all like to have great power so that we could do whatever we pleased, but thanks to our Lord, most of us are not willing to pay the Devil's price." His voice became hushed and ominous. "We would lose our souls."

Betsy pondered this for a moment. "Is that bad?"

For the next ten minutes, Sam told Betsy about her soul. She was disappointed that he could not tell her what it looked like nor even where it was, but she was impressed by the deep solemnity of his voice and listened attentively.

Finally, Sam, running out of words, asked hopefully, "Now do you understand what your soul is, my child?"

"A little," Betsy said thoughtfully. "It's like your maidenhead; like Mama said, you better keep it as long as you can."

Sam's mouth dropped open in shock. His impulse was to punish her, but then he told himself that the word was not an obscene one, and the sentiment, at least, was moral.

Although Betsy's definitions of witches and souls remained hazy, her ability to read, write, and spell improved with a speed that amazed and delighted her teacher. Her behavior, too, underwent a sudden change that Sam considered nothing less than miraculous. The obscenities disappeared from her speech. There were no more outrageous acts of pillage and destruction. She was sweet of temper and dutiful. She seemed, for the first time, to be happy.

Sam thanked God fervently for the miracle He had wrought. But it was not a miracle. It was just that Betsy had made a discovery.

It happened one evening as the writing lesson was nearing an

73

end. Betsy had been especially bright and attentive. She had written her own name so that it was completely legible, if somewhat ink-splotched from her awkward upstrokes of the long quill pen, whose feather tickled her nose. She had sputtered her way quickly and easily through the staccato grunts of the syllabarium in the *New England Primer*. She had recited the rhymed alphabet that began with "A for Adam—In Adam's fall/ We sin*ned* all" and ended with "Z for Zaccheus—Zaccheus he/ Did climb the tree/ Our Lord to see."

Last of all, and to Sam's amazed gratification, she spelled a long list of words he had given her only the night before and did it without making a single mistake.

The drawn lines in his angular face smoothed with pleasure, and the blue of his eyes became warmly alive and penetrating. He stretched out his arms toward her, and, his voice soft, he said, "Come to me, lass. You are an apt pupil, and you have made your uncle both happy and proud."

He smiled one of his rare, slow smiles, and she moved quickly within the orbit of his arms, which encircled her and drew her toward his chest. Then, unexpectedly, his thighs closed on her, viselike, and pinned her against him. The sudden, almost fierce movement alarmed her, and she looked searchingly at his face.

She was relieved to see that it showed no anger or displeasure. His eyes were closed, his face immobile, except that the little vein on his forehead pulsed rapidly. She was watching it in fascination when he abruptly moved his head close to hers. She felt his lips pressing roughly against her forehead, her hair, and finally on her mouth. The familiar slow warmth began to flow through her body—that happy, protected feeling that until now she had known only during the aftermath of a beating.

His breath came fast and irregularly, and he strained her so tightly to him that she squirmed in discomfort. Then, quite suddenly, his whole body shook convulsively, and after a moment, went slack. He thrust her away from him roughly, almost angrily, one hand pressed against the front of his osenbrig breeches.

The change in him puzzled her, and she looked up anxiously, fearing that she had done something to displease him. But it seemed to her that his face was neither angry nor happy. It had become a mask. His eyes were veiled now, faraway and cold. She stood uncertainly before him, as though waiting for instructions.

"Come!" he said gruffly. "It's time for bed." He rose awkwardly from the chair, still holding one hand just below the waist of his breeches.

To Betsy, his actions, though peculiar, were no cause for concern, and she was elated by the discovery she had made. She would no longer need to misbehave and endure punishment in order to feel his arms about her, to be kissed so that she would feel happy and warm.

She need only learn to spell well.

Her life continued on its new and angelic course until Thanksgiving Day, a time that she had looked forward to with great excitement and anticipation. In Providence, as in all parts of New England, it was the only real holiday of the year, when festivity was not merely permitted but was given free rein. The celebration of Christmas as observed in England, with feasting and merriment, was considered "a wicked papistrie." Here, it was marked only by religious services such as those that took place at Easter.

But Thanksgiving was happily free of the taint of Rome, and so after a morning of prayer in the meetinghouse, the day was given over to feasting and jubilation. The kitchen of the Allen house, along with every kitchen in well-to-do houses throughout Providence, became a place of magnificent and intoxicating aromas—from the spicy, molasses-sweetened pumpkin pies baking in their square tins, from the sizzling turkey roasting before an open fire.

It seemed to Betsy that the house overflowed with all the things that she liked most to eat—raisins and citron, walnuts and popcorn, apples and cider. And when at last it was time for the dinner to begin, she fidgeted and squirmed in her chair while Sam said the especially long grace that the holiday demanded. Her mouth watered and she had to clench her hands to keep them from making a dive for the nearest edible object.

When at last she had eaten herself into a state of torpor, she wanted only to fall into bed and sleep. But Sam had other plans. As a pleasant surprise for her, and in keeping with the conviviality of the holiday, he had arranged to visit the Wyatt family so that Betsy might have a joyful reunion with her sister, Polly.

Betsy greeted the invitation anything but joyfully until she remembered that the Wyatt boys would be there. The prospect of the outing became even more agreeable with Lydia, pleading a headache, asked to be left at home.

Betsy was curious to see the inside of the elegant house on Angell Street, partly because its exterior was so imposing and partly because she had never been in any well-to-do home except the one she lived in. As she and Sam went up the double flight of steps leading to the ornate doorway, she looked up in wonder at the heavy, elaborately carved pediment. Sam lifted the shining brass door knocker and let it fall.

"Is Mr. Wyatt the richest man in Providence?" asked Betsy.

"Not quite, lass," said Sam with a smile. "But he is a shipbuilder, and he does very well."

The inside of the Wyatt house was even more awe-inspiring to Betsy than its majestic entrance. As she moved through the spacious hall, with its wide and curving staircase and solid mahogany rail, her eyes lingered curiously on the figure of a partly naked woman who stood, with arms upraised presumably to heaven, on the newel post. And from above the double-doored entrance to the drawing room, the busts of two other women looked down at her from their marble placidity. She did not know that these were Roman goddesses named Juno, Ceres, and Diana, but she was greatly impressed by them just the same because she had never before seen women made of marble, women who were dead but who looked almost alive.

The huge drawing room, with its French rococo marble fireplace and mahogany pilasters, its rich and colorful hangings, its gleaming furniture of highly polished woods, seemed to be part of a palace in a fairy tale. The people in the room were so beautifully dressed that they looked like a royal family instead of those Wyatts whom she had always seen, until now, dressed in dark clothes on their way to church.

The three boys and Polly sat primly, like a row of bright-colored spring tulips, on chairs that were lined up at the far end of the room. Henry Wyatt and his wife, Ellen, stood not far from the entrance, near a table on which there was a large silver punch bowl and innumerable little trays of macaroons, sugared almonds and green ginger, candied lemon peel, caraway comfits, and exotic-looking sweetmeats such as Betsy had not imagined in her wildest dreams at church.

Sam introduced her to Mr. and Mrs. Wyatt, and she executed her deepest and most elaborate curtsy. Mrs. Wyatt then took her by the hand and led her over to Polly and the boys. At the sight of Polly, Betsy's face showed a surprise that was quickly succeeded by embarrassment, for Polly was nothing less than resplendent. She wore a pale-yellow dress of silk, and it was embroidered at the shoulders with tiny, intensely golden flowers. Her trim little shoes of striped calamanco glittered with diminutive silver buckles. Her dark hair was tied back with a scarlet ribbon of pompadour silk, and most beautiful of all, there was a string of pink coral and miniature seashells about her neck.

Polly dutifully extended her cheek for a sisterly kiss, but Betsy did not respond. Her eyes moved from Polly's gay holiday costume down to her own plain white linen dress—the dress that had pleased her so much when Sam gave it to her. She felt like a dun-colored sparrow confronted with a peacock that shone with jeweled plumage. She wanted to run from the room and hide, and it was only with a great effort of will that she held back tears of shame that started to her eyes.

The kindly voice of Mrs. Wyatt was saying, "Come now, Betsy, aren't you going to kiss your sister in greeting after all these months?"

The Wyatt boys were watching her curiously, and so was Sam. She lifted her head and forced herself to smile and say, "Hello, Polly," and then, stepping quickly forward, brushed her sister's cheek with her lips. Polly smiled insipidly, like a queen receiving the respects of a dutiful subject. Betsy turned abruptly away and fastened her attention on the boys.

Mrs. Wyatt performed the introductions. "Peter, this is Miss Betsy Bowen." The youngest boy bowed stiffly, while Betsy curtsied mechanically. "And this is Richard." The boy in the middle moved awkwardly toward her, gave her a mischievous look as though he were about to laugh, then did a quick bow, which she acknowledged with another brief curtsy. "And this," Mrs. Wyatt continued, "is my eldest son, Matthew."

For a moment, Betsy forgot her concern about the drabness of her appearance as she gazed curiously into the boy's pensive gray eyes, which for a few seconds lost their usual faraway expression. He looked at her with a piercing directness that seemed to read her mind, to see the envy that was making her so miserable. This increased her embarrassment even more, and before he had even begun his bow, she lowered her head and did a deep curtsy to escape his knowing eyes.

When Mrs. Wyatt led her to the table and offered her a glass of punch and a choice of cakes and sweetmeats, her enthusiasm for the refreshments had all but disappeared. She wanted only to leave this magnificent house with its handsomely dressed people—to go home, throw herself on her bed and cry.

She sipped the punch listlessly, munched a cookie without relish, and looked fixedly at the floor. When Sam and the Wyatts tried to engage her in conversation, she looked up at them sullenly, answering their polite questions as briefly as possible.

Mrs. Wyatt invited her to join the other children in a game of blindman's buff, but she hung her head and shook it negatively.

Mrs. Wyatt's voice took on a coaxing tone. "Are you not happy to see your dear sister, my child?"

"Yes, ma'am."

"Then why don't you go play with her?"

"Because I don't want to," said Betsy with a note of peevish irritation in her voice.

"Very well. Perhaps you would like to sit here." Mrs. Wyatt indicated a chair. Betsy moved toward it, aware that Matthew's eyes were following her, as alert and curious as a cat's. She sat down and smoothed the skirt of the hated white linen dress.

Sam was watching her with a beginning scowl of annoyance at her strange and unsociable behavior. He felt that some sort of apology was in order, and turning to Mrs. Wyatt, he said, "She's been a bit peaked of late, ma'am. A matter of the bile, I believe, but nothing serious."

Betsy gave him a look of surprise and then went back to staring at the floor. For the remainder of the visit, she continued to sulk, politely refusing further invitations of refreshment and flatly declining to join the other children in their game. She was relieved

when it was time to go, when all the polite goodbyes and thank
yous had been said, to the accompaniment of more bowing and
curtsying.

The door had hardly closed behind them when she turned
abruptly to Sam and asked, "What is bile?"

He looked at her quizzically. "It is a fluid made in the liver.
When there is too much of it in the blood, it makes for ill temper
and sickness."

"But I'm not sick," she said. "Why did you tell Mrs. Wyatt I
was peaked?"

"Because your sullen behavior was not seemly in a guest." He
looked at her sternly. "What ailed you, child?"

Betsy said nothing. With her hand in Sam's, she kept on walking
and stared before her at the half-frozen ruts in the road.

"Well," he asked again, "what *was* it?"

Suddenly, Betsy halted and turned her head up to him. Her face
was fierce and determined. "I want a ribbon for my hair!" she said
loudly. Then, in a breathless rush, she added, "And a silk dress
with flowers on it! And shoes with silver buckles! And a pretty
necklace of seashells!"

To Sam, the intense feeling in her voice was surprising, and
somehow annoying. "Envy and vanity," he said drily, "are sins
before our Lord."

"I don't care! I want to look pretty like Polly!"

"We must cast out vanity, Betsy, as we cast out all sin."

Mocking the singsong gravity of his voice, she said, "It's a sin to
lie, too!" She turned to him angrily. "You lied to Mrs. Wyatt!
You said I was sick with the bile! Liar! Liar!"

"It must be that you are indeed sick with the bile—to talk in
such a manner to me!" said Sam with growing exasperation. "No
doubt a physic is needed."

"I need no physic!" Betsy shouted. "I need a ribbon for my hair
and a necklace of shells and—"

"Enough!" Sam commanded angrily. "You will have no gew-
gaws and vain fripperies that are becoming only to children of
Satan!"

Betsy laughed at him. "Then is Polly a child of Satan? And will
Mrs. Wyatt burn in hell-fire?"

" 'Tis enough, I said!" Sam shouted and seized her by the arm, propelling her forward, but she shook herself free and then planted herself squarely in front of him, stubborn and defiant.

"Liar, liar!" she screamed. "You'll burn in hell-fire along with Polly and Mrs. Wyatt, and all of you will stink like burned chicken feathers and shit!"

He slapped her hard on the cheek, but instead of crying, she laughed at him again, and this turned his anger into uncontrollable rage. He grabbed her roughly by the shoulder, swung her around, and shoved her ahead of him on the road.

Betsy recovered her balance and, still laughing, ran awkwardly ahead of him, like a chicken in flight. And Sam, muttering furiously to himself, ran after her.

Later that afternoon, after Betsy had received her punishment in the upstairs bedroom, she became more than ordinarily affectionate in the prayerful aftermath of a beating. As she and Sam rose from their knees after asking the Lord's forgiveness for her sins of vanity and rebellion, she rushed into his arms. She glued her body against him, pressing the soft ringlets of her red-gold hair against his cheek, placing the warm moistness of her mouth on his neck, just below his ear.

Sam's sinewy arms closed about her tightly, but before he could imprison her between his legs, she managed to spring away from him. She turned penitent eyes toward him and said, "I love you, Uncle. I am sorry I sinned and called you bad names. Mayhap a scarlet ribbon in the hair be a sinful thing."

Sam nodded in a pleased way, meanwhile trying to pull her toward him with his outstretched legs, but again she moved away just far enough to elude him.

"But in truth, Uncle, I did not want a scarlet ribbon like Polly's." She moved quickly within his arms, and thrusting an innocent, pleading face toward his, she added, "A green ribbon—be that sinful, too?"

He did not know whether it was the sweet innocuousness of her question or the sudden proximity of her young, warm body that made him say, "Perhaps not, child, perhaps not."

CHAPTER 8

B Y the time the first heavy snowfall arrived in mid-January, a green silk hair ribbon was only one of several adornments that Betsy received in the weeks that followed the Thanksgiving visit to the Wyatts. Not long after the gift of the hair ribbon, and following an especially excellent spelling lesson, a new dress had appeared—of cream-colored silk, with a purple rose and a golden crown of thorns beautifully and piously embroidered on the bodice. A few weeks later, there was a pair of gloves of pale-green wool; and on the very eve of the snowstorm came the most beautiful gift of all—a necklace of small stones that glowed with deep sea-green color.

On the morning after the storm, when Betsy was getting ready to go with Sam to watch the breaking out of the roads, she wanted to wear the new necklace, but Sam said it was not a proper occasion for such finery.

"But Uncle," she pleaded, "it's so pretty, and I haven't yet wore it."

"It can wait," Sam said. "It is more important to dress warmly than elegantly for the breaking-out. It's not likely that you will take off your coat in any case, child. And supposing you were to lose your new necklace in the snow?"

The last argument was convincing, and inasmuch as she had never watched a breaking-out before and hardly knew what to expect, she was quite ready to accept Sam's opinion as to what she should wear. Reluctantly, she put the necklace back in its Chinese lacquered box.

Earlier in the morning she had watched the team of oxen pull the heavy iron snowplow down Benefit Street toward the meeting-house. The road to church was among the first roads to be opened, second only to Towne Street, the location of the respectable taverns where the men would go for warmth and rum potions while they worked. After Towne Street, the way to Dr. Bentham's house on George Street was cleared, and then all the other main streets of town.

Betsy put on her newly acquired winter clothing—a warm coat of hand-woven blue wool and a round hat made of squirrel fur. But she was not allowed to wear the new pale-green gloves and had to content herself with red mittens, which Sam said would be warmer and more appropriate for the occasion.

Finally, in a state of high excitement, she settled herself next to Sam in the small sleigh drawn by his stomping and impatient sorrel mare, called Dorrie. It was Betsy's first ride in a sleigh, and she loved it. Until now, she had only watched from the side of the road while sleighs glided by, bells jingling, and she had envied the well-dressed and smiling people who rode by so gaily.

Now, she was one of them, and she turned an enraptured face up to Sam and closed her hand affectionately over his arm. She reveled in the feel of the icy air against her face, in the sight of the sparkling shower of snow thrown up by Dorrie's fast-moving hoofs, in the giddy sensation of sailing so silently and swiftly over the white expanse all around her.

They went south along Benefit Street and then turned left into Power Street, from which direction the shouting voices of men could now be heard. When at last they arrived at the scene of the plowing, Sam brought the sleigh to a halt, lifted Betsy out of her seat, and set her down on the road.

The sight of the huge oxen filled her with awe and wonder. Clouds of steam poured from their nostrils as they lumbered powerfully forward, dragging the wide, heavy plow behind them. They were amazingly sure-footed, and only when the angle of the road rose slightly did they begin to slip, struggling and straining to keep their balance.

The alternately commanding and cajoling cries of the drivers and the men on either side of the team filled the air with an excitement so contagious that Betsy yelled and screamed along with them. She was enjoying herself so thoroughly that when it came time to change the team of oxen and for the men to repair to a tavern for warmth and refreshment, she wanted to go along with them. But Sam explained that a tavern full of men, sitting around an open fire drinking flip and rum toddy, was no place for a little girl. He set her back on the sleigh, and they started for home. But Betsy, as usual, did not give up easily.

"But *why* can't I go with them?" she wanted to know.

"I have already told you that it is not proper," said Sam. "When men are alone together, they talk roughly in language that is not fit for a lady's ears."

"But I'm not a lady," said Betsy. "Anyway, I *know* how they talk because I heard them when they came to see Mama—"

"Hush!" said Sam. "Your mama was not a lady."

"Then why should I have to be one?"

"Because it is better. You will be more acceptable to the Lord, and you will also be happier, Betsy."

Betsy considered this for a moment. Then, with a note of sadness in her voice, she said, " 'Tis true that Mama did not have clothes as pretty as mine. And she never rode in a sleigh."

"These are only small ways in which the Lord rewards virtue," said Sam sententiously.

Betsy could not think of any larger rewards at the moment— except possibly the possession of a pair of ice skates. "Do you think the Lord might give me some skates, Uncle?" she asked.

It took the Lord a little over two weeks to deliver the skates, but when they came, they were very handsome. Of brass, they had come all the way from Holland, and they fastened to her small feet with neat leather straps. She was very proud of them and learned to skate, under Sam's patient instruction at Dexter's Pond, almost as quickly as she had mastered the alphabet.

She was pleased to learn that virtue was rewarded so promptly, and at last, she was sure that she knew what virtue was. It was an affectionate response to Sam's odd behavior at the conclusion of a letter-perfect lesson in spelling.

For Sam, these brief moments of ecstasy brought in their wake hours of conscience-stricken torture, sleepless nights when he gave himself over to endless self-recrimination. With the coming of spring, he made new and more determined efforts to escape the fleshly temptations that Betsy's presence provoked in him.

He prayed constantly for the strength to conquer his sinful weakness, and there would be times when he seemed to be winning his battle. And then a night would come when tenderness for the child would suddenly overwhelm him, and her physical nearness would, in a rush of passion, sweep aside all his resolves in a flood of lust that momentarily drowned his reason.

In the aftermath of disgust and guilt, as he prayed God for forgiveness, he would tell himself that though he was corrupting himself, he was not harming Betsy. He came to believe that in spite of all the precocious knowledge she seemed to have acquired during her life with her mother, she had remained curiously innocent. Although she knew the obscene words that had been part of the language from earliest Anglo-Saxon times and had now learned that they were forbidden, she had, he was sure, only rather vague notions of the meaning of some of them. He was certain, at least, that she had no idea of what happened to him physically when he held her closely in his arms. At first, she had seemed surprised by the intensity of his affection, but now she accepted his behavior as something quite normal.

He could not escape the realization that she used these incidents as a means of extracting gifts from him, but he did not mind. It was hardly blackmail because she did not know that he was doing anything that might be wrong.

Actually, he had begun to enjoy giving her these presents of clothing, of trinkets or skates, or whatever. He loved to watch the look of delight that came into her eyes, the quick smile that made the dimples appear in her cheeks. He liked, too, the feeling that he was rewarding the serious devotion she gave to her studies, which continued to progress with a speed that astounded him. More deeply, and in a most curious way, he felt that a gift, especially if it was made only by denying himself the purchase of something he wanted, magically helped to atone for his moments of wantonness.

And yet, the sense of sin never left him. It was so pervasive that for days at a time he would live with a brooding melancholy that colored all his thoughts. But he did not give up his struggle, and for every time that he was overpowered by desire, there were a dozen victories, when he battled against temptation and won.

He told himself that if there had been a public school in Providence, he might have sent her there for instruction, and so have avoided these nightly sessions alone in the parlor. But the town's only public school had burned down in 1774, and a new one had never been built. He considered hiring a tutor but immediately decided that he could not afford it. Instead, he made himself believe that in time he would be able to control himself completely. Meanwhile, he was sure, he was doing no harm to Betsy.

Increasingly, he found that she had become the very center of his existence, his only connection with life and feeling, an outlet for the love that had always been in him and that had never found as full expression before. Never, until now, had his love been returned by anyone, spontaneously and without conditions. It was a response of which Lydia was incapable. She did not love people, she loved things—the house and all the inanimate objects it contained, from the furniture to the pots and pans in the kitchen, and without his wishing it, she had somehow made him part of this lifeless world. Most of their conversation had centered on it, and whatever companionship they had had together had revolved around it. And now, with his complete absorption in Betsy, they had even less to say to each other, and relations between them became more formal and distant than ever.

His love of the child spread far beyond the bounds of his fitful and guilt-laden moments of passion. Through her he was able to escape, if only vicariously, from his drab world, from the round of monotonous duties that had once made up his whole existence. Through her eyes, life took on color and movement.

Her boundless enthusiasm and energy, her insatiable curiosity about everything, her bubbling delight in the small events of living—whether it was the Saturday-night bath or a sleigh ride—were infectious, and the hours he spent with her had a fresh, new-minted luster. They were the only happy ones he knew. He began to seek out occasions, aside from the nightly lessons, when they could be together.

On a Saturday morning in April, when one of his ships had just docked, he decided to take Betsy with him to the port. Saddling up Dorrie, he lifted the child onto the seat before he mounted himself.

Lydia, watching from her bedroom window, was sure that he had taken leave of his senses. The child would surely fall, she thought to herself, and it would serve them both right if she did. But to Lydia's disappointment, Betsy did not fall. She followed

Sam's instructions to hold her legs tightly against Dorrie's flanks, and when he had mounted and his left arm went around her to hold her in position, she looked back toward him and grinned triumphantly.

Though Sam had expected her to be somewhat frightened, she showed not the slightest sign of fear. Except for her elation and excitement, she might have been sitting in a chair in the kitchen. When Dorrie moved down the road, Betsy squealed with delight at the unfamiliar rocking motion.

And by the time they reached the port, she seemed thoroughly at home on horseback. Sam watched her in admiration as she sat there perched so jauntily in front of him, dressed in her finest clothes, her head lifted high.

Her face was pensive and preoccupied. She was imagining that she was the Queen of Sheba, whom she had just read about in the Bible. From her lofty position high on the horse, she looked at the towering masts of the ships anchored in port, and she thought, I am the Queen, and all these boats belong to me.

In disdain she looked down at the sailors and ships' officers and dock workers who walked along the muddy streets. They were her subjects, all of them, and at her command, they would do her slightest bidding. Once, she recognized a face as one of her mother's friends. When it looked back at her and smiled, she quickly turned her gaze to the horizon, as though something of great interest had suddenly appeared there.

It disturbed her that Dorrie did not look at all the way a queen's steed should. Someday, she decided, she would have a horse befitting the Queen of Sheba—a high-stepping palfrey of purest white and with golden trappings, not a broken-down old sorrel mare like Dorrie. Then, with sudden guilt for her unkind thoughts, she reached forward and patted Dorrie on the head.

When they reached India Point and the ramshackle building where Sam had his shipping office, he dismounted and tied Dorrie to a hitching post. Then, lifting Betsy down, he led her by the hand into the building and up the rickety stairs to the office where he kept his books. He sat her down in a high-backed chair and went over to his desk. He asked her to be quiet while he worked, and she was. But soon, growing weary of watching him leaf through his books of cargo listings and bills, her eyelids began to droop, her head nodded, and she fell sound asleep.

When she awoke, Sam was still working. She was hungry, and Sam told her they would leave for home very soon. She grew restless with waiting and moved to the window that looked out on Narragansett Bay. The clean salt breeze, damp and faintly fishlike, ruffled her hair. It carried the spicy odor of pitch, turpentine, and pine boards, and she breathed deeply, enjoying the smell. She watched the men unloading cargoes from the ships that were docked at the nearby wharves. Their bodies were stripped to the waist, and their sweating backs glistened in the spring sun. They shouted and sang in rhythm with their movements, and these sounds, with the mewing of the sea gulls wheeling overhead as an unceasing chorus, produced in her a kind of ecstasy and enchantment.

She decided that the port was a far lovelier place than the heaven that the Reverend Arnold described on Sundays. He and his churchgoers could go there when they died, if they wanted to. She would go to the port.

All the way home, she plied Sam with questions about ships and the men who sailed in them. Where did the ships go to? What did they carry down deep inside them? Pearls, rubies, silks, and satins? Pepper, spices, oranges, and lemons? How long would the *Lydia A.* be gone after she sailed again? Could they meet her when she came back? Where was China? Had he ever been there? How big was a whale? Had he ever been in a storm at sea? How high were the waves? Could he dance the hornpipe like her mother's friends? Could he sing sailor songs? Why did he stay in Providence when he could go to sea if he wanted to?

Sam was amused and oddly flattered by her curiosity, answering all her questions seriously and in detail, with a flow of words and a vividness of description that did not ordinarily color his conversation. For the moment, he was reliving the years of his youth, when he had gone to sea, and quite unexpectedly, he rediscovered the sailor's pleasure in telling a yarn. He described typhoons and hurricanes, strange lands and brown-skinned people, and Betsy listened spellbound, her eyes shining.

That night, at their lessons, he took a teacher's advantage of the interest that he had awakened. Taking out a collection of old maps and nautical charts, together they pored over them in the candle-light. And on succeeding nights, she learned more than just the rudiments of geography. Sam explained to her the phases of the moon, the movement of the planets around the sun, the constellations that guided ships at sea, the vast galaxies in the heavens, and most especially the one that was called the Milky Way.

Betsy listened and learned, her mouth sometimes dropping open in wonderment, until the lesson became so prolonged that she would begin to yawn and nod, finally falling abruptly into sleep while she still sat in her chair. Then, Sam's voice would become still and for a moment he would look at her in tenderness and pride. At last, he would arouse himself, take her up in his arms, and carry her to her bedroom.

Betsy, as drowsily limp as a sleepy kitten, would make no move to undress herself, and so Sam would take off her clothes gently, one by one. Then he would pull her nightdress on over her head and push her snugly down under the bedclothes.

Only half-awake, she still made a desperate effort to keep her eyes open. She was waiting for the faint brush of his lips on her forehead to tell her that she was loved.

CHAPTER 9

T HE summer was hot and dry that year. There was so little rain that brooks stopped running and wells went dry. On farms the crops in the fields shriveled and turned brown, and the soil lay hard and baked under a broiling sun. Clouds of dust swirled up from the roads of the town, settled on buildings, blew through open windows and doors.

To Lydia's despair, the furniture and floors of the Allen house were covered with a daily deposit of powdery grime. She scrubbed and dusted and polished in a frenzy of cleaning. Finally, she closed up the house entirely against the onslaught of dirt and, in spite of the heat, she opened the windows only at night, when the movement of horses and carriages on Benefit Street had stopped.

On a morning early in August, while she was in the midst of her never-ending battle against the dust, her right leg suddenly stiffened with such a spasm of pain that she cried out and fell. She found that she could not walk on the leg at all. With Nellie's help she hobbled to her bedroom and collapsed. Dr. Bentham was called and prescribed hot compresses.

After two days, the pain had subsided, but she walked with a severe limp, dragging the leg stiffly behind her, as though it were a useless appendage. She had the feeling that it was bound by a heavy chain, on the end of which there was a weighted iron ball.

And then, in a flash of revelation, she knew what it was. It was indeed a chain, but an invisible one, and it had been shackled to her foot by witchcraft. She ordered Nellie to bring Betsy to her room.

"Why have you done this to me?" she demanded.

Betsy looked at her blankly. "Done what to you, ma'am?"

89

"You know very well. You have put a ball and chain on my foot!" Lydia gestured dramatically in the direction of her leg.

"I don't see any ball and chain," said Betsy.

"Well, 'tis there, all the same. Take it off at once, I command you!"

Betsy stared at her in bewilderment. "How can I take it off if I can't even see it?" she asked. She turned to Nellie, who was staring at Lydia's leg with squinted eyes, doing her best to see a ball and chain. "Do you see anything, Nellie?"

Nellie shook her head solemnly, and then, catching Betsy's eye, began to giggle nervously. "I don't see nothin' except your leg, ma'am."

"Of course, you don't!" shouted Lydia. "It's an *invisible* ball and chain!"

Betsy exploded into laughter, and Nellie joined her. Lydia sprang from the bed and tottered to her feet. She was quaking with fury.

"Get out, both of you!" she screamed. "You've joined together against me! *I* know what's happening in this house, and don't think I don't! Get out, get out, get out!"

Still hysterical with laughter, Betsy and Nellie fled downstairs. Lydia returned to her bed. She sank back against the pillows, and in spite of the heat of the day she drew the coverlet up over her body, as though to protect herself from further injury. She stared at the ceiling and tried to calm herself. She tried to sleep but could not.

Finally, she picked up her Bible from the bedside table and leafed through its pages in search of a comforting verse. She found herself in the First Book of Samuel, and this seemed an omen, because she immediately remembered the story of Saul and the witch of Endor. Not only that, it *was* in the book of Samuel, and that was her own husband's name. Breathing quickly in excitement, she turned to the twenty-eighth chapter and started reading.

She found herself thinking that Saul had been exceedingly wicked to seek a witch's help, but then, she told herself, the poor man must have been desperate. It was the day before his last battle against David, and when he saw the forces of the Philistines drawn up against him, it was no wonder that he became frightened. And then, when he prayed to the Lord for help, the Lord did not see fit to answer him because he had been getting arrogant and disobedient.

She shuddered as she read: *Then said Saul unto his servants, Seek me a woman that hath a familiar spirit, that I may go to her, and enquire of her. And his servants said to him, Behold, there is a woman that hath a familiar spirit at Endor.*

Lydia had almost forgotten the rest of the story—how the witch had conjured up the spirit of Samuel, who then foretold Saul's death in battle the next day. A chill ran through her as she remembered that the witch's prophecy had come true.

But the end of the story was disappointing, for the witch of Endor had turned out to be a kindly witch. When she learned that Saul was hungry, she had killed a fat calf and made unleavened bread so that he could eat. Lydia was loath to believe that any witch could be so charitable, but then perhaps Old Testament witches were different from the kind that had always plagued New England.

She closed the Bible and sighed, resigning herself to the fact that she would have to wage a lone battle against Betsy and could count on neither Sam nor Nellie for help. She told herself that she did not really need human allies because the Lord was on her side. Unlike Saul, she had not been disobedient, and so He would surely answer her prayers.

At once, she began to pray, not only for Betsy's destruction but for her own deliverance from the sorceries all around her. She was aware that she, too, could fall beneath the spell of this innocent-appearing child who was possessed by Satan.

In the days that followed the arrival of the ball and chain, she saw new and more ominous manifestations of the witchcraft that had settled over her household like a noxious fog. On a cool, moonlit evening in September, another black cat appeared—not a kitten, but a huge, wild-looking creature that sat on its haunches in a clump of frostbitten marigolds and gave forth unearthly wails followed by screams of fury. When Lydia ran to the window and threw a shoe at the cat, it did not run away, but merely disappeared into the moonlight.

The milk that Nellie brought on her breakfast tray was always sour, although Nellie vowed that it had been bought at the market only the day before and was as sweet as could be. It was clear to Lydia that Betsy's witchcraft had not only soured the milk but had perverted Nellie's sense of taste as well, for the milk was certainly sour as swill. She refused to touch it.

When Indian summer arrived in October, the weather turned warm and sultry, and Lydia opened the window of her room at bedtime. She was awakened from sleep one night by the sound of wings beating frantically in the dark and of ear-piercing squeaks that echoed through the room. She was so terrified that when she tried to scream, no sound came from her throat. She prayed desperately for the Lord to save her from the evil thing that Betsy had sent to her room. Immediately, she found her voice, and her screams rang shrilly through the sleeping house.

Sam came running into her room. In the flickering light of the taper he carried, she saw a large bat that lay, stunned and flapping, at the foot of her bed. The sight made her scream more loudly than ever, and she covered her head with the bedclothes.

Even after Sam had removed the evil-looking creature, she continued to shake in convulsive spasms of terror. Sam sat by her bed and held her hand until she had calmed down and her trembling had ceased. But she did not go back to sleep until dawn, when the growing light finally dissipated her fears. After that, she never dared to open her window again.

More and more, as the weeks of autumn passed, she lived almost entirely in her bedroom, which had become a kind of sanctuary where she could escape the contaminating presence of Betsy. She lost all interest in the cleaning chores that had consumed so much of her energy during the whole of her married life. She no longer took her meals in the kitchen as a member of the family. Pleading illness and weakness, she had Nellie bring food to her on a tray.

This brought in its wake new and more perplexing problems. Food that she had not cooked herself began to develop strange tastes and aromas. She came to believe that the most innocent of dishes contained a witch's brew of some sort, and those that contained sweetening were especially suspect since they might be laced with distillations of deadly poison, artfully disguised by the sugar. And so she emptied all puddings and custards into the slop jar without even daring to taste them.

She ate less and less, and by Christmas time, her already thin body had become emaciated, her face of an unprecedented paleness. She was plagued by constant headaches and seemed never to be without a cold. The more Sam and Nellie urged her to eat, the more convinced she became that they had become Betsy's accomplices in the plot to bring her to their own state of bewitchment. When Dr. Bentham was called in to see her, his exhortations that she must eat made her certain that he, too, had fallen beneath Betsy's powerful spell.

In mid-January she developed a severe inflammation of the chest. She coughed so violently that she brought up small amounts of blood. For a week she was delirious with a high fever, and Dr. Bentham feared for her life. And then, as though miraculously, she recovered. Immediately, she asked Sam to place a strong lock on her bedroom door, and not long after that, she ordered that a stout wooden cross be nailed above the entrance to her room, and over it she asked Sam to hang a little necklace of silver that had belonged to her mother.

Sam knew that the cross and an object made of silver were believed to offer protection against witches, but he saw no harm in humoring her and dutifully carried out her requests. Indeed, he did all the things that a solicitous husband might be expected to do during his wife's convalescence from an almost fatal illness. He made frequent visits to her. He brought her gifts of fruit and sickroom delicacies. He inquired about her health and did his best to be sympathetic while she described at length her long list of maladies.

But he no longer could bring himself to feel any real concern for her. The long paroxysms of coughing that shook her thin body made him nervous and restless at her bedside. It was only with an effort that he concealed his impatience with her endless infirmities.

Finally, after a few minutes, he would rise, saying, "Discourse has a poor effect on you, my dear. It seems to bring on an attack of coughing. It is better that you do not talk overmuch. Try to sleep."

Try to sleep, indeed, Lydia would think to herself. Although she tried desperately to recall visions of those happy childhood days when Mama and Papa were still alive, she could not. Instead, new and horrible nightmares began to invade her fitful periods of sleep. She was pursued by all kinds of grotesque and evil creatures who

93

tempted her to sin—and sometimes by Satan himself, disguised as a cat or a voracious wolf with gleaming fangs.

On a night late in February her father appeared to her in a dream, so real that his presence seemed to fill the room. He held out his arms to her in tender affection and called her name aloud again and again in soft and loving accents. Behind him was her mother, dressed neatly in black homespun, with snow-white cuffs and a collar of fine lace. Like a frightened child, Lydia ran to them for comfort. They seemed to stand in a circle of pure white light that offered sanctuary from all the evil that surrounded her.

Her father's arms at once enfolded her. But then, as her eyes lingered fondly on his familiar and dear face, its features began slowly and horribly to change. The placid brown eyes became dark pools of lust, the sedate mouth turned scarlet and sensual. Suddenly he seized her roughly in his arms and kissed her passionately, thrusting his tongue past her protesting, innocent lips.

Screaming, she pushed him away and turned to her mother for protection. But her mother, too, had undergone a monstrous change. Bedizened with garish jewels, face painted like a harlot's, her mother laughed jeeringly at her, and then, with an abruptly lewd movement, tore open Lydia's bodice so that her thin, pitiful breasts were revealed for all the world to see. Lydia cowered in shame and then fell to the floor, which had inexplicably become slimy and stinking with human excrement. As she lay there in the filth, she screamed out her horror until there was no breath left in her.

She was awakened by Sam's hand patting her shoulder, but his sudden presence at her side only threw her into a further spasm of terror. Leaping from the bed, she shrank against the wall, pressing herself into the corner of the room near the window. Quaking, baring her teeth in a desperate rage, she had the look of a wild animal at bay.

"Lydia! Lydia!" Sam murmured soothingly.

At last, his voice seemed to reach her, and abruptly she came out of her dream. Her figure went slack, and she began to weep uncontrollably. Sam helped her to her feet and led her back to her bed. He spoke to her cajolingly, trying to comfort her, but when he moved to take her in his arms, she flung herself away from him violently.

"No! No!" she screamed. "Don't touch me! Your hands—your hands! They are red with sin! May God smite thee in thy wickedness if you so much as lay a finger on me!"

Sam looked at her in pity, a puzzled frown knotting his forehead. "But I wish you no harm, Lydia. You had a nightmare and cried aloud, and so I came to comfort you."

Lydia sat up tensely in her bed. She thrust her arm out toward him, her bony forefinger pointing at him accusingly. "Liar! Fiend! You came to corrupt me—to push your filthiness into my virgin's womb! But you cannot! You cannot! Because I am strong with the purity of the Almighty!"

Sam sighed and rose from the bedside chair. He looked down at her sadly for a moment, then quietly left the room, shutting the door softly behind him. In the hallway, by the flickering light of his taper, he saw Betsy standing uncertainly in the doorway of her bedroom. She was frightened and ran to him quickly. He picked her up in his arms to carry her back to bed.

"Is somebody hurting Aunt Lydia?" she asked.

"No, child. She has bad dreams. You must go back to sleep."

He tucked the bedclothes about her, but she would not lie down. She sat up and looked at him pleadingly. "I'm scared," she said. "I don't want to be alone."

"The Lord is always with thee, child."

"But I can't feel Him and touch Him. Can I sleep with you in your bed?"

Sam stood up quickly. "No. No, Betsy."

"But why not?"

He paused at the door. With a shock, he realized that he would like to have her next to him in bed, but he closed his mind to the pleasurable and disturbing thought.

"Why not?" she repeated, moving to leave her bed and come to him.

"Because—because 'tisn't proper," he mumbled. He left the room hurriedly and closed the door with resolution behind him.

Betsy, left alone, was wakeful and restless. She stared at the window near her bed. Outside in the frosty moonlight, the bare branches of a tree moved stiffly in a light wind.

She was puzzled and confused by Lydia's strange behavior. She knew what illness was. Her mother had often been sick, especially after a long night of carousing and drinking with a sailor friend. The memory of her own illness, too, was still fresh in her mind. But Lydia's sickness was different. The cries that came from her bedroom and shattered the night silence were not cries of pain but of terror.

And Betsy had begun to feel a terror all her own. It had begun one day when she passed the open door of Lydia's bedroom. Unable to repress her curiosity, she had hastily looked in, and Lydia's eyes had stared out at her in such a curiously fixed and penetrating way that she had caught her breath in sudden fear.

From that moment on, she had had the strange feeling that Lydia's eyes followed her everywhere, spying on her every movement, searching her out no matter where she might be. They reminded her of the eyes of a cat watching a bird, intent and unblinking in that long moment before the lightning pounce.

Again and again, she told herself that Lydia's eyes could not really follow her because Lydia was in her bedroom and never left it now. But the illusion would not go away. No matter where she went, the eyes still seemed to be there, just behind her.

And though she could not see them, she could feel them. They seemed to be focused, aimed like a gun, at a spot in her spine exactly between her shoulder blades.

CHAPTER 10

O N a morning in the middle of March, a gale blew itself into Narragansett Bay with such suddenness that two ships and four fishing boats were driven aground and were wrecked before they could reach safety. The great wind struck Providence with the impact of an explosion, wrenching and tearing at trees, sending shingles flying. It was followed by a heavy torrent of rain that pounded against the windows of houses and whirled itself down chimneys so that fires smoked and refused to burn.

The roar of the gale around the Allen house drove Lydia into such a frenzy of fear that for the first time in months she left the sanctuary of her room. She tottered down the stairs and burst into the kitchen, where Nellie hovered over the fireplace, vainly trying to coax the fire back to life.

"The house is blowing down!" Lydia screamed.

Nellie turned and gave a sudden start at the unexpected appearance of her mistress, who had the look of some supernatural wraith blown in by the wind. Her uncombed, tangled gray hair streamed out in all directions like an unruly wig, and her eyes twitched wildly in her pale face.

Nellie went over to her and put a protective arm around her, trying to lead her toward the stairs. "Oh, Missus Allen! Whatever be you doin' down here? You must go back to bed before you take a chill!"

"I'll not go upstairs and be blown to kingdom come when the roof comes off!" said Lydia.

"But the roof won't come off, Missus Allen. 'Tis only a big wind like we've had many a time before."

"Big wind, indeed!" said Lydia. " 'Tis a witch's gale, and unless it is stopped at once, none of us will be left alive! Where is that cursed child?"

"She's in the parlor with Mr. Allen, doing her lessons. He didn't go to the port, what with the storm and all."

Lydia turned suddenly and ran toward the parlor. She paused at the door and looked in. Sam and Betsy sat across from each other at the small table they used as a desk during lessons. Betsy was writing in her copybook, while Sam watched quietly. Their silence and the fitful light that came from the taper on the table gave them a mysterious air. To Lydia, they looked like conspirators and she was sure they were drawing up plans for her destruction.

"I know what you are doing!" she screamed at them.

As they raised their heads in surprise, she advanced into the room, clenched fists raised above her head. She turned blazing eyes toward Betsy. "I'll kill you—once and for all—just as I killed your evil black kitten!"

She lunged toward Betsy and crashed into the table, sending papers and candle flying. Sam got up quickly and seized her by the arms. He lifted her to her feet while she struggled helplessly in his embrace. Betsy had retreated to the corner of the room and was watching them both in bewilderment. The fallen taper had set fire to the foolscap on which she had been doing sums and the sight of the flames seemed to kindle a new excitement in Lydia.

"Burn, fire, burn!" she chanted hysterically. Flecks of saliva appeared at the corners of her mouth. "Burn, witch, burn! Burn! Burn!"

Sam slapped her hard across the mouth. "Have done with this nonsense! Have you lost your reason?"

Lydia's eyes closed. She did not cry out at the blow, but crumpled and slid to the floor, and Sam let her lie where she had fallen. He turned his attention to the fire that had begun to creep along the floor and stomped out the flames. Then he went over to Betsy, who still stood fearfully in the shadows, and patted her on the head.

"Do not be frightened, child. She will not harm you. Go to Nellie in the kitchen and have some tea. There will be no more lessons this morning."

Betsy looked down at Lydia's prostrate body. "What's the matter with her, Uncle?"

"Her illness has destroyed her reason. It is nothing for you to fret about. Go to Nellie now, and don't ask any more questions."

Betsy left the room with reluctance, pausing at the door to look back at Sam, who was staring down at Lydia, his face set and expressionless. Finally, he heaved a sigh and then knelt down to pick her up.

Betsy wondered if Lydia might not be dead, and she found herself hoping that it was true, because that would make everybody happy, she was sure.

It was clear to her now that Lydia wanted to kill her, wanted to make her dead like Blackie, to turn her into something that was stiff, cold, and unmoving. It was because she was a witch. And yet Sam had told her that she was not a witch. It was all very puzzling. Maybe she was a witch, and maybe she wasn't. But there was one thing she was sure of. She didn't want to be dead because then she would be buried in the ground and couldn't play games and eat sweetmeats anymore.

She comforted herself with the thought that Sam would protect her from harm, just as he always had. But if Lydia should try to hurt her when Sam was away, then she would have to fight back. Maybe she would even have to kill Lydia before Lydia killed her. The thought made her smile with pleasure.

After the gale had blown itself out, Lydia's hysteria disappeared as quickly as it had come. She became calm and even reasonable. And the next day, when the sun came out, she sat up in bed and looked about her with new interest, developed a sudden appetite for food, and ate voraciously. In the evening, when Sam paid her his daily visit, she greeted him cheerfully. The lines in her face had smoothed, and her cheeks were faintly pink. When, for the first time in months, she smiled at him, Sam could scarcely believe his eyes.

"Stay a moment, Samuel," she said softly. "I have something to say to you."

He sat down dutifully by her bedside, still too surprised by her changed appearance to speak.

"I have been wicked and sinful," she said. "I have done great injustice to an innocent child. I believed that she was a witch. I thought she had raised winds to destroy us all. I was wrong. It was only a March gale. The madness has left me, and now I am going to get well."

A great joy filled Sam, and he fell to his knees by the side of her bed. "Thank God, thank God," he said. "The Lord has seen fit to heal you. It is a miracle."

He seized her bony little hand in his and fell silent. Lydia's smile became even more beautiful at his demonstration of affection. She closed her eyes and murmured, "Amen, O Lord, amen."

Although Sam usually accepted the Lord's grace without question, this time he could not repress his curiosity. "But how did this happen, Lydia? Tell me."

Lydia's eyes took on a faraway look. "It was a—vision, Sam. The Lord came to me in my sleep and showed me the error of my ways. Then He told me that I must regain my health so that I could once again do His will." She paused and turned her head away from him. "And He even told me what medicine I must take to effect my cure."

"What is it, Lydia? I shall have Dr. Bentham get it for you at once."

Lydia turned her face back to him and smiled. "Perhaps Dr. Bentham will not approve of it. It sounds rather foolish. I am to eat two raw carrots four inches long each day for two days."

Sam nodded in approval. "There are carrots in the root cellar, my dear. I shall have Nellie fetch some."

Lydia sighed. "The rest is not so pleasant. I am to eat a teaspoon of clay before each meal for thirteen days running. Do you think Nellie could find some clay? Has the ground thawed?"

Sam had often heard of clay-eating for ills of various kinds, but the practice had long since been discontinued by men of medicine. It seemed strange to him that the Lord should have recommended a remedy that doctors had decided was ineffective. However, if the Lord had appeared to Lydia—and the miraculous change in her seemed to leave no doubt of that—it was clear that the Lord knew more than the doctors. In any case, the eating of clay had never seemed to harm anyone. His own mother had always taken it during the weeks when winter was changing into spring.

"I am sure Nellie will be able to find some good clean clay," said Sam.

"I'll need a ball of it, enough to last a fortnight." She cupped her hands together, making a circle. "About the size of a baby's head, that should be enough."

Lydia laughed in amusement, as though she had said something funny. The sound of her laughter struck Sam as being unnatural, but he decided that this was merely because he had forgotten what it sounded like. It had been years since Lydia had laughed at all. Perhaps it was a good omen and she would recover completely.

The next afternoon Lydia told Nellie that she was going to take a nap and did not wish to be disturbed. She locked the door of her bedroom and drew the blinds. Then, in the darkened room, she lighted a taper on her bedside table. Humming excitedly to herself, she got down on her hands and knees and from under the bed hauled forth the ball of clay and the four carrots that Nellie had brought her.

She sat down on the bed and put the objects in her lap, patting them lovingly. Her eyes glittered in excitement. With nervous, quick-moving hands she began to knead part of the clay into the likeness of a small human head. She gouged out hollows for eye sockets and smoothed the clay above them into a forehead. She pinched some of the clay together into a rough approximation of a human nose, and below it she dug out a mouth with her fingernail.

Lifting the primitive sculpture in her right hand, she gazed at it for a moment, critically and even proudly. Then, with a short nod of her head by way of approval, and still humming to herself, she affixed dabs of clay to both sides of the head and fashioned them into ears. Once again, she surveyed her handiwork critically, and then, apparently satisfied, she set it aside.

Next, she took the rest of the clay in her hands and molded it into the rounded oblong shape of a human torso. With a sudden, chuckling laugh, she again used her fingernail to scoop out a tiny piece of clay from the center, so that the depression vaguely resembled a human navel. Her mouth fell open in absorbed concentration and saliva spilled from her lips as she pinched two places above the navel to form small breasts.

Then, breathlessly, she seized two of the carrots and jammed them into the soft clay to form legs. The other two carrots became arms. Abruptly, she got up and ran across the room to her sewing table, searching frantically in a drawer until she found a bodkin and a pincushion studded with pins. From the top drawer of her dresser she got two handkerchiefs, one of lace and the other of dyed linen.

At last, she returned to her bed and, grinding her teeth together pleasurably, speared the effigy's head with the bodkin and affixed it to the torso. The linen handkerchief became a skirt around the body of the doll, and the lace one, folded diagonally, was fitted around the shoulder as a shawl.

She grasped the doll under the armpits and held it up before her, in the way a mother lifts her baby when she makes cooing noises to it. But the doll bore little resemblance to a living child. It had the half-formed, idiot look of a grotesque fetus.

Its evil appearance threw Lydia into an ecstasy that was oddly like affection. She clasped the misshapen thing against her flat and withered breasts and crooned, "Oh, my poppet, my sweet baby poppet!"

Suddenly, the look of love on her face turned into one of bitter hatred. She seized the doll by its middle and pushed it down against the pillow on her bed. Her voice rose in a weird singsong as she spat out the words. "Your name is Betsy! And I hate you, hate you, hate you!"

She began to jabber then, a hodgepodge of syllables, a mad gibblegabble that spewed from her mouth without a pause. Her lips and tongue moved rapidly in a parody of human speech. Then her gibbering stopped as abruptly as it had begun and she fell silent, her mouth hanging open. Her hand moved slowly to the pincushion, and her fingers pulled out the longest pin they could find. She poised it, like a dagger, above the prostrate doll. Then she plunged it violently into the spot on the poppet where a heart might be.

"Die! Die! Die!" she whispered hoarsely. "May your black witch's heart stop beating!"

Beside herself with fury now, she seized more pins and began plunging them one after another into the doll's body. "Right through your head and into your evil brain! Two for your dirty witch tits! And a big sharp one for your vile quiff of a whore!"

Her rage finally exhausted itself. Her hands went limp, and she stared down at the poppet in contempt. It seemed to smile malignly at her with its idiot mouth, and so she spat in its face. Then she grabbed it up roughly in her hand and got to her feet. She looked around the room, her eyes searching for a place where she might hide it—somewhere accessible and yet out of sight. She decided to keep it under her bed, where no one could find it without her knowing it.

But Lydia was asleep the next afternoon when Nellie came up to empty the chamber pot under the bed. When she saw the poppet, lying there in the shadows, she was mystified. She pulled it out into the light and looked at it curiously.

"The missus be havin' her second childhood for sure," she thought to herself. And then she saw the pins that had been stuck into the doll's body, like small daggers, and she shuddered.

Nellie had never before seen an actual poppet, but she knew very well what poppets were for. She had heard grim tales of how they had brought mortal illness and death to innocent, law-abiding people. Terror-stricken, she shoved the malign thing back under the bed and wiped her hands on her apron as though she had just touched a leper and might already be infected. She fled from the room in such a panic that she forgot to take the chamber pot with her.

When Sam came home for dinner, she announced to him flatly that she would no longer work in his house, and that was that.

Sam sighed wearily. "What is it now, Nellie? What's happened?"

"More evil doin's, that's what! I'm a-gettin' out of this cursed house before somebody lays a spell onto me and does me in for good and all!"

"But, Nellie, you no longer believe that Betsy—"

Nellie interrupted him impatiently. "I don't know if it's Betsy or who it is. All I know is that upstairs right this minute there's a witch's poppet layin' under Missus Allen's bed!"

"A poppet? What do you mean?"

"I mean a poppet as ever was—and stuck full of pins!"

Sam frowned. "But, Nellie, nobody makes poppets anymore. Surely, you must be mistaken—"

Nellie turned on him angrily. "Mistaken, am I? Then go up and look for yourself! It's right there under the bed!"

Sam started up the stairs. Nellie's voice trailed after him. "Look behind the chamber pot and you'll see!"

Lydia was still asleep when Sam knelt down and pulled the poppet out from under her bed. He looked down at it incredulously and then at Lydia's tranquil face. For a moment he paused in indecision. Then he shook her gently by the shoulder, and she awoke with a start. Her sleepy eyes focused on the doll in his hand and then quickly closed again. Her heart began to beat violently, but when she spoke, her voice was controlled and calm.

"What is that thing you're holding?" she asked.

"It is a poppet," he said.

Lydia's eyes raised themselves to his, all questioning innocence. "A poppet? What is that?"

"You know very well what it is," he said. "Surely, your extensive knowledge of witchcraft includes the use of a poppet."

"No, it does not. What is it for?"

"It was once used by witches to work black magic on their enemies."

"There is only one witch in the house," said Lydia.

"I am not so sure of that, my dear." He looked at the doll reflectively. "It is curious, I think, that this thing is made of the clay and the carrots you asked for, and that it is dressed in two of your kerchiefs."

Lydia became indignant. "Are you accusing *me* of making that wretched object?"

"I am. Who else could have done it?"

Lydia smiled sweetly. "Why don't you ask Betsy?"

"I shall do that," said Sam and he left the room.

Sam was sitting behind the table in the parlor when Betsy came in to him. She looked at him apprehensively, because when Nellie had brought her into the house, she had said ominously, "The master wants to see you in the parlor."

That announcement usually meant trouble, and so Betsy hesitated when she reached the parlor door. Sam seemed unaware of her and stared at something in his lap.

"I am here, Uncle," said Betsy softly.

Sam looked up. "Come in, child."

Betsy moved forward and sat down nervously on the edge of the chair opposite him. She was wondering what she had done to displease him.

"I want to ask you some questions, Betsy. It is very important that you answer them truthfully. Do you understand that?"

"Yes, Uncle."

He paused. Then, with a sudden movement, he picked up the poppet from his lap and placed it on the table between them. "Have you ever seen this before?"

Betsy looked at it curiously, and then a smile spread over her face. "Why, it's a doll." She raised her eyes to his and smiled. "Is it for me?"

"No, Betsy. And it is not a doll."

She frowned and looked back at the poppet. "It looks like a doll to *me*, Uncle. But it's not a very pretty one." Her eyes suddenly fastened on the pins. "Oh, I see. It's a pincushion."

"No. It is neither a doll nor a pincushion. It is a poppet. Do you know what a poppet is?"

Betsy shook her head, and Sam continued. "In the old days, it was used by witches to bring harm to their enemies."

"You mean they *threw* it at people? Why didn't they use a rock?"

Sam smiled in relief. "You've answered my question, Betsy. You may go now."

As she got up to leave, she said, "Where did you get that thing, Uncle?"

Sam hesitated. "Oh, I—I just found it." His eyes narrowed in suspicion. "Would you like to have it, Betsy?"

"But I don't need a pincushion," she said. "And it isn't pretty enough for a doll. It's got a mean face. Maybe Nellie would like it."

"I hardly think so," said Sam, and he smiled again with relief. But after Betsy had left him, his face grew solemn again. He stared down at the doll, wondering what, if anything, he should do about it. It seemed strange and ironical to him that Lydia, with her fear of witchcraft, had ended by trying to practice it herself. There was a time when he could not have believed such a thing to be possible. But he saw now, with an absolute clarity, that Lydia was hopelessly mad and quite beyond the help of either Dr. Bentham or the Reverend Arnold. Though he would continue to pray the Lord that she might by some miracle recover, he did not really believe that she would. She was lost forever in the tangled jungle of her daft fancies, and his concern now was only for Betsy. If Nellie were to leave, as she threatened, he could not let Betsy remain in the house alone with Lydia. He would put his wife in the madhouse first.

But as it turned out, there was no need for him to take such a drastic step. He was able to convince Nellie, after a long and earnest argument, that there was no witchcraft in the house—only a woman who was sick in mind as well as body. As a dramatic finale to his lecture, he tossed the poppet into the fire on the hearth.

As they watched it burn, he turned to her again. "Though there be no witchcraft here, there is danger. Not for you but for Betsy. I believe Mrs. Allen would harm her if you were not here."

"Oh, Mr. Allen, she wouldn't!"

"In her right mind, she wouldn't. But she is mad, Nellie, truly mad. She hardly knows what she does." He paused, hoping that his words had penetrated Nellie's dull wits. "Do you understand that?"

"Oh, yes, sir. She do seem to have a hole in her wig, right enough. Her head be full of chinkapins, poor lady. I do feel sorry for her."

"That is Christian of you, Nellie. But see to it that your charity of heart does not lead you to trust her alone with Betsy. Not *ever*, do you understand?"

"Oh, yes, sir. In her daftness, she might do harm to the child."

Sam rose and seized Nellie's fat hand in his own. "Thank you, Nellie. I have trust in you."

Nellie flushed with pleasure at this unaccustomed show of feeling on the part of her master. She bowed her head in embarrassment and mumbled, "I will do my best, sir. I'll not so much as let the child enter her room. I'll take my oath on't!"

CHAPTER II

L YDIA brooded about the loss of her poppet. She could not very
well ask Sam to return it without tacitly admitting that it was
indeed she who had made it. But she wondered where it had
gone and feared that it might have fallen into Betsy's hands.
Finally, as casually as she could, she asked Sam what had become
of it. He replied quite truthfully that he had burned it and assured
her that even if it had possessed magical powers, it could no longer
do any harm. He did not accuse her again of making the doll herself, having decided to let the whole matter drop in the hope that
she would forget all about it.

But for Lydia, the poppet remained still mysteriously alive and
potent. She did not for a moment believe that it had been destroyed, and proof of her suspicion soon manifested itself. One
rainy day, not long after daybreak, she was awakened by stabs of
excruciating pain in her chest and roused the whole household
with agonized screams. Her wasted body was convulsed with
violent coughing that left her gasping for breath, and soon her bed
sheets were stained bright red with the blood she brought up from
her burning lungs.

The sight of the blood alarmed Sam so much that he got Dr.
Bentham out of bed and brought him, sleepy-eyed and half-
dressed, to Lydia's bedroom. The doctor's face was grave as he
applied hot poultices to her chest. He then punctured a vein and
bled her profusely. Sam frowned as he watched the blood flowing
into a cup. "But she is already bleeding from the lungs, Dr.
Bentham," he said.

Dr. Bentham, annoyed that Sam should question the accepted
rituals of his profession, said tartly, "I can see full well that she is

already bleeding, Sam Allen. That is why more blood must be removed, to relieve the pressure. Now, be good enough to prepare another hot poultice!"

Sam felt like a reprimanded schoolboy and left quickly to do the doctor's bidding. Dr. Bentham turned his attention once again to Lydia, who was thrashing about weakly on the bed like a bird with a broken wing. He was relieved that her coughing had subsided for the moment, but he continued to watch her with a perplexed frown. He was startled when she unexpectedly sat up and thrust her white face toward his.

"Dr. Bentham, you must help me!" she gasped.

"I am trying, my child," he said soothingly. "But you must rest."

He tried to ease her back on the pillows, but she shrugged away from him angrily. "No, no! You don't understand! They have taken the poppet, and they have named it *Lydia!*"

Dr. Bentham had no idea what she was talking about and tried to calm her by saying, "Yes, yes, I know, I know."

"Then why don't you do something about it?" Lydia cried. "Even now, they are sticking pins into my breast!" She caught her breath as a new stab of pain cut through her. She beat her hand weakly against her breast and fell back against the pillows.

"Gently, Mrs. Allen, gently now. The pain will pass."

Lydia's eyes looked at him in utter hopelessness. Tears began to trickle down her sallow cheeks. "You, too?" she whispered in a voice so low that he could scarcely hear her. "You, too, are in league with them against me. O God, there is no one to save me now!" Her eyes closed and her body went limp as she lost consciousness.

When Sam returned with the hot poultice, Dr. Bentham placed it against her withered chest, already a vivid scarlet from the applications of heat. The poultice was steaming hot, but Lydia seemed not even to feel it.

Dr. Bentham sighed and looked toward Sam. "I am sorry, Sam, but there is little to be done. I fear that she will not be with us for long."

Sam looked up in surprise. "But surely, it is only another congestion in the chest brought on by a cold—"

"No, Sam, I believe it is more serious than that. This hemorrhage from the lungs—it is caused by a canker that will soon consume her utterly. God's will be done."

Sam stood silent, with bowed head. Pity for the poor creature who lay there in pain engulfed him. He was almost unaware of Dr. Bentham's departure, of the hand that was briefly placed on his shoulder in a gesture of sympathy. He stood motionless at the bedside, his head still bowed. Then his lips began moving in prayer as he beseeched the Lord to be merciful, and if it was His will, to take Lydia to Him before the pain became too great and the suffering too prolonged.

In the days that followed, Lydia's condition worsened. She lay unmoving on her bed, her face waxen. Her eyes were almost always closed, and when they did open, they looked out in an unseeing way. They seemed made of stone with glassy centers of blue agate, their gaze turned inward, as though fixed on some world deep inside—private, inviolable, and self-contained—safely beyond the nightmares that visit the sleep of the living.

And then, one afternoon Lydia came abruptly out of her trancelike state. The pain had completely disappeared, and she was fully conscious. Mustering all her strength, she got waveringly out of bed and sank to the floor. Then, in a loud, expressionless voice she began to pray, thanking the Lord for restoring her to life and rescuing her from the pit of hell into which the black magic of the poppet had thrown her. Her voice rose in a hoarse and strident singing. It was so loud that Nellie heard it in the kitchen, and she ran up the stairs in the grim certainty that the end had finally come.

Lydia tottered weakly to her feet and glared at Nellie from feverish eyes. Spots of color had appeared on her cheeks like hastily applied dabs of red dye. "The Lord has saved me!" she cried. "The evil poppet has been destroyed by His awesome power! I am saved, saved, saved!" Then in sudden exhaustion she collapsed into Nellie's arms.

"Oh, mistress, mistress," said Nellie, "you must get back into bed and rest. Here, now."

Nellie led her gently back to bed and coaxed her to lie down again. But Lydia did not close her eyes. A delirium of excitement still possessed her, and she continued with her litany of thanksgiving. "I am saved! Oh, praise be to God, I am saved! Rejoice with me, Nellie, rejoice!"

"Oh, I do, mistress, I do," said Nellie. "Mayhap—mayhap you would like something to eat?"

"Yes. Oh, yes! Bring me bread! Bring me wine! I will partake of the body and blood of our Lord Jesus, for He renewed my strength that I may carry out His will!"

"Wine? Do you think it wise to drink wine, mistress?"

"Yes, wine! Red wine, shining and pure as the blood that He shed for me! Bring it to me at once."

Nellie shrugged her shoulders. Wine hardly seemed a proper thing for someone who had been so close to death, but perhaps it would restore the appetite at least. She remembered the ruby port that was kept in the cellar for special occasions. It was very red and pretty. She left to get it.

Lydia drank two glasses of the wine, draining them in single gulps. She ate ravenously of the bread that Nellie had brought on a plate. Her spirits soared dizzily, and she jabbered in ecstasy and jubilation. She had Nellie fill the wineglass once more and then ordered her to bring her the large pair of scissors from the sewing table.

"The shears?" said Nellie incredulously. "But whatever for, Missus Allen? This be no time for sewing and such."

"Fool! I am not going to sew! I am going to trim my hair! I must make myself comely for the Lord!"

Nellie hesitated, wondering just how far she should go in humoring her mistress, who was clearly more daft than ever, in spite of her cheerful spirits.

"Well, why do you stand there?" said Lydia imperiously. "Go get the scissors, I tell you!"

Nellie decided it was easier to obey a madwoman than to argue with one. But when she returned with the scissors, she said, "You are still weak from your illness, my lady. Mayhap I could trim your locks—"

Lydia snatched the scissors from Nellie's hands with a lightning movement. "Weak! How can I be weak when the strength of the Lord fills every part of me?"

Before Nellie had time to interpose, Lydia had sheared off the frowzled ringlets that dangled over her forehead. She threw them triumphantly to the floor.

"Oh, mistress," wailed Nellie, "you mustn't—your lovely hair—"

Lydia laughed hysterically and continued to lop off huge gobbets of hair. "Vain adornments, begone!" she sang out shrilly. "Away, vanity! Behold the bridegroom cometh! I will come unto His presence even as an innocent child!"

Nellie covered her eyes with her hands and moaned, "Oh, mistress, whatever will Mr. Allen say? Oh, that you should disfigure yourself so—"

But the scissors in Lydia's trembling hands frenetically continued to cut and snip at random, and she chortled in glee as the hair fell about her onto the bedclothes. At last, she flung the scissors down on her bedside table and sank back on the pillows.

"It is done, O Lord! Thy will be done! I come to thee a virgin once again, undefiled by worldly wantonness and the filthy lusts of men!"

Nellie looked at her mistress with a shocked expression, her hand on her mouth. She shook her head back and forth and clucked her tongue. Then, as she gazed at Lydia's shorn head, a vague pity stirred in her. The poor woman looked like some abandoned doll, cruelly scalped and disfigured by an angry child. Quick tears rolled down her fat cheeks as she murmured, "Oh, lady, lady, whatever have you done to yourself?"

Lydia put her forefinger to her lips and whispered, "I have made myself ready for the sacrifice." She paused and listened, cocking her head to the side, then, abruptly, in a harsh voice, she said, "Now, get back to your duties, you slut, and leave me to my prayers!"

Nellie, relieved that she had been dismissed and would no longer need to listen to the ravings of her almost-bald mistress, left the room without a word. Lydia's eyes followed her to the door and then moved lazily toward the scissors that lay gleaming on her bedside table. She reached out her hand to them and stroked their cold, smooth surface with her fingertips. Then she opened the drawer of the table and dropped them into it. A slow smile turned

III

up the corners of her pale lips, and she hugged herself with sudden joy.

Betsy listened in openmouthed wonder to Nellie's highly colored story of how her mad mistress had cut off her hair. To Betsy, bald men were commonplace and therefore uninteresting, but she had never seen a woman without hair. She was filled with curiosity, and as soon as Nellie had left the kitchen to lay the evening fire in the parlor, she sneaked quietly toward the stairs. Sam had forbidden her to visit Lydia, but this was a sight that she had to see.

The stairs creaked ominously beneath her feet, and the gathering shadows of the spring twilight had turned the upstairs hallway into a suddenly fearsome place. She paused, her heart beating with a dread that was somehow exciting. She remembered again Sam's stern words of caution. For a moment, she considered turning back, but the prospects of seeing her enemy so comically divested of hair turned her fear into a gleeful anticipation, and she moved on up the stairs.

When she found herself in the hallway, she paused again. The door to Lydia's bedroom was swung open invitingly. Without further hesitation Betsy tiptoed over to it and peeked into the room. Lydia was lying on her side, her face turned toward the hallway. She did indeed look ridiculous. Betsy clamped a hand to her mouth to stifle the delighted laugh that rose in her throat.

She jumped in surprise as Lydia's voice, sweet and unusually friendly, said, "Come in, my child. I was hoping you would pay me a visit."

Betsy stood in frozen immobility at the door. Like someone unexpectedly confronted by a coiled rattlesnake in his path, she wanted to run but couldn't.

"Come in!" The voice became even more gracious and welcoming.

Against her will, Betsy found herself moving toward the cadaverous figure that lay on the bed. She stared in fascination at the grotesquely shorn head that lolled against the pillow. She no longer felt like laughing.

Lydia's eyes regarded her in a kindly way. "It is indeed a long time since I have seen you, child," she said softly.

"Yes'm," said Betsy.

"I prayed that you would come, and now you are here." Lydia stretched out her hand to Betsy's and pulled her gently toward her. Fear rose in Betsy, and she swallowed hard. She stood firm, not allowing herself to be brought any closer.

"I have been very ill, oh, so very ill," said Lydia.

"I know, ma'am—I'm sorry."

"If you are truly sorry, there is something that you can do for me—and for the Lord."

"What's that, ma'am?"

Lydia folded her hands and looked into Betsy's eyes. Her voice became quietly commanding. "Open your bodice, child."

Betsy's heart beat faster as she stammered, "What for?"

"So that God's radiance may reach your sinful flesh and purify it! Open your bodice, witch-child!"

Betsy pulled her hand away and said, "I will not! And I'm not a witch-child!" She turned to leave, but Lydia suddenly sprang from the bed and seized her by the hair. It was as though the violent motion released in Lydia a flood of pent-up hatred, and it poured forth in obscene and violent words.

"Child of filth!" she screamed. "Spawn of a whore! May God damn your harlot soul to stinking hell!" Her left hand reached out for the drawer of her bedside table. Before she could open it, Betsy had wrenched herself free and fled down the stairs.

At supper that night, when Betsy told Sam what had happened, he looked at her sternly and said, "But I have told you not to go anywhere near your Aunt Lydia. Why did you disobey?"

Betsy regarded her plate guiltily. "I—I didn't mean to, Uncle."

"But you did! Why?"

Betsy looked up at him, her eyes pleading. "Well, I wanted to see what she looked like without any hair. I just wanted to peek, that's all. Is peeking a sin?"

Sam knew that it would be quite useless to explain to her that inquisitiveness was sometimes natural and sometimes wicked. Instead, he told her the story of Lot's wife, whose curiosity had led her to disobey the Lord and to look at the sinful city of Sodom.

"And so," Sam concluded, "the Lord punished her. He turned her into a pillar of salt."

Betsy pondered this. "Salt?" she asked. "You mean salt like what's there in the salt dish?"

"Even so," said Sam.

"But how could He turn a woman into a pillow of salt, Uncle?"

"The Almighty can do anything, Betsy."

"But He won't do it to me because I looked at Aunt Lydia, will He?" she asked in alarm, feeling her hand to make sure it was still solid.

"No, I think not."

"Anyway," she said, "*I* didn't look back at a sinful city."

"No, child," said Sam, "but your curiosity led you to disobey me."

"But you're not the Lord, Uncle, and so you couldn't turn me into a pillow of salt, even if you had a mind to."

"No. But like the Lord, I give you orders for your own good. You must remember that your Aunt Lydia has lost her reason. She knows not what she does and she wishes you harm."

"Oh, I know that, right enough," said Betsy.

"It is why I have forbidden you to visit her or to go near her. I want no harm to come to you, Betsy."

She smiled up at him. "Is it because you love me, Uncle?"

Sam did not answer. He lowered his eyes to his plate, and his pale face became suffused with color. The little vein in his temple stood out and began to throb. To Betsy, it was a comforting sign, a kind of barometer that told her when the emotional weather was fair, and she smiled happily to herself.

But that night, after Sam had tucked her into bed, she was restless and wakeful. The image of Lydia's head, so weirdly mutilated in appearance as it lay there as though disembodied on the bed, kept coming back to her. And then, it mysteriously attached itself to the figure of Lot's wife, which instantly crumbled into a neat pillow of glistening rock salt.

Betsy turned and tossed, trying to escape her eerie visions. She tried to think of something comforting, some ordinary, daylight thing that had nothing frightening about it. Immediately, Sam's face rose before her, the way it looked when he was kindly, when his blue eyes softened as they gazed into hers. And then all her dark fancies were blotted out, like shadows vanishing when bright sunlight suddenly fills a room. A golden radiance filled her, and she drifted into sleep.

Some hours later, she could not have told how many, she was awakened by a feeling of utter terror. It was as though she had just had a nightmare, but she knew that she had not been dreaming. Without reason, a great fear was making her heart hammer against her ribs. She sat up in bed and looked around her in bewilderment. The vague outlines of the room and the furniture were familiar enough, but they did not comfort her. She began to tremble violently as she became aware, without knowing how, that she was not alone in the room.

She turned her eyes toward the window for the reassurance of its faint light. A figure stood there, so shadowy and gauzy that she could not believe it was real. She tried to convince herself that she was dreaming, that it was only the curtain blowing in the wind.

And then the figure moved slowly and purposefully toward her bed. Now there was no mistaking the silhouette that limned itself black against the growing light beyond the window. It was Lydia.

Betsy tried to scream, but her throat had gone dry and there seemed no air in her lungs at all. The blood pounded so loudly in her ears that she did not even hear the hoarse, rasping sound that came from her throat. Her whole body had stiffened in numb paralysis, so that even the tiniest movement seemed an impossibility.

The figure of Lydia advanced on her swiftly, right arm raised above her head. The scissors that were clenched in her hand gleamed dully in the half-light. At the sight of them, Betsy tried again to cry out, but could not. She shrank back against the headboard of the bed, her arms upraised against her breast, her fists clenched. A bony arm shot out and grabbed her by the hair. The sudden shock of pain came as a blessed release. At last, she was able to scream, and her cry, like the splintering of a windowpane into jagged pieces of glass, shattered the dark silence of the house.

Her terror found words at last. "Uncle! Uncle! Help me!"

The sound of Betsy's voice was like a battle cry to Lydia. Her left hand clutched Betsy's hair in a new and more painful grip, and she pulled the screaming child toward her with a convulsive, yanking motion. Then she drove the scissors straight at Betsy with all the strength that was in her. With a desperate movement Betsy jerked herself out of the way. She did not even feel any pain when she left whole strands of her hair in Lydia's clenched fist. Kicking out wildly, she managed to get free, running out the door with Lydia in pursuit.

Sam stood in the hallway, dazed and bewildered, his nightcap askew, and Betsy ran to him and cowered behind his legs. Lydia hurled herself furiously against his bulk, and he seized her writhing body and held it against him. Then he twisted her wrist until the scissors clattered to the floor.

Betsy had retreated to the wall, pressing herself against it as though she could make herself disappear. She could hear but only dimly see the figures that scuffled and grappled in the darkness. There was a cry of pain from Sam as Lydia sank her teeth deep into the lobe of his ear. She broke free of him and ran toward the stairs. In the darkness she slipped and fell, and there was a sound as though someone had thrown a bundle of kindling wood down the stairs.

Betsy stopped her ears against the anguished cry, half scream, half moan, that seemed to hang interminably in the darkness. In the terrible silence that followed, she felt Sam's hand reaching for her and she moved quickly toward the solid warmth of his body. When he picked her up in his arms, she pressed her head against his chest.

He spoke to her softly and comfortingly. "I am taking you back to your bed, child. I want you to stay there."

"I'm afraid," she whimpered and began to cry.

He carried her to her bedroom, stroking her head. "There is nothing more to fear, lass," he said, setting her down gently on the bed.

The quiet authority of his voice calmed her, and though she still trembled, she stopped crying and allowed him to tuck her into bed. Then he brushed her forehead with his lips and stood up. "Try to sleep now. I must look to your Aunt Lydia."

He started to close the door behind him, and Betsy said, "Please Uncle, will you leave it open?"

He nodded and left. She heard him go to his room and in a

moment saw him reappear in the hallway with a lighted taper. She watched him as he stood for a few seconds at the top of the stairs, the candle raised above his head as he peered down into the darkness. She heard his footsteps going slowly down the stairs, saw the light from the taper become fainter and fainter. Once again there was silence.

She closed her eyes, but before she could get back to sleep, she heard Sam coming up the stairs again, slowly and laboriously. The light of daybreak was stronger now, and she could see that he was carrying Lydia. Suddenly, she could not endure being alone for a moment longer, and she ran to Lydia's room.

Standing at the bedside, she stared down at the motionless figure of Lydia on the bed. Her usually pale face was red and swollen, the veins in her scrawny neck engorged and throbbing. Her eyes, open and staring, were made alive only by the pinpoints of light reflected in them from the taper's flame. Her nose looked very small and pinched, somehow like the beak of a small bird.

Betsy reached out her hand for Sam's, but he seemed unaware that she was in the room. Wonderingly, she gazed at the still figure on the bed, fascinated and then repelled by the sight of the nightdress soaked with blood, of the bluish legs that stuck out from beneath it in such a twisted unnatural way, like the matchstick legs of a broken marionette. Suddenly sickened, she jerked her head away.

The movement roused Sam from his trance. "I must get Dr. Bentham," he said to himself. Then he looked down at Betsy sternly. "I told you to go back to bed. Now, go at once!"

His voice told her that she had better obey, that there would be no use in telling him that she was afraid. Anyway, she wasn't afraid, not anymore. She knew that Lydia was dying, and she was glad. It served her right. Maybe God had finally decided to punish her for breaking the commandment that said "Thou shalt not kill," for Lydia had drowned her kitten, and now she had even tried to kill her.

Although God's appearance remained vague in Betsy's imagination, His love of vengeance was very real to her. In story after story that Sam read to her from the Bible, He smote down those who broke His commandments or disobeyed Him, sometimes a whole townful of people all at once. It gave her great satisfaction to know that He had at last risen in His wrath and had decided to smite Lydia down. The only thing that she couldn't understand was why He hadn't done it a long time ago.

Alone in her bedroom, she waited for Sam to return with Dr. Bentham. She would like to have gone back to sleep as though the fearful scene in the dark at the top of the stairs were only a dream. But the sound of Lydia's tortured breathing from the room next door would not let her forget. The rhythmic gasping went on and on, as monotonously as the ticking of the big clock downstairs. She tried putting her hands over her ears so that she wouldn't hear, but it was no use.

Finally, she decided to sing, hoping that her own voice would blot out the sound of Lydia's deep-drawn struggles for air. The only songs she knew were the ones that her mother had taught her, and loudly and shrilly she sang the one that had so shocked Lydia on the day she had first come to the Allen house.

> " 'Oh, Lily was a sailor's lass,
> She liked the boys to pat her arse.
> She allus took 'em to her bed,
> And when they got undressed, she said—' "

Her high treble voice rolled into the chorus with spirit.

> " 'Ho, sailor boy! Heave it to!
> Your mainmast's swingin' in the breeze—' "

Her voice suddenly trailed off to a whisper as the song brought back the memory of her mother so vividly that it was almost as though Phebe were there in the room.

Suddenly and magically, Lydia and her clean white house were gone. Lydia and her agonized struggles for breath evaporated into the air, leaving a blissful silence behind. Betsy, in a ramshackle bed that sprawled in the middle of a mud hut, lay curled against the warmth of her mother's body. She smelled once again the strangely comforting odor of rum breath and wine-stained clothing. She felt peaceful and happy, and at last, she slept.

118

It seemed that no time at all had passed when she opened her eyes. Morning sun had turned the walls of her bedroom into slabs of bright gold, and the twittering and chirping of birds beyond the window filled the room. She felt a hand gently pressing on her shoulder.

Sam stood at the bedside, looking down at her. His eyes were tired, his face was haggard. "It is time to get up, Betsy. Your Aunt Lydia has gone."

Betsy sat up. "Where did she go?" she asked sleepily.

"She has gone to God," said Sam quietly. "She is dead, Betsy."

"Oh." She sighed, not in sorrow, but in relief, and then asked, "Did you bury her?" Sam shook his head, and Betsy asked, "Well, don't you think we ought to, just like we buried Blackie under the tree?"

"Not yet, child. First, we must have a funeral."

Betsy was not sure what a funeral was for, but she knew that there were such things because she had seen funeral processions move slowly by the house on Benefit Street, while church bells tolled and filled the air with a sound that was lonely and sad, not at all like the merry pealing of bells on Sunday morning.

But sad or not, a funeral was an event, and therefore something she could look forward to. She looked at Sam almost joyously and said, "I have never been in a funeral before."

Sam's eyes reproved her as he said, "A funeral is not a happy thing, Betsy. It is not meet that you should smile."

Betsy's face immediately assumed an expression as solemn as Sam's, for she sensed that the occasion demanded the same kind of decorum that was expected of her in church during prayers. His nod of approval told her that she was doing the proper thing, but her feelings of excitement persisted—the happy anticipation that always filled her when a new and strange event loomed on the usually monotonous horizon of her small world.

Lydia's funeral did not disappoint her. She enjoyed it immensely. The house was filled with people, many of whom she had never seen before. She stood gravely at Sam's side as he greeted the visitors and in a hushed voice thanked them for their condolences. Betsy, proudly conscious of the new black dress that had been

119

bought for the occasion, executed deep curtsies with bowed head. It was too bad, she thought, that the new dress had to be black, but at least, it was new, and that was something.

Then, her hand in Sam's, she went with him into the parlor so that the visitor could look at Lydia as she lay stiffly in her pine coffin, her face as waxen and expressionless as a French china doll's. She could not understand why all these people would want to look at Lydia. She herself had found the sight vaguely disturbing at first because she could not help remembering the huge scarlet stain on Lydia's nightdress and her ugly bluish legs. She was sure that if these people knew how Lydia really looked, underneath the plain white-satin burial gown, they would have run from the room in horror.

In a way, she did not really believe that the effigy in the coffin was Lydia at all or that it had ever been alive and made of flesh like everybody else. And so, during a moment when she found herself briefly alone in that shuttered room, which was lighted even during the day by flickering candles, she hastily reached out and touched her hand to Lydia's. She withdrew it as though she had been bitten. The hand was as cold and stiff as the claw of a dead chicken.

After that, Betsy's pleasure in the social occasion was somewhat dampened by her awareness of the coffin and what was in it. But her spirits quickly rose again when the Wyatt family came in to call. All three of the boys were on hand, along with her sister, Polly, and she curtsied with special grace while each of them reeled off the words of sympathy that they had carefully memorized for the occasion.

It was for Matt, of course, that she reserved her most elaborate curtsy, as low to the floor as she could get without losing her balance, her skirts spread so fully that they had the look of the wings on an enormous black butterfly. When she rose slowly to her feet, her eyes looked deeply into his, and his own quiet gray eyes returned her stare with that steady, strangely studious look that always unsettled her.

"I have come," Matt intoned solemnly, "to express to you my sorrow in your great bereavement, Mistress Betsy. I cannot find words to tell you of my feelings of—of—" He paused awkwardly, trying desperately to recall the rest of his speech.

"Oh, that's all right," said Betsy, a little too cheerily.

"I cannot find words to tell you—" he repeated, and then floundered again, while his mother and father looked on anxiously.

"But you have already told me, dear Matthew," she said graciously, "and I wish to thank you from the bottom of my heart for your kind wishes."

Matt breathed freely again and nodded his head. The quick look of gratitude that he sent in her direction made her glow. She started to smile, and then stopped suddenly as she felt Sam's hand close over hers with an admonishing pressure. Her face became solemn again and she lowered her eyes to the floor—the very picture of a little girl overwhelmed by sorrow.

The church service on the following day both bored and baffled her. During the Reverend Arnold's sonorous and long-winded eulogy, her mouth dropped open in surprise. As Lydia's many virtues, minutely described and praised, were endlessly enumerated, Betsy could not believe that the Reverend Arnold was talking about the Aunt Lydia she had known. Either it was someone else or he was making up stories. But Lydia's name kept recurring, and there could be no mistake. She decided that the Reverend Arnold, like so many people, was a liar.

She was glad when the service was over and the congregation filed slowly out of the church, while the bell tolled overhead, with long pauses between its notes, like the slowed beating of a tired heart that might stop at any moment. After the stuffiness of the church, the smell of the spring air, damp and earthy, was refreshingly sweet to Betsy and somehow cheering. She wanted to run and skip, leaving the slow-moving procession of mourners far behind her. She wished that the whole thing might be over and done with. She was tired of looking gloomy and pretending to a sadness that she did not feel.

And then, quite unexpectedly, at the graveside, while the coffin was slowly being lowered into the earth, she did feel sad for the first time since Lydia had died. The hole that had been dug in the muddy earth seemed far too deep to put a body into, even if it was dead and its name was Lydia. The coffin went down, down, down, out of sight, and she clutched Sam's hand in panic. She looked up into his face questioningly, as though to say, "Are you going to let them do this? Why don't you stop them?"

She saw the tears rolling slowly down Sam's gaunt face as he stared fixedly at the freshly turned wet earth. His head was bent to his chest and his shoulders sagged. She had never seen him cry before. It had never occurred to her that he could, and the sight shocked her, filling her at first with shame for him, and then a melting tenderness such as she had not known till now. She wanted to hug his head against her, to console him, to make him stop crying. She squeezed his hand hard in her own, and now, he looked toward her, his eyes blurred and red-rimmed, his mouth contorted in a stifled sob.

She began to cry too, loudly and inconsolably. Not for Lydia now, because Lydia was forgotten, but for him, because he was in pain and she loved him.

His arms swooped down and gathered her up. He pressed her shaking body hard against his chest. Then, lifting his head toward the sky, he began to pray.

CHAPTER 12

I N the weeks that followed the funeral, Sam became remote and faraway. He moved slowly, like a man walking in his sleep. He arose earlier than usual in the morning, and by the time Betsy came down to breakfast, he had left the house. When he returned home at dusk, he disappeared until suppertime. Then he sat down to the table mechanically and, after he had said grace, ate in silence.

Betsy's efforts to engage him in conversation brought only vague noddings of the head by way of response, as though he had scarcely heard what she said. She was puzzled and began to wonder if she had done something to displease him.

One night, when she could bear his silence no longer, she said, "Uncle, why don't you talk to me? Have I done something bad?"

He looked up in surprise. "No, child, you have done naught that is wrong."

Then hesitantly she asked, "Don't you like me anymore?"

His face softened, and his eyes seemed aware of her for the first time in days. "I like you. Don't fret yourself."

"But then why don't you talk to me like you used to?"

He paused, not knowing how to make Betsy understand the melancholy that had closed over him. There were no simple words to describe the guilt he felt about Lydia's death, the irrational conviction that somehow he had been responsible for it. He told himself that if he had not neglected her, if he had given her the love that he had given so freely to Betsy, she would not have retreated into her lonely world. He began to look upon her violent and painful death as a judgment upon him, a punishment for his wickedness and most especially for his lustful feelings toward Betsy. And now the child's very presence had become a sharp physical reminder of his sinfulness. Although he knew that she was in no way to blame, that the grievous fault was all his own, not to be shared with anyone except his God, he found himself withdrawing from her, as though to ignore her very existence.

Sometimes, during lessons, he would realize how unfair he was, and he would make an effort to be more friendly. But he would freeze in the very attempt. Her nearness, the innocence of her face, only added to his self-contempt, and he would turn away hastily from the questioning in her eyes and resume an air of cold detachment.

Betsy's bewilderment deepened, and her interest in her lessons all but disappeared. She studied hardly at all and did not care whether she answered questions correctly or not, especially when she began to realize that much of the time Sam was not listening to her anyway.

As the days went by, she became more and more lonely. She turned to Nellie for warmth and companionship, but Nellie was her usual unresponsive and stolid self. She looked upon children as a kind of livestock that had to be fed, to be kept clean, and to be fenced in. Actually, she preferred livestock to children, because animals, at least, were useful, providing eggs, butter, milk, and meat. And food, for Nellie, was the single most important aspect of living, a fact that manifested itself only too clearly in the folds of fat that encased her lumbering body.

In an attempt to break through Nellie's indifference, Betsy began a campaign of small attentions and favors. She picked bouquets of violets from the spring garden and ceremoniously offered them to Nellie in outstretched hand, while she executed an elaborate curtsy. She took special pains with all her chores, and even volunteered to prepare afternoon tea. And Nellie acknowledged these small acts of homage with a surprised lift of an eyebrow and a grunt of satisfaction, as though such favors were only her rightful due.

Since it did not occur to her to give Betsy an affectionate pat or even to say thank you, Betsy abruptly gave up her blandishments and declared war. Rage filled her against Sam, against Nellie, against the whole unloving house and everything in it. She had long ago discovered that being naughty was a sure way of getting attention. And so, when she was sent to the well for water, she threw the pitcher down the well. After feeding the chickens, she opened the gate, and within an hour there were hens everywhere, clucking excitedly in newfound freedom. A few of them even found their way into the kitchen through the open door, and to Nellie's horror, left their droppings on her freshly scrubbed floor.

At first, Nellie ascribed these acts to childish carelessness, but on the day when she found that the fire in the hearth had been doused with the contents of a chamber pot so that the stench of excrement filled the air, she recognized that Betsy was off on one of her tantrums again. She lost no time in telling Sam about it.

When Betsy went to the parlor to answer for her sins, she was not in the least frightened. Defiantly jubilant, she strode into the room without knocking and sat down in the chair opposite Sam without invitation.

"Nellie says you wanted to see me," she announced.

Sam looked at her studiously, and the directness of his gaze made her glow with pleasure.

"What ails you, child?" he asked quietly.

"I am naughty," she said.

The forthrightness of her reply made Sam pause. Finally, he said, "Methought you had outgrown such childishness."

"No, sir. The devil still tempts me!"

He looked at her small figure, taut with challenge, and was suddenly aware of its budding maturity. Turning his eyes away, he said, "You are too old for punishment. You are twelve."

"Maybe so. But I am *wicked*—more wicked than I was when I was eleven!" She threw him a look that was both challenging and contemptuous and added, "I *like* being wicked, you big jackass!"

Sam's eyes, gently chastising until now, narrowed in anger. "Hold your tongue!" He waited, fighting to control his temper. After a moment, in a cajoling voice, he said, "Come now, Betsy. Say that you are sorry!"

"No, I will not! I am not sorry! I hate you and I hate Nellie, and I'll keep right on doing bad things, and I won't stop—ever! So there—you stupid muttonhead!"

She had risen from her chair now and spat her words at him contemptuously. Sam jumped to his feet and slapped her hard across the mouth.

"Go to my bedroom at once! If you cannot behave like a young lady of twelve, you will not be treated like one! Perhaps the birch rod can still thrash the evil from your heart!"

She laughed and ran almost gaily from the room. He could hear her feet eagerly tripping up the stairs.

He found her sitting nonchalantly in a chair in his bedroom. She looked up at him coolly as he approached, his temper all but disappeared now as he made a last effort to be calm and reasonable.

"I do not wish to thrash you, Betsy. If you will say that you are sorry—"

"Why should I say I'm sorry when I'm not? Anyway, I will not *let* you thrash me! And don't you dast try!"

A new wave of anger rose in him, and he strode to the closet, returning with the birch rod clutched in his trembling hand.

"Take off your dress and stand before the chair!" he ordered.

"No! I will not!"

He seized her by the shoulder and forced her to her feet, so that she faced him. "Do as I command! If you don't, I'll tear the dress from you!"

The prospect of a ruined dress made her pause. Slowly, she began undoing the buttons. She felt a sudden shyness, for she had not been naked before him since her breasts had begun to swell. As her clothing fell to the floor, she crossed her arms over her bosom and began to blush. The uncomfortable warmth moved from her face and then seemed to suffuse her whole body.

Sam's eyes showed surprise, and he moved away from her. With his eyes fixed on the floor, he said in a shaking voice, "You are indeed too grown for bodily punishment." Then, with an effort of will, he raised his head and looked at her. His eyes had become fixed and staring, like those of a blind man. "This willful rebelliousness must be beaten out of you, once and for all! Bend over the chair!"

Betsy leaned dutifully over the chair, strangely relieved that the posture enabled her to hide her breasts from his eyes, but she had become genuinely frightened now, not so much by his threat as by the look in his eyes and the sound of his voice. Her legs began to tremble uncontrollably.

The first blow fell. It was harder and more stinging than any she could remember, and she screamed in pain. But her cry, instead of

126

placating him, only inflamed him further. He brought the rod down again and again, as hard as he could, and welts rose up in scarlet stripes across her buttocks. At last she could stand the pain no longer and ran to a corner of the bedroom, where she collapsed in sobbing terror.

Blinded by sweat and rage, Sam lunged after her. She cowered before him like a small animal, cornered and defeated. As he raised the birch rod to strike again, she raised her head toward him, eyes piteous and streaming with tears. His arm went suddenly limp, and the rod fell from his hand to the floor. He turned his head away abruptly, and his body sagged as hot, unexpected tears poured down his face. A convulsive sobbing tore at his lungs, and he fell to his knees at her side. He reached out his arms toward her, and as he picked her up, she shrank away from him in fear. He carried her to his bed and set her down tenderly.

She turned her back to him, burying her face in the pillow. Her back, with its thin shoulder blades protruding in a somehow pathetic way, shook with sobs. As he looked in mounting shame and horror at the swollen ridges where the rod had bitten into her soft flesh he began to pray, begging God's forgiveness for this monstrous cruelty to a defenseless child. At last he became calm and silent, but he did not move from his position, burying his head in his crossed arms.

Moments later, when Betsy turned her head from the pillow and looked at him, he was still there, as though frozen into this posture of remorse and penitence. She stared at him in silence from troubled, swollen eyes. Impulsively then, she reached out her hand and stroked his head in the way that a puppy, after being beaten, may tentatively lick its master's hand. Sam raised his head slowly as he felt her hand against his hair.

"Forgive me, forgive me," he said, and there was a note of pleading in his voice.

She pulled his head toward hers and kissed him on the mouth. As he moved onto the bed beside her, she pressed herself violently into his suddenly enfolding arms. His lanky body sprawled over hers, and he began kissing her frantically. His lips moved from her mouth to her face, to her hair, and then in a storm of affection down to her neck and to her budding breasts. Her small nipples, of a delicate shell-pink, stood erect, and his mouth closed over one of them with such hungry fierceness that she stirred in pain. He had begun now to move himself against her in an accelerating rhythm.

The movement was not strange to her. For as long as she could remember, she had seen men, naked and sweating, thrusting their hips in this same repetitious motion toward the prostrate bodies of women. It was for this that they paid money, and it was described by a word that Sam Allen had forbidden her to use. And she remembered how one night, while she and her sister had watched from behind a door while their mother lay with a naked sailor, Polly had given her a whispered and vivid description of the way a man and woman joined themselves together when they played this strange game in bed.

Now, more than ever before, she wanted to please Sam. She wanted to bring him out of his remoteness and silence and back to the warm responsiveness he had once given her. Nervously but deliberately, she glided her hand beneath his writhing body and touched him between his legs.

Sam reacted so savagely that she became momentarily alarmed. He tore at the opening in his breeches and was all at once astride her, exploring her with frantic fingers. She cried out in pain as he thrust himself deep inside her. She beat her hands helplessly against his chest, crying, "No! No! You're hurting me!"

He did not even hear her, and his movements became wilder and more hectic than before. Then his body grew taut with a final thrust that turned all his muscles to stone. He shook and sobbed as though in pain. At last he lay quiet, so quiet that she thought he must have fainted. He was breathing long and deeply, the way she herself did after she had run up a hill.

"Are you all right, Uncle?" she asked anxiously.

The sound of her voice made him start, as though she had awakened him from sleep. He looked distractedly about him and then down at her. Then he sprang quickly from the bed and almost ran from the room. The awkward way in which he moved, with one hand holding his breeches together at his waist, made her want to laugh. But she didn't. She was too surprised by his sudden departure, knowing that this was not the way the game was usually played. After it was over, the man and woman went to sleep in each other's arms and stayed that way until morning.

She felt alone and deserted, and the wounds from the birch rod had begun to hurt. Since she could not be comfortable lying down, she got up and looked down wonderingly at the coverlet on the bed. It was stained with blood. She realized with a shock that it must be her own, but she was not alarmed. Polly had told her that this was what happened when a girl lost her maidenhead.

As she began putting on her dress, she fell to wondering whether Sam would give her money now, the way her mother's friends had always done after the game was over. Or sometimes, they had presented Phebe with a bolt of cloth, even some silk from China. Maybe Sam would buy her a new dress—a dress of shimmering green satin—or better still, a necklace of real pearls.

For a while, her pains miraculously vanished as her imagination conjured up visions of beautiful clothes and dazzling trinkets, but then she came abruptly out of her dreaming as pangs of hunger made her stomach rumble. Conscious of a great empty feeling inside her, she suddenly remembered that she had had no supper and ran downstairs to the kitchen.

It was dark and deserted. Nellie had left long ago, and Sam was nowhere about. Lighting a candle, she peered into the parlor, but he was not there. She shrugged and returned to the kitchen in search of food. There was a pot of some kind of stew that Nellie had prepared and left on a trivet. She started toward the hearth, and then remembered that Nellie had baked a cake that afternoon. She found it and, stuffing it greedily into her mouth with her fingers, almost finished it.

Sated and feeling strangely happy now, she began to hum to herself. Then she began to sing. The saga of Lily, the sailor's lass, filled the shadowy kitchen with bawdy merriment. Finally, she stopped singing, but still humming happily to herself, she picked up the candle and moved back up the stairs to her bedroom. She left the door open, hoping that maybe Sam would come back to her soon. But she fell asleep almost at once, a quiet and still-innocent smile of contentment hovering about her lips.

Betsy did not see Sam again for two days. On the morning after the beating and its passionate sequel, a boy unexpectedly appeared at the door and gave Nellie a note. Since she could not read, Betsy had to decipher the message, which said merely that Sam had to remain at the shipping office indefinitely to supervise the unloading of a new cargo. Nellie received this news with a puzzled look, for her master had never stayed away overnight before. But the ways of commerce were a mystery to her, to say nothing of the ways of men themselves, and so, she shrugged her shoulders. Without Sam to think about, there would be less work to do.

When Sam finally put in an appearance at twilight two days later, Nellie was shocked by his appearance. More gaunt than ever, there were dark blotches beneath his eyes, as though he had gone a long time without sleep. His hair was tousled, and he was unshaven. His step was so unsteady that if Nellie had not known him better, she would have said that he'd spent two days in a port tavern, drunk and disorderly. She decided that he must have been working so hard that he had made himself ill, and she set herself to fussing over him to nurse him back to health.

Sam had indeed been drunk, very drunk. Not in a port tavern, but alone in his shipping office with a cask of rum from the *Lydia A.*'s cargo. Tortured by conscience, consumed with self-loathing, he had sought oblivion, and he had found it. He had eaten nothing, and whenever consciousness began to return, he had reached blindly for the rum, drinking it down in long, burning gulps that made him gag. Sometimes, to keep the stuff down, he followed it with long draughts of water. He drank desperately against the return of memory and the still-vivid horror of what he had done.

But finally, late in the afternoon of the second day, he had become violently ill. Retching again and again, his body was drenched with sweat. Awareness, throbbing with pain, returned, and he welcomed the pain almost joyfully. The physical agony that wracked him was a heaven-sent punishment that he deserved and must now bear. Shaking uncontrollably, he was at last able to pray, imploring God to send down further suffering upon him, in this world and the next. He did not ask for forgiveness, because forgiveness for the enormity of his sin seemed forever impossible.

He no longer looked on his sin as merely his own. He convinced himself that Betsy was his partner in evil, playing Eve to his Adam. It was clear to him now that she had been corrupted long before he had rescued her from the old gaol on that summer night so long ago. What she had done with him she would surely have done long since with some other man, perhaps some sailor friend of her mother's. But he, at least, could make restitution for the damage done her. In time, perhaps, he would marry her.

But the deep and inward evil that he had done—the sin against God Himself—that sin he would carry to his grave. And it must not, at all costs, be repeated. He contemplated ways in which he could mortify his flesh. He would eat no meat. He would sleep on the bare boards of his bedroom floor. He would avoid being alone with the child on all occasions. His spirits rose as he saw himself conquering his lust, finally and absolutely, once and for all.

He told himself these things desperately, to make it possible to return to reality at all, forgetting for the moment that they were the same things he had promised himself again and again in the past. Nor did he ask himself how it would be physically possible for him to live in the same house with Betsy and yet never be alone with her. Most of all, he did not reckon with Betsy herself.

For Betsy's view of what had happened was quite different from Sam's. She was not aware that the passionate consummation between them had been a sin. It was a natural event. She had lost the maidenhead that her mother had told her about, but she did not even see it as a deprivation. According to Black Bets, a girl of twelve was "ready," and so Betsy looked upon the whole episode as a sort of achievement, a seal set upon childhood once and for all. Now she could start becoming a woman.

This knowledge elated her, made her strangely proud, and she could not imagine why Sam did not share her feelings, especially since he had made it all possible. She could not understand, in the days that followed his disappearance, why he should now become more distant than ever, going to great pains to avoid her company and hardly even talking to her. When it became clear that the lessons she loved so much had been not just temporarily suspended but were not to be resumed at all, her puzzlement turned to anger.

One night, as she lay in bed unable to sleep, the anger gathered itself into a tight ball of furious resolve. Jumping out of bed, she ran across the upstairs hallway and burst into Sam's bedroom without even knocking.

He was sitting at his desk, reading the Bible by the light of a candle. Turning startled eyes to the doorway, he saw her standing there, ghostlike in her white nightgown—but a small and determined ghost, with its feet planted apart in a stance of defiance.

He stared at her in surprise. "Are you sick, child?"

"No, I am not sick."

"Then go back to your bed. It's late."

"No. I wish to talk to you, Uncle."

He got up nervously. "There is nothing for us to talk about, child."

"I am not a child! Not anymore." She looked at him so directly that he turned his eyes away.

"There is nothing to talk about—" he began again.

As persistent as a bee that would not be brushed aside, she said, "But there is! That thing you did to me—"

He closed his eyes, as though to shut out memory, and whispered, "It was monstrous, unforgivable—a crime against nature, against you, Betsy. It was a horrible sin."

He sat down wearily at his desk again, and his hand reached out for the reassuring touch of his Bible. Betsy moved to his side and stared into his face with serious, questioning eyes.

"Why was it a horrible sin? My mother did it all the time with the sailors, and so did Black Bets and Debbie and Esther. And they got money and pretty things for it."

Sam looked at her sadly and a compassionate tone softened his voice. "Oh, Betsy, my poor child. You were exposed to the sins of the world before you ever knew virtue. How can I make you understand?"

"But I understand it already," she said cheerfully. "I know about babies, too. I saw Esther's baby come right out of her, while she was screaming and crying. Why, I'm old enough to have a baby myself!"

"Don't say such things. You are still but a child."

"My mother had John Thomas when she was only thirteen, and I already have the bleeding every month."

He regarded her in stunned silence. "When—" he began nervously, "—when did you have—your—your last flux?"

"Last week. It always happens in the full of the moon."

Sam sighed his relief. When he spoke again, his voice had become firm and decisive. "I see that you stand in need of education in other things than reading and writing. We must begin your moral education."

"When?" asked Betsy delightedly. She was not entirely sure what "moral" might mean, but education and lessons of any kind were pleasurable things. "Can we begin now?"

"No. It is too late. Go to bed. But tomorrow night after supper I will tell you a story from the Bible—about Adam and Eve, the first man and first woman created by the Lord."

"Oh, please to tell me now," she pleaded, circling his neck with her arms.

Her voice was so eager that he agreed to tell her the story, but only on condition that she would sit in the chair opposite him and be very quiet. She obeyed instantly, and so Sam embarked on the story of Adam and Eve in the Garden of Eden.

Betsy sat spellbound. She was enthralled by the fatal apple and the tempting serpent. But as Sam dwelled on the moral implications of Eve's choice, she began to grow drowsy, and long before Adam and Eve had been banished from the Garden, she had fallen sound asleep in her chair.

Sam lifted her in his arms gently so as not to waken her and carried her to her bedroom. After he had tucked her in, he looked down for a moment at the lovely, angelic face, so tranquil now, so absurdly innocent. He felt again that overwhelming tenderness that filled him whenever he saw her asleep. But now, suddenly, a dark river of shame flowed through him. He left the room quickly, shutting the door firmly behind him as though to blot out the still-vivid picture of his sinful act, so loathsome and ugly in cold retrospect. He saw the panting, sweating figure of a middle-aged man in frantic and ridiculous movement over the body of a twelve-year-old child and he was filled with sudden nausea.

For Betsy, moral education was as pleasurable as she had expected it would be, but for Sam it was a nearly hopeless undertaking. He discovered that the taken-for-granted principles that he had lived by for so long could be all but demolished by Betsy's often repeated "Why?" Why, she wanted to know, did the Lord bless the love game only when the players were married? And if the game was sinful, then it must always be sinful. How did getting married change it into something good? And if the Lord knew everything, then he must have known that the serpent was going to tempt Eve, and so why didn't he just kill it to begin with and save Adam and Eve all that trouble?

And when Sam, to justify the whole illogical situation, introduced Satan into the story, he was immediately faced with a new problem. Betsy conceived an immediate liking for the Prince of Darkness and it took three sessions of moral education before she reluctantly admitted that he *might* be bad if he really made people unhappy. But she was not entirely convinced. She had known too many people, mostly women, who succumbed to Satan's wiles and seemed quite happy about it.

There was her mother, for example. She could hardly blame Phebe for siding with Satan when God didn't give her anything to eat and Satan did. And then, what about Lydia, who loved God and would have nothing to do with Satan? She went mad and died in agony.

Sam argued and explained, trying to refute her common sense with the more theoretical logic of his theology. When Betsy finally announced that she understood, he breathed a sigh of relief.

"Now I see," she said in a highly serious tone. "It's good to play the love game when you're married and want the begats. But if God don't give you anything to eat, then you *have* to play it to get some money or you would die. So the only time it's a *real* sin is when you do it just because you want to." She paused reflectively and then added, "Like you and me did."

Sam looked away in confusion at the uncomfortably personal turn her explanation had taken. He could think of nothing to say, and meanwhile, Betsy continued. "I expect that if you gave me a pretty new dress, then the Lord wouldn't be so angry at you, would he?"

Sam frowned in bewilderment, trying to figure out how all his arguments had landed him in this quagmire of logic. He did not even attempt to answer her question. Instead, he started the story of Adam and Eve all over again—from the beginning.

And as the days passed, he went back to the beginning again and again. Sometimes, he would believe he was making progress. Betsy would start making the right responses, her mind following his as

134

he described the origin and nature of sin. Momentarily, she would see the necessity of loving God and hating the Devil, if only because that way she might have a happier life than her mother had.

And then, in a twinkling, Sam's hopes would be splintered into a thousand pieces as Betsy triumphantly stated her original interpretation of what constituted sinful behavior between men and women.

Betsy's convictions on this score were not merely theoretical, as it turned out. A few weeks after her moral education had begun, she was able to put her newly acquired principles into action—to behave, in fact, quite morally.

The opportunity came at the end of an especially lively discussion of right and wrong. Betsy and her persistent "Why?" had succeeded in shaking some of Sam's own long-accepted convictions, and he had responded by defending his faith with the passionate eloquence of a man on trial.

He abandoned logical argument altogether and in his zeal to make her understand, he seized her by the shoulders and shook her.

Betsy, not intimidated in the slightest by the picture of hell-fire in store for her, became infuriated by this physical approach to argument. Jumping out of her chair, she kicked him in the shins. Sam stopped talking in mid-sentence and slapped her on the face. All at once, they tangled, tussled, and fell to the floor, fighting like a pair of angry tomcats. Finally, Sam sat astride her, with his hands pinning her arms down to her sides. They stared at each other, panting and sweating. Then Betsy went obligingly limp and looked up at him archly. She squirmed her hips against him in an effort to get up.

"Let me up, you fool!" she said.

He shook his head doggedly. As his eyes moved slowly along the lines of her quick-breathing body, lust flamed up in him again, without warning. The weight of his body came down upon hers as though propelled by a force altogether beyond his will and control.

"No!" she cried. " 'Tis sin, 'tis sin! Git away!"

He held her all the tighter and then began to tear at her clothing with shaking hands. Betsy fired a stream of invective at him. His descriptions of hell's tortures were returned to him in words more vivid, if less proper, than his own.

"You'll burn, burn, burn!" she shrieked. "The Devil will stick a red-hot poker right up your arse, and he'll put boiling pitch on that ole snake between your legs!"

"Be quiet and lie still," he muttered. "I'll not hurt you."

She became more pliant and her voice took on a wheedling tone. "But, Uncle, 'tis indeed a sin." She paused and then continued more softly. " 'Tis a sin lessen you buy me a new dress."

He had yanked open her bodice, and his lips were covering her small breasts with kisses.

"Did you hear me?" she asked.

"Yes, yes," he mumbled through lips wet against her skin.

"A green dress—of silk," she added, helping him as he fumbled at his breeches with trembling hands.

"Yes, yes," he said. "Ah, Betsy, my sweet little lass."

She shrank away from him as he entered her, anticipating pain. But there was none, and she arched herself toward him instinctively but without enjoyment. She found the weight of his body oppressive and hoped that the game would be quickly over. The only pleasure she experienced came from the picture that shone in her imagination—a shining, shimmering dress, as green as the sea in early morning. Transported by this vision, she was hardly aware of what was happening.

She was brought back to reality by the anguished moans that came from Sam in those few seconds before his body went slack. The sadness of the sound evoked a curious tenderness in her. She clasped his head against her breast and moved her fingers soothingly through his damp and tousled hair.

When at last he stirred and made a move to relinquish her, she still clung to him. Then, placing her mouth close to his ear, she whispered, "You promised—a pretty green dress—remember? Silk."

"God forgive me," he said. "Oh, God, forgive me."

"Oh, He will, Uncle," she assured him. "Why, soon as he sees that dress He will know you done right, and the sin will all be washed away. For thy God is a just God—"

"Hush," he said and placed his hand gently over her mouth.

Sam could hardly subscribe to the logic of Betsy's ideas about sin and atonement. He could not even follow it. But he believed that a promise was a promise, even if it had been made under circumstances that were, at the very least, unusual.

The new dress was green, and it was made of silk, and it was highly becoming to Betsy. The color enhanced the fiery red-gold of her hair, and beneath this burnished and resplendent halo, her eyes seemed more violet-blue than ever. The whole effect might have been angelic, had it not been for the cut of the dress itself, whose silken folds clung sensuously to the maturing lines of her body.

In the months that followed, other adornments made their appearance, one by one. First, there was a pair of golden-striped cloth slippers; then a rust-colored bonnet astream with white ribbons; with the coming of fall, an elegantly cut coat of forest-green wool; and just before Thanksgiving, after a particularly stormy session of moral education, a modest and discreet necklace of tiny seed pearls with a golden clasp.

Sam refused to allow her to wear this finery to church, and a long and continuing battle ensued. He pointed out that color was absolutely forbidden in Sabbath dress. But there was a deeper reason for his objections. Even if colorful clothing for women had been quite acceptable in church, he would still have refused to let her flaunt before God these symbols of the dark lusts that over-whelmed his reason with such unhappy regularity.

But in the end, Betsy won this battle, too. If she could not go to church in colorful clothes, then she saw no reason why he should not provide her with a whole new Sabbath wardrobe in black and white. And so, garment by garment, the new acquisitions arrived. By the time winter came, her Sunday appearance put even her sister, Polly, to shame.

The clothes were so simple, unrevealing, and primly cut, that Sam was finally able to forget their guilt-laden association, telling himself that after all, the child should look as neat and attractive as possible before God during worship. He was relieved, too, that the women of the congregation did not send stares of disapproval in

137

her direction. If they were aware of her changed appearance, they did not show it.

As for the male parishioners, whatever Baptist objections they might have had to such vain feminine adornment were quite swept away by the glow of Betsy's beauty, by the charm of her manner. A shy look from the innocent violet eyes, a graceful curtsy of greeting, a smile of flattering attention, and the most Puritan of male hearts melted into taffy tenderness.

Betsy herself was well aware of the masculine eyes that lingered for an abstracted second or two on her upturned face, on the slight curve of her bosom, before they moved blinkingly away to a vague spot apparently just above her head. She wondered if these men, too, might enjoy sinfulness as much as Sam, moaning and groaning over the bodies of their wives. But the thought of these prim and starched women playing the love game was somehow absurd. The very thought of it made her giggle.

By the time spring came again, Sam and Betsy had settled into a secure and tidy domesticity. For the first time, they lived together in comparative peace and serenity. Betsy had, in fact, begun to think of herself as Sam's wife, although his plans to marry her still seemed as vague as ever.

She developed an unexpected interest in the feminine arts of cooking and sewing, cajoling Nellie into teaching her how to make tarts and gingerbread. From the sweet things that she liked so much, she went on to learn the more complicated mysteries of roasting and making stews.

Her experience with sewing began with the making of small articles of dress for herself. Within the year, she had added mending to her accomplishments and could darn Sam's socks or put a patch on the seat of a worn pair of breeches.

Sam praised her and encouraged her to develop these talents so eminently suitable to young ladies of gentle breeding. She basked in the warmth of his approbation and spurred herself on to even greater efforts. She learned to hatchel flax and to card wool. She knit him a pair of stockings, which were a little too small, but he wore them anyway, pride overcoming discomfort. In autumn, she helped Nellie make soap, and in spring she dipped candles.

Sam looked on these activities with great approval and renewed his pledge to the Almighty to make Betsy his wife just as soon as the social amenities permitted. He was, after all, still a widower in mourning, and though Betsy was not too young for marriage by custom and convention, the difference in their ages seemed disparate. All things considered, it would be better to wait.

Meanwhile, he was relieved of some of his feeling of sinfulness. Although he still lusted, repented of his lust, and lusted again, he began to look upon himself as the divinely appointed agent for Betsy's eventual salvation. It was true that he had led her into sin, but he would also be, when he married her, the means of extricating her from the Devil's toils. Sometimes he could even see himself as a man with a mission—a lover with a purpose beyond the immediate satisfaction of his sensual needs. God, he firmly believed, works in mysterious ways.

There were times during those sessions of moral and religious instruction when he felt that Betsy herself was making spiritual progress. Glimmers of understanding would unexpectedly light up her eyes. The idea of Christian charity appealed to her, in theory, at least, and she told him that she liked Jesus, even if she didn't always understand the strange things He did, like walking on water for no very good reason.

She found God more acceptable than His Son. She saw Him as a kindly old man, not at all the angry, avenging God that she had first heard about in the Baptist meetinghouse. Her God chided her gently when she did wrong, but He was never mean and violent. Sin, for her, was very simply doing anything that hurt somebody else, and that included animals as well as people. As for the love game, she did not believe that He looked upon it as sinful at all, just so long as the proper rules of fair exchange were observed by both players.

The game, as it was played by her and Sam, had begun to change. She no longer rebelled against him and defied him. There were no more beatings. His passion came as a result of a sudden rush of unexpected tenderness toward her, and she responded with a tenderness of her own. And yet, at the moment of their coming together, the thought that was uppermost in her mind was still the reward that she could look forward to after the game was over.

139

She was not demanding about the reward itself. It might be large or small, perhaps even something trifling. But it had to be there, waiting for her, something promised in advance and quite definite. She had learned, however, that the initiator of the game had to be Sam, because once, when she had greatly desired a new comb, she had deliberately sat herself on his lap and attempted to rouse him with calculated squirmings and a hand placed caressingly well up on his thigh. Sam had become inexplicably angry, thrusting her away from him with violence. He had called her harlot and Jezebel.

That was the first and only time she ever started the game herself. The day, the hour, and even the place were for Sam to decide. She learned how to wait, and she never had to wait overlong.

PART TWO

In August 1790, not long after Betsy's fifteenth birthday, Providence was the scene of a great celebration. Rhode Island, the smallest but most stubbornly independent of the original colonies, had finally ratified the Constitution of the United States, thereby becoming the thirteenth state of the Union.

The event was so noteworthy that President Washington left the new nation's capital in New York, boarded a sloop named the *Hancock*, and sailed for Newport and Providence so that he could personally welcome the new state into the Union. After a tumultuous reception in Newport, he arrived in Providence, and the townspeople, after their prolonged hesitancy, went suddenly wild with enthusiasm.

When the *Hancock* tied up at Hacker's Wharf, it was greeted by a thirteen-gun salute of cannon. After an elaborate greeting by Governor Arthur Fenner, Mr. Washington and his entourage rode up Benefit Street in a procession of gaily decorated carriages.

The town was on holiday. The taverns, stores, and other places of business were deserted, and the street was thronged with jubilant crowds. Everyone in Providence seemed to have come to catch a glimpse of the President of their newly adopted nation. They cheered as Mr. Washington's carriage passed, and he inclined his head graciously toward them, his face friendly but unsmiling. They liked his grave dignity and responded to it by cheering and applauding more fervently than ever.

Betsy and Sam stood waiting behind the gate to the Allen house. Sam had brought out a footstool for her to stand on so that she could see over the heads of the people who lined the street. She was decked out in her most fetching dress and wore an elaborate plumed bonnet that sat jauntily on the massed russet curls of her hair. She stood there so quietly that she might have been a statue of some queen, loftily perched on a pedestal. At her side, Sam, neatly formal in Sabbath clothes, held himself in an erect posture of attention.

But when the President's carriage came into view and then finally rolled by, Betsy's regal calm was instantly shattered. She went into such a frenzy of waving and cheering that she lost her balance and would have toppled inelegantly to the ground if Sam had not been there to catch her. Undaunted by this momentary loss of poise, she pulled excitedly at his coat as the carriage moved on.

"Oh, let's follow him!" she cried. "I want to see him up close!"

She pushed the gate open and joined the stream of people following the carriage, Sam trailing protectively at her heels, urging her to return to the house. She did not even hear him, and he resigned himself to joining the pushing, jostling crowd.

The procession came to a halt at the Golden Ball, the most sumptuous and imposing inn in Providence, four stories high and with an ornate upper balcony along its façade. Alpheus Ammidon, the proprietor, had spared no expense to make the occasion worthy of the most distinguished guest his hostelry had received in its six years of existence.

A fife-and-drum corps was stationed at the entrance, and as the members of the President's entourage stepped out of their carriages, it burst into such a high-spirited rendition of *Yankee Doodle* that the tempo almost ran away with the tune. On the other side of the entrance a band of Negro fiddlers added a quota of rhythmic but untuneful scrapings that made the din even more impressive, if not entirely musical.

Loud huzzahs burst forth again as Mr. Washington descended from his carriage. Once more he acknowledged the applause with grave nods of his head and then moved stiffly and militarily up the steps toward the door of the inn. Unrecognized by the crowd, Thomas Jefferson walked at his right side and Governor George Clinton of New York at his left.

Betsy had edged herself well to the fore and was so close that she might have reached out and touched Mr. Jefferson's flapping coat-

144

tails. Sam, still breathless from the exertion of chasing her the length of Benefit Street, stood at her side.

As the last member of the Presidential party disappeared into the inn, there was a sigh of disappointment from the crowd. They had hoped that Mr. Washington would address a few patriotic words to them, praising them for their long-delayed consent to become part of the United States.

Betsy looked at Sam in disappointment. "Oh, dear, he's gone, and I did want him to notice me."

"Notice you? But why should he, lass? He is a very great man—the father of our country."

"But he's *my* father, too," said Betsy.

Sam smiled one of his rare smiles. "Now why should you say a thing like that?"

Betsy gave him a look that was serious and slightly indignant. "But he *is* my father! Mama told me so!"

The implication of this statement shocked Sam, and he said, "Hush, Betsy! You must never say such a thing again, for it is a lie that your mother told you."

Betsy became furious. " 'Tis not a lie! 'Tis true! And someday I will *tell* him that I am his daughter!"

Sam began moving her gently away from the inn, following the rapidly dispersing crowd. It was not beyond his imagining that then and there she might run into the inn and present herself to the President as his bastard daughter.

Cajolingly, he said, "Well, perhaps you are. But it would hardly be proper for you to tell him on a great occasion like this, now, would it?"

As her sense of the fitness of things told her that Sam was probably right, regretfully she fell into step beside him as they turned back along Benefit Street toward home.

Sam noticed with amusement that she walked proudly, with erect carriage and head held high. As though in disdain of the townspeople around her, her small upturned nose was lifted slightly. But Sam did not smile. He knew better. Although he had never heard Phebe's legendary tale until now, he saw that Betsy believed it implicitly.

There was, to be sure, an odd resemblance between the two,

especially evident in the firm squareness of their jaw lines. But the idea that they might be father and daughter was ridiculous. Even granting that the great George Washington might have had the sinful moments that come to most men, it was unthinkable that he would have stooped so low as to succumb to the raffish charms of Phebe Bowen.

The celebration continued the next day when Mr. Washington and his entourage were entertained in the homes of the town's leading citizens. At a luncheon given by Governor Fenner they drank innumerable toasts: to the President, to the new republic, to Rhode Island, to the town itself, and then to every member of the President's party and to every official in Providence.

Late in the afternoon they walked weavingly down Benefit Street to John Brown's house, where they were expected for tea. Even the President was seen to lean rather too heavily on the arm of Mr. Jefferson. But instead of tea, they partook of Mr. Brown's renowned rum punch, and when at last they left to return to the Golden Ball, there were many gentlemen who had to be carried to the waiting coaches.

That night there was a great banquet at the State House, attended by more than two hundred members of the town's prominent families, and Betsy and Sam stood in the crowded square to watch the elegantly dressed guests arrive in their newly painted and polished carriages.

Betsy caught her breath in excitement when she saw the Wyatt family's coach line up with the others near the entrance. She craned her neck to see who was inside. When the coach finally stopped before the door to the State House, Mr. and Mrs. Wyatt alighted, followed by Matt Wyatt and Polly.

Betsy was filled with such consuming envy that she could not contain herself. "Look at her!" she said. "My sister Polly! And she's going to meet President Washington!" She turned on Sam in anger. "Why didn't you take *me* to the banquet?"

"Because I wasn't invited. I am not an important and rich man like Mr. Wyatt."

"Well, why aren't you?" she screamed.

"Hush!" said Sam, embarrassed by Betsy's outcry. People in the crowd were turning their heads to look curiously at them.

One of the faces was disturbingly familiar to Sam, and he searched his memory in an effort to place it. And then he remembered. It was Phebe Bowen.

The five years that had passed since that day when she had appeared before the Town Council had not been kind to her. The Irish prettiness had all but disappeared, and her pale, thin face was careworn and prematurely lined. Sam judged by her bloodshot and swollen eyes that she had been drinking, thanking heaven that she did not recognize him and that Betsy, so preoccupied with her jealousy of Polly, had not seen her.

Seizing Betsy's hand, he said sternly, "We are going home now."

"Going home? But I want to watch the people—"

"We are going home," he said more firmly.

"Well, you can go home if you've a mind to. But I'm staying here!"

"You will do as I say," said Sam, pulling her by the hand and dragging her, protesting, through the crowd.

As Betsy found herself being propelled backward against her will, her fury at Sam mounted and she struck at him, landing a glancing blow on his ear. Sam retaliated with a hard clout that hit her full in the face and knocked her down. Then he dragged her away until they were free of the crowd.

Breathlessly, they faced each other. Sam was preparing to carry her, if necessary, back to the house when he saw that it was too late. Phebe Bowen had detached herself from the mob and was approaching them. She swayed as she walked and came to an abrupt halt behind Betsy.

"Who gives you the right to strike me child?" she bellowed hoarsely.

Betsy turned at the sound of the familiar voice. She stared at her mother in amazement and then, in a rush of emotion, threw herself into Phebe's outstretched arms. Phebe strained her to her breast, and Betsy began to cry.

Sam watched them in embarrassment. The scene he had hoped to avoid had happened, and there seemed nothing to do but wait until it had played itself out. Patiently, he listened to the murmured endearments, averting his eyes from the unseemly display of emotion.

When they had at last quieted down, he nodded politely to Phebe and said, "It is past Betsy's bedtime." To Betsy he said, "Are you ready to go home now, my child?"

Betsy turned her tear-stained face to him pleadingly. "Can my mother come with us—please, Uncle?"

"No," said Sam firmly. "I think not."

"But she's my mother, and I haven't seen her in so long! I won't go home and you can't make me!"

Sam's voice was quietly resolute. Although he spoke to Betsy, he fixed his eyes on Phebe. "I am your legal guardian. I would very much dislike having to call the town sergeant to make you return home, but I will do so if you force me to."

Phebe's bleary eyes flickered with a momentary fear. Drunk though she was, she knew that she had been forbidden to return to Providence and that a brush with the authorities would land her in gaol.

"You had best go, lovey. We want no trouble now, do we? What Mr. Allen says is true."

"I don't care!" said Betsy. "I won't go unless you come too!"

Phebe's voice became stern. "Now, you listen to me, Betsy love. If the town sergeant finds me here in Providence, he'll throw me back into gaol. You wouldn't want that to happen, would you?"

"No, but—but when will I see you again?"

"Soon, my darlin', very soon. Now don't you worry. Just you go back home with Mr. Allen." She turned to Sam. "And if you so much as lay a hand on her, I'll report *you* to the town sergeant, and don't think I won't!"

Sam drew himself up with dignity. "Your daughter is well treated, ma'am. She is chastised only when she is disobedient, I assure you."

There followed a prolonged leave-taking with more emotion and more tears. Then Phebe disappeared into the crowd, and Sam and Betsy started up Benefit Street toward home.

Betsy walked slowly and in silence. Sam would have liked to offer her words of comfort because the sight of her tear-stained face and her now rather bedraggled little figure filled him with pity. Her fanciest dress was torn and dirty from their scuffle, and her

148

hair was in disarray. But the firm thrust of her jaw and the fierce look in her eyes told him that a storm was coming, and he did not know how he would cope with it.

Betsy, at fifteen, was no longer a child to be fobbed off with easy, authoritative answers backed up by force. Sam was learning that he must now deal with her as an equal. She had always been rebellious, but he understood that her rebellion now was not so much childish and willful as it was a part of her growing up. The memory of his own adolescence was still vivid to him, and he recognized, as his own father had not, that if he resorted to force, he would be risking utter defeat.

Until now, no question had arisen between them so potentially explosive as the one posed by Phebe's unexpected reappearance. He knew that he might easily lose Betsy to Phebe, not merely because she was her mother but because she was the only human being beside himself for whom Betsy had felt love.

Jealousy played no part in the decision that he now made to prevent a renewal of the relationship, by force if need be. Though he did not condemn Phebe for what she was, he saw her quite simply as a source of corruption for Betsy, someone who could undermine and even destroy all his efforts to mold the child into a civilized and moral young woman.

He dreaded the battle that was sure to come because it was a battle that he was not confident of winning. He did not underestimate the power of his adversary, and he was prepared to fight with whatever weapons he could find, fair or not. Of one thing he was sure. There would not be room for two victors.

When they got home, Betsy refused to go to bed. She sat stubbornly in a chair near the kitchen hearth and would not move. Sullen and silent, she stared ahead of her, elbow on knee, chin cupped in her hand. She seemed scarcely to hear Sam as he begged her to be reasonable and come to bed.

"You are tired and upset," he said soothingly. "We can talk about this tomorrow."

Betsy looked up. "Why can't we talk about it now? I want to know why my mother couldn't come home with us!"

"Because—well, for one thing, Betsy, she was drunk."

"Maybe she was. She is still my mother, and I have not seen her in five years."

149

"It is best that you should not see her at all."

"Why?"

Sam paused. Though he was tired and in no mood for argument, he knew that he must choose his words carefully. "I do not wish to condemn your mother, Betsy. She is as she is, God help her. But that does not mean that I approve of her."

Betsy's voice roughened with anger. "Approve, condemn! Who are you to approve and condemn? 'Judge not, and ye shall not be judged'! St. Luke, Chapter Six."

"My judgment concerns only what is good for you, my child. Your mother's salvation is beyond my reach. Yours is not."

Betsy rose and glared at him. "Salvation? What do you care about my salvation?"

"I care deeply about it," said Sam quietly. "And I believe that association with your mother would be a corrupting influence upon you."

She looked at him scornfully. "And you are *not* a corrupting influence? 'Twas you who took my maidenhead!"

Sam looked down at the floor in shame, momentarily silenced. When he looked up, her mocking eyes gazed into his with cool questioning.

"I acknowledge my sinfulness," he said at last. "And I have promised you that I will rectify the wrong I have done you. You know I intend to make you my wife, Betsy."

"When?"

"When you are a little older—when it will be more seemly."

"I am already fifteen. Many girls in Providence are married at thirteen."

"But not to men more than twice their age, widowers who have only recently lost their wives."

"Aunt Lydia has been dead three years," said Betsy.

"I know," said Sam. "But, Betsy, you must understand the circumstances—"

"I understand the circumstances very well. You get into bed with me whenever you feel like it. You speak with the forked tongue of a serpent! You will not permit my mother to enter your house because she is a drunken whore. But it is all right to keep your *own* whore! I'd like to know what God thinks about that!"

Sam knew full well what God thought about it. He also knew, quite suddenly, that he could not evade the issue any longer. He took a deep breath. "Very well, Betsy," he said. "I shall marry you without further delay."

"You will?" She looked at him in astonishment. "You will marry me now?"

"Yes. That is a promise."

His unforeseen proposal left her feeling oddly deflated and at a loss for words. She felt that her strongest weapon against him had been taken away, leaving her defenseless. And then, as she began to envision the reality of becoming Sam's wife, a sense of power welled up in her, not unlike the feeling she had immediately before she played the game with him, when she stipulated the reward to be given her in return.

She foresaw that as Sam's wife she would be able to make demands of him that, as husband and protector, he could not deny. She had often envied Lydia's power over him, and the thought that these privileges could now be hers filled her with joyful anticipation. She wanted to run to him, throw her arms around him, and give a jubilant assent to his proposal. And then something instinctively and perversely feminine in her made her pause. She knew somehow that she should not accept his offer too enthusiastically.

He had presented marriage as a great gift that he chose to bestow out of the generosity of his heart. He was like some king in a fairy tale offering to make a princess out of a beggar. Whenever, in her daydreams, she had envisioned a proposal of marriage, it had been given by a handsome prince, on bended knee before her, begging her to become his princess and help him rule his kingdom.

Not only did Sam bear little resemblance to this suitor of her dreams, but he had not even troubled to ask her if she would consent to be his wife. His bland assumption that she would gratefully fall in with his plans annoyed her.

Without coquetry and with a look of calm appraisal, she said, "I am not sure that I want to become your wife."

He looked at her in disbelief. "What—what do you mean?"

She shrugged. "I know it will make things look good to your God, but—"

"But surely my God is your God," he sputtered.

151

Unexpectedly, she smiled. "I know that *you* think so. I am not so sure. If there is a God, I don't know how it is that only you always know exactly what He wants."

"Because He speaks to me, my child."

"Then why don't He ever speak to me?"

"Because you do not listen. Betsy, surely you can see that even if there were no God, we are already man and wife, and it would be desirable for us to be joined together legally in wedlock."

"Why? My mother slept with men and did not marry them."

Sam paused in embarrassment at the thought that now presented itself as an argument. "There is something that you must remember, Betsy. You—you are now old enough to—to conceive a child."

"I know," she said. "I am a woman. I have been having the monthly flux for three years now."

He winced, not liking to contemplate her bald statement, and continued, "If you were to become with child—"

"Then I suppose I would give birth to it."

"But it would be illegitimate."

"So it would." She cocked her head to the side and laughed at his discomfiture. "But then, I am a bastard child myself. George Washington—"

His temper snapped. "That's nonsense!"

"It is not nonsense, either!" she said, bridling.

"Nonsense or not, I cannot risk your giving birth to a bastard child in this house!"

"Then I would have to give birth someplace else, I guess." She paused and looked at him acutely. "Why are you all of a sudden so worried about getting me with child? You've been jigging me for three years now."

Ignoring the vulgar word, he said, in a placating tone, "I have been greatly worried about you, Betsy."

"But not so worried that you stayed away from me, I'll be bound." She got up from the chair and moved toward the stairs. "I think I will go to bed now."

He followed her imploringly and seized her hand. An unexpected wave of emotion swept over him and poured itself forth in a torrent of words. "Betsy, I beg of you—marry me! I know I have wronged you, and now I want to make amends for the evil I have done you. I love you, Betsy. I have always loved you from the moment I saw you that night in the old gaol so long ago. And every year, as I watched you grow, I have loved you more. Please—please be my wife!"

Taking her in his arms, he pulled her tight against him. Her heart had begun to beat fast in response to this unexpected and strange outburst of feeling from him. Surprise had given way to a feeling of happiness, and she felt herself melting into compliance beneath the touch of his caressing hands. The unaccustomed words of love fell like needed rain on some dry and arid part of her being, and she sighed gratefully.

And then something hard and unyielding rose up in her—a fear that her very weakness would betray her. She found herself growing taut in his embrace. She pulled herself gently away from him and this made him even more frantic in his attempt to hold her to him.

"Betsy—Betsy—for God's sake, as I love you, marry me."

She had gotten free of him and now ran toward the stairs. Halfway up, she turned. "Yes—yes, I will marry you, Uncle—but first you will have to get my mother's permission!"

Sam came to an abrupt halt at the foot of the stairs. She could not have stopped him more effectively if she had doused him with a pitcher of cold water from the well.

Quietly and with great dignity, she continued up the stairs, lifting her begrimed skirts daintily. With head held high, she disappeared around the corner of the upstairs hallway.

For a moment, Sam stood there, looking after her in bewilderment. In his imagination, he could hear the opening guns of battle, and he was as frightened as any soldier at that panic-stricken moment when the signal comes to move out into the fray.

On an afternoon two days later, Betsy sat in the parlor mending Sam's stockings. The hot and sultry breeze that came through the open windows and the droning of bees in the flower garden made her feel drowsy. The stocking that she had been darning dropped into her lap, her head nodded forward, and she dozed.

She was awakened abruptly by the sound of a voice calling in the street.

"Yarbs an' greens! Yarbs an' greens t'sell!"

The voice sounded somehow familiar, and sleepily she tried to place it. Suddenly, her body tensed, and she sat up very still and straight in her chair, scarcely breathing, waiting for the voice to call out again.

When it came, she ran from her chair to the window. Phebe stood on the street, leaning against a small handcart full of vegetables and herbs. Her face was turned full toward the house, and she seemed to be waiting. She did not wait long. Betsy ran to the front door, flung it wide, and sped down the path to the arms of her mother.

"Oh, Mama, Mama! You've come at last!" She thrust her face against Phebe's bosom and began kissing her with the frantic affection of a puppy. The smell of her mother's rum-soaked breath, hot on her cheek, stirred old memories, reassuring her that his woman was indeed her mother, however little she resembled the Phebe of five years ago.

That woman had been young and pretty, thin in body and full of animation. Now, only Phebe's eyes looked the way Betsy remembered them, and even they had a different expression—of pain, of weariness. Her face was bloated, her once-fair complexion was mottled now with patches of red. Her figure had lost its gracefulness and become stolid, almost fat.

Finally, she held Betsy at arm's length and surveyed her. Brushing the tears from her grimy cheeks, she said, "Lord, how you growed!" Then shaking her head in admiration, she added, "So womanly you've become—I'd hardly have known you, lovey. Such a beauty as you are!"

"Oh, am I, Mama? It must be that I take after you." Betsy paused and looked at her mother. She tried to keep her eyes casual, to conceal the shock she felt. "You're looking—quite well, Mama."

Phebe smiled her wide smile that always seemed to contain a hint of mockery. "Oh, come now! You don't hardly need to lie to your own mother. Me good looks is gone. Why else would I be peddlin' greens like an honest woman? The men from the ships can get more tender blossoms than me. And anyway, I'm a respectable married woman now!"

"Married? Oh, Mama, I'm so glad! Come into the house and tell me about it. We'll have tea together!"

Phebe hesitated. "I don't think Mr. Allen would want me to—"

"Mr. Allen isn't to home," said Betsy. "And anyway I don't care whether he'd like it or not!"

Phebe sat awkwardly on a Queen Anne side chair near the fireplace in the parlor and ate ravenously. Above her the oil portrait of Lydia's mother stared out into the room with its eternal icy disapproval of everything it saw. But Phebe, impressed though she was by these clean and elegant surroundings, was not intimidated. She had fortified herself with a swig of rum from a small flask she carried in her apron pocket, and this, along with the tea and the cake that Betsy had filched from the kitchen, made her talkative and expansive. She launched into a detailed account of her marriage to Captain Jonathan Clarke, from the moment of their not altogether sober meeting in a tavern in Rutland to the dramatic "shift marriage" that had taken place in Newport a few months later.

"But what's a shift marriage, Mama?" Betsy asked.

"Oh, 'tis a very legal thing, child. It was requested by the Captain, you see, because I had been married before—to your father, I mean."

"Is he dead now?"

"Oh, yes, at the bottom of Narragansett Bay these four years— me poor John Bowen. But Captain Clarke did not wish to be responsible for any debts he might inherit by marrying me, and so we had a shift marriage." She paused solemnly. "I came to him nekkid right there in the street."

Betsy gasped. "You were in the street getting married—without any clothes on?"

"Stripped to the buff, lovey, except for me shift, and, of course, me hair lace. And I walked across that street right into the preacher's house, where we was joined in holy matrimony—and me free and clear with no burdens for me new husband."

Betsy breathed an ecstatic "Oh!" Then, envisioning the whole town of Newport as witness to this daring act on her mother's part, she asked, "And all the people watching! What did they say?"

"They didn't say nothin' because there wasn't any people there. 'Twas in the dead of night. And so, that's how I became wife to Captain Jonathan Clarke!"

On this triumphant note Phebe ended her story, settling back in her chair regally, as though awaiting applause.

"But Captain Clarke, Mama—is he really a captain?"

"Oh, yes, daughter. He was an officer in the Continental Army, fightin' the Revolution with Mr. Washington. And what's more, he's an educated gentleman! He reads books. Printed books!" She allowed a moment of awed silence to pass.

"But, Mama," said Betsy, "if he's an officer and a gentleman, why must you go through the streets hawking greens?"

Phebe sighed. "Alas, the Captain is presently ill. And penniless."

After the dramatic account of the marriage, Betsy felt disappointed, but she said cheerfully, "But he will get better and be rich again?"

Phebe's gay spirits quickly departed, and she said dolefully, "He was never rich, lass. He is a cobbler by trade."

"Then he will get well again and work."

"I believe he will never be truly well, child. He is a high-livin' man, the Captain is. He has taken too much of the bottle in his time, and truth to say, he likes work as little as I do meself." She smiled and with an attempt to be more cheerful, she said, "We be two of a kind—and very well suited each to the other." She reached for the flask in her apron and took another gulp of rum. Then, exhaling her breath in a rasping "Aaah!" she said in a sanctimonious tone, "Stay away from the rum, lovey, for it'll take away your good looks just as it did mine."

"But if it does that, Mama, why do you drink it?"

"You wouldn't understand, me darlin'. I scarce understand it meself."

A silence fell between them, and Betsy was filled with sadness as she looked again at her mother, contrasting the woman she had known as a child to the one who sat opposite her in the Allen parlor. Until now, the fact of aging had had little meaning for her. Somehow, it was as though people who were old had always been old, just as the young seemed always to have been young. And now, in a mere five years, her mother had moved, as though by magic, from one group to the other. She was old.

Betsy had never felt pity for her mother, but she felt it now. In all her dreams of a reunion, she had seen herself as a child, receiving once again the love and protection she had always found in her mother's arms. And now, quite suddenly, it was the other way around. She wanted to take care of Phebe and help her though she did not know exactly how.

She rose silently from her chair and went over to Phebe, putting her arms around her. "I love you, Mama," she said simply. "I want to—I want to do something for you."

Phebe's eyes misted with tears, but she blinked them back. She forced herself to laugh—the mocking laugh that Betsy knew so well, the laugh that always appeared when Phebe was deeply moved.

"Now what in God's heaven could you do for *me*, child?"

"Do you—do you have enough to eat, Mama?"

"Phebe Bowen ain't never yet gone hungry." She gave a playful punch in the direction of her belly. "Fat, nothin' but hawg fat." She grinned suddenly. "Or did you maybe think I was in a condition?"

Betsy found herself blushing in embarrassment. "Oh, don't say such things, Mama."

"And why not? You're forgettin'—I'm a respectable married woman now." She paused and frowned. "But not so respectable that I be welcome in the town of Providence, I fear me."

"You're not leaving, are you?" asked Betsy anxiously.

"Oh, no. Y'see, we don't be exactly livin' *in* the town. We're out on the Old Warren Road—in a mud hut."

"A mud hut? Oh, Mama—"

"T'ain't so bad." Phebe looked at her daughter suspiciously. "You ain't grown so elegant that you've forgotten how it used to be, have you?"

"Oh, no. I didn't mean that, Mama. But I'd like for you to live more—more comfortable—"

"Like a lady, hey?" Phebe laughed. "Well, it ain't likely, not now or ever, lovey. Your Ma is a draggletailed baggage, a traipsin' wench whose home is where she lays her head." She paused, and then looked at Betsy with a sudden intensity. "But that ain't for you, daughter! You've got beauty and wits now—and you always had spunk. You'll be a great lady, if you've a mind to!"

"I have a mind to," said Betsy solemnly. "And when I am, Mama, I will take care of you."

Phebe got up abruptly. "I don't need takin' care of! I can make do—don't you fret. So I'll say goodbye to you now, daughter."

As Phebe moved toward the door, Betsy ran after her, throwing her arms around her mother's waist in an effort to keep her from leaving. "Don't go, Mama! Please don't go!"

Phebe disengaged Betsy's arms gently. "I got to, lovey. 'Twould never do for your Mr. Allen to come home and find your ragamuffin of a mother stinkin' up his parlor."

"Oh, I don't care!" said Betsy.

"Well, you'd better care! He's given you a fine home and brought you up like a lady. You can't throw all that away just because you happen to meet your mother on the street. I came here because I wanted to see you. Well, now I seen you. But I can tell you this—I won't be comin' here again!"

Betsy began to cry and clung to Phebe. "Mama, Mama, I don't want you to go away! Ain't I never to see you again, Mama?"

Betsy's show of affection was not without its effect on Phebe. She stroked Betsy's hair soothingly and said, "There, there now, child! It ain't as bad as all that. If the town sergeant don't catch me and throw me into gaol, you'll be seein' me here and there. And mayhap you could walk out the Old Warren Road some afternoon for a visit."

Betsy's sobs quieted, and at last, with reluctance, she moved with Phebe toward the door. They walked down the steps of the house and toward the street, and there they embraced again. Phebe seized the handles of her vegetable cart and began to move away.

She turned her head for a farewell look at Betsy, and a broad smile lighted up her face. "Now, you be a good girl," she said. "You'll turn out a real lady for sure and be the pride of me heart!"

Betsy nodded and tried to smile, but a great sadness filled her. Standing there at the gate, she watched Phebe's pathetic figure until it was out of sight. The sound of the voice calling "Yarbs an' greens!" became fainter and fainter, but it echoed in Betsy's ears until she went to bed that night. And even later, while she slept, she heard it in her dreams—a haunting music that sang forever somewhere on the edge of love.

Phebe's visit did not go unobserved or unmentioned. Nellie reported it to Sam in full detail that night as soon as Betsy had left the kitchen to go to bed. Sam listened, his face thoughtful. His impulse was to call Betsy downstairs immediately and forbid her ever to see her mother again, but he decided to wait. He wanted time to plan his strategy. He knew that he would have to be firm, and yet the situation must be handled with delicacy and gentleness.

And so, the following evening, after Nellie had left to go home, he invited Betsy into the parlor for a talk.

"What about?" asked Betsy, though she knew very well what it would be about. She had expected that Nellie would lose no time in reporting her mother's visit.

"I think you know what it is about," said Sam. "It is best that we reach some kind of understanding in this matter."

She followed him dutifully into the parlor and sat herself down in the chair opposite him, settling back quietly and waiting for him to begin.

"You have disobeyed me, Betsy," he said. "You have seen your mother."

"Yes, I have seen her. And I shall see her again if I've a mind to!"

He let the challenge pass and spoke softly in an injured tone. "Evidently, my wishes in this matter are not to be considered."

"No, because you aren't being fair. She is my mother, and nothing you can say will stop me from seeing her. I love her."

He paused and said sadly, "And do you not love me?"

She was. silent for a moment. "Can't I love both of you?" she asked.

"Yes, it is natural that you should love her. You would be undutiful if you did not. I ask only that you do not *see* her."

"Why not?"

"I have already told you. Her influence on you, her sinful way of life—"

"She is no longer sinful. She is a respectable married woman!"

"Married? To whom?"

"To Captain Clarke! He was an officer with Mr. Washington in the army, and he is a gentleman!"

Sam gave her a tired smile. "Captain Jonathan Clarke—so now he calls himself a captain, does he? It is a matter of doubt if he ever raised himself to the rank of corporal. The Town Council knows him well. He is a vagabond and a ne'er-do-well."

"He is a cobbler," said Betsy defensively.

"Yes, and I am sure that he cobbles when he is not too drunk to do so. He was ordered to leave Providence several years ago after repeated appearances before the Council. I fear that your mother has made an unfortunate match, Betsy."

"He's still her husband—legal and proper—and my stepfather." She paused, and then she looked up at him with amused eyes. "I expect you will have to ask *his* permission if you want to marry me."

"I'll do no such thing!" Sam said in annoyance.

"Then I won't marry you, and that's that!"

"Betsy, you are acting like a child."

"If I am, it is because you treat me like a child, telling me what I can do and can't do!"

His irritation changed to anger as he said, "I want it understood that as long as you remain under this roof—"

"And who's to say I must remain under this roof?" she flung at him.

He waited, debating whether it was time to use force. At last, he said, in as casual a tone as he could, "You realize, Betsy, that both *Captain* Clarke and your mother could be taken into custody for their mere presence here in Providence?"

"They are not *in* Providence! They live out on the Old Warren Road."

"No matter. It would be an easy matter for me to report their whereabouts to the Town Council."

Betsy got up from her chair angrily. "But that's unfair! You wouldn't do that!"

"To protect you from evil, Betsy, I would do almost anything," he said quietly.

She turned and faced him, quivering with rage. "If you dast do that, I will go to the Town Council myself! And I'll tell them how *you* have been protecting me from evil—by taking my maidenhead and keeping me as your doxy—"

"They wouldn't believe you," he said, but his voice lacked conviction. Her threat had unsettled him, making him uneasy and fearful. He made the mistake of saying, "You—you did not tell your mother about—about us, did you?"

"No," she said. "But I will if you bring trouble to her!"

160

She had countered his threat with one of her own, and she glared at him challengingly. He looked away from her, momentarily beaten.

When he spoke again, a placating tone had come to his voice. "Very well," he said. "We will leave the Town Council out of our disagreement."

"Then I have your permission to see my mother?" she asked.

"No, you have not!" he said.

"Then I shall see her anyway, and be damned to you!"

"As my wife-to-be, I order you—"

"I am not going to be your wife!"

"But of course, you are. Surely you understand that we must rectify our sin in the eyes of the Lord—"

"It's your sin, not mine," she said. "If it troubles you so much, then stay out of my bed!"

The words stung him because they were true. She had bested him again, and he began to drum the table with his fingers in frustration. He knew that if she won now, he would surrender whatever control he had over her, to say nothing of her respect for him. He breathed deeply in a vain effort to calm the impotent fury that rose up in him.

"I will not have you talking to me like this!" he said angrily. "I will not be told what to do by a child of fifteen. This is my house, and I am master in it! As long as you stay here, you will do what I say!"

She moved suddenly to the door, and as he rose to follow her, she turned and faced him. "Then I will not stay here!" she spat at him.

"And I say that you will!"

"I'll go to my mother! And you can't stop me!"

She fled into the kitchen and out the door. He pursued her and caught up with her at the gate. When he seized her roughly by the shoulders, she turned on him and delivered a stunning blow to his cheek. This enraged him, and he grappled with her. She began to scream then, and he dropped his hands, afraid that she would rouse the neighbors and cause a scandal.

Finally, utterly defeated, he let her go, staring after her hopelessly until she had disappeared into the shadows of the dark street.

As he turned and walked dejectedly back to the house, he tried to convince himself that she would come back as soon as her anger had cooled, like a frightened and penitent child. But she was no longer a child. It was this simple fact that frightened him more than anything else.

CHAPTER 14

Betsy turned away from Benefit Street, with its quiet, respectables houses and neatly curtained windows, and went down Bank Lane toward Water Street and the port. She had only a vague notion of where the Old Warren Road might be and small hope that, in the dark, she could find the mud hut where her mother was living. But she was sure that Phebe, respectably married or not, would still frequent the taverns along the waterfront.

She had known Water Street well as a child. By day a busy, workaday thoroughfare given over to the business of loading and unloading ships, it became at night a cheerful place of taverns, which had always seemed friendly and inviting. But now, the street had become a new and strange world, darkly mysterious and somehow forbidding.

The ships were still there, lined up at the docks as far as her eye could reach, but this familiar sight did not reassure her. The ships looked abandoned and oddly forlorn, their masts rising in gaunt, crisscrossed patterns that moved eerily against the dark blue of the sky. Across from them, the taverns that had always seemed to her to blossom like night flowers after sunset now seemed to glow with a baleful light. The sounds that came from them—the brawling voices of sailors, the sea-gull cries of women, the bursts of raucous singing—filled her with apprehension.

She shivered at the thought of going into one of these places and exposing herself to the stares of strangers. She knew that though her years with Sam Allen may not have made her a lady, they had at least given her the appearance of one, and ladies did not go to taverns. Her dress was too clean and fresh, her hair too neatly combed for her to pass as a sailor's wench.

Coming to a halt in the middle of the dark street, she looked about her cautiously, like an animal that finds itself unexpectedly in dangerous territory. She had an impulse to run back to the sedate security of Benefit Street, but she knew that she could not turn back now. She had set out in search of her mother, and she could not leave without at least trying to find her. Taking a deep breath, she moved resolutely down the street.

She remembered that the Bulldog Tavern had been one of Phebe's favorite haunts, and she set out to find it. At last she saw the sign in the dim light that came from a tavern's second-story window; the faded black silhouette of a bulldog ready to attack, its eyes and open jaws painted blood-red. The sight was not reassuring, and she moved toward the tavern's door hesitantly. It was only with an effort of will that she could bring herself to open the door and cross the threshold.

She found herself in the middle of the taproom. It was neither as crowded nor as boisterous as she had expected. A quick survey of the room determined that her mother was not there. Two sailors and their girls sat at a table not far from the door. On the long, high-backed bench at the side of the fireplace, over which there were crossed sabers, a musket, and a powder horn, three men of the town were drinking flip. She recognized one of them as Bobby Brown, the town sergeant. In the far corner of the room a man of middle age with a curly black beard sat by himself, quietly drinking wine.

Ignoring the appraising stares of the men and the hostile, competitive glances of the women, she headed for the small bar in the corner, behind which stood Nate Mason, the proprietor. Though he was partially screened from view by the fencelike slats that lined the end of the bar, she recognized him and, with as much dignity as she could muster, presented herself to him.

"I am Miss Betsy Bowen," she said in a businesslike manner. Then, with a quick smile, she added, "Mayhap you remember me, Mr. Mason."

Nate Mason took his pipe from his mouth, cocked his head to the side, and regarded her studiously. At last he said, "Phebe Bowen's daughter, be you?"

Betsy nodded eagerly, and now Nate surveyed her in a more leisurely way, his eyes moving slowly and appreciatively the length of her trim figure.

"Quite a young lady you've become, lass. I hardly would ha' knowed you."

"I'm fifteen," said Betsy, and then added, "going on sixteen."

"My soul!" said Nate gently. He ran his hand through his thinning hair, as though suddenly reminded of the passing of time. "I don't know where the years go to. And what brings you here, lass?"

"I'm looking for my mother. Have you seen her tonight?"

Nate shook his head. "She don't stop by in the taverns like she used to—not since she married Captain Clarke." He did not add that there would be small point in her coming anyway, since she was no longer attractive enough to find someone to pay for her drinks. This would certainly not be true, he reflected, of the pretty young girl who stood in front of him. But she was a little too young, and Nate hoped she would leave before one of the men invited her to sit down with him. "This ain't a fit place for a young lady like you. Don't you live over to Sam Allen's?"

"I did," said Betsy. "But now that my mother is back in town, I'll be staying with her."

She was suddenly aware that Bobby Brown was standing by her side. Drawing himself up officiously, he said to Nate, "It ain't safe for this girl to be out alone on the streets at night. I'll see that she gets home."

Betsy turned toward him and said, "But I don't want to go home, and I'm not afraid to be on the streets alone."

She remembered the town sergeant, and she was afraid of him. On that night so long ago when the townspeople had burned down the old gaol, she remembered how he had struck Debbie on the jaw and sent her sprawling. She remembered, too, that she herself had kicked him in the shins and spat in his face. She had hated him then and she hated him now. His bleary light-blue eyes were fastened on her in a way that made her uneasy. Although his face was innocuous enough, formlessly flabby and mottled red in color, there was something about it that frightened her. It had the look of a bird of prey—the thin, aquiline nose and the voracious lips, red and swollen, that parted suddenly, when he smiled, to show sharp-pointed upper teeth and pale-pink gums.

He smiled now, as he said softly, "So you don't want to go home? Then where *will* you go, my lass?"

"I'll find my mother and stay with her."

Bobby Brown laughed. "Come now! It's too dark a night to go looking for your mama. You'd best come with me."

"No!" The word came out more forcefully than she had planned, and it rang sharply in the room. The bearded man in the corner looked up, and for the first time his eyes regarded Betsy with interest.

Bobby Brown drew himself up authoritatively, hands on his hips. "Do you know who I am, girl?"

"Yes. You're the town sergeant, and I don't need your help, so please to mind your business!"

The firm dismissal in her voice annoyed him. "That's what I'm doin'. 'Tis my duty to protect the citizenry, and like it or no, you will come with me or I'll take you into custody!"

Betsy turned to Nate. "Please, Mr. Mason—I don't want to go with him. Ask him to leave me be."

Nate pulled at the lobe of his ear in embarrassment. "You'd best go with him, Miss Betsy. He's the law. You can look for your mother tomorrow in the daylight. Meanwhile, if I should see her, I'll tell her you was lookin' for her."

Bobby Brown had seized Betsy by the arm now. He began to propel her toward the door.

"Leave go of me!" she cried, shaking herself free of him. "I'll go, but just don't you touch me, that's all!"

She gave him a look of contempt and walked with dignity toward the door. He shrugged his shoulders with forced amiability and followed her. As they disappeared into the darkness outside, the bearded man's eyes stayed fixed on the doorway for a few moments, his face set in a speculative, frowning expression. He had not liked the way the sergeant had looked at the young girl.

He knew that as a stranger in this port it was none of his business. And as a Frenchman and a sailor, he viewed rape and lost maidenheads as such common events that they were hardly worth worrying about. What bothered him was that the girl was so lovely and the man so repulsive. Cursing himself for a fool, he finished his wine in one gulp and went over to Nate to pay for it.

As Nate put the change down on the bar, he looked up and said in a low voice, "Be careful, M'seer Captain. He is the law."

The Captain gave a quick smile. "*Merci, monsieur*. I will be careful."

As he went out the door, the smile was still on his face. But he was smiling now at himself. The picture of Capitaine Jacques de la Croix as a defender of female honor amused him. He told himself that he had drunk far too much Madeira, and it would indeed be wise for him to be careful.

And so, he followed them, not too closely, but near enough so that his presence might be known and perhaps discourage the sergeant from taking advantage of the girl. He saw that Betsy had separated herself from the sergeant and walked two paces ahead of him in a disdainful way, as though ignoring his presence. The sergeant seemed content, for the moment at least, to trot along behind her, his rump stuck out officiously.

Betsy stopped suddenly and turned to face him. "It is no use for you to take me to Sam Allen's house because I'm not going to stay there!"

He pursed his lips, and then, in what he believed to be a seductive whisper, he said, "Mayhap you would prefer to stay at my house on Olney Lane?"

"At your house?" she asked, feigning innocence. "What for?"

"'Tis late," he said, "and you must sleep somewhere." He paused, and then added casually, "Unless you prefer to sleep in the gaol."

The threat frightened her, and she said, "Please help me find my mother. She lives on the Old Warren Road."

He ignored the plea in her voice. "My bed is very comfortable, lass." He put out a hand and stroked her shoulder. "I will take good care of you."

"Keep your hands off me, Bobby Brown!" she said.

Impatiently, he seized her and pulled her to him, planting a hot, slobbery kiss on her mouth. She beat her fists against him and tried to get away, but he held her hard against him.

"Listen to me, you little bitch! If you won't come to my bed, I'll take you right here on the street!"

He dragged her, protesting and screaming, toward the darkness of an alley. He clamped a hand over her mouth to stifle her screams and then, giving her a clout on the head that knocked her off balance, he wrestled her to the ground and got astride her. When she tried to wriggle free of him, he struck her again, a hard blow on the mouth. She was no match for him and she lay helpless as he ripped open his trousers and pulled them down. As she began struggling again, he tore frantically at her skirt, so preoccupied that he did not hear the footsteps that were coming down the alley.

The Captain's voice, mildly curious in tone, caught him by surprise. "What are you doing, *monsieur le sergent?*"

Bobby looked at the intruder furiously. "Get the hell out of here and mind your own business!" he snarled.

"It is not good what you do," said the Captain.

Bobby was on his feet, one hand pulling his trousers over his nakedness while the other searched frantically for his pistol. But the Captain did not wait for him to find it. He delivered a powerful blow to Bobby's jaw, and Bobby fell down in ignominious disarray, his bare bottom coming to sudden and unexpected rest on the hard ground. Betsy lost no time in getting to her feet and taking refuge behind her rescuer.

Bobby shook his head as he recovered from the blow and then slowly raised himself to a sitting position. "You are under arrest, Captain!" he bellowed.

"*Très bien*. You will take me to the gaol, *en ce cas*, and I will tell what is happen here."

"And I'll tell 'em, too!" said Betsy.

Bobby said nothing. He had no intention of facing a rape charge, especially when there was a witness. With as much dignity as he could manage, he stood up, trying to button his pants without seeming to do so and then brushing himself off carefully. Finally, he raised his head and glared at Betsy, anger replacing the lust that had been in his eyes.

"As for you, slut, you've made your choice. You won't let me take you home, so you can spend the night in gaol!"

"No," said the Captain. "I will take her to her house."

Bobby laughed. "So you can finish what I started? Like hell you will!"

The Captain bowed. "Then we will *both* take her to her house."

Betsy looked at the two men and laughed. "But I'm not going to my house, and I can look for my mother without help from either of you!"

Suddenly, she turned and ran, disappearing quickly into the darkness of the street. Bobby moved to follow her, but the Captain's hand gripped his shoulder.

"You go back to the tavern and have a drink, yes?" He smiled. "The virgins—they are much trouble, *monsieur le sergent*."

As Bobby shrugged, the Captain extended his hand and said, "I am sorry to hit you. We are friends, no?"

Bobby shook the offered hand begrudgingly and then set off in the direction of the Bulldog Tavern. The Captain looked after him for a moment, a pleased smile on his face. He began to whistle as he started down the street to the dock where *L'Étoile de Marseilles* was tied up.

As he neared the ship he heard footsteps behind him. It occurred to him that the town sergeant had changed his mind, but the footsteps were too light to belong to Bobby Brown. He slowed his pace, finally coming to a halt. In a moment or so, Betsy stood before him.

"I was waiting for you," she said. "I wanted to thank you."

"Is nothing," he said. "You must go to your house before another bad thing arrives to you."

Betsy was silent, staring into the darkness in an effort to see his face more clearly. The sound of his voice, with its foreign flavor, had seemed to her kindly and pleasant. She had waited for him not to thank him for rescuing her so much as because she was frightened and did not want to be alone.

Her tussle with Bobby had demonstrated only too clearly that Sam was not the only man who desired her, and she realized that on a dark and deserted street she might be forced to play the game with whatever partner presented himself. And with no reward, promised or given. And yet, as frightened as she was, she had no intention of returning to Sam and admitting defeat.

"I cannot go back to my house, sir," she said at last.

"Why not?" asked Jacques.

"Because—because my master will beat me."

"You are *servante*?" Jacques asked.

"Yes, I am a servant," she lied. "My master is very cruel." She pointed to the spot on her chin where Bobby's blow had landed.

"Ah, *ma pauvre petite*," said Jacques.

She looked at him sorrowfully. "I ran away, and if I go back, then he will beat me again."

"But where will you go, *ma chère?*"

"Tomorrow I will find my mother, and I will stay with her."

"But tonight—is no good to sleep in the street."

She lowered her eyes and murmured, as though in embarrassment, "I—I thought maybe you could give me a place to sleep, sir."

"But I have no house. I sleep on my ship."

"I wouldn't mind sleeping on a ship," she said.

Jacques laughed. The thought of smuggling a young girl aboard his ship for the innocent reason of giving her a place to sleep struck him as being as absurd as the chivalrous role he had already played as a defender of her womanly virtue. It would be equally ridiculous, he thought, if he were now to take the maidenhead he had been at such pains to preserve.

And so, he said, "But there is no place, *mon enfant*. I have only one bed in my cabin."

"Then I will sleep on the floor. Please to take me with you!"

He could not resist the pleading look in her eyes, which, he had already noted, were very beautiful. He shrugged his shoulders and said, "*Très bien*. Come!"

They moved onto the dock, and when they reached the gangplank of the *L'Étoile de Marseilles*, he picked her up in his arms to carry her, ignoring the astonished look on the face of the sailor on watch. He smiled again to himself, this time philosophically, thinking how odd it was that the most innocent of actions could appear evil.

By the time he had arrived at his cabin door and had set Betsy on her feet once again, he was already reconciled to the fact that his chivalry was evidently as boundless as it was inexplicable. He knew that he would end by giving her his bed and sleeping on the floor himself.

To Betsy, the Captain's cabin was a place of enchantment. She had always loved ships, but until now she had never been permitted to penetrate the mysteries of their interiors. Sam had always refused to take her aboard the *Lydia A.* because he felt that this was a rough and uncouth man's world that should be forbidden to ladies, unless they happened to be passengers on a packet ship, where they would not come in close contact with the crew and their coarse language.

And so she looked about the small room in delighted wonder. With its dark-paneled walls, only faintly illumined by the rays of the lantern Jacques had lighted, it was a place of secret shadows that gave her, nevertheless, a feeling of being protected from dangers of the world outside. She gazed in fascination at a porthole that gleamed like a great benign eye from the darkness of one wall. It gave forth a bluish light that fell across the Captain's desk, which was large and handsome, made of West Indian mahogany and fitted with shining brass knobs.

Against the opposite wall was the Captain's bunk, and the sight of it, so neatly made and covered with a thin red quilt, made her realize how very tired she was. She went over to the bunk and, without waiting for an invitation, sat down on the edge of it with a sigh of relief.

Jacques looked at her thoughtfully, a half smile on his lips. "You are *fatigué*."

"*Fatigué?*"

"Tired."

"Yes." She paused. "I am hungry, too. Do you have anything to eat?"

Her boldness amused him, and he laughed a quick, explosive laugh that made her jump. "I have here not much food. You like the salt cod—and some bread and cheese?" She nodded enthusiastically, and he added, "And wine? You drink wine?"

"Oh, yes," she said. "All the time!"

He did not believe her, because the people of this new world did not take wine with their meals the way Frenchmen did. But he shrugged his shoulders and set out for the galley to get her some food.

As soon as he had gone, Betsy stretched out full length on the bunk and closed her eyes. She had not sat down since she had left home, and her feet felt tired and hot. She kicked off her shoes, and then, because the cabin was warm, she loosened her dress around her shoulders.

There was a light breeze coming through the open porthole, and though it was not cool, it felt fresh and soothing against her face.

It was almost like being caressed, and that made her think of the Captain. She supposed he would want to play the game with her, and though she was so tired that she did not look forward to it, she was curious about him. Except for the fact that he was a man, he was not in the least like Sam. Instead of being tall and thin, he was rather short and stocky. And yet he was not fat. When he had lifted her in his arms to carry her up the gangplank, she had felt the strength in his arms and shoulders, the solid hardness of his chest.

She liked his face, in spite of the black frizzly beard that covered most of it. Most especially she liked his eyes, which were friendly, like his smile. She was not in the least afraid of him, and yet, along with her curiosity, she had a vague uneasiness about playing the game with him. She did not expect that he would give her a reward. He was, after all, giving her his bed, and at the moment, that was something she wanted more than anything she could think of—except food.

When the Captain reappeared, she sat up eagerly on the bunk. He was carrying a tray that he set down on his desk and then motioned her with his head to sit down in the chair before it.

"Eat, *mon enfant*. Is not much, and I make apologies."

There was the promised salt cod, a kind of cheese that she did not like the smell of, and several slices of crusty bread. Best of all, there was wine, and she was very thirsty. Jacques did not need to apologize for the wine. It was his best Madeira. She drained the glass almost at one gulp, and he poured more for her.

"Not too much wine, *chérie*," he cautioned, "or it will make you turn in the head."

She nodded and then began stuffing cod and bread into her mouth as though she had not eaten in a week. He watched her with a slightly astonished air of concern.

"*Doucement, doucement!*" he said. "More slow, or you will make the *estomac* sick." He patted his belly and shook his head warningly. She paused only long enough to grin at him and went back to devouring the food.

When she had finished the cod and most of the bread, he pointed to the cheese and said, "You do not like this?"

She pinched her nose with her thumb and forefinger and said,

"It smells bad." Smiling, he moved it away from her. Suddenly, she looked at him and said, "What's your name?"

"Jacques. Jacques de la Croix. I am captain of the ship."

She finished the second glass of Madeira and held the glass out to him to be refilled.

"No," he said. "Is enough. You must not be drunk."

She shrugged and regarded him, cocking her head to the side. "Dellycraw—Captain Dellycraw. Is that French?" When he nodded, she said, "I would like to speak French. There are a lot of Frenchies in Providence."

"Yes. Many Frenchmen begin now to part from Santo Domingo in the West Indies."

"Why?"

"Is trouble—the black men do not wish anymore to be slaves."

She thought of Black Bets and, after a moment of reflection, she said, "The blacks are not slaves here. They are free. But people are not good to them. Why is that?"

"I do not know."

She yawned, stretched, and then, getting up from the desk, she went to the porthole and looked out. The water of the harbor gleamed with the pale light from a new moon that had risen. As she gazed at the gently moving water, she had the feeling that the ship was at sea and had left Providence and Sam far behind. This thought, along with the effects of the wine, gave her a sense of exhilaration and freedom. On her bare feet, she almost danced back into the middle of the cabin, where she stood in front of the Captain.

"I love your ship, Captain Jack! What is her name?"

"*L'Étoile de Marseilles,* which is meaning 'The Star of Marseilles.' "

She slowly repeated the name after him, imitating his accent with surprising fidelity. "There. I have already learned two words—*étoile* means 'star,' and *de* means 'of.' I am quite smart." She paused and then added, "I can read and write too—but only English."

He smiled at her like a pleased parent. He was reminded of his two daughters back in Marseilles, and he congratulated himself again on having saved her from the town sergeant. And yet it was

173

not difficult for him to understand Bobby Brown's desire to possess her. The girl was not merely pretty, she was beautiful, and young though she was, her figure was almost that of a woman. Yes, she was very desirable, and although she might remind him of his daughters, she was certainly *not* his daughter, and—

He stopped the thought before it could go any further and said hastily, "Is good that you read and write, *mon enfant*. And now, the time is here for you to sleep." He pointed to the bunk. "Go to the bed now. I will sleep out there." He waved his hand toward the door.

"No," said Betsy. "I said I'd sleep on the floor, and I will."

Captain Jacques de la Croix drew himself up to his full height. "I am gentleman," he said, "and gentleman must have politeness for the ladies." He bowed abruptly, and not very gracefully, from the waist.

"No," repeated Betsy, more firmly. "I don't want to be alone. All by myself here I would be afraid."

It was at least partially true. Though she was not really afraid, the thought of spending the night alone in a strange room, and aboard a ship at that, did made her vaguely apprehensive.

"But there is not reason for fear, *chérie*. Nobody will come here."

"Please—*please* stay, Captain de la Croix."

She moved to him quickly and put her arms around his neck. His body became tense, and he raised his arms to push her away. Her nearness and the touch of her hands on the back of his neck unsettled him. He tried to move away, but she clung to him.

"I will sleep in the bed," she said softly, "if you will sleep there too. Then nobody will have to be on the floor."

He was about to protest, but her lips were suddenly on his, and as he moved to free himself once again, she turned herself slightly so that her hip pressed itself hard against his groin. He tried to make himself believe that it was an accident, but the thrust was continuous and insistent. He cursed himself for a naïve, romantic fool, and with momentary anger mixing with his rising lust, he seized her roughly in his arms and pulled her to him. Covering her face and bare shoulders with kisses, he held her so close in his powerful arms that she could scarcely breathe.

His violence frightened her. In a panic she struggled to free herself, beating her fists against his chest. Then, unexpectedly, he let her go, and she ran toward the bed. The sight of her shrinking back against the pillows at the head of the bunk made him lose control again, and he threw himself against her, his mouth seeking hers.

"Please—please!" she whimpered. "You're hurting me."

He became all gentleness, and momentarily his body seemed to relax, but he stayed close to her, sliding his right arm under her shoulders, so that he held her loosely in his embrace. His eyes looked into hers, and the tenderness in them reassured her.

"I am sorry," he said softly. "I am *bête*. I do not desire to hurt you."

His hand began stroking her forehead, pushing her hair back and smoothing it caressingly. She sighed in relief and smiled up at him. Now he kissed her more gently, his lips lingering on hers. His hands had begun to move over her body. He pulled the dress down from her shoulders until her young breasts were exposed, and his mouth fastened on one of her nipples. Then passion rose in him again, and though he tried to be gentle, his hands began to pull at her clothing.

She let him have his way, lying back limply, waiting for the moment when the game would begin. When at last he had her naked in his arms, he tore open his breeches. Quickly, she moved her hand down to help him enter her, and then she pulled back her hand in terror.

"'Tis too big!" she gasped. "I cannot! Please!" She wriggled herself away from him.

"*Doucement, doucement!*" he murmured. Again there was a tenderness in his voice that reassured her. His hand sought her and began caressing her softly between her thighs. Gradually, her body lost its tenseness, until at last she felt herself becoming limp and compliant beneath him. Slowly, he began pushing himself into her. She held her breath in suspense, waiting for pain. But there was no pain, and finally in a warm wave of surrender, she gave herself up to him completely. He had begun to move upon her now with a leisurely deliberateness. She threw her legs up, locking them over his buttocks, and waited for the quick climax that Sam

175

always experienced when she did this. But moments passed and he continued to ride upon her, slowly and inexorably, with smooth, unhurried thrusts. She was impatient because she wanted it all to be finished and over so that she could go to sleep. When it became clear to her that this man was different from Sam not only in body, but in the way he played the game, she resigned herself to being patient. Unexpectedly, she found herself feeling a vague pleasure that was new to her, like a slow drifting away on a sleepy sea of well-being. She had, in fact, almost gone to sleep when she was jolted into consciousness by the Captain's arms tightening around her body. He was breathing hard, and his thrusts had accelerated to a wild and frenzied tempo.

He cried out then, and his voice was like the roar of a bull raging in its pen for freedom. Involuntary shudders shook his heavy body again and again in rhythmic spasms, and he fought for breath. Incoherent words of endearment tore at his throat. Then the paroxysms that had shaken him came farther and farther apart, and his breathing became more regular. At last he was quiet.

Betsy was glad that the game was over. She felt crushed and uncomfortable under the dead weight of the Captain's body and hoped he would go away soon.

When finally he withdrew from her, he looked at her face with gentle eyes. "*Comme tu es belle!*" he said softly and kissed her hair. She squirmed herself away from under him and then curled herself against his side like a weary kitten.

She turned her face to him questioningly. "What did that mean? What you just said to me in French."

He had to think a moment to remember. "I said you are very beautiful."

"*Belle* means 'beautiful'?"

"*Oui*—if it is a girl."

"But a boy can be beautiful, too."

"A boy—he is *beau.*"

She nodded gravely. "I'll remember that. And how do you say 'you are'?"

"*Tu es.*"

She repeated it after him and was silent a moment, finally looking up at him with solemn eyes. "*Tu es beau,*" she said.

This delighted him, and he hugged her to him. "You are very

young. I should have shame, but I do not. How many years have you?"

"Eighteen," she lied.

"*Méchante!* You must tell Jacques the truth. How many years?"

"Fifteen," she mumbled. "But I am a woman!"

"Yes. Is true. You are woman."

She felt sleepy and closed her eyes. She had almost dozed off when she felt his hands moving over her, his lips kissing her breasts, and then his hardness pressing against her thigh. She could not believe that he wanted to play the game again. Sam always waited a whole week, sometimes two. She tried to move away from him, but she could not escape. He was already over her, and so she sighed resignedly and let him have his way. Again she had the pleasurable feeling of floating away. She fell half-asleep and was only dimly aware of his movements. When his passion broke and he cried out again in ecstasy, she scarcely heard him.

When Jacques awoke, he looked curiously at the young girl who still slept at his side. The sight of her innocent and lovely face, flushed with sleep, gave him a feeling of remorse that was strange to him. With an automatic movement of his hand, he blessed himself as though to ask God's forgiveness for a sinful act.

Then he laughed and called himself an idiot. No matter how young and pure this girl might appear, she had certainly been no virgin. And yet, looking at her there beside him, he did not feel the cynical satiety that usually came to him after a night of love-making—the urge to get on with life, to leave the suddenly dis-tasteful warmth of bed for the clean, cold pleasures of work. There was something about the girl that made him feel sad. Wincing at the thought that so lovely a creature had been abused or beaten, he found himself impulsively reaching out his hand to stroke the reddened bruise on her cheek.

He withdrew his hand quickly as she stirred in her sleep, telling himself that he must stop acting like a sentimental fool and get the girl out of his cabin and on her way. He did not want to risk getting himself involved with the ridiculous laws of these Ameri-cans, for whom sin seemed to exist only when it was found out. They were all of them hypocrites, like the town sergeant of the night before.

177

And so he decided to get the girl off the ship as soon as possible. But first he would give her some breakfast. He got out of bed quietly, put on his clothes, and went to the galley.

A few moments later Betsy was awakened by a shaft of sunlight that streamed through the porthole and came to rest on her face. She opened her eyes and sat up, looking around her in confusion. In daylight, the cabin was even more pleasing to her than it had been the night before. She sank back contentedly into the warmth of the bedclothes. The gentle swaying of the ship at anchor made her drowse, and she was not aware of Jacques' return until she felt his hand stroking her neck. She opened her eyes and smiled up at him.

"I have for you some *petit déjeuner*," he said.

"What's that?"

"It is what you call the breakfast." He pointed to the desk where he had set down the tray. "It is there," he said.

She sprang out of bed, and the sudden sight of her nude young body made him blink. She seemed not only unashamed of her nakedness but even unaware of it. An unaccustomed sense of propriety made him throw one of his jackets over her shoulders. She grinned at him, her mouth stuffed full of bread and butter.

"I'm not cold, Jacques. It's nice and warm in here." Shrugging off the jacket, she launched a new attack on the plate of thick-sliced bread and butter and stared curiously at a steaming mug of hot chocolate. Finally, she picked it up and gulped down some of it, burning her tongue. "Oh, I like that!" she said. "It tastes like sweetmeats at Thanksgiving."

"It is *chocolat*," said Jacques.

"Don't Frenchmen ever drink tea for breakfast?"

He shrugged. "Sometimes tea, sometimes *chocolat*, and coffee, too."

"When I am a lady and very rich," she said, "I will always drink *chocolat* for breakfast."

She became silent then, entirely preoccupied with the food, and as he watched her with speculative eyes, he found himself admiring the loveliness of her breasts, the soft maturing lines of her body. But oddly, desire did not stir in him. Instead, he found himself thinking that there was a unique and strangely tremulous beauty in the body of a girl poised on the brink of womanhood. It made him think of the almost mysterious, still hidden loveliness of a rose that has not yet burst into radiant bloom.

As Betsy finished eating, she became aware of the Captain's eyes fixed on her. Inexplicably, she blushed. It was as though Sam had suddenly walked into the room. She made a move to cover her breasts with her hands.

"Oh, I am sinful!" she said.

"No," said Jacques. "*Tu es belle*, and it is not good to have shame for it."

She turned toward him and smiled. "*Tu es beau*," she said. "Did I say it right?"

He laughed. "*Parfaitement*."

"Perfectly?"

"*Oui*."

She got up from the desk suddenly. "I must get dressed now. I have to look for my mother."

He nodded. "And your mother—where is she?"

"She lives in a mud hut on the Old Warren Road. I am going to stay with her if she will have me."

While she dressed, she told him how she had gone to live with Sam five years ago, when the old gaol had been burned down and her mother had been sent away from Providence.

"And now, she is back," she concluded, "but Mr. Allen will not let me see her. That's why I ran away last night."

When she had finished dressing, she stood before him and stretched out her hand to say goodbye. It occurred to her that she might ask him for a gift, but she decided not to. He had, after all, given her a place to sleep and something to eat, and perhaps that was enough.

As he took her hand, she said, "Will you show me how to get off the ship, Captain Jacques?" inclining her head slightly and smiling at him.

Something about the way she stood there waiting, almost as though she were on tiptoe, kindled desire in him, and he seized her roughly in his arms and kissed her. Startled, she tried to free herself, but he held her tightly against him. As he pressed his legs against her, she could feel the growing hardness in his breeches.

She broke away from him, laughing. "Oh, not again, Jacques. I must go. Not now, please."

179

"When then? When?"

"Oh, I don't know—"

"Tonight? You will see me tonight, *ma chérie?*"

"Yes. If you like—"

"I will wait for you on the dock by the ship at six o'clock." He paused, remembering his resolve to be free of her and avoid entanglement with the law. Then he told himself that as long as he did not appear in public with her, he had nothing to fear.

"We will have dinner in my cabin," he said.

"With wine—and *chocolat?*"

"*Oui.*" He laughed delightedly and took both her hands in his. "We will have—everything!"

She became silent and looked at him pensively. Although he had given her a place to sleep and supper and breakfast, he had not truly given her a reward for having played the game with him, a reward that she could touch and keep.

"My mother likes to drink wine very much," she said.

He looked at her questioningly and said, "That is good."

She turned her eyes away from him, simulating shyness. "It would be—*beau*—if I could bring her a present. Do you have an extra bottle of wine?"

He looked at her curiously, surprised by her unexpected request. "*Oui.* I have some wine," he replied, moving to a cupboard that stood in a corner of the cabin. When he opened its door with a key, she saw that inside there were shelves lined with bottles of many shapes and sizes.

"Your *maman* likes the *vin rouge*—the red?"

"How do you say please in French?" she asked.

"It is *s'il vous plaît.*"

"Then, *s'il vous plaît,* I would not like the red, but the Madeira, like we had last night. It was very good."

He smiled to himself, thinking that the child had expensive tastes. But he shrugged and took a bottle of Madeira from a shelf. After relocking the cupboard, he went over to her and handed her the bottle.

With a timid gesture that she considered appropriate, she reached out her hand hesitantly to take it. "How do I say 'thank you'?"

"*Merci bien.*"

She repeated the words after him softly, and then, with the bottle tucked more firmly than necessary under her arm, she turned to go. As he led the way through the door, she followed, smiling happily to herself. It made her feel better to know that the rules of the game had been properly observed.

When they arrived on deck, he took her hand and they moved toward the gangplank. Two sailors on watch regarded them with astonished eyes. They nodded at Jacques in greeting, but their gaze rested admiringly on the small figure of Betsy.

She was aware of her effect on them and smiled at them demurely. Then, on impulse, she picked up her skirts and dropped an elaborate curtsy in their direction. Somehow it seemed the lady-like thing to do.

CHAPTER 15

THE day was hot and sunny, and by the time Betsy reached the spot where the Old Warren Road led out of town, she was already weary. Nate Mason at the Bulldog Tavern had given her directions, and the road had been easy enough to find, but the distance was already greater than she had imagined, and she still did not know how far out on the road the Clarkes' mud hut might be.

She had walked perhaps a mile when she saw it, standing on the edge of an open field, close to a patch of uncleared woodland. It seemed very small to her, with a forlorn look, like something that had been built in a hurry and then abandoned. But a rope strung between two trees and crowded with freshly laundered clothing told her that the place was inhabited.

The hut itself had a familiar appearance. She remembered living in a number of such hovels during the early years of her childhood—with their smoky interiors, their square-cut small holes that passed for windows. In the winter the holes were kept closed by heavy pieces of oiled paper tacked to the walls inside, and inside it became even smokier. But on a summer's day such as this one, the holes were left open and looked, she thought now, like empty eye sockets.

She rapped on the half-open door with her knuckles. There was a groan from inside, then a shuffling of feet, and finally Phebe stood before her, swaying slightly and looking at her blearily from red-rimmed eyes that showed no signs of recognition.

"Mama, it's me!"

Phebe's eyes came to life and, dramatically, she took a step backward. "Ah, 'tis me daughter Betsy, come to see her mother!"

Then hurling herself forward, she clasped Betsy to her breast.

Tears rolled from her eyes, and her voice murmured endearments. Betsy, almost smothered in the embrace, began crying too. When the turbulence of Phebe's greeting had subsided, Betsy said quietly, "I've come to stay with you, Mama."

Phebe looked at her in surprise. "To stay? But your home is with Mr. Allen—"

"Not anymore," said Betsy. "I've run away from him for good and all, and I'll not go back, even if he was to marry me, like he promised."

"Marry you?" Phebe's eyes widened. "Mr. Allen wants to marry you?"

"Yes. But if I do, he said I could never see you again. And so I ran away." Betsy paused. "I *can* live with you, can't I?"

"Well, yes," Phebe said with a frown. "But child, think what you're doin'. A gentleman like Mr. Allen ready to take you to wife—I wouldn't be standin' in the way of that. I ain't worth you givin' up a chance to be a real lady—"

"I'll be a lady anyway!" said Betsy. "And it's for me to say whether I'll marry him—not you, Mama!"

Phebe decided not to argue the point. She took Betsy by the hand and led her through the door into the hut. A man lay sprawled in a dilapidated armchair near the fireplace. He was asleep, and his snores filled the room with a rhythmic rumbling. Phebe nodded in his direction.

"That be Captain Jonathan Clarke," she said. "Your stepfather."

Betsy studied the sleeping figure. She saw a man in his middle forties, large-boned and heavy-set. He had a grizzled beard in need of trimming, and his cheeks, which puffed out every time he exhaled, were red and weather-beaten. It would have been a nondescript face if it had not been for the well-formed brow that jutted out from a high forehead. His eyes now unexpectedly opened. They were bright blue, penetrating—and bloodshot.

Captain Clarke slowly and painfully raised himself on an elbow and stared at Betsy. "And who may this person be?" he growled.

Phebe tried to make her voice casual. "Why, Jonathan, 'tis me daughter Betsy, and she's come to stay with us."

Jonathan snorted. "That she's not!"

"But the child has nowheres else to go and—"

"Let her go back to the street where she came from."

Phebe prepared herself for battle. "She'll do no such a thing, Jonathan Clarke! She's a ladylike child and no common whore of the port. She's here and here she stays!"

Jonathan chose to ignore this announcement. He bent over and dolefully studied the toes that protruded through the holes in his stockings.

"And why do you never mend my footwear, woman? Can it be that you consider such wifely chores beneath you?"

Phebe's voice became conciliatory. "Oh, no, me love. This afternoon, this very afternoon, I'll be—"

Betsy stepped forward briskly. "I am very good at mending, Captain Clarke. It would be a pleasure for me to mend the stockings of my new stepfather."

"I'm not your new stepfather, and don't be trying the thin edge of the wedge on me to get into my good graces. There's no room in this house for another mouth to feed, and that's an end on it!"

"It's not an end on it," said Phebe quietly. "She stays!"

Jonathan rose to his feet unsteadily and advanced on Phebe in a menacing way. "So I'm not to be the master in my own kingdom, is that it?" he bellowed. "I'm to be treated like a lickspittle knave in the home I've built with my own two hands? Stand back, woman! And take your bastard offspring away or I'll thrash the two of you!"

Jonathan, for all his years of drinking and idleness, was still a powerful man. Seizing Phebe roughly by the shoulder, he spun her around toward the door. Then he glowered at Betsy and began moving toward her.

Betsy stood her ground. She looked Jonathan squarely in the eye, and when he was within a foot of her, she said gently, "I'll not be a sponge upon you, Stepfather. I have money enough to keep myself. I have a—a benefactor."

"Benefactor, indeed! That's a pretty word—" He stopped, suddenly curious. "And where did you learn a long word like that?"

"I must have read it somewheres."

Jonathan looked at her in astonishment. "You know how to *read?*"

"My uncle taught me," said Betsy. Suddenly she remembered

the bottle of wine that she still carried under her arm and added, "I have brought a present for you, sir. Here."

Jonathan took the bottle. He studied the label and looked up incredulously. "And where, may I ask, did you get so excellent a bottle of Madeira?"

"From my benefactor. Taste it, Father. *C'est beau!*" She tossed off the French words airily, and Jonathan looked at her in surprise.

"You speak French, too?" he asked in an awed tone.

"Oh, yes, very well," she lied, adding, "My benefactor is a French sea captain. He is very rich."

"I see," said Jonathan, swaying and clapping his hand to his forehead in sudden pain. He retreated to his chair and sat down heavily. "I am sick and queasy. I have partaken too much of the grape."

Phebe turned to Betsy. "The Captain is a learned man and often speaks in odd fashion. He means that he was drunk last night."

"Aye." Jonathan nodded. "Say it how you may, it is God's truth."

"Then why not have a nip from the beast what bit you?" asked Phebe, seizing the bottle from his hand and looking at it lovingly. "I could use a swig of it meself. Why, 'tis time for a toast to all three of us—and to our happy days together from now on!"

Jonathan looked up. "I haven't said she could stay," he grumbled.

Betsy walked over to Phebe and calmly took the bottle from her. "Mama, the wine is Father's, not ours. It is for him to make a toast, if he wishes."

Jonathan nodded. "The lass has manners, at least, though where she came by them I know not—certainly not from a trull like her mother."

Before Phebe could defend herself, Betsy addressed herself to Jonathan in her most ladylike manner and said solemnly, "Father, I ask thee permission to stay for only a few days. If it be too close quarters for all of us, I will seek other accommodations."

Jonathan straightened himself and with an effort strove to match her elegance of manner. "Your speech, lass," he said pompously, "falls trippingly from the tongue—that's from *Hamlet*—and so let us have a toast at once!" He turned commandingly to Phebe. "Take the bottle, woman, and withdraw the cork without further ado!"

The long speech seemed to have exhausted the Captain because he fell back in his chair, closed his eyes, and breathed heavily.

Betsy went quickly over to him and asked, "Is there anything I can do for you, sir?"

"Yes," he whispered. "Leave me be."

While Phebe struggled to get the cork out of the bottle with a bone knitting needle, Betsy surveyed the hut appraisingly. One end of it had been curtained off with burlap sacking, and she supposed this might serve as a bedroom. Not far from the fireplace, where Jonathan lay sprawled in his chair, there was a straw-filled mattress. Betsy smiled to herself, thinking that at least there would be a bed for her here. Above the mattress, a wide shelf had been attached precariously to the mud wall. Supported by wooden pegs, it held up a long row of battered books of every imaginable size and thickness.

At the crudely constructed table of unfinished yellow pine in the center of the room Phebe still labored over the wine bottle. Betsy went over to her and said, "Can I help, Mama?"

"I'm gittin' the blasted thing," said Phebe breathlessly. "I'm a-gonna push the bugger right down into the bottle!"

Betsy sat down in one of the three chairs drawn up to the table, which was evidently used for dining, and waited. Suddenly Phebe gave a cry of triumph and waved the bottle joyously in the air. Then she poured generous amounts of the wine into three goblets that apparently were as permanent fixtures on the table as the salt dish.

"Jonathan! Jonathan! Come and git it!" screamed Phebe.

Jonathan rose and shook himself. Lurching toward the table, he picked up one of the goblets in a trembling hand.

"Wait, Jonathan!" said Phebe, raising her goblet in the air. "Wait for the toast!" As Betsy and Jonathan raised their glasses, Phebe said, "To the health of all three of us—and to the happy life we'll be living *together in this house!*"

Jonathan drank the wine steadily until he had finished it, but the emphasis that Phebe had placed on the last words of her toast was not lost on him.

" 'Twas only a toast," he said. "A life together it will not be. But for a few nights, yes, I'll consent to it." He extended his goblet and added, "And now, wife, a bit more of my Madeira."

"*S'il vous plaît,*" said Betsy softly, with a wink at Jonathan.

"*Oui, mademoiselle,*" said Jonathan. And for the first time he smiled at her.

Betsy found Jacques waiting for her when she arrived at the dock where *L'Étoile de Marseilles* had tied up. It was well after six o'clock, and he seemed overjoyed that she had at last appeared.

As he took her hands in his, he said, "It is so late. I thought you are not coming."

"Oh, I am sorry. But there is no clock where my mother lives and I didn't know what time it was."

"*De rien,* you are now here," he said, putting his arm around her and leading her toward the ship. "And my cook has made for you *un dîner magnifique!*"

The dinner was indeed magnificent. Édouard, the ship's cook, had been turned loose in the galley with instructions to prepare a small feast, and he had outdone himself—a clear soup fragrant with herbs, haddock in a rich cream sauce, a roast *gigot* of lamb studded with garlic cloves, then a *mousse au chocolat,* followed by wedges of Brie.

For Betsy, who had tasted only dinners prepared by the unimaginative hands of Nellie, the dishes seemed deliciously exotic and, as course succeeded course, endlessly surprising. After ravenously consuming the fish, she had settled back in the belief that the meal was over, and then the roast arrived.

She was equally dazzled by the succession of wines that Édouard served her: a cool golden Chablis, then a rosé followed by champagne, and finally a glass of the Madeira that she liked so much. It especially impressed her that each wine was served in a fresh glass. She fell instantly in love with champagne, was not so sure about the Brie, but ate it anyway.

When she had finished, she became so sleepy that her eyes kept closing and her head nodded. Although Jacques had carefully limited the amount of wine she drank, the alcohol and the heavy meal finally proved to be too much for her, and she fell sound asleep while still sitting at the table.

Jacques picked her up in his arms and set her down gently on his bunk. Then, while Édouard cleared away the dishes, he sat down at his desk near the open porthole, lighted his pipe, and made an attempt to busy himself with the bills of lading that were stacked in a pile on his desk.

But his eyes kept returning to the sleeping figure on his bunk. At last he abandoned his books and gave himself up to his thoughts. He had always been an uncomplicated man, not much given to rumination—especially when it came to women. He had met his wife at eighteen and married her a year later. She bore him two daughters and a son in rapid succession, and then, inexplicably, conceived no more. He loved his wife, and during those periods when he was at home, he was faithful to her. The rest of the time, which was also most of the time, he was not. He took women where and as he found them, using them as his needs demanded, seeing the same one more than once only if that was convenient.

But never, in all the years since his marriage, had he courted a woman, and most certainly not to the point of having dinner à deux prepared in his cabin. In fact, he had seldom even brought a woman aboard his ship, and he was well aware of the stir that Betsy had caused among his crew.

He could have understood his actions better if he were one of those men—and he had known many—who took a special delight in very young girls. But he was not one of them—at least, he told himself, not until now. He had heard it said that as a man grew older and more jaded, he developed a taste for young flesh to whet his appetite. But his own appetite was hardly in need of whetting.

So he was forced to the conclusion that it was the girl herself. Her very presence enchanted him, not only her beauty, but the way she looked at him, the way she smiled, the odd combination of utter innocence and the perfectly conscious seductiveness of a woman of the world, fully aware of her power to charm, even calculatingly so.

She was, he decided, one of those women who were destined to be someone's mistress, and he could think of no reason why she should not be his. She might, of course, become pregnant, but such things could always be taken care of if money was forthcoming. The only possible stumbling block to his taking her as his mistress might be the girl's mother. He was in the process of drowsily resolving to learn more about this situation before he committed himself when he, too, fell asleep.

188

It was after nine o'clock when Jacques awoke. He shook himself and looked around the cabin blearily. Betsy still slept on his bunk, lying on her side with her knees drawn up almost to her breasts. She looked, he thought, like a kitten, and the soft sound that came from her throat might almost have been purring.

He studied her for a moment, a half smile on his lips. At last, he got up, went over to the table, and poured himself some wine. He drained the glass in one gulp and then went over to the bunk.

"Betsy, *chérie*," he said, placing his hand gently on her shoulder.

She opened her eyes, looked at him blankly, and then closed them again. When he increased the pressure of his hand on her shoulder, she finally roused herself. She stretched, throwing her hands above her head in a sensuous gesture.

"I fell asleep," she said matter-of-factly.

"*Oui.*"

"You gave me too much to eat."

"You had too much wine, *je crois.*"

"Oh, no," she said firmly. "Not enough." She sat up. "And now I would like some more."

"No, it is not good that you have more."

"Champagne. I want more champagne!"

"It is all gone—*fini*," he lied.

"Then Madeira." She pointed toward the table and added, "There—just a little, *s'il vous plaît.*"

He sighed, and reluctantly rising, poured half a goblet and brought it to her. She seized it from his hands and drank greedily, spilling some of the wine on her bodice.

"Now, see how you have wet your dress, *mon petit cochon*," he said. His hands moved to open her bodice, and she looked at him speculatively.

"What does *cochon* mean?" she asked.

"Pig."

"Pig! That's not a nice name to call me." She watched his hands as they pulled her dress down, exposing her breasts. "I think," she said with a smile, "that you are the *cochon*."

He laughed and playfully placed his mouth on one of her breasts, caressing the nipple with his tongue. She lay back on the bunk and closed her eyes. Then his hands began working the dress down over her hips until he had gotten it off.

189

She opened her eyes and looked at him gravely. "I suppose you want to play the game again," she said.

"The game?" He paused in the midst of removing her petticoat and looked at her questioningly.

"You know—the game that men play with women when they push their thing into you and bounce up and down until they breathe hard and have a fit." Then, in an imitation that was both accurate and innocently satirical, she breathed hard, snorted, and then thrust her hips back and forth convulsively. Then she groaned, cried out, and gasped for air.

Jacques laughed uproariously. Betsy was pleased that she had amused him, even though she had not intended to.

"I don't understand it," she said gravely. "When you make so much noise, is it because you're angry? Or maybe it hurts. But if it hurts, then why do you want to do it?"

He smiled. "It does not hurt, *chérie.*" Then, in a rush of affection, he began kissing her again—on the lips, on the breasts, on her neck and ears. His hands tore frantically at her petticoat until he had it off. Suddenly he became quiet. Raising himself, he looked down at her naked, unmoving body. There was a tenderness in his voice as he said, "Then you would like to play the game with the old *cochon?*"

"I don't mind," said Betsy, "but please don't take too long. You're heavy."

When he had taken off his clothes, he lay down next to her and began caressing her again. Between kisses, he murmured, "You like me to touch you, *chérie?*"

"Oh, yes. But it does make me sleepy."

"Then we must wake you up," he said. He moved to enter her, and she put out a restraining hand. He responded by slowing his movements, pushing himself into her gently but relentlessly. She lay back and arched her legs over his buttocks, as she had done the night before. And again, while he worked over her, with his slow and penetrating strokes, she felt a sleepy contentment moving through her body. Pleasant though this was, she was relieved when the spasms of his climax shook him because she wanted more than anything else to be let alone so that she could sleep.

When at last he had shifted his weight from her and lay at her side, he continued to caress her, whispering endearments into her ear.

"Do you love the Capitaine Jacques?" he asked.

"Oh, yes," she said drowsily.

"But I do not think you like very much to—to play the game."

"It's all right," she said. "But I think one game a night is enough."

"I will wait then until morning," he said.

Suddenly she sat up and looked at him thoughtfully.

"What is it, *chérie?*"

"I was wondering, Jacques—"

"Yes?"

"Well, I don't know how they play the game in France, but in Providence, after the game is over, the man gives the lady a present."

"I see. Who has teached you this?"

"My mother always got presents after she played the game with the sailors, and then, when I started playing the game with my uncle, he always gave me pretty things afterward."

"Your *uncle?*"

"Mr. Allen, I mean. He's not really my uncle, but that's what I call him. He wants to marry me, but I'm not going to."

Jacques was thoroughly bewildered now. "But why not?"

"Because he won't let me see my mother. He says she's a whore and will make me sinful, but that's not true. She's married now to Captain Clarke. So I ran away, and I'm going to live with my mother because I love her. Anyway, how can she make me sinful when I am already sinful?"

Jacques could not keep from smiling. "*Tais-toi, mon enfant.* You are not sinful." He patted her cheek. "You are *adorable.*"

"That must mean adorable," she said.

"*Oui.*"

She yawned and said, "I'm tired. I think I'll go to sleep now."

He watched her as she crawled to the top of the bunk and pulled down the coverlet. When she had squirmed herself down under it, she looked at him with a pleased smile and then closed her eyes.

He rose from the bunk and moved toward the desk. After he had poured himself some wine, he stood by the porthole looking

191

out reflectively at the water. The sight of its slow and rhythmic rippling in the faint light from the low-hanging moon would ordinarily have made him feel peaceful, but now he felt restless and ill at ease. The knowledge that Betsy was not only the mistress of her so-called uncle but could, if she wished, become his wife had unsettled his half-formed plan to make her his own mistress. He had no wish to become embroiled with the fiancée of one of the town's apparently respectable citizens, nor did he want to run the risk of an entanglement with the law. He had a sudden picture of himself standing before a judge who reviled him as a corrupter of young maidens.

He told himself that the sensible thing to do was to bring the relationship to an end as quickly and kindly as possible, send the girl back to her Mr. Allen or her mother or wherever, and set sail for France. But he had barely finished unloading his cargo, to say nothing of taking on a new one for his return trip to France. More than that, he knew that he did not want to break off with Betsy at all. The thought of the town whores who might take her place while he remained in port filled him with disgust. It was not only the youth and freshness of her body that so excited him. Her childlike sweetness, her naïve honesty, awoke in him a strange combination of tenderness and lust that he found irresistible. Even her odd notion that love was a game in which a tangible reward must be given delighted him.

And it was not really so odd, after all. Did not all women, including wives, consider this a proper and necessary arrangement, no matter how carefully they concealed it from themselves and the men with whom they went to bed? Wives as well as mistresses tacitly expected some kind of reward, whores merely set the price in advance. To Betsy, it was a rule in a child's game. The idea, instead of giving him the feeling that he was loved only for the material benefits he might give, amused him.

He turned from the porthole and looked back at the small and quiet figure on his bunk. Her face, flushed with sleep and framed by tousled red-gold curls, was turned toward him. He found it hard to believe that only moments earlier he had seized this innocent-looking ethereal creature in his arms, plunged himself into her softness and pounded out his lust, sweating and grunting like some beast in a barnyard.

A flicker of shame went through him, but as the memory of their love-making became vivid in his imagination, it was succeeded by a quick stirring in his groin. He looked down at his growing hardness in cynical amusement and muttered to himself, *"Comme tu es vicieux, toi!"*

He moved to the bunk with the intention of awakening her. And then, as clearly as though she had spoken, he could hear her saying, "But I think one game a night is enough."

"Very well, then," he told himself. "It is a game, and I will honor the rules, mam'selle."

He got quietly into the bunk, resolutely turning his back to her. But it was an hour before he finally fell asleep.

The next day Betsy decided that she would go back to the Allen house to get her clothing. She was still wearing the dress she wore on the night she had run away, and it had become wrinkled and soiled during her tussle with the town sergeant.

She dreaded the thought of another scene with Sam, and so she planned to go to the house during the day, while he was at the port. The problem would be how to move her things from Benefit Street out to the mud hut. And then she remembered the handcart that Phebe used for carrying the herbs and greens that she sold on the streets of the town. All of her belongings, including even her winter clothes, would fit into the cart easily, and she would be able to move out of Sam's house completely, once and for all.

It was midafternoon by the time Betsy arrived at the mud hut, and Phebe had not yet returned with her cart. But Captain Clarke was there, seated at his cobbler's bench, where he was busily nailing new soles onto a pair of boots. He looked up at her, annoyed at this interruption of one of his rare periods of industry.

"Your mother's not to home," he said irritably. "She's still out peddling her herbs and greens."

"I'm glad you don't call them yarbs," said Betsy.

Jonathan regarded her curiously. "Now why should you be glad about a thing like that?"

"Because yarbs is not the proper way to say herbs."

"And how would you know that?" he asked idly, fixing his interest on the boot in his hand.

193

"Because my uncle taught me. He said I should try to speak like a lady."

"He sounds to be a sensible man. Why do you want to run away from the good home he's given you?"

Betsy paused for dramatic effect, waiting for Jonathan to look up from his work again. When at last he did, she managed to make her eyes fill with sudden tears.

"He—he beats me," she said softly.

Jonathan sat up abruptly. "Beats you? Why? Are you disobedient, lass?"

"Oh, no. I do my best to please, but no matter what I do, he gets angry and fetches the birch rod—" She shuddered as though the thought were so terrifying that she could not continue. She remembered the bruises that she had suffered at the hands of the town sergeant, and pulling her dress down from her shoulder, she displayed them.

Jonathan looked at the black-and-blue marks and reacted with indignation. "For shame! For shame!" he said dramatically. "What manner of man can he be so to mistreat a child?"

"A cruel man," said Betsy. She dried her eyes with the back of her hand and then said, "But let's not talk about it. I won't have to go back to him since you have been kind enough to give me shelter for a few days, until I can make other plans."

Jonathan said nothing and picked up the boot he had been working on.

At last, Betsy said, "Do you think my mother will be here soon? I want her to go to his house with me so that I can get my clothes. Mayhap we can use her handcart."

Jonathan looked up suspiciously. "Do you have so many clothes then—enough to fill the handcart? Where will you put them?"

"Oh, not that many, Captain Clarke." She looked around the room hastily. "I could just pile them over there in the corner."

"They'll get dirty." He shrugged noncommittally. "I suppose we could find you a box somewhere."

Betsy reached out her hand and touched him lightly on the arm. "That would be very kind of you, Captain."

A silence fell, and Jonathan resumed his work on the boots. Betsy looked around the room nervously. When her eyes lighted on the shelf that held Jonathan's collection of books, she rose from her chair and went over to look at them. Aware that Jonathan was watching her, she read the titles to herself in a whisper.

At last she turned to him and said, "Why do you have so many little books with the name Shakespeare on them?"

Jonathan set down his hammer in surprise. "You say that you know how to read. How is it that you don't know the name Shakespeare?"

"My uncle would let me read nothing except the Bible," she said demurely.

"The idiot! The Bible is a fine book, but it is not the *only* book!" He swept his hand through the air in a grandiose gesture. "There is a vast treasure of great lit-er-a-toor waiting for human eyes to devour! A vast treasure, I tell you!"

Betsy could think of nothing to say except, "Well, I'm glad to know that."

"Glad, indeed!" Jonathan rose dramatically from his bench and pointed his forefinger at Betsy almost accusingly. "Then explore that treasure without further ado!"

He strode to the bookshelf, and brushing her out of the way, he seized a thin volume and thrust it at her. "Here, then, my lass. Make the acquaintance of the greatest mind the human race has yet produced! Shakespeare!" He paused and repeated the name slowly and majestically. "Will-yum Shake-speare!"

Betsy looked down at the book in what she believed to be a properly reverential way. "*Hamlet*," she read aloud. "What is that?"

Jonathan smote his forehead with his open palm. "What is *Hamlet?* Good God in heaven, girl, *Hamlet* is the greatest play in the English language! Sit down in that chair there and read it!"

Betsy wanted to ask him what a play was, but, deciding not to display her ignorance any further, she retreated to the chair, sat down, and opened the book.

Jonathan went back to his bench, and as soon as he had seated himself, he stretched out his arms as though to embrace all of Elsinore. " 'Who's there?' " he began, almost shouting the question. " 'Nay, answer me: stand and unfold yourself.' "

Betsy looked up in surprise. "Why, that's just what it says here. How did you remember that?"

"I have committed the entire play to memory," said Jonathan with quiet pride.

Betsy rippled the pages with her fingers. "All that? You remember all that?"

"Certainly, my dear." As though to prove it, he continued. " 'Long live the king! Bernardo? He. You come most carefully upon your hour. 'Tis now struck twelve; get thee to bed, Francisco. For this relief much thanks—' "

Betsy interrupted him, reading, " ' 'Tis bitter cold, and I am sick at heart.' " She paused and looked at Jonathan in genuine admiration. "How long did it take you to remember it all?"

Jonathan waved his hand airily. "Oh, a matter of weeks—I have forgotten."

Betsy shook her head in disbelief. "Who are these men—Francisco and Bernardo? Why do they talk that way?"

Jonathan abandoned his work completely and went over to her. He described the setting at Elsinore, the darkness of the night and the guards at their post on a platform of the castle. In ominous tones, he explained how the king had been murdered by his own brother, how his ghost had been seen and would appear again.

Spellbound, Betsy listened, and when Jonathan paused for breath, she said, "But what's going to happen when the ghost comes? Will the guards get scared and run away?"

Jonathan smiled at her in a lofty and mysterious way. "I shan't tell you. Read and find out for yourself."

Betsy was disappointed. Jonathan's rolling voice and dramatic gesturing made the words in the book before her seem dull and boring. "It's too hard to read it, and I don't know what all the words mean. Please tell me instead."

He shook his head and returned to his bench and sat down. "No, I will not tell you. The reading will come easier the more you do of it. Unlock the door to the vast treasure house of lit-er-a-toor!" With that, he resumed work on the boots, and the sound of his hammer made further conversation impossible.

With a sigh, Betsy went back to the book and began reading.

When Phebe returned to the hut late in the afternoon, she found Betsy asleep in the chair with an open book on her knees. Jonathan lay sprawled on the floor near his bench, an empty wine bottle and glass beside him. He was snoring loudly.

Phebe was one of those people who cannot stand the sight of others sleeping during the daylight hours. If she was up and about, even though she might be doing nothing, she felt that everybody else should be too. She went over to Betsy and shook her by the shoulder, then moved on to Jonathan, shoving at his large rump with her foot. Jonathan snorted and went back to snoring more loudly than before.

Betsy roused herself. "Oh, Mama, you're here! I was waiting for you, but I fell asleep reading a book Jonathan gave me. Is your handcart here?"

"Sure, it's here. Why?"

"We've got to go to Sam Allen's and get all my clothes and bring them here."

"Whatever for? Did he throw you out?"

"Oh, no. But I'm not going back to him, and I haven't any clothes except the dress I'm wearing. You will go with me, won't you, Mama?"

Phebe sighed, wiping the sweat from her forehead with a grimy hand. "I'm tired, daughter. We'll make it another day."

Betsy was insistent. She pleaded tearfully until Phebe wearily agreed to go. At last they set off down the road, with Betsy pushing the cart and Phebe trailing behind her.

When they arrived at the Allen house, Betsy ran up the path and tried the door. Finding it open, she went in. The house was quiet and deserted. When she called up the stairs, there was no answer. She went back to the door and beckoned Phebe to come in.

Together, they went up the stairs to Betsy's bedroom, opened the closets, and gathered the clothing in their arms. After three trips the closets were bare, and the small chest in which Betsy's winter clothing had been stored had been emptied. The cart by this time was full to overflowing and heavy, but Phebe took one handle and Betsy the other and together they were able to move it down the street.

They had progressed almost as far as Angell Street when Betsy suddenly dropped her handle. "My jewelry!" she screamed. "I forgot my jewelry!"

Leaving Phebe to guard the cart, she ran back to the house and once more climbed the stairs to her bedroom. The box in which she kept the trinkets that Sam had given her was not in its usual place. She searched hurriedly through all the drawers of her chest, but the box was nowhere to be found. She realized, at last, that Sam had taken it, and the thought made her furious. While debating whether she should stay and demand the box or leave without it, she heard the downstairs door open and close. She waited in silence. When she heard Sam's familiar footsteps on the stairs, her heart began to beat fast. There was no avoiding him now. She moved resolutely to the door of her bedroom.

As Sam rounded the corner of the stairway, he saw her and stopped, dead still. His eyes, swollen and bloodshot, stared at her coldly, without surprise. Then he continued his way up the stairs until he had reached her.

"So you've come back," he said tonelessly.

"No. I came to get my clothes."

"Well, you can't have them."

She laughed. "It's too late. They're already gone. If you don't believe me, look for yourself." She pointed into the bedroom toward the empty closet with its door ajar. "And now, I want my jewelry. You took the box."

He swayed toward her, and she saw now that he was drunk.

"Yes," he said. "I took the box, and I shall keep it. The jewelry is not yours."

"You gave it to me!" she said angrily.

"Yes. And now I am taking it back. And that's an end on it!"

She turned away, for the moment defeated. And then in her imagination she saw the necklace of small sea-green stones, the gift that she had loved above all the others. When she turned to him again, her face was set and determined.

"You will give my trinkets back to me or I will go to the Town Council and tell them—"

"Go tell them, then. Tell them anything you want. I will not be blackmailed! Anyway, they will not believe you." He paused, and his voice became unexpectedly soft and pleading. "Betsy, I have asked you to be my wife. I love you."

"You don't love me. You only want to—"

"Don't say that, Betsy. You don't understand."

"I understand that you gave me jewelry for playing the game with you, and now you won't give it back!"

"But it will be yours again if you will come back and be my wife."

"And my mother? You will let me see her?"

Sam's voice lost its conciliatory tone and became firm. "No. She would end by making you a whore like herself."

Betsy looked at him with a mocking smile. "But I am already a whore. I spent last night in the arms of a French sea captain!"

Sam looked at her blankly. "I don't believe you."

"Then look!" She pulled at her bodice and thrust her bared breasts at him, pointing to the blue marks around her nipples where the Captain had kissed her roughly.

She laughed derisively at Sam's shocked face. "The Captain kisses hard, Uncle. Three times he had me last night, and he's twice as big as you."

He struck her across the mouth with such force that she fell to the floor. He was on top of her then, like an enraged beast coming in for the kill. His long fingers locked about her throat, and she struggled for air, trying to cry out, and her legs thrashed about helplessly.

Then, as Sam raised himself above her on hands and knees, she desperately mustered all the strength left in her and landed a violent kick square in his groin. Sam screamed in pain. His hands went limp around her throat as he doubled up in agony and lay finally prostrate and groaning on the floor beside her.

Betsy filled her lungs with great breaths of air, and when the thudding of her heart had quieted, she got slowly to her feet. Sam was sobbing now like a hurt child, and she looked down at him with mingled feelings of pity and remorse. When he turned his face toward her, his eyes still full of pain, she knelt quickly by his side and cradled his head in her lap. Inexplicably, she too had begun to cry.

Sam closed his eyes, and when the pain had subsided and he was able to breathe evenly, he began praying in a voice so low that she could scarcely hear his words.

"Oh, God, merciful God, forgive me. I have had murder in my

heart . . . murder . . . murder . . ." His voice trailed off into a whisper and he was silent.

When he opened his eyes at last, he stared at Betsy with a strange intensity. His voice, when he spoke, was filled with a kind of hopeless sadness that Betsy had never heard in it before.

"I cannot see you more, Betsy. The time has come when I must cast you from me for my own soul's good—and yours. There can be no atonement in marriage vows for you and me. The wages of sin—" His voice seemed to dry up, unable to go on.

Betsy shook her head from side to side as though trying to shake off the confused feelings that filled her. "Oh, Uncle—Uncle, I didn't mean to hurt you, but you would ha' killed me."

Sam nodded. " 'Twas the Lord's intervention that gave you the strength to save yourself—and me." He paused, and then with an effort he said softly, "Go now, Betsy, and as God loves you, do not come back."

She rose uncertainly, looking down at him in indecision. Groping for words, she said, "Uncle, I do love you—somewhat—but I—I love my mother too."

"Go!" he whispered with a hoarse urgency. "Go! Leave me to my punishment!"

She started toward the stairs and then abruptly stopped. She looked back at him and said quietly, "And my jewelry—will you give it to me?"

"Take it. It is accursed, and I do not want it here to remind me of my sinfulness. It is in the top drawer of the chest in my room."

She ran quickly into Sam's room, opened the drawer of his chest, and with shaking hands grabbed the jewelry box. In the hallway she paused once again, feeling that she should say something but not knowing what.

At last, she murmured, "Thank you, Uncle. You are good. God will forgive you." She turned her head toward him and added with gentle finality, "Goodbye, Uncle."

As she descended the stairs, she straightened her dress and tried to smooth the tangle of her hair. She could hear Sam's voice droning in prayer above her, and she stopped for a moment, listening.

"God bless thee, Betsy. May He lead thee out from the temptation and sinfulness around you and into the ways of virtue and righteousness for all the days of thy life . . ."

She smiled to herself, as one might smile at the make-believe games of a child at play. Then unaccountably her eyes filled with tears again, and she began to run, clutching the jewelry box tightly under her arm.

CHAPTER 16

THE moods of Captain Jonathan Clarke were determined by the amount of wine or rum he had been able to lay hands on the night before. But drunk, sober, or in the throes of recovery, he preferred reading to the pursuit of his trade as a shoe cobbler. Only one of Phebe's more blistering harangues or the physical threats of an irate customer succeeded in making him lay aside his book and sit down at the cobbler's bench. Then he would sigh, grunt, and consign the world of practical and ignorant men to eternal hell-fire.

His love of books was equaled only by his fondness for talking about what he had read in them. For this, he needed an audience of a very special kind, one that would listen and interrupt only to applaud his long, rolling sentences. And in Betsy he found the most nearly perfect audience he had ever discovered.

Since the arrival of her clothes in Phebe's handcart, she had been tacitly accepted by Jonathan as part of the household. Her nights were spent aboard *L'Étoile de Marseilles*, but her afternoons, while Phebe was out selling herbs and greens, were spent alone with Jonathan.

As he spouted forth the streams of his learning, Betsy would sit quietly by his side, like an attentive mouse. She was dazzled by the flow of his words, and even when she did not understand what he was talking about, she would listen, often in openmouthed wonder. Sometimes, during a pause, she would ask a question.

If Jonathan was reasonably sober, this delighted him, and he would go to great pains to explain, but if he was drunk, he would become impatient at the interruption and call her a stupid slut with hog guts for brains. Then Betsy would bow her head and wait for the torrent of words to begin again. And it always did.

One afternoon, in an expansive mood, he led her over to his rickety bookshelf and proudly displayed what he called "my private collection of works of lit-er-a-toor." Volume by volume he pulled the books from the shelf and insisted that she read the titles aloud. Aside from Shakespeare, there was a dog-eared and weather-beaten copy of *Plutarch's Lives*, printed in London in 1741; a cheap edition of *The Dialogues of Plato* and almost half of a broken copy of *The Republic*; two small volumes from the works of Aristotle; and Books IV and VII of *Paradise Lost*.

These books he encouraged her to read, but there were others that he forbade her to touch: cheaply printed descriptions of life in the more profligate courts of Europe, both French and English; purported confessions of highwaymen, prostitutes, mistresses of great men, dissolute priests, and lustful nuns. The fact that these books were forbidden made them extremely attractive to Betsy, and later, on those days when Jonathan was sleeping off a drunk, she stealthily took them from the shelf and devoured their sensational contents.

Jonathan's library was rounded out by stray volumes on a multiplicity of subjects that ranged from astronomy to horticulture. For Jonathan, anything that had been set into type somehow had value, and he had collected books in any way he could. Few of them had been bought; some had been borrowed, never to be returned; some had been salvaged from rubbish piles; many had been filched or stolen.

For Betsy, all of Jonathan's books were more interesting than the Bible, which was the only book she had known until now. At first she read only to please Jonathan, or to provoke one of the long and often dramatic declamations that she liked so much.

She had found a new teacher, and one whose methods of conveying knowledge were vastly more enjoyable than Sam's had ever been. He not only encouraged her to read but would sometimes ask for her opinions, praising her when these resembled his own, cursing her for a fool when they did not. But as time went on, she became impervious to his curses and finally contradicted him openly.

After reading most of *A Midsummer Night's Dream* she said, "I don't care what you say, the whole thing is daft!"

"Daft!" repeated Jonathan. "It is you who are daft! If you have not the imagination to—"

"I have plenty of imagination. But I think it's daft because nothing would have happened if it wasn't that this stupid boy Puck hadn't gone around putting some kind of juice on people's eyelids. Anyway, there isn't any juice like that, is there?"

"Certainly not! But this is like a fairy tale. Mr. Shakespeare himself calls it a dream."

"I don't want to read about a dream unless it's a real dream."

Jonathan shook his hands despairingly over his head. "And what, pray tell, do you mean by a *real* dream, my dear girl?"

"A dream that somebody dreamt, and they tell you about it, but you know it's a dream and not really what happened."

Jonathan sat down suddenly. "Oh, my God," he groaned. "How will I make this oaf of a girl understand?"

"I'm not an oaf. You said yourself that I was very smart."

"That was day before yesterday. Today, you are a stupid, ignorant slut, completely without imagination or humor." He paused and then decided to try again. "Don't you see, Betsy, that the person who dreamed the dream is Shakespeare himself—Shakespeare, the finest poet in the English language? He wrote down this dream for you, d'you hear me? And you sit there like an addlepated goose and say it's daft!"

"But why did he bother to write it for me or anybody else?"

Jonathan thought a moment, and when at last he spoke, his voice was quiet, somehow sad. "He wrote it to show us what fools we are when we fall in love."

"Is that why Puck says 'What fools these mortals be'?"

Jonathan jumped from his chair so ecstatically that he almost fell face down on the floor. "That's it! Now you understand at last!"

Betsy sighed. "But I don't think I do, Captain."

"Yes, you do. Think of Queen Titania waking up and falling in love with the head of a jackass."

"That was stupid too," said Betsy.

"Exactly! But more than stupid, my girl." Then he shouted, "Love is blind! Blind, blind, blind! The head of a jackass or the head of a beautiful woman who brings us nothing but pain—what's the difference if we're blind?"

Betsy was silenced at last, dimly beginning to understand what the Captain was saying. "You mean, it's like Mr. Shakespeare is making up this dream to—well, to show me how love is blind?"

Tears of joy rolled down Jonathan's cheeks. It was one of those rare occasions when he found himself at a loss for words, and so he sat down and poured himself a goblet of wine.

Betsy watched him silently while he gulped down the drink. She could not understand his tears and waited for him to say something.

At last he muttered, "Betsy, my girl, sometimes you are—brilliant. And that makes me very happy."

The words pleased Betsy, but she still said nothing. She was thinking about Queen Titania and the ass's head. The image had become suddenly vivid. She saw the Queen cradling the head in her lap, heard her whispering words of love to the ugly and lifeless thing. She thought of Sam and Jacques, murmuring endearments while they pumped up and down on her and breathed hard.

Then the thought struck her that she herself was the ass's head, and this idea made her laugh.

"What are you laughing at?" asked Jonathan.

"Nothing," said Betsy. But she kept on laughing.

Later that night, while Jacques was astride her in the midst of love-making, she found herself laughing again. The thought of herself wearing an ass's head appealed to her still-childlike sense of the ridiculous. Her laughter stopped Jacques as effectively as a pitcher of cold water doused over his naked back.

"What is funny?" he demanded.

"I have a jackass head," she said.

He looked at her in bewilderment. "Ah, you have had too much wine, I think."

"Yes," said Betsy, still giggling.

Jacques was piqued. "You do not like what I do?"

Betsy realized that he had thought she was making fun of his love-making, and so she said, "Oh, yes, I like it. Don't stop, Jacques."

Reassured but still puzzled, he continued until at last, satisfied, he rolled away from her. He fondled her gently, all the while looking at her in a thoughtful way. Even after she had fallen asleep, he continued to stare at her.

"A jackass head," he said to himself. He could not explain it, but then she said many things that astonished him: observations that were a curious combination of childlike ingenuousness and a wisdom far beyond her years. It was this ability to surprise him that lightened the boredom that so often set in as soon as his lust was satisfied.

He was amused rather than annoyed by her maneuvers when she wanted something but abandoned her usual frankness for a transparent deviousness. Although he had long ago accepted her notions about love being a game with certain rules, notably that the man should in some way offer a tangible reward for pleasure, she sometimes resorted to indirect methods to gain her ends.

He remembered the sunny afternoon when they had gone out for a walk, and she had adroitly steered him past the clothing shops of Cheapside. She had clapped her hands together in ecstasy at the sight of a pair of shoes with little cloth-covered high heels. Her upturned face, with eyes glistening, had been altogether irresistible and he bought her the shoes. And on successive expeditions she had acquired a pair of gloves, a new bonnet, and a gaily colored little shawl.

And yet these demands, unvoiced as they were, were never excessive. She did not presume on his generosity and expect a reward for every bout of love-making. She had, he decided, her own special way of keeping books, and soon he was able to anticipate, almost to the day, just when he would find himself standing outside a shop window where some coveted article was on display.

She had succeeded, too, in getting him to take her to dinner at the Bulldog Tavern. She could hardly complain about the food served in the Captain's cabin, but she remarked from time to time that she would be proud to go to the tavern with him. At first he let these hints pass without comment because he felt cautious about making their relationship too public. But as time passed, and neither Sam Allen nor the town sergeant made trouble for him, he decided that there could be no harm in taking her to dinner.

On that first night he had felt a bit nervous as he walked into the taproom of the Bulldog Tavern with Betsy clinging to his arm. She had dressed for the occasion and seemed anything but nervous. Impervious to the stares of the customers, she looked back at them casually and with a trace of disdain. The eyes of the men lighted up in appreciation of Betsy's youth and beauty, but their women, who for the most part had neither, sent openly hostile glances in her direction. None of this interfered with Betsy's appetite. She enjoyed the attention and ate voraciously, much to the delight of Jacques.

In the days that followed, they became regular and expected customers. Nate Mason, in his role as proprietor, made a great fuss over Betsy, as though she might indeed be a young lady of the town, instead of what she so obviously was—the Captain's doxy. And yet he realized that she was different from other women who frequented the tavern, not only younger and prettier, but soft-voiced, polite and dignified.

From the very first it was clear from Betsy's manner that she belonged exclusively to the Captain and was not interested in other conquests. The other women relaxed, and their escorts of the evening limited their attentions to envious stares. Only Bobby Brown, who stopped by at the tavern from time to time, was openly hostile. If he looked at Betsy, his upper lip lifted in an expression that was meant to convey disgust, but when the Captain moved his eyes toward him, he quickly turned his head away, as though he had never seen him before.

Betsy enjoyed it all. Her life, for the moment, was happy. She felt free—free of Sam and the quarreling, free to see her mother as often as she wished, free to have her own way without restraint. She enjoyed her evenings with Jacques in the tavern, but just as important to her were the afternoons she spent at the hut with Jonathan.

And then, quite unexpectedly, Jonathan's daughter, Polly Clarke, made an unheralded appearance at the hut one afternoon as Betsy was sitting in a chair reading, while Jonathan sprawled on the floor asleep.

As Betsy looked up from her book, Polly said, "Who are you?"

Betsy rose and went to greet the visitor. "I'm Betsy Bowen, Phebe's daughter."

"Oh. Then I expect I'm your stepsister."

"But I have a sister named Polly—"

"I said *step*sister." She nodded toward Jonathan. "That's my father. I'm Polly Clarke."

Betsy made an attempt at politeness. "How do you do?"

"Not very well. I got in a condition and had to go to see the midwife to get rid of it. I feel sick."

Betsy tried to disguise her feelings of embarrassment at Polly's frankness. "Oh. I'm sorry. Maybe you better sit down."

"Lie down would be better," said Polly.

"Here, take my bed. I hardly use it." She led Polly over to the corner of the room where her straw pallet lay on the floor.

"You call that a bed?" asked Polly.

"It's all I have. I'm sorry. Could I make you some tea?"

"I wouldn't say no," said Polly. She looked curiously at Betsy and added, "Thank you."

Tea seemed to make Polly more friendly, and Betsy, unable to repress her curiosity about this daughter of Jonathan's, plied her with questions.

"Do you live in Providence?" she began.

"I'm living here now, I guess. I was up to Newport for quite a while, but when I began to get big, business wasn't so good."

"What business are you in?" asked Betsy.

Polly laughed. "Why, the whore business. What did you think?"

"Oh," said Betsy, and then added, "you don't look like a whore."

"And how is a whore supposed to look? I'm only eighteen, and I've got good looks. I go easy with the rum, and I can be choosy about who I go with. Sometimes I stay with one man for a while. But when you get in a condition and it starts to show, a man don't want you around. So I went to the midwife in Newport and decided to come back here and stay with Papa till I felt good again. So here I am."

"I hope you'll be feeling better soon," said Betsy.

"Oh, I will. It takes a couple of days. You lose a lot of blood, you know."

Betsy shivered. "I've never—well, I've never been pregnant."

"Well, it happens." Polly looked at Betsy acutely and said, "You look pretty young. Do you go with men?"

The directness of the question unsettled Betsy. She found herself blushing as she said, "Well, yes. With one man. He's a French sea captain. I stay with him on his ship every night. So you can see I won't be using my bed, and you can have it."

Polly looked over at the straw pallet. "Well, I expect it's softer than the floor and not so damp." She got up, went over to the pallet, and stretched out. "I'm tired. Excuse me if I go to sleep now. And thanks for the tea."

Betsy found an old quilt, dusty and full of holes, and covered Polly with it. "It gets cool here when the sun goes down," she explained.

Polly nodded her head in a grateful way and was soon sleeping. Betsy looked at her studiously. The girl looked older than her eighteen years. Her figure, with its wide hips and ample bosom, was that of a fully developed woman.

Her face was pretty without being really beautiful. The features were ordinary, the nose a little too large, the mouth a little too wide. Her dark-brown hair, curly and uncombed, gave her a careless appearance that was somehow attractive.

Betsy had liked the bluntness of her language, her lack of affectation. But beneath the outward nonchalance Betsy had sensed both warmth and kindliness. Betsy had liked her immediately, and her concern was genuine. She knew about these visits to the midwife and their painful aftermath because her own mother had gone to Freelove Ballou on two occasions to rid herself of unwanted children. She also knew that in spite of Freelove's expert manipulation of slippery-elm sticks or knitting needles, it was a dangerous business, and the women sometimes died as a result.

And so, during the next week, she spent a good share of her time nursing Polly back to health. This was not entirely unselfish on her part because she had decided to win Polly's friendship, having long felt the need of having a girl of her own age in whom she could confide. Her own sister, Polly, had always been cold and unfriendly, and Phebe, so often drunk or recovering from drink, was for the most part incapable of fulfilling the role of confidante.

But Betsy's campaign to make Polly her friend was not easily won. Of Jonathan's seven children by his first wife, Polly had always been his favorite, if only because of her unwavering loyalty. She had followed him in his gypsy wanderings from town to town, accepting his abuse and affection with tolerant good humor. And after her mother's death, four years earlier, she had assumed responsibility for him. She begged for food, stole it if she had to, and finally, as she grew older, sold herself for money. She had long ago accepted the fact that rum would always interfere with his shoe cobbling.

When Phebe had appeared on the scene, Polly felt relieved of responsibility and went to Newport with every intention of starting a new and independent life. But now that she was back, her old feelings of possessiveness toward her father returned, and she quickly realized that in Betsy she had a rival for his affections. When she compared her own rather ordinary good looks with Betsy's delicate beauty, she felt inferior and unattractive, although she knew that she was neither.

But it was not Betsy's beauty that made her jealous; it was Betsy's intelligence, which Jonathan obviously admired so much. Here, she felt out of the running and did not even attempt to compete. Like most women, in fact, like most of the population of Providence, she could neither read nor write, and Betsy could do both. At first, her envy expressed itself in derision of Betsy's accomplishments. She called her "Mistress Bookworm" and mocked her accent and her occasional use of French phrases.

Betsy accepted the situation with good humor. She stopped using French phrases and made a conscious effort to coarsen her speech. She told Polly about her affair with Jacques and asked for advice in matters of love and love-making. And when Polly had regained her health and was ready to go back to the streets, Betsy celebrated the event by making her a new bonnet. Most important of all, she limited her literary conversations with Jonathan to times when Polly was not at home.

At Polly's request Betsy made an attempt to teach her to read and write. But Polly proved to be a scatterbrained pupil, and more often than not these sessions dissolved into laughter and an exchange of gossip. When it came to gossip, Polly excelled. There was nothing that happened in Providence, whether in the taverns along Towne Street or in the elegant houses on the hill above, that Polly did not know about. If Mrs. Joseph Nightingale, in the new house on Benefit Street, threw a soup tureen at the Colonel in a fit of rage, Polly would hear about it within twenty-four hours and duly report it to Betsy, along with colorful conjectures as to the bawdy reasons for such unseemly behavior on the part of Mrs. Nightingale.

It was from Polly that Betsy learned that Sam Allen had left Providence shortly after her parting from him. He had shut up the house on Benefit Street and taken his ship on her first trip to China, and this at a time when voyages around Cape Horn to China were uncommon and considered highly adventurous. Only four years earlier, John Brown had been the first shipowner in Providence to undertake the ten months' journey to Canton.

Sam's departure was welcome news for Betsy. Sometimes she still had nightmares that woke her screaming, nightmares of Sam, wild-eyed and vengeful, seeking her out to murder her.

She had told the whole story to Polly, exaggerating it for dramatic effect. Polly, listening in fascination, had been alternately indignant at Sam's cruelty and enraptured by his transports of passion, followed by gifts of jewelry.

One Sunday afternoon, as the two girls promenaded along Towne Street, Betsy, in a burst of intimacy, began questioning Polly about the ways of men during love-making.

"Why is it," she wanted to know, "that they get so much fun out of it and women get none?"

Polly looked at her in disbelief. "You mean you don't *like* it?"

"Well, I don't hate it," said Betsy shyly, "like I did at first, when it hurt me."

"It always hurts at first," said Polly, "but after a while it begins to feel good, and the time comes when you want it so much it's like being hungry."

"Maybe I ain't a true woman yet," said Betsy.

"You're sixteen. You got a woman's body almost." Polly paused and then added thoughtfully, "Mayhap you ain't done it with the right man yet."

"But the Captain's doodle is very big."

"Big has nothing to do with it," said Polly with authority. "It's how they work it and how long they can last—and how much you like the man to begin with."

"You mean—love?" asked Betsy.

"I guess so. Do you love your captain, Betsy?"

"I like him. He is good to me. He takes me to dinner every night. He gives me little presents for playing the game with him."

"Game? What game?"

"Oh, you know, letting him do it to me. Then he gives me—well, a reward. It all started with Sam when he'd give me presents afterward because he felt bad for his sins. And so I got the idea it was like a game, and I always asked for something I wanted while he was doing it to me."

Polly threw back her head and laughed. "A game!" she repeated. "Betsy, my girl, you'll make a fine whore!"

"But I don't want to be a whore," said Betsy.

"And what will you do when your Frenchy captain sails away? How will you eat, and where will you get your pretty dresses then?"

"I don't know. Maybe he'll give me some money to use while he's gone."

"You're a silly goose," said Polly. "Why should a man support a woman while he's away at sea for a couple of months and can't get to bed with her—unless he's married to her, that is. But maybe you think he'll marry you."

"Captain Jacques already has a wife in France," said Betsy.

"So how do you expect you're going to get him to leave money with you?"

"I'll ask him," said Betsy.

It had always been easy for Betsy to ask for things during or after making love. It was part of the rules of the game that she had invented. But to ask for something when her partner would not be there to participate was a new situation and one that she did not know how to deal with. Strangely enough, it violated her sense of fair play, and she was unable to bring up the subject.

As the day of Jacques' departure drew near, she became nervous and ill at ease. In her mind she rehearsed conversations in which she managed very easily to ask Jacques whether he would provide for her while he was away, but in actuality the right moment never arrived and she remained tongue-tied.

On the night before *L'Étoile de Marseilles* was to sail, she had dinner with Jacques at the Bulldog Tavern. For Jacques, it was a festive occasion, and he ordered food and drink lavishly. But Betsy toyed with her food and drank little of the Madeira in the glass before her. She was silent and preoccupied, and when Jacques looked into her eyes, she lowered her gaze to her plate.

Jacques regarded her curiously. At last he said, "You do not eat the plover pie. You do not even drink the Madeira that you love so much. You feel sick maybe?"

"No," said Betsy, still not looking at him.

"You are *triste*, then. You are sad because your Jacques is going away."

She nodded her head vigorously. Jacques moved his hand across the table toward hers. Then in a gentle voice, he said, "I will be sad, too. And I will think much about you when I am at sea." He paused and looked at her thoughtfully. "Tell me," he said, "how will you eat while I am gone?"

Betsy looked up at last. Her eyes met his directly. She nodded her head in the direction of two of the whores who came to the tavern regularly with sailors. "I will do—what they do," said Betsy. Her voice was quietly matter-of-fact.

"That is what you wish to do?" he asked.

"Oh, no! I would hate it! I don't want any man but you."

He was pleased. It was what he had wanted to hear her say. He smiled at her and said, "You will not need to sell yourself, my Betsy. I will leave you with silver, enough to last until my ship makes the return."

She was relieved to know that now she would not have to ask the question, and she sighed. But she was also moved, and her voice was tremulous as she asked, "You would do that for me?"

"Yes," said Jacques, "because I know you will be good girl and wait for me. Only five, maybe six, weeks, and I will see you again."

Her eyes filled with tears.

"Why do you cry?" he asked.

"I don't know. Maybe it is because you trust me. Nobody has ever trusted me. Why should you?"

Jacques was silent for a moment. "Because I love you. I trust you the same way I trust my daughters."

"But I am not your daughter," said Betsy.

Certainly there was nothing paternal about the passion that

seized Jacques later that night, after they had returned to his cabin. There was a desperate quality to his love-making, as though he might never live to make love again. He took her again and again, sleeping scarcely at all. She would be awakened by his caressing hands, along her shoulders, on her breasts, between her legs. And then his warm mouth would close over hers, his beard scraping her cheek, and he would be astride her again. Sometimes she was so sleepy that she hardly responded, wishing only that he would finish once and for all. But she never pushed him away. The memory of his offer of silver glowed in her like a small but very warm flame.

The next morning, when he had dressed and was ready to leave the ship, Jacques gave her a little chamois bag filled with silver coins. It was more than enough to take care of her while he would be away.

She looked at him gratefully, at a loss for words. At last she murmured, "*Merci bien.*"

"And you will be good girl, *ma chérie?* If you go with other men, they will maybe give you a sickness, and then I will get the sickness from you. Do you understand what I mean?"

She nodded seriously, remembering what Polly had told her about the "clap" and the "pox."

"I will stay only for you, *ma chérie*," she said.

"*Mon cher*," he corrected her, smiling. "*Chérie* is only for woman."

"*Mon cher*," she repeated after him, and then added, "*Tu es mon brave capitaine!*"

He laughed and on impulse swept her into his arms.

As he carried her toward the bed, she said pleadingly, "*Oh, non encore, non encore!*"

"*Si, si!*" said Jacques, not stopping now to correct her grammar.

And once again, he had his way.

214

PART THREE

CHAPTER 17

D URING the three years that Betsy was the mistress of Captain Jacques de la Croix she bloomed. The slight angularities of her adolescent body gave way to the delicate curves of womanhood. Her breasts grew larger, swelling voluptuously in her bodice; her hips widened and lost their boyish straightness; she added three inches to her height and carried herself proudly and gracefully.

But it was her face, mature and astonishingly beautiful now, that made strangers turn their heads and look after her when she passed them on the street. Even the townspeople, to whom she was a familiar sight, often stared at her openly.

The stares were not always approving, even from the men. It was generally known that she was the mistress of a French sea captain. Few people knew his name, but they did know the name of his ship. They had noted that when *L'Étoile de Marseilles* was not in port, Betsy was never seen with another man. She walked alone.

On Sunday afternoons when the weather was fair, she could always be seen on a promenade that took her from one end of Benefit Street to the other. Alone though she might be, she was always beautifully dressed in the latest fashions. Women of the town watched from behind window curtains and wondered who her dressmaker might be. It never occurred to them that Betsy might be her own dressmaker.

Lydia Allen had been unable to give Betsy love, but her sewing instructions had been excellent, and Betsy easily copied the styles worn by the wives of the rich shipowners who lived on the south side of town.

On these Sunday strolls along Benefit Street, Betsy liked to imagine that she was not only dressed like one of these elegant ladies but that she herself was one of them. She would pause before the imposing house of John Brown on the corner of Benefit Street and Hopkins Street and then see herself as the real Mrs. Brown, with a parasol of Chinese silk over her shoulders, moving slowly up the walk toward the ornate and handsome doorway.

She envisioned the drawing room with all its luxurious furnishings and saw herself sitting in the room's most beautiful chair, which had, of course, been imported from a château somewhere in France. The room was filled with an assemblage of the town's most established and respectable citizens. Then, seated regally before a gleaming solid-silver tea service and a set of hand-painted Chinese cups, she poured tea.

But these fantasies soon became rather tame, and for this Jonathan Clarke was responsible. She not only listened breathlessly while he described the splendors of Rome, of Athens, and of the French and English courts, but now she had begun to read for herself the books that re-created these wonders in high-flown, exciting words.

And as she read, she was not merely a spectator in the court of Elizabeth or Cleopatra or Isabella. She herself was the queen. Beautiful, powerful, and triumphant, she was surrounded by throngs of her subjects. Whether they were nobles or peasants made little difference. They were all devoted to her. For she was always a benevolent empress, generous with her largess and favors, compassionate to the poor and downtrodden, wise and fair in all the judgments she rendered.

Most of all, she enjoyed being one of those legendary women who rose from low beginnings to become the favored mistress of a king. She knew them all and was as familiar with the details of their rise to fortune as Jonathan's books allowed her to be. Anne Boleyn, Pompadour, Du Barry and Nell Gwynne—these were her favorites. She rose to glory with each of them individually, but she never fell from eminence. She rewrote history: Anne Boleyn was rescued from the headsman's block; Pompadour and Du Barry, both having outlived their consorts, were given titles and great wealth; and Nell Gwynne, at the death of her beloved Charles, became Queen Nell by acclamation of the English people.

Even the great Cleopatra was spared the asp's bite, was reunited with Antony, and was certainly never dragged through the streets in chains. It was not too clear why the asp did not bite—perhaps someone had drugged it or removed its fangs. But such details did not matter. All endings had to be happy, not tragic.

During Betsy's excursions into the world of wealth and power, the muddy streets of Providence dissolved into pavements inlaid with gold and jewels; the houses, drab or beautiful, became palaces, châteaux, and baronial manors; passers-by in the street were elaborately costumed courtiers and ladies in waiting. The sky was perpetually blue, it was always spring, and the air was perfumed with the falling petals of apple blossoms.

Although Betsy recognized her fantasies for what they were, she saw no reason why she could not someday become as renowned and famous as any of these women of history. But there were days when her fantasies deserted her, when the ugliness of her surroundings pressed in on her from all sides, when the sights, sounds, and smells of workaday Providence became so pervasive that her imagination became earthbound, incapable of flight.

At such times she gloomily wondered how—in a country that prided itself on the very absence of kings and nobles—she was going to be another Nell Gwynne. There was not even a theater where she could sell oranges. Theaters had been outlawed in Providence for many years, and oranges were so rare as to be almost unknown.

But eventually her natural optimism always took over. She would tell herself that even here, in these thirteen states pledged to the ideal of democracy and the common man, there was already an aristocracy. There were most certainly men of power, of wealth, and of accomplishment. She still remembered that celebration three years ago, when President Washington and his entourage had visited Providence. The socially prominent people of the town had been invited to the governor's great ball, while Sam Allen, a good citizen and respected man, had not received an invitation.

She determined that somehow, some way, she would become part of that world of privilege and wealth. Most certainly she would not become another Phebe—poor, hungry, and abused to the point where rum was her only refuge. She had watched her mother change from a pretty and desirable wench into a fat and sodden slattern, and all within a very few years. She found it hard to believe that she, too, would age, but she knew that it would happen and that there was no time to be wasted.

Meanwhile, there was Jacques—passionate, generous Jacques, who was her means of survival. He offered her affection, too, and in their three years together he had also, at her urging, taught her to speak a little French. In some of her daydreams she made plans to visit France, which for her was the very essence of romance. In spite of the fact that at the moment it was torn apart by revolution and that its king and queen had been guillotined that very year, Betsy felt sure that it would be only a matter of a few years before royalty would be restored and life in Versailles would go on as before. She intended to be part of that life, and she saw Jacques as a means of turning her dreams into realities, a step on her way up a ladder of gold.

But in that summer of 1793, when Betsy became eighteen, her dreams of glory were shattered, to be replaced by dreams of a new and different kind.

That summer Betsy fell in love.

During her promenades about town, alone or with Polly, she had met many young men. They were attractive and they had money to spend, and during the long summer evenings in Market Square, where they gathered, she allowed them to buy her sweetmeats or other refreshments. She would lead them on, and then just short of conquest, she would say good night, abruptly and firmly, leaving them feeling frustrated and cheated.

But with the unconquerable vanity of the rutting male, they always returned to the battle, confident that this time she would surely find them irresistible. But she never did. To Betsy, they were like friendly, amusing puppies. She enjoyed playing with them and teasing them, but when they became too rough, she cuffed them and sent them on their way.

Betsy found them curiously alike. They began with flattery, followed by attempts at love-making that became a familiar and monotonous ritual: the hand that wandered from arm to bosom to thigh; the mouth that moved from lips to ear to neck. It was as though they had all gone to the same school and learned their lessons by rote. Whether it was Ned or Tom or Ebenezer, they were the same.

Matthew Wyatt was different. Although Betsy had seen him about town from time to time and had watched him grow through adolescence to young manhood, she had not talked with him since that day so long ago when he had come to the Allen house at the time of Lydia's funeral.

He still seemed quiet by nature, holding himself aloof from the others. He did not join them in their running fire of crude jests followed by immoderate laughter. His pensive gray eyes, when they looked at her, were not hungry and bold in their appraisal of her face and figure. They were almost shy, moving away from her quickly, as though dazzled by too much light.

And yet he seemed neither frightened nor in awe of her. One evening when she calculatedly moved away from Polly and the others and stood looking out at the river, he came to her side quickly, as she had hoped he would. She had not realized until now how tall he had grown. He looked down at her silently, lowering his head toward her face as he began to speak.

"You're Betsy Bowen," he said. She nodded and he went on. "Your sister, Polly, lives with my family. I'm Matthew Wyatt." He spoke casually, but there was a tension in his voice that was anything but casual. The way he looked at her made her unexpectedly ill at ease.

"How is Polly?" she asked quickly, in an effort to be as diffident as he was.

"Polly is very well."

There was a pause, and then, as though forcing himself to keep talking, he said, "I remember you. Mr. Allen brought you to our house one Thanksgiving Day when you were a little girl. You were very ill-tempered."

She laughed, and he smiled back at her—that odd smile that seemed to light only one side of his face, while the other side remained serious.

"You were dressed in homespun," he said, "and you were jealous of Polly's pretty clothes."

She looked at him in surprise. " 'Tis true," she said. "How did you know that?"

"Your eyes looked at nothing but Polly's dress, not even at me."

"But I did look at you. That's why I was jealous. And I remember you that other time, when you came to the house to give a speech when Aunt Lydia died—and you got all mixed up."

They laughed at the memory and then fell suddenly silent again. Finally, Betsy said, "But that was six years ago. How be it that you remember a little girl you saw only twice?"

His eyes moved to hers now in a steady gaze, no longer shy and wavering. "She was the prettiest little girl I ever did see," he said.

She moved away from him and then looked back at him coquettishly over her shoulder. "And now?" she asked, raising her eyebrows in studied naïveté.

He did not respond to her flirtatiousness in the way she had expected. "What a daft question! You must know that you've grown to be a beautiful woman."

His directness and the serious tone of his voice unsettled her. She could think of nothing to say in reply. She found herself hoping that he would make an impulsive movement toward her, seize her hand, put his arm boldly around her waist, perhaps even try to kiss her. Then she would be able to put him off and deal with him as she did with her other suitors. But the silence continued, and she disliked this quickening of her heartbeat, this tremulous feeling that made the palms of her hands moist, this strange breathlessness and lack of poise.

"Will you go walking with me on Sunday afternoon?" he asked.

She wanted to say "Yes! Yes, I'll go walking with you now—why wait till Sunday?" But she remained silent, trying to regain her composure. At last she said, "I don't know. Your family would not like it. I'm—I'm—"

"I know what you are," he said. "You belong to a French sea captain."

The words, so flatly stated, angered her. "I belong to no one!" she said.

"Then you will? You'll go walking with me on Sunday?"

Her anger dissolved into laughter. "If you say so," she said with a smile.

"I'll be here in Market Square at three," he said. On impulse, he seized her hand, and bending over quickly, he brushed it with his lips. She thought he was making fun of her and she withdrew her hand in annoyance, but as he straightened and looked at her, she saw that his eyes were serious.

He left her quickly. There was a look of astonishment on her face as she watched his departing figure. No man had ever kissed her hand before. Indeed, no man had ever treated her as though she might possibly be a lady. And yet he knew not only who she was but what she was and had said so quite openly, without a smirk or concealed amusement.

As she turned to leave Market Square for home, she raised her head in a movement of pride. She felt warmed, as though a shaft of sunlight had singled her out, lighting her in a radiance that was exclusively her own. And her eyes were shining.

Sunday was a clear and beautiful June day. Though warm, a fresh spring breeze blew across the river from the west, gently moving the trees that were all bright and new-leaved. Later, as full summer took over, life would drowse under a sun that moved higher and higher in the sky, but now everything was awake and moving. Birds sang love songs, quarreled noisily, or chattered about nothing.

Betsy matched the day in spirit and appearance. She wore her newest and prettiest dress, carefully copied from an illustration in a New York newspaper that had arrived by packet only two weeks ago. The light-green silk had been a present from Jacques, the ruffles and ribbons had come from a shop in Cheapside, the amethyst necklace and brooch were mementos of her life with Sam Allen.

She had never been more radiant and vivacious, and the effect on Matt Wyatt was intoxicating. His habitual solemnity was lightened with bursts of gaiety that came upon him suddenly, as though taking him by surprise.

Later, she could not remember what they had talked about. Their conversation made little sense and swept them into gales of inexplicable laughter. It was as though they had discovered a secret language, a way of communication known only to themselves, and a mystery to all the other and less fortunate people in the world.

They walked the streets of Providence like a pair of young animals on a tour of exploration. They looked at the familiar houses as though they had never seen them before. They sniffed the air, looked at each other with admiring eyes, smiled, talked, and kept walking. They left South Water Street and then went along Towne Street and up the hill to Benefit Street. As they passed Transit Street, Matt stopped and looked at her challengingly.

"A shilling you don't know why they call it Transit Street," he said.

"I don't even know what transit means," said Betsy. "I don't go to the Rhode Island College like you do."

Matt scratched his sandy hair. "It's—well, it's a passage. Right here is where they set up a telescope and watched the transit of Venus—before I was born, it was."

"Who did?" asked Betsy.

"Joseph Brown, Stephen Hopkins, and Jabez Bowen. Maybe he was a relation to you."

"There are plenty of Bowens in Providence," said Betsy, "and very upstanding, too, but no kin of mine. My father was John Bowen, but that's not for sure. Anyway, he was a sailor who drownded off Newport. Mama says he was knocked overboard by the boom of his fishing sloop."

This unfunny fact sent them both into a new fit of laughter. Weak and wet-eyed with mirth, they moved on hand in hand. When Benefit Street came to an end and the sparsely settled marshes of East Providence stretched before them, Betsy took off her fashionably high-heeled shoes and tucked them under her arm.

They came to rest at last on a dry hillock, not far from the point where the widening Seekonk River poured itself into Providence Harbor. Here, in the waning light of the afternoon, they stretched out on the warm earth. Looking at the flawless blue of the sky above them, as though not daring to look at each other, they became curiously silent.

Matt rolled over on his belly and rested his chin on his hands. Quiet as a cat dozing in the sun, he watched her through half-closed eyes. She was aware of his prolonged scrutiny and of the fact that her heart was beating too fast. She closed her eyes against the brilliance of the sky and waited.

224

At last he reached out his hand and his long, slender fingers closed over hers with a steady pressure. She answered with a tightening of her own hand, and they did not stir for several moments. When he moved toward her, he was so quiet that she was scarcely aware of him until his head was close to hers. His lips were smiling, and she could see the tips of his very white teeth. She began trembling, but now she did not even try to control the feelings that surged inside her.

His kiss was not like any she had ever known. It was not hungry, not burning, not demanding. His lips met hers firmly and lingeringly, as though setting a seal of possession on her, inevitable and permanent. She felt strangely pliant and yielding. Always before, her response had been tense, a tightening within herself in anticipation of what she knew was going to follow. Sam Allen and Jacques had been rough and hurried in their love-making, but Matt was gentle, almost leisurely, as though their time together had no limitations.

Strangest of all, he talked to her, murmuring her name over and over again, as though he loved the very sound of it. His whispered endearments were simple words of love, the words that she had read in Jonathan's books but never had heard before. Feelings that she had not known she possessed welled up in her—most of all, a pervading tenderness, not unlike what she had once felt toward her dolls as a child. She took his head in her arms, cradling it against her breasts, and his mouth moved along her skin, moist and searching. His hands fumbled clumsily at her bodice, as though he were blind, and slowly his fingers drifted down toward the white globe of a breast, caressingly, lovingly.

She was scarcely aware of how they had left the confinement of clothing and found themselves meeting, skin to skin, bodies tight against each other, arms straining to bring each other closer. When she felt his hardness pressing between her thighs, it seemed only natural to welcome him, to enfold his flesh in hers, and to give herself up to him utterly.

As his lean, tanned body rose and fell above her, he was like a graceful rider, tempering his motion to that of the steed beneath him. An ecstasy began to flow through her, beginning with his rhythmic thrust and then moving up from her loins to her breasts, her arms, her very fingertips. An almost unbearable suspense seized her. It was as though she had started on a journey that must be completed or she would die. She found herself holding her breath in anticipation of she knew not what. And then, as his movements became faster, his thrusts harder and more savagely possessive, her head moved restlessly from side to side and she began to moan.

When his body went taut in a convulsive spasm of final pleasure, he grasped her buttocks and pulled them against him with all his strength. She screamed as the floodgates of her passion broke, as though a wild torrent coursed through her, smashing and over-turning everything in its path, leaving her shaken and weeping after it had passed.

They lay together, panting and exhausted, deeply happy. Matt raised his head, and his mouth touched hers again, tenderly now and gratefully but still with that quiet possessiveness. And she clung to him with a possessiveness of her own, wanting him never to leave her, but to stay as he was, enfolded by her, held forever close.

It was not until the next day that it occurred to Betsy that not once during their love-making had she thought of what her reward would be. What had happened with Matt bore no resemblance to what she had until now thought of as a game—and with Jacques as simply a means of survival.

She was puzzled and vaguely frightened. The prospect of sub-mitting to the panting and frequent lusts of Jacques was suddenly and unaccountably disgusting. It was not that she disliked him, merely that he had become physically repugnant, somehow alien and undesirable. He would be back in Providence within a fort-night, and she did not want to see him. But how, then, would she live?

It was to Polly that she went for advice. As she told the story, she found herself stumbling for words, and to Polly's delight, she even blushed.

"It's happened!" crowed Polly triumphantly. "You're in love, my lass, and you don't know it!"

"I know it, right enough," said Betsy. "It's like what I've read in your papa's books. But what am I going to do?"

"Do? Enjoy it—long as it lasts, anyway."

"But the Captain. What am I going to do about *him?*"

Polly seemed puzzled. "Ain't no need to do nothin' about him. He don't have to know about it, do he?"

"But you don't understand, Polly. I don't want to do it with him anymore."

"Lord, you *do* be love-bit! Or maybe you're just a-feared that Matt will find out about the Captain."

Betsy shrugged. "He already knows. It ain't that. It's me. I don't want Jacques to even touch me!"

"And how do you expect to buy your bread if you drop your Frenchie over the boatside?"

"That's what I'm asking *you*, Polly."

"This here Matt—his papa owns that big shipyard down the bay. He ain't no poor boy."

"I don't want money from him," said Betsy. "Anyway, he don't work yet. He's at the college getting educated."

"Damn his eddication! If he loves you like you love him, he'll go to work and set you up in style. Hook him, lovey, while the hookin's good!"

Betsy sighed. "I'm a-feared as I'm the one that's hooked, Polly."

As the time of Jacques' return to Providence moved closer and closer, Betsy grew anxious. She longed to ask Matt openly about what she should do, but the idea of talking with him about money disturbed her. He might well wonder about the sincerity of her love. But more disturbing was the thought of continuing to be Jacques' mistress.

Finally, one night as they lay together in a field, in the expansive moments that followed their love-making, she turned to him abruptly and said, "Matt, you must tell me what to do about Jacques."

"Who's Jacques?" he asked.

"My French captain," she said.

Matt, who had been lying on his back, idly chewing a blade of grass, sat up suddenly. "What about him?"

"He'll be back from the West Indies any day now."

Matt tried to keep jealousy out of his voice. "Do you want to see him then?" he asked as casually as he could.

"No. Not ever." She looked into his eyes seriously. "I love you, Matt, I want to be no other man's woman."

His arms went quickly around her, and he kissed her passionately, the pride of possession all at once in his lips.

"Then don't be any other man's woman. Be mine, Betsy."

She looked away from him in embarrassment. "But you don't understand, Matt. He gives me money. It's how I buy my food and clothing."

He got to his feet and looked down at her, almost as though he were angry. "I'll give you money."

"But I don't want money—not from you, Matt."

"Then where will you get it?"

"Maybe I could be a servant—a maid—"

He knelt before her, his eyes tender and faintly amused. "My Betsy a slavey? No, it wouldn't do."

His look of amusement annoyed her. "Why not?" she demanded.

"You're too—too beautiful. What woman with a live husband would take you into her house? Why, the minute the mistress was away, he'd be a-chasing you from room to room."

Matt laughed, but Betsy remained serious-eyed and thoughtful.

"But I'll make myself plain and be as prissy as can be."

"Oh, Betsy! You're as daft as a donkey in the full of the moon. How would you make yourself plain? Cut off that pretty snip of a nose, perhaps? Well, don't you dare—I love it!" He kissed her nose lightly and went on. "I've made a few plans of my own, my love. I'll go to work in my father's shipyard as soon as can be, and there'll be money enough for both of us to live great and high!"

"And your education—what about that?"

"I want no more of it," he said. "I'm twenty-one and a man. I want to work. It's my father's plan to turn me into a lawyer, but I hate studies. I would not like to spend my days on a judge's bench, settling petty quarrels and punishing the dull sins of others. So don't fret yourself about silver, Betsy darlin'. You've a new provider, and a lustier one than your Frenchy man of the sea!"

"That be for sure!" Betsy said gaily. "Oh, Matt, I do love you!"

He took her in his arms, and soon they were lying on the earth once more, sealing their new pact in a fresh burst of loving.

228

Henry Wyatt was a simple and virtuous man who had succeeded by following all the Puritan disciplines instilled in him by stern but loving parents. He rose at dawn, he worked hard, he avoided strong drink and temptations to sinfulness, and he went to bed early and slept soundly. He lacked both humor and imagination, but he prospered.

And yet it bothered him that he was not a gentleman born and that he had no education and was not acquainted with Latin and algebra. There had never been time for schooling, since he had begun working for a shipbuilder when he was still a boy, and by the time he was thirty-four he had a small shipyard of his own.

Now, at fifty-one, he owned a very large shipyard indeed. As the shipping trade in Providence expanded during the years that followed Revolution, he had invested his savings in the purchase of some wharves along Towne Street, and now, when China trade was opening up, Henry was on his way to becoming one of the richest men in Providence.

But he still knew nothing about Latin and algebra, and so he sent his three sons to school to acquire them. Matt and Dick were both full-time students in Rhode Island College, and Peter, only sixteen, would leave his private school in another year or so and join his brothers in the pursuit of higher education.

Although Henry's money made him far from unacceptable in the better homes of Providence, he was painfully aware that he was not descended from one of the old families that had settled there in the period when Roger Williams, banished from the Massachusetts Bay Colony under threat of deportation to England, had found sanctuary on the banks of the Moshassuck River and established a settlement that he named in gratitude for "God's providence to me in my distress."

Henry, who had been born in the straggling village of Cowesett, on East Greenwich Bay, had not even arrived in Providence until 1759, when he was seventeen. He was a Johnny-come-lately, but he intended to compensate for that unfortunately unchangeable circumstance. His wife, Ellen, had produced for him three sons— attractive, bright boys who were approaching a marriageable age— and he foresaw quite correctly that the daughters of the town's best families would hardly be averse to mating with the sons of a well-to-do Henry Wyatt.

Henry's plans for his sons had long been formulated, and he did not anticipate any change in them. And so, when Matt calmly announced to him that he wanted no more education and wished to go to work in the shipyard immediately, the family explosion that followed was only to be expected.

Ellen Wyatt was horrified that her first-born could so lightly abandon a chance to become what she called "a true gentleman," and Henry was not only horrified, he was furious. In opposing Matt's announced intentions, he was tenacious and stubborn, but so was Matt, and the two of them locked in a high-shouting struggle that almost ended in physical violence.

But there was a chink in Henry's armor, and Matt knew exactly what it was. He was aware that although his father had felt a lifelong uneasiness because of his lack of gentility, he was also inordinately proud of what he had achieved through his own efforts, without education and beholden to no one. He might be envious of an acquaintance with Latin, but in his heart, he despised it. This had become apparent to Matt as soon as he and his brothers advanced beyond their father in the education he was at such pains for them to acquire. He made fun of their square roots and equations and defended his own grammar hotly when they were so bold as to correct it.

And so, when the argument waxed hottest, Matt quietly turned to his father and asked, "Sir, what is the true worth of a man?"

Henry looked up, puzzled and frowning. "What are you talking about?"

"Work. I believe that a man's worth lies in what he can do with his bare hands. Education is all very well for those who need it in order to survive. But a real man survives by what he can do with his hands."

Henry looked at Matt in astonishment. "And what, may I ask, can *you* do with your hands?"

"Nothing. But I can learn. Like you, I want to build ships—later on, with some education, maybe design them. I have no taste for law. Are not a country's ships as important as its laws?"

Speechless, Henry sat down in a chair to prepare a reply. But feelings of pride had begun to stir in him. He had always been proud of his own very real accomplishments, but the fact that his eldest son not only respected his achievements but wished to emulate him had turned all his arguments into jelly. Education? Henry knew in his heart that he would not sell a single one of his ships for all the education in the world. He loved his ships for· what they were and for what they could do. Vicariously, he went through storms and typhoons with them, sailed into exotic harbors where they rode at anchor, rising and falling with the tide. Through his ships, Henry somehow possessed the world.

When, finally, Matt looked at him in a piercing way and said point-blank, "Don't you, sir, think that I already possess enough education to qualify as a gentleman?" Henry could think of nothing to say in answer to that somehow plaintive question. He bowed his head in a strangely happy defeat and nodded silently.

At last he said, "It may be true, Matthew. More education will not teach you to build ships, if that be truly your heart's desire."

"It is, Father," said Matt, and slightly perjuring himself, he added, "I swear it."

Immediately Henry became brisk and businesslike. "There'll be no fancy berth for you at the yard just because you be the owner's son. You understand that?"

"Yes, sir. I'll begin as you did. How else will I grow to understand the building of ships?"

The answer was, of course, exactly the right one, and Henry was pleased by it. He rose abruptly from his chair. "Very well, Matthew. You will present yourself to Joe Higgins tomorrow morning at seven."

Matt drew himself up in an attempt to be as businesslike as his father. "Yes, sir." He paused. "And Mama—she will not oppose this?"

"Let her oppose. I am master in this house. I make the decisions. Good day to you, Matthew."

Henry left the room quickly, and as soon as the door had closed behind him, Matt moved to the window. He looked down the hill toward the harbor.

Smiling his odd, one-sided smile, he said aloud to himself, "Well, my Betsy, you'll have fine food and clothes, and no Frenchy's silver will pay for it, either!"

CHAPTER 19

L'*étoile de Marseilles* docked in the Providence River two days later, and late in the afternoon Betsy went down to the wharf to look for Jacques. She found that he had already left the ship, and so she went to the Bulldog Tavern.

He was there, sitting alone at a table, drinking rum and obviously waiting for her. He rose quickly as soon as she entered and motioned her to join him.

When she reached the table, he seized her hand in his and drew her toward him. She gently pulled herself away from him and sat down in the chair opposite.

Jacques shrugged and then smiled. "You are not so happy to see me, I think. Maybe you are learning, *ma chérie*, to play coquette with your Jacques, *oui?*"

She shook her head and was silent. She had taken care to dress poorly, to make herself as unattractive as possible. Her hair was untidy, and her cheeks were pale and unrouged. She had planned the whole meeting in her imagination, and it had seemed easy. Now, sitting opposite this friendly bear of a man, with his affectionately amused blue eyes beaming on her so steadily, she found herself unable to begin the little speech she had prepared.

As she continued to say nothing, staring down at her hands, which clenched the side of the pine table in nervousness, he studied her with observant eyes.

"You have been sick?" he asked, with concern in his voice.

"No, Jacques. I—I—do not know how to tell you. I do not wish to make you unhappy."

He leaned toward her attentively. "You are maybe going to have a *bébé?*"

She shook her head, and then, with an effort of will, she blurted out, "Jacques—I will not see you anymore."

"You go away?"

"No. I—I have met someone—a young man."

Jacques looked at her in silence for a moment, and then he sighed. "Young. Yes. It was going to happen."

"Not just young, Jacques. I am in love with him."

Jacques seemed to ponder her words, and then he cleared his throat and smiled sadly. "*Je comprends, ma chérie.* You are what they call in love. You will marry him and be a woman *respectable?*"

"I don't know. He comes of a good family. He is rich. I am—" She shrugged.

Jacques nodded in sympathy. "And you have made love with him, and he will give you money to live?"

Betsy reached out her hand toward him impulsively. "Oh, Jacques, you have been so good to me, and now I make you *triste.*"

"*Oui,* I am *triste*—for me. But for you too."

"For me?"

"Yes, Your Jacques know the world is not kind to young girls like you, with much beauty but no money. This young man love you very much?"

"Oh, yes," said Betsy. "Why he stopped his schooling and went to work in his father's shipyard for me, Jacques, just for me!"

"And if he stops being in love with you and finds a girl rich like him, what will you do, *ma chérie?*"

She answered him vehemently, with a conviction born partly of fear. "But that won't happen, Jacques! It couldn't happen! He will never stop loving me. Never, never!"

"I hope not," said Jacques softly. "Perhaps he will love you *toujours* and will make marriage with you and you be very happy and rich."

She pressed his hand in gratitude. "Oh, thank you, Jacques. I will never forget you. You are a good friend."

He got up from the table abruptly. "*Oui,* I am good friend." Then, as though to distract himself, he rummaged in his pocket and brought forth a silver chain from which was suspended a shining piece of cut jade. "I bring this for you, a *petit cadeau*. You will take it, then give old Jacques a kiss of goodbye, *oui?*"

She rose and went over to him. She took the jewelry in her hand and held it up to the light admiringly. When she turned back to him, her eyes were moist. Then she kissed him lightly on the forehead. Without saying another word, she fled.

Jacques stood looking after her, his eyes tender and pensive. Heaving a long sigh, in which there was both weariness and resignation, he turned toward Nate, who stood behind the bar shining glasses and mugs in preparation for the evening's trade.

"*La jeunesse*," said Jacques. "Youth—how sad it is, so full of hope. *Quelquefois je suis content que je suis vieux.*"

Nate, who understood no French, nodded in agreement. But he did understand that Jacques wanted to get drunk, and so he took a bottle of rum from the shelf and moved it forward hospitably.

The days of the summer passed quickly. When the weather was fine, Betsy and Matt met during the hour after sunset on the hillock where they had first made love. It would have seemed almost sacrilegious to them to move their passion to the comfort of a bed. They liked the open sky and stars above them, the fresh smells of marsh grass and pines in the air.

But as the days of late summer gave way to the crisp nights of fall, the chill in the air reminded them that winter was not far off and that soon they would need a room, a bed, and the warmth of a fire. In their summery dream of love, they had been so preoccupied with each other that the prosaic realities of life had scarcely existed.

Matt worked, and he worked hard, to his father's great satisfaction, but his thoughts were never very far from Betsy and the prospect of an evening alone with her. As for Betsy, the hours of her day were spent in making herself as alluring as possible. Every morning she washed her clothes in the icy waters of the stream that wandered through the meadow that lay just beyond Jonathan Clarke's hut, and it was there, on sunny days, that she bathed. Afterward, shivering and gasping for breath, she would lie naked in the long grass, letting the sunlight dry her hair and warm the fair skin of her body, rosy from the cold of the water. Lying outstretched, she would dream idly of Matt, feeling in imagination the hard slimness of his taut young body pressed against her, his hands stroking her breasts lightly and tenderly, the moistness of his mouth closing over her nipples. But most of all, she would feel his slow, rolling motion within her, so unlike the hasty, impatient jabbing of Sam and Jacques. It was rhythmic and insistent, a movement undulating from his legs to the very center of him and controlled somehow gracefully by the muscles of his buttocks.

But her love for him did not begin and end with the pleasure he gave her during love-making. She loved everything about him: his quick intelligence, his sense of the ridiculous and the way he laughed, and most especially the odd, one-sided smile that he had had even as a young boy.

His gray eyes still had their pensive, faraway look, which seemed to have deepened now that he had reached manhood. She loved the look, but sometimes its elusiveness would upset her. She would have the feeling that he had suddenly left her alone, and she wanted to say, "Where have you gone? Come back to me." But instead, she would say only, "What were you thinking about, Matt?" Then his eyes would meet hers, and the answer was always the same. "Why, nothing," he would say. "Just daydreaming, I guess."

She knew that her need to share his every thought was possessive and foolish, but she also understood the reason for it. Her relationships with men seemed to her until now as having been somehow superficial. There was the love-making and the material reward for playing what she had childishly called "the game." There was friendliness, the fun of eating good food together, but always her feeling that, regardless of her mood, she must be entertaining and calculatedly amusing for the benefit of an audience.

With Matt, all of these things had become unimportant. Love-making was no game now. It was real. For the first time with a man she felt that she could be truly herself and still be accepted. And with Matt she always was, even when she was irritable or even unfriendly, especially during those times when she endured the discomfort of her monthly flux. At such times, Matt was as sympathetic as Polly might have been, and he was always solicitous and protective toward her, as though he might be the father she had never had.

Almost without knowing it, she had developed a deep and abiding respect for him, as though he might be some kind of god in human form. Often, this made her feel unworthy of him, especially because he had education and good breeding, both of which she lacked.

She was woman enough to know that she must keep herself as beautiful and alluring as possible, but she was convinced that this was not enough to hold him to her. And the thought of losing him filled her with fear. Now that she had found him, she could not imagine living without him.

She was well aware that she was intelligent, but she was also aware that her intelligence needed cultivation. And so, every afternoon, she sought out Jonathan Clarke. She told him bluntly that she wanted instruction in grammar and correct speech. Although Jonathan was slightly surprised by the earnestness of her request, he enjoyed the role of teacher, and so he was both pleased and flattered. Sometimes he even postponed the pleasures of the bottle until later in the day so that he could be reasonably alert.

Although Jonathan hardly spoke with the accents of a gentleman and had long ago abandoned grammatical rules for the colloquial and slipshod talk of everyday, he still knew the difference between correct speech and the vulgar jargon used by the people around him. He taught Betsy to pronounce the final "g" sound on her "ings," to avoid "ain't" except as a substitute for "am not," and he explained the popular confusion between past tenses of verbs and their past participles. Above all, he urged her to drop the time-honored but indecent monosyllables that had served the English tongue so long and dishonorably.

When Betsy protested that an arse was an arse and what else could you call it, he presented her grandly with the word "posterior." In place of her other Anglo-Saxon four-letter words, she learned to say "the male part," "excrement," and "intercourse." As usual, Betsy was an apt pupil, and with her mind constantly on the watch for her double negatives and other grammatical lapses, her speech did, in fact, improve. She began also to imitate the more cultured accent of Matt himself, who often rocked in merriment at the small elegances that began to creep into her speech.

One night when, exhausted by two wild sessions of love-making, he leaned toward her and moved himself sensually against her thigh with the obvious promise that a third session was not far off, she turned to him in concern and said, "Oh, no, Matt. You will overdo yourself. Your male part is tired."

"My what?" he asked, laughing.

"Your male part," she repeated with prim dignity.

He collapsed over her, half in laughter, half in renewed desire, and said, "My male part is shipshape and ready to sail. Feel it, love. It's as stiff and stout as would skewer any maid and lift her a foot off the ground!"

She wondered how he, a young man of education and good family background, could speak so coarsely, but about the abilities of his "male part" she had no questions. His boasts were not idle.

And yet, even Matt's ardor cooled in the increasingly frosty air of autumn. One night, as they walked, shivering and chilled, back toward town, he said between chattering teeth, " 'Tis no time to be making love in the fields anymore. We must find a room for the winter that's coming."

Betsy nodded and smiled. "Your male part might get the frost-bite," she observed seriously.

"That it might," he said, his arm circling her waist and hugging her to him. "Where could we get lodgings?"

Betsy pondered. She knew that Jonathan's hut was out of the question. There would be little privacy there, and anyway, she did not want Matt to see the squalor of her circumstances. She knew that the sight of the inside of that ramshackle hut, primitive, dirty, and perennially untidy, would shock him. More than that, it would make all too clear the wide social gulf that lay between them. Betsy was already aware of that gulf, and in her more thoughtful moments, it worried her. She wanted to become Matt's wife, but she did not see how this could happen—at least, not yet.

She answered his question about lodgings by saying, "We could engage a room at an inn or tavern, Matt. One that would not be too dear for you."

"At an inn? With every man jack in the place noising it around that Matt Wyatt was keeping his doxy upstairs?"

Betsy regarded him coolly. "I am not your doxy, Matt."

The word had slipped out without his knowing it, and he hastily apologized. "Forgive me. You know I'd not call you that, but it's the word the gossips would use. And use it they would, and when my father got wind of it—"

"What if he did?" asked Betsy.

He kicked a stone out of his path irritably. " 'Twould be the devil to pay. I can't afford an offense to the old man and to my mother."

"Am I an offense, then?"

"Oh, Betsy, use the wits God gave you!" he said impatiently. "My father is a rich man. Someday I will own a good share of his shipyards and wharves."

"And where shall I be then, Matt?" she asked in as casual a tone as she could manage.

He looked away, and after a pause, he said, "With me." His voice had gone strangely soft, but his tone did not carry conviction.

They walked the rest of the way in silence, and when they parted, his kiss seemed falsely reassuring, and her lips did not answer the pressure of his with their usual yielding.

After Betsy got back to the hut that night, she found it hard to get to sleep. The conversation with Matt about his father had deeply disturbed her. The word "doxy" had slipped out before Matt was even aware of it, and although he had apologized, she feared that this was really the way he thought of her. And then they had walked the rest of the way in a kind of silence that had never come between them before.

It was not the question of marriage that was her greatest concern. Always, it was the thought of not seeing him, of losing him, that made her fearful. But for the first time now, she began to think that perhaps he was beginning to look upon her as a possession bought and paid for, and one that could be dispensed with if his interest should wane.

And so, for the next two nights, although the weather was fair and not too cool, she did not appear at the usual time and place of their meeting. She did not need Polly's counsel to tell her that it was time to remind Matt that her love could not be taken for granted.

But she did seek Polly's advice about lodgings for the winter. Polly looked at Betsy's predicament with a kindly but slightly cynical eye. Although she had not been asked for advice on Betsy's probable future, she gave it anyway.

"Just remember," she said, "that you're his doxy and not his fiancée."

"But I love him," said Betsy.

"Then the more fool you. He'll not marry you, if that's what you be dreamin' of."

"Why shouldn't he?"

"Because they don't. Do you expect your Matt will be throwin' away a chance at a fortune to marry with a baggage he found on the streets?"

"I'm not a baggage, and he don't—doesn't think of me as a baggage either!"

"Oh, you're a fine lady, I suppose, from an old family with money and a house on the hill! Leave off your dreamin', Betsy. You'll only get hurt."

"I'm not dreaming. I can wait a bit, if I have to. Meanwhile, we must have a room to go to."

"Well, an inn ain't good, and no respectable house would give you a room where you could be private. That leaves Sally Marshall's."

"Sally Marshall's! But Sally runs a whorehouse, that is—a house of ill fame!"

" 'Tis a whorehouse, right enough, and never mind the fancy words that Papa's been teachin' you. But Sally lives alone in the little house next door. There's a room she had built onto the back of it. Mayhap she'd let it to you and your fine gentleman."

Polly was well acquainted with Sally Marshall, inasmuch as she had become one of that enterprising businesswoman's more successful protégées. Although Polly thought of the hut on the Old Warren Road as home, her place of business was a sparsely furnished upstairs room on Olney Lane. Part of her earnings went to Sally in return for a place to take her paying customers. It was a room with a battered bed and an equally battered washstand on which stood a cracked earthenware pitcher and washbowl.

Sally's career had been that of the traditional madam. When she had been young and reasonably pretty, she had been a whore herself, but unlike most of her professional sisters, who lived in the

240

moment, she recognized from the start that a time would come when she would no longer be in demand. Like that other prosperous citizen, Henry Wyatt, she had observed some of the cardinal virtues that lead to success. She did not put her trust in luck. She saved her money and she avoided strong drink. Though she worked late hours and could not go to bed as early as Henry, she was up betimes, planning and scheming for the future.

By the time she was forty, she was able to buy a house of her own and rent rooms to the town's better class of prostitutes. Four years later, she decided to retire and purchased the small house that adjoined her now established house of pleasure on Olney Lane. Furnishing it comfortably, she moved in. She acquired a dog, two cats, and an air of respectability. With that combination of acuteness and lack of sentiment that is indispensable to what is called "business sense," she chose girls who were young, attractive, and willing to work hard. And if because of an addiction to drink, a loss of charm, or through sheer laziness, they failed to turn over a good profit, they were sent back to the street to make their living as best they could.

Sally had been careful to make friends with those who could protect her: the overseers of public morality and guardians of the law. They were given alcoholic refreshment and feminine companionship when they wanted it, and in return they turned a blind eye to her illegal business activities. Sally kept a disorderly house that was, in fact, as orderly as she could make it. Customers who were too drunk or potentially quarrelsome were refused admittance by Cato, a giant of a young Negro who was more popularly known as Black Tom. Naked to the waist, muscles flexed and shining, all six feet five of him stood guard at the door. Like all Negroes in Providence, he was a freed slave, and in return for his services, he was given food, a place to sleep, eight shillings a week, and an occasional night of love with Sally herself, who liked his manliness, his doglike and tender devotion—and his size.

When Polly presented Betsy for Sally's inspection, Sally gave her a long stare of appraisal, then said she would be happy to take Betsy in as one of her girls.

"But she ain't for the house," Polly explained. "She has a fine steady gentleman of her own."

241

"Then what she want to be doin' here?" asked Sally.

"They need a room for love-makin'," said Polly. "It be cold out in the fields now. That room of yours out back—"

"But that's in *my* house!" said Sally with indignation. "I aim to keep it respectable!"

Polly assumed a lofty air. "And is not a son of Henry Wyatt a respectable enough lodger for you?"

Sally's sharp little eyes came to attention. "A son of Henry Wyatt?" She breathed the name reverently as well as questioningly, and then looked at Betsy with new interest. "Well, missy, you've caught a fine fish, ain't you? And you hopes, no doubt, to be married with the young gentleman?"

"Yes," said Betsy with assurance.

Sally's cackle of high-pitched laughter jangled through the room. "I won't hold me breath waitin' for the weddin' day, pretty though you be. How much will your bully-boy pay?"

Betsy became suddenly wary. She was prepared to bargain and even haggle, if necessary. "Mr. Wyatt will pay what the room is worth, ma'am. He works in his father's shipyard as a laborer, and he cannot afford lodgings too steep in price."

Sally looked at her prospective tenant with a new respect. "Well, now—we're as pinchpenny as a real lady, even if we ain't one."

"Would you wish to show me the room, ma'am?" asked Betsy. "But mayhap you do not wish to let it."

Sally looked at her acutely. "Are you clean and tidy in your habits?"

At this point, Polly rejoined the conversation with a recommendation of her own. "As tidy as a wren in its nest, she is. I been living with her at me father's, and I'll swear to it, that I will. And she don't git noisy and drunken and keep folks awake, neither."

Sally fixed Betsy with a candid eye. "And do you make love quiet, too? I'll have no screamin' and moanin' and bangin' of the bed in the middle of the night, hear?"

Betsy avoided an answer to this vulgar question. "Mr. Wyatt," she said quietly, "will not stop overnight, ma'am. He lives to home with his family on Angell Street."

Sally, finally satisfied that Betsy and her lover might not interfere with the running of a proper household, led the way through the house to the room that she had added at the rear. At the moment, it seemed to be used as a storeroom, for it was crammed full of assorted pieces of abandoned furniture and tattered bedding, in which several families of field mice had set up living quarters. One skittered for cover as Sally approached, and Polly screamed.

Sally said, "I'll put the cat in here tonight and there'll not be a mouse by morning."

The room was comfortably large, with a fieldstone fireplace and chimney at the end. Windows in opposite walls looked out on overgrown, unweeded flower gardens that had already been mostly blackened by heavy frost. Betsy was pleased by the room, but she masked her enthusiasm so that the price would not rise beyond Matt's limited means.

"It will do," she said brusquely. "Shall I send Mr. Wyatt to make terms with you?"

Sally nodded, as though the matter were settled. "Now, about furnishings, missy, there be plenty here to choose from. What will you be needin' aside from a double bed with a strong frame?"

She leered suggestively at Betsy and winked, and Betsy could not repress a smile. The effect on Sally was immediate. The cackling laugh split the air again, and she swatted Betsy playfully on the rear by way of sealing their bargain.

"You ain't such a lady as you looks, me girl. You quiet ones is always the kind what keeps the boys rocky in the groin."

Betsy, feeling that the limits of intimacy had been reached, became once again serious and unsmiling. "If an agreement is arrived at, Miss Marshall, when will the room be in readiness?"

Sally quickly assumed the air of a dignified landlady. "Methinks," she said in an attempt to match Betsy in elegance, "that you might take up residence by the end of the week."

At the end of the week, Betsy moved in. She had instructed Matt in the ways of bargaining, and he and Sally had finally settled on a price that did not put too much strain on his meager earnings in the shipyard.

Phebe was wild with joy at the good turn her daughter's fortune had taken. On the day of the move, she loaded her handcart with

Betsy's wardrobe, and together they journeyed from the hut on the Old Warren Road to the comparatively genteel surroundings of Olney Lane.

Fortified by several swigs from a bottle of rum that Betsy had given her, Phebe exuberantly began to outline her plans to leave Providence and seek a better life back in Massachusetts, which she considered her "only true home."

"But, Mama," Betsy pointed out, "things were never good for you in Taunton either."

"Mebbe not," Phebe admitted. "But Providence ain't me home, and the constable is always a-houndin' us, nippin' at our heels like a sheep dog. So we'll be leavin' before they calls us before the Town Council again and threatens us with gaol."

Betsy gathered that this might already have happened, for Jonathan, drunker than usual, had been absent for two days. In all probability, he was at this moment sobering up in a cell at the gaol.

"And so you see," Phebe concluded, " 'tis a stroke of fortune that the good Lord has seed fit to give you a new home and sent such a fine rich young gentleman to take you under his wing."

Betsy listened while her mother conjured up rosy dreams for the future. Phebe was sure that a change of scene would have a near miraculous effect on Jonathan. Free of the bloodhounds of the law, he would stop drinking, settle down to his trade, and become a good provider. She herself would drink but sparingly and become a proper housewife, and when she came to visit Betsy in the spring, Betsy would no longer need to be ashamed of her.

"But I am not ashamed of you, Mama," said Betsy and gave her mother a reassuring hug. "Though your wits may often be addled by spirits, your heart has always been warm. 'Tis what counts the most."

As Phebe's view of the future grew even more iridescent, a sadness began to settle on Betsy, for she saw no hope that her mother's life might change for the better but would, in all probability, become even worse. But she nodded smilingly and said nothing to dampen Phebe's enthusiasm. There seemed little point in reminding her mother of a reality that she had long ago refused to recognize.

"And Polly?" Betsy asked. "Will she go with you?"

"Oh, no. She does mighty well at Sally Marshall's and she finds Providence to her taste." Phebe paused, considering Polly. "She's a good girl and a dutiful daughter to Jonathan. And she works hard. Why, sometimes she has five and six men of a night and is up to all hours! And I believe she is a good friend to you, my daughter."

"That she is," said Betsy.

Phebe sighed and sentimental tears filled her bloodshot eyes. "When I am far away, 'twill make me easier in the mind to know that Polly is here watchin' over you and takin' your poor mother's place."

Emotion overcame her entirely, and she stopped in the middle of the road, sobbing loudly and wiping her eyes with her grimy apron. Betsy set down the cart and took her in her arms, kissing her bloated face, so prematurely seamed and old. She whispered encouraging words that expressed a cheerfulness she did not feel.

When at last Betsy's belongings were unloaded and it was time for Phebe to return to the hut, there was another scene, this time of farewell, and therefore, even more tearful. At last, with the aid of several more swigs from the rum bottle, Phebe picked up the handles of her rickety cart and set off for home.

It was a picture that would stay in Betsy's memory for a lifetime: the stocky but somehow frail figure, staggering and lurching down the road, stopping again and again to wave frenzied goodbyes, until she turned the corner and was lost to sight.

Betsy knew, somehow, that she would never see her mother again.

CHAPTER 20

THE room in Sally Marshall's house was the first real home that Betsy had ever known. It was hers, and hers alone. Although Matt might be paying for it, and it was in Sally's house, it was still Betsy's domain. Spurred by this new and delicious feeling of possession, she went into a fever of activity, making curtains for the windows and a coverlet and canopy for the four-poster bed. She swept, cleaned, and scrubbed with brushes and brooms borrowed from Sally, who also lent her an assortment of old cooking pots and pans.

From a corner of the garden she rescued a plant of red button chrysanthemums that had somehow escaped the frost, potted it, and placed it in a sunny window. The fact that she had saved it from the cold of winter gave her a feeling of pleasure, and she watched its growth like an overfond mother.

Matt made fun of her and called her a proper little housewife, but he was pleased just the same. He looked forward to going there in the evening, after the cold formality of dinner with his family. He would find Betsy curled like a kitten in a threadbare wing chair that faced the bright warmth of the fire. His shoes came off, then his coat, and soon they were sprawled on the hearthrug, making love as enthusiastically as though they had just met. When the fire died down, he would lift her in his arms and carry her to the bed, and there they would stay until the night watchman's bell told him it was time to get home before the Wyatt front door was latched for the night.

Henry objected to his son's late hours and sometimes lectured him on the importance of living a more regular life. Matt would agree with him, but he did not change his ways. Henry finally gave up, comforting himself with the thought that at least his eldest son was not addicted to strong drink and that he had not once been late for work at the yard.

During the Christmas holidays, Matt's social life interrupted the frequency of his visits to Betsy. It was a season of parties and balls among the people who lived on the hill, and Matt was popular, especially with the families that had marriageable daughters. During Matt's absences, Betsy was lonely, and she began to be jealous, too, questioning him closely about the young ladies he met. She wanted to know their names, what they wore, how well they danced, but most of all, how pretty or plain they were.

Matt tried to evade these cross-examinations by assuring her that the girls he met did not compare with her, that he was bored by social functions and attended them only to please his parents.

But Betsy was not easily reassured, and she was envious as well as jealous. It infuriated her that but for the accident of birth, she might be one of these socially acceptable girls, dressed expensively and beautifully in clothes made by the best dressmakers in town, her hair curled and trimmed in the latest fashion by a professional hairdresser, her feet trained to dance by a French dancing master. It seemed unjust that she had to make her own dresses, curl her hair as best she could with a pair of primitive tongs, and did not know any dance except an Irish country jig that her mother had taught her long ago.

On these lonely evenings, when Matt was away at a fancy ball on the hill, Polly's words would echo in her ears. . . . *"You're his doxy and not his fiancée. . . . Do you expect your Matt will be throwin' away a chance at a fortune to marry with a baggage he found on the streets? . . . Leave off your dreamin', Betsy. You'll only get hurt."*

Once, after three nights had gone by without a visit from Matt, she was certain that he had found a girl that pleased him, that he had become engaged, and that she would be abandoned. When he finally did appear, she greeted him without warmth. He sensed what the trouble was and went to great lengths to apologize for his neglect, explaining that at many parties, supper was not served until eleven and the guests did not leave until three in the morning.

Betsy listened quietly, studying his face as though to find the truth there, and she remained aloof and cold. Matt abandoned words as a means of reassurance. Over her protests, he kissed her and fondled her and murmured endearments in her ear. He placed her hand on his hard bulge and said, "And does that look like I've been making merry with the girls on the hill?"

Betsy drew her hand away abruptly as she felt sudden desire for him. "Oh, the girls on the hill be too smart to let a man take liberties before the marriage vows are said. And anyway, you'd always be ready for more love, even if you were fresh out of another hussy's bed."

He threw her a mocking smile. "Is it my fault I was born hot-blooded?"

She felt herself warming toward him and strove to maintain her calm. "Born hot-blooded, indeed! 'Twas years of experience in upending every jade in town that made you a stallion!"

"There you're wrong, my lass," he said.

"If that be so, then how did you learn so well how to pleasure a woman, Matt Wyatt?"

He reflected a moment and said, "From my aunt."

Betsy was shocked. "Your *aunt?* You f—, I mean you bedded with your aunt?"

"Yes. My Aunt Deborah. She taught me how to do it."

"And I suppose," said Betsy, "that she's still teaching you."

"Oh, no. She's not in Providence anymore. They sent her off. There were some as said she was a witch and possessed of the Devil, and others believed her to be mad. But there was nothing wrong with Aunt Debbie except that she had a hearty appetite for loving."

"What happened to her?"

"My father sent her to Boston to be shut up in a madhouse. On the way there, she was taken with the plague and died." He paused, and when he spoke again, his voice had softened. "I was sorry. She was pretty and she loved me. But maybe it was better that the plague took her off than that she should be put away with mad folk and die slowly."

The sadness in his voice moved Betsy, and the old feeling of warmth toward him flowed in her. In sympathy, she reached out her hand for his. Quietly, then, he took her in his arms, and now she did not resist him. He smiled at her gratefully, like a small boy who has been forgiven and accepted back into his mother's good graces.

He stayed later than usual that night, long after the watchman's bell had sounded. He made love to her again and again, as though to prove that there was no one else in the world he could ever care for. As for Betsy, the warning voice of her reason dissolved in the flood of giving that engulfed her.

CHAPTER 21

B Y the end of February Betsy could no longer ignore something that she had suspected for several weeks. She was
pregnant. At first she had made herself believe that the extremely cold weather was responsible for the fact that she had
missed her regular flux. She had escaped for so long what other
girls regarded as a penalty for their sins that she had come to
believe that it was not possible for her to conceive. Even now, when
there seemed little doubt of it, the idea was unreal. She had thought,
the way most people think about death as something that happened
to other people, that pregnancy was an impossibility for her.

She delayed telling Matt as long as she could. In her plan for
eventual marriage to him, she had played for time, and now, without warning, time had run out. The question would be out in the
open now, and she was afraid of the answer. Although she had no
doubts about his love for her, she was not at all sure that he loved
her enough to break with his family and marry her.

She considered going to a midwife and ridding herself of the
problem. Many girls did, enduring the agony of knitting needles
and sticks of slippery elm stuck into them, and the miscarriage that
followed. Sometimes they died. The idea filled her with horror.
She did not want to die.

And yet, an abortion would postpone that moment of decision
when Matt would either make her his wife or tell her that
marriage was out of the question.

Finally, she consulted Polly, who, with her usual forthrightness,
cut through Betsy's daydreams and faced her with the unpleasant
truth.

"Time?" she asked. "What d'you want time for? Will he love
you any more in a year than he does right now? Rid yourself of

the thing, if you've a mind to, but it won't bring you any nearer to weddin' vows with your bully-boy. If he won't marry you now, he never will!"

Betsy had no counterarguments to oppose Polly's hard sense of reality, remembering Matt's neglect of her during the holidays. Though he was a long way from being tired of her, she knew that she had become taken for granted. As Polly pointed out, a year from now she would have become even more clearly a possession that could be replaced without too much difficulty. She was well aware that the rapture of their early days together had not so much cooled as it had become habitual. The excitement of strangeness and discovery had given way to a placid, if comfortable, familiarity.

And so, that night she told him. He looked at her in disbelief. Like her, he found the idea unreal and even impossible. He tried desperately to put the whole thing down to a mathematical miscalculation on Betsy's part, to a passing indisposition, to the weather, to anything, in short, except the inescapable fact that they had conceived a child.

Betsy tried to be as realistic as Polly. She said there was no possibility of a mistake. She was indeed with child, and in less than nine months he would be a father and that was that.

He looked at her in distress. "But what will you do?" he asked.

"I will have the baby, unless I find a midwife to rid me of it by poking things up inside me," Betsy said in as factual a manner as she could.

"But that's dangerous!" cried Matt. "You might die!"

Betsy nodded solemnly. Matt sat down in the wing chair, his brow furrowed in thought. She went over to him, sitting on the floor at his feet. Circling his legs with her arms, she rested her head on his knee. She stared pensively into the fire and said nothing. Soon she felt his hand stroking her head gently. She looked up at him then and saw that his eyes were contemplating her with a studious seriousness. He had never looked at her in quite that way before, and a glow of hope stirred in her. When he spoke, his voice was gentle.

"I'll not have you risking your life, Betsy. I want no butchering midwife to tear at your body. If you must have the baby, why then you must have it. It's mine and I will care for it."

His words, so reassuring and unexpectedly mature, made her feel strong and certain of herself. She looked at him directly, her eyes serious.

"And me, Matt? Am I yours too, then?" she asked.

"You have always been mine," he said. He lifted her up and took her in his arms.

"But I'm not yours to the world's way of thinking," she said.

She felt his arms grow tense as he said, "Never mind the world, with its laws of marriage and respectability. The world can go to blazes for all of me!"

She waited, like a gambler in the final moment of play before he lays down a last card. "And the child?" she asked. "The world will say it has no name. It will be Betsy Bowen's bastard from now to kingdom come."

She turned her head away. She knew that this was the moment for tears, but she had none. Desperately, she conjured up a vision of this poor, unwanted child, reviled in the streets by its playmates, shunned and unhappy. And then she thought of her own miserable childhood, and soon her eyes brimmed with tears that were both real and spontaneous.

Matt had never seen her cry, and the sight moved him. "Oh, Betsy, don't cry. We'll do something. You know how my family would oppose a marriage, no matter how much I wished it. They would cast me out with never a penny. There'd be no living in this town for us, and well you know it."

Betsy nodded. Then, with a lift of her head, she said, "We could always go somewheres else."

Matt stared at her in astonishment. For him, such an idea was unthinkable. His hand stopped stroking her head and he stared unseeingly into the fire.

As the weeks went by, Betsy's hopes that Matt indeed might marry her began to dissipate. Although he talked bravely and encouragingly, he did nothing. No plans for a wedding were discussed. He did not even tell his family of the situation. The only thing he was at all definite about was his insistence that she not go to a midwife.

Their love-making took on a subdued quality. It was as though they had both become suddenly aware of the life that was forming itself in her body, and they could not abandon themselves to passion as recklessly as before.

Sometimes Betsy would catch him staring at her naked belly in a curious, frowning way and she would say with a smile, "Oh, Matt, you can't see it, not yet, anyway."

But Matt did not smile. He looked away, embarrassed that she had observed him, and said nothing.

Gradually, the laughter that had been one of the surest bonds of their intimacy began to disappear. They became almost solemn in each other's company, and the silences between them became more frequent and more prolonged. It was as though they had become empty of things to say to each other, like friends who have not seen each other for many years grope for words when they meet.

Matt's visits were as regular as usual, but he left her earlier, with excuses that he was tired or had a headache or had to rise earlier than usual the next day. As time went on, he did not even apologize for his precipitate departures, but after a rather perfunctory farewell, he merely left.

The whole climate of their relationship had changed, and in this cool atmosphere Betsy felt lost and frightened, uncertain of what to say or do. In her anxiety to take some kind of action, she began to urge him to tell his father about their situation so that at least they could know exactly where they stood and make plans.

One night Matt exploded in a fit of temper. "Know where we stand? I *know* where we stand! I know what he'd say, if you don't!"

"But, Matt, you could at least tell him—"

"Tell him that he's going to be a grandfather to a bastard?"

To Betsy, the word seemed to strike at the defenseless bit of life that was growing within her, and she reacted with a quick, protective anger of her own. "He won't have to be a bastard if you'll marry me!"

"Oh, my father would *like* that, he would, with his plans for me to marry into a fine family on the hill! And so I bring home a wife who was fathered by a common sailor on a town whore!"

Betsy struck him hard across the face. "You'll not talk that way about my mother, you son of a bitch!"

Matt stared at her in disbelief, his hand moving to his stinging cheek. He had never seen her so angry, nor so beautiful. Her eyes, alive and shining in fury, blazed into his.

In an inexplicable rush of passion, he seized her in his arms and kissed her full on the mouth. She struggled against him briefly and then went limp, suddenly in tears.

He held her close, her head against his chest, his hand smoothing her hair in a gesture of tenderness. "Betsy, my Betsy, my love," he murmured, and then, "I'm sorry, but you don't understand—"

"But I do understand," she said. She reached her hand up to his cheek and stroked the reddening welt where her hand had struck him. "Oh, Matt," she began, but he silenced her with a kiss. She felt his body straining against hers as he bent her backward toward the bed.

They gave themselves over to love-making with an abandon they had not known for weeks, as though they had met again, as strangers. He tore at her clothing with frenzied fingers, impatient to possess her. Her heart beat wildly as she lay unresisting in his arms.

And then, at the moment when he was forcing himself into her, she went suddenly cold. A strange calm flowed through her. She felt that it might as well be Sam Allen or Jacques whom she was holding between her thighs. The tremors of pleasure stopped abruptly. It was time to play the game.

"Oh, Matt," she breathed softly, "I do love you."

His only answer was a renewed thrust. But she did not respond to it, and he paused, looking questioningly into her eyes.

"Matt," she said, "you will promise to see your father?"

"Yes, love," he murmured. He moved on her again, but she still resisted his rhythm.

"Tomorrow?" she asked plaintively.

"Yes, love. Tomorrow."

At once, in a loving motion of welcome, she arched herself up to meet him. She clenched his hard buttocks in her hands and pulled him toward her fiercely. Then she gave herself to him completely with a soft moan of pleasure.

CHAPTER 22

THE waning light of the March afternoon slanted through the blinds in Henry Wyatt's upstairs sitting room. Sunlight fell in golden slabs across the waxed pine boards of the floor, and a light breeze fluttered the white Chinese silk curtains of the window.

Henry sat before his handsome Goddard mahogany desk and looked idly at the papers before him: his wife's scatterbrained accounting of the monthly household expenses. He had no patience with people who could not do simple addition, and Ellen's squiggles for figures were almost undecipherable.

The unseasonable warmth of the day made him sleepy. His eyelids began to droop, and drowsily he fought off sleep with the delicious foreknowledge that he would eventually give in to it. A knock at the door interrupted him. It was not loud, but it was insistent, and he knew he would have to answer it. Stirring himself, he muttered a mild oath.

The voice on the other side of the door said, "It's Matthew, Father. May I come in?"

Henry sighed and tried to look alert. "Come in, Matthew, if it's important."

The door opened, and Matt stood there hesitantly, as though waiting for a further invitation. "It is important, sir," he said tensely. "I may say, it is *very* important."

Henry motioned him to a chair near the desk. "Well, be quick about it. I'd like a nap before dinner."

Matt sat down uneasily in the chair and looked nervously at his father. He was silent, not knowing how to begin.

"Well, what is it, son?"

"Father, I have done a bad thing. I have sinned. I am guilty of

255

wrongdoing, and I pray for your forgiveness." He came to an embarrassed halt.

Henry drummed his fingers impatiently on the desk. "Well, out with it, man! What have you done?"

Matt gulped, then plunged. "I have gotten a woman with child!"

Henry had anticipated many things: a botched job at the ship-yard, a fight with a foreman, even the pilfering of some petty cash. But if Matt had announced that he had just murdered his foreman, Henry could not have been more jolted than he was at the news that his son had proved his manhood in the most decisive and inconvenient way possible.

Henry paused for breath, and then said, rather unnecessarily, "You have lain with a woman?"

"Yes, Father."

That Matt should already have done something that Henry himself had not accomplished until safely married at twenty-five seemed somehow unthinkable. And so he asked, again quite unnecessarily, "But how could you?"

Matt blushed. "In the—the usual way, Father."

"I do not stand in need of instruction in the begetting of children!" said Henry. "I am asking you how you could *do* such a thing! What devil possessed you?"

"No devil," said Matt simply. "I fell in love with a girl, and it happened."

"You fell in love?" said Henry incredulously. "With a girl who became your doxy?"

"She is not my doxy. I want to marry her, Father. I have come to ask your permission."

"Permission? You ask my permission *now*, sir? After the dark deed is done, you come to me asking leave to whitewash your sin? Who is this hussy who has seduced you?"

"Her name is Betsy Bowen, and she didn't seduce me."

"Betsy Bowen!" Henry thundered. "Betsy Bowen! The girl whom the men in the yard call Bouncing Bet? Betsy Bowen!"

Henry stared in silence at the papers on his desk. His acquaint-ance with Betsy was not strictly limited to her name and what the men at the yard called her. He had seen her on the streets of the town, had watched her with hooded eyes as she passed, had sensed the voluptuousness of her body and seen the compelling beauty of her face. Here, before him, sat a man who had kissed those fresh young lips, smoothed that red-gold hair with passionate hands, known the secrets of that white body and possessed it completely. And the man was his son.

Henry quelled the unwelcome feelings of admiration and envy that so unexpectedly welled up in him, but his voice, when he spoke, had become soft. "Matthew, my boy," he said, "you are not seriously thinking of marrying this girl?"

"Yes, sir. I love her."

Henry shifted uneasily in his chair. "You wish me to believe that you could bring her into this house and introduce her to your *mother?*"

Matt was silent for a moment. At last he said, "It would be difficult. But I would do it. I am the father of Betsy's child."

"And how can you be sure of that?"

"I know her very well, Father."

"That much is very clear," said Henry. "But with a woman like that, a Jezebel who gives herself to everyone—"

"Not to everyone, Father. Only to me."

"And that French sea captain she used to be seen with—to him, too? And to how many others?"

"That's in the past, over and done with, forgotten."

"Well, it's not forgotten by the people of this town, I can tell you. People have long memories when it comes to sinful females. I daresay they still remember her wanton mother, and that the girl herself lived alone with Sam Allen after his wife's death. Why, there was talk that—"

"But she was only a child, and there is always talk about a beautiful woman. I think my mother would understand."

Henry's voice became firm and uncompromising now. "Your mother will not be given the opportunity of meeting her, and I doubt if she'd be as understanding as you think. Women, my boy, *good* women, are even less charitable toward creatures of this sort than men."

"My mother is a Christian woman, and Jesus himself said—"

"I know what Jesus said. But this is Providence, Rhode Island, not Jerusalem, and I will not insult my wife by introducing her to a woman like your Betsy Bowen, let alone welcome her as my daughter! There is no need for further discussion, Matthew!"

"I think there is, sir," said Matthew. "If you are so concerned about what people will think, perhaps you should consider the fact that next autumn you will have a bastard grandchild!"

Henry stood up suddenly, trembling with fury. "*I* will have a grandchild! I, who have not tasted the obscene pleasures of this wanton's body! *I* am to have a grandchild! Thank you, thank you very much, Matthew!"

"You sound almost envious, Father!"

"Quiet!" Henry thundered. "Hold your tongue! Unless you apologize at once, leave this house and leave it forever! Marry your strumpet and give your bastard a name!"

"Which also happens to be *your* name, sir!" said Matthew.

Henry went suddenly limp. He sat down in weary resignation and became silent. At last he said quietly, "My name, until this moment a good name, and one that you have seen fit to dishonor." He looked at Matthew sadly, his eyes filling with tears. "How could you do this to me, Matthew? I have taken great pride in you, tried to bring you up properly, instill in you a conscience."

Against his will, Matt found himself moved. Going over to Henry, he rested his hand lightly on his shoulder. "I am sorry, Father," he said. "I am truly sorry. But it is because I have a conscience that I wish to mend the evil I have done."

"By marrying this girl?"

"Yes, sir."

Henry bowed his head in thought, and Matt stood before him in silence. Perhaps Betsy had been right. The idea of marriage might not be altogether impossible, after all.

But when Henry spoke, his voice was as cool and impersonal as though he were reading out the specifications for a new ship to be built at the yard. "There are many kinds of evil, son," he began, "and many ways of mending it. We must consider all these things in reaching a decision."

"Yes, sir," said Matt, aware that his father was about to embark on one of his long and ponderous lectures. He sighed and sat down in his chair to listen. At the tone of his father's opening words, all hope of marriage had fled, and he waited resignedly.

Henry stood up, taking the belligerent, persuasive stance of a lawyer addressing a jury. "Yes, Matthew, there are many kinds of evil. There is the evil of the sin of the flesh you have committed with this—this woman. But now, to mend this evil, you are willing to do more evil. You are willing to bring shame upon your mother and on me. You are willing to ruin your own standing, your very future in the town where you were born, your good name itself!"

Henry paused for breath, and Matt said, "But what else can I do, Father?"

"I am coming to that. I said there were many ways of mending evil. Let us look at them. First, must this poor nameless child be brought into the world *at all?* There are ways, I believe—"

"I know," said Matt. "I can send Betsy to a midwife and have the child destroyed, which may, in turn, destroy Betsy. I would remind you, Father, that the sixth commandment says 'Thou shalt not kill.' "

Henry cleared his throat loudly. "Of course, of course. I am merely counting off the possibilities. So let us say that the child comes into the world. Money could be provided for its care and for the mother."

"For how long?"

"Until the child is of an age to work, at fourteen, let's say."

"And who will provide the money?"

Henry looked at his son sharply. "You, of course. It is not *my* child. You are a workingman, you have wages. And, of course, you would give me your promise not to see the woman again, ever."

"It's a promise I could not keep because I know that as long as she was in Providence I would go to her."

"Then we will see to it that she leaves Providence."

"She would refuse!"

"In that case," said Henry, "there is only one course—to send *you* away."

"And if I refuse to go?"

Henry paused before playing the trump card that he held. He decided not to threaten until he had tried a milder approach. "You are my eldest son, Matthew. You have already decided that ship-building is what you want most to do. Someday my shipyard—"

"But I lied to you," Matt said quietly. "I have no interest in shipbuilding or in your shipyard."

Henry was taken off guard. "But then why did you—"

259

"I needed money to support Betsy, and so I went to work."

"You were willing to give up your education just for that?" asked Henry in astonishment.

"I loved her."

Henry's ears, so well attuned to the nuances of bargaining, did not hear the statement so much as the past tense of the verb it contained, and he seized on it. "*Loved* her?" he repeated. "Then perhaps you do not love her now quite so much? And it might even be that given a second chance you would not be so eager to give up my plan of your becoming a lawyer?"

Matt, too, was momentarily taken off guard now. He stammered, "I did not mean that I had stopped loving her—that is, well, naturally, I am not as hotheaded as I was at first. It is the same with people who marry."

Henry looked at his son approvingly. "You have discovered early, Matthew, what most men discover late, some of them too late. But in marriage there are rewards, as the Lord meant there to be: a home, children. But the passions—they do cool, don't they?"

Henry gave his son a conspirational smile, and Matt could not help responding to it with a wry smile of his own. With this encouragement, Henry went on. "In this life, son, we do not often get a second chance." He paused dramatically, before adding softly, "But I am willing to give you one."

Matt was not without some bargaining instincts of his own. He looked up quickly but carefully disguised the interest that his father's statement had aroused. "How do you mean, a second chance?" he asked casually.

"I was thinking," said Henry, "of Harvard College. It is, of course, an older institution than we have here. Many signers of the Declaration—"

"I know what Harvard College is," said Matt, "and *where* it is. It would be a convenient way of getting me out of town, wouldn't it?"

"And also expensive," said Henry drily. "But I am willing to—"

"And if I say to hell with your offer and marry my Betsy?"

Henry was silent. The moment had come for the trump card, and Henry played it with confidence and authority. "Then I shall disown you, Matthew, socially, morally, and in all the lawbooks of this town, state, and nation. And the door of this house will be closed to you, together with the society of your mother, your brothers, and me. Not just now, but forever!"

An implacable ferocity had roughened Henry's voice, and the words echoed with a dry ringing through the room. For Matt, it was as though a door had suddenly opened on a winter landscape and a blast of icy, freezing air had engulfed the room and everything in it.

In all his imaginings of this scene, he had not anticipated the stunning effect his father's threat would have on him. He had not foreseen the wild, frightened beating of his heart, the sweat that broke out on the palms of his hands, and most terrifying of all, the arid emptiness that filled his whole being. As though in a nightmare, he felt like someone who finds himself unaccountably wandering alone in a strange and barren country.

His throat was so dry that he could not speak, and he struggled for control of himself. He was aware of his father's eyes on him, as confident as those of a cat that has caught its mouse and awaits the pleasurable moments of playing with it. Not since he was a small boy, brought howling to this room for punishment of some childhood misdemeanor, had he felt so abjectly in the power of the man who sat opposite him.

And then something in him rebelled. He would not sit here and be triumphed over so completely. Some way, somehow, he would beat this adversary at his own game. He would salvage what he could of pride. He would become greater, more powerful than this little man who sat so smugly on his shipyard and his money, and he would use him mercilessly in the process.

The image of Betsy, the very feeling of his love for her, melted into nothingness in the burning sun of this new necessity for power, for control of whatever life lay before him, an undiscovered country that must be his to possess and own. Never again would he allow himself to be placed in the position of watching his world turn into ice at someone else's command. It would be he, Matt Wyatt, who would give the commands.

He looked up and his eyes met those of his father without flinching. "I will go to Harvard," he said coldly.

Henry smiled his satisfaction. "And the girl?"

"You will provide for her and the child," said Matt flatly.

"I did not agree to that!" Henry objected.

"But you will, sir," Matt observed, as though the matter were settled.

Henry scowled, and then a smile lighted his face. "You're a better horse trader than I thought, my boy." He paused. "I think you will go far."

Matt did not smile. "I mean to," he said.

CHAPTER 23

W HEN Matt went to Betsy's room that night to tell her of his decision, she knew, even before he had taken off his coat, that he had talked with his father and that marriage was out of the question. There was a remoteness in his manner, more frightening than his coolness of the past few weeks. His eyes looked at her vaguely, almost as though they did not see her, and when they did focus upon her, there was in their depths a calculating look of appraisal, as though they might be setting a price on a possession shortly to be disposed of.

She sat in a chair opposite him, waiting for him to speak. At last, in a low, toneless voice, he said, "It is all over, Betsy. My father has forbidden our marriage. He will disinherit me if I disobey his orders."

"And you will obey them, I suppose."

"What else can I do? He has also arranged for me not to see you again."

"Arranged? How can he do that?"

"I am to leave Providence and go to Boston. I will resume my law studies at Harvard College."

Betsy had been prepared for Henry Wyatt's disapproval of their marriage, but she had not foreseen Matt's disappearance from her life. An emptiness stretched itself before her, as though she had suddenly found herself at the edge of a cliff that she had not known was there.

Her mouth went dry, and her voice quavered as she asked, "When will you go?"

"As soon as may be. I will study with a tutor until such time as arrangements for entrance can be made and a new term begins."

"But you could do that here. There are teachers at the college—"

In a voice that was cold and factual, Matt said, "My father wishes me to go to Boston immediately."

Betsy had recovered from the shock of Matt's news, and now she felt a rising anger. She foresaw that she was fighting a losing battle, but it was a battle that she would fight anyway.

"Your father wishes it! Are you a child who must do anything its father tells it to? You're twenty-one, Matt, old enough to be a man. And old enough to father the child I'm carrying!"

His voice softened as he said, "The child will be cared for, Betsy, and so will you. Your needs will be provided for."

She despised the tears that filled her eyes, but she could not stop them. "Do you think my only needs are for food and a roof over my head? I've been foolish enough to love you."

"We have both been foolish," said Matt, reaching for her hand.

She snatched her hand away from him, and a tide of fury engulfed her, a fury that seemed compounded of all the hurts and humiliations she had ever suffered.

"Don't touch me!" she screamed. "I want no part of you. What kind of man do you call yourself, Matt Wyatt, that you can let an old man's silver turn your balls to water, a milksop gelding that can't stand on his own feet!"

The words drew blood, and anger filled Matt as he shouted, "I'm my own man! Not my father's, not yours, nobody's! And I won't be shackled by a woman with a brat! I've got my own way to make it in the world, and by God, I'll make it!"

"Well, make it, then!" she spat at him. "And up your arse with it, world and all!"

A silence fell as they glared at each other like enraged animals caught in the same trap who turn on each other in frustration.

Matt breathed deeply to control his rage, and at last, in a voice still shaking with emotion, he said, "Betsy, love, there's no good in this."

The term of endearment sent her into a new storm of weeping, and she flung herself on the bed. Matt moved toward her. He wanted to take her in his arms and comfort her, but with an effort of will, he checked himself. Sitting down on the edge of the bed, he touched her arm lightly in a gesture of friendliness.

"Betsy, try to think, please try to think," he said, echoing the eternal male plea for reasonableness in the face of feminine hysteria. "What would become of us if we married? Where would we go? What would I do for work? What am I fitted to do? It would be a life of poverty and struggle. How long do you think our love would last?"

She stopped crying suddenly and turned her tear-streaked face to him. "Love? When a man loves, he don't run at the first sign of trouble. He stays with his woman and takes care of her, and her brats, too. What's love to you, Gentleman Matt? It's nothing but shoving yourself into a woman to pleasure yourself, and the Devil take the consequences!"

"But I'm providing for the consequences."

"You? No, not you, my bully-boy. It's rich Henry Wyatt with a house on the hill. And why? Is it because he has taken pity on the baggage his son has gotten with child? No. It's to protect his honorable name and leave his son free to marry some fancy filly with a good family name. And that will be what love is for you, Matt, another quiff with another name!"

Matt froze at the viciousness of her attack, sensing in the vulgar flow of words the truth that lay behind them. He assumed a dignified air and moved in the direction of the door.

"We have said all we need to say," he said. "Goodbye, Betsy. Though you may not believe it, I wish you well."

As he opened the door, she sprang across the room at him and flung herself into his arms. The door shut with a slam, and she was hard up against him, pressing her body against his in a last effort to hold him, her lips seeking his in desperation as her arms encircled him. He strained to escape her, but at last she found his mouth and kissed it violently. All at once his resistance evaporated, and she felt his tongue forcing its way past her lips. His arms grew taut about her, and she moved one of her hands down his leg, manipulating him with frantic movements.

Then, without warning, he pushed her away from him violently. "Stop it, Betsy! For God's sake, let things be!"

She threw herself at him again, fell to her knees and tore at his clothing savagely, until at last her searching mouth had found its object.

He pulled away from her and struck her jaw with such violence that she fell to the floor. "For the love of Christ, Betsy, don't play the two-shilling whore!"

The sound of the slamming door came to her only dimly as she lay there face down on the floor. Long, indrawn sobs racked her body, and she was filled suddenly with an overpowering nausea. She raised herself on an elbow and vomited. The act gave her a sense of release, as though she were purging herself of all the disgust she felt for herself. Matt's last words rang in her ears, filling her with revulsion and demolishing whatever was left of her pride.

For the better part of an hour she lay still and unmoving. In her imagination the nightmare scene with Matt played itself over and over again in all its painful, somehow unreal detail, from the moment he arrived and announced his shattering news, through the whirling angry words, to her final ignominious effort to prevent his leaving. Once completed, the scene would start again from the beginning in idiot repetition, like the singsong jingle of a childhood game that went on and on interminably.

At last she sat up and shook her head angrily, as though to break the monotonous chain of contorted images and strident voices. Forcing herself to her feet, she moved to the washstand, poured water into the washbasin from the earthenware pitcher, plunged her face into the cold water and held it there for a few moments. Then, as she dried her face with a towel, she looked at herself in the mirror above the washstand.

In spite of the swollen red eyes and the matted tangle of her hair, it was still a beautiful face. She lifted her chin, smoothed her cheek, and pushed the hair back from her brow. She patted the bruise that Matt's blow had left on her cheek.

Anger rose up in her, and to that disheveled image of herself, she said, "Not a two-shilling whore, Matt Wyatt! A two-dollar whore, and too good for the likes of you!"

Sally Marshall lay back in her elegant four-poster bed and sighed in grim satisfaction. She had spent the early part of the evening sitting uncomfortably in a straight-backed chair with her ear glued to the wall that separated Betsy's quarters from her own prim sitting room. She enjoyed dramatic scenes, especially when they involved lovers, and the one she had listened to tonight met her most extravagant demands for unbridled passion and violence.

Although her sympathies in a situation of this kind were most certainly with the wronged woman, she could not have endured a happy ending, the happy ending that fate had denied Sally herself. And so, it was with a perverse pleasure that she heard the slamming of the door and Matt's hurried footsteps echoing down the corridor.

She had stifled a fleeting impulse to go to Betsy and comfort her. But after all, the girl had gotten only what she bargained for. She had had her season in the sun, and now she must pay for it. More than that, she was a prideful little fool to turn down her lover's offer of silver so scornfully. Well, she would learn. But not at the expense of Miss Sally Marshall.

And so the next morning Sally paid an early visit to her tenant. She came neither to sympathize nor to gloat, but to look out for her financial interests.

She entered the room without knocking and said, "So your highborn gentleman will be taking off for Boston."

"How did you know?" Betsy asked in surprise.

" 'Twould be a wonder if the whole town don't know, the way you was yowling and screeching at each other like two alley cats."

"I'm sorry," said Betsy. "Matthew Wyatt is not such a gentleman as you might think."

"Nor you such a lady," added Sally. "Well, what will you be a-doing now, missy, left high and dry and with a bun in the oven, too?"

"I can take care of myself."

"Or find somebody else to do it, at least until you start to get big." Sally narrowed her small eyes and looked at Betsy appraisingly. "You'd turn a better profit on the open market."

Betsy turned and faced her. "I mean to!"

Sally, in anticipation of a business talk, sat down on the edge of a chair without invitation. "But you'll not be carryin' on your trade in *this* room, my girl."

"But this room is like home to me," said Betsy with a note of pleading in her voice. "I'll pay the rent. You can be sure of that."

"No doubt. But I'll not have men's feet tramping in and out of the house all night long. 'Tis a respectable house here. The whorehouse be next door."

"But I'll be quiet, Miss Marshall. Please do let me stay. It's my home—"

"Not anymore it isn't! And you might as well call me Sally. That's what my other girls call me."

"You're asking me to be one of your—your girls?"

"I ain't asking you, Miss Priss. I'm a-telling you. If you take a room in my whorehouse, you're one of my girls, and I takes a slice of your wages."

"And if I don't want to be one of your girls?"

Sally shrugged. "It be no concern of mine if you want to take a tavern room every night and end up in the town gaol." Her thin body straightened with pride. "My girls is pertected by the constable because I run a seemly house, no brawlin' and disturbin' of the peace."

Betsy remembered her mother's unhappy association with the constabulary, the periodic hustling off to gaol, the hunted-animal furtiveness of her existence. And she wanted no part of it. She was ready to do business with Sally, but she was not going to be bullied into it.

"And how much is your slice?" asked Betsy.

Sally smiled, not even attempting to hide the pleasure of conquest that lighted her eyes. "That depends on how much the girl is worth. With you, I'll take four shillings a customer. Anything you can get over that is yours to keep."

"That's too much. Three shillings."

"Four."

"Three and six."

Sally laughed. "If you're as sharp at the quiffing as you are with a penny, you'll end up rich, Miss Priss. All right, three and six. And no tricks and no lyin'. I got my spies."

"I do not lie," said Betsy in disdain. "I am not an ordinary whore."

"Whores be whores," said Sally. "I know. I was one myself. I'll ready a room for you tonight."

"Don't bother," said Betsy with firmness. "The rent is paid through this week, and here I'll stay till then!"

"Have it your own way, me ladyship." Sally got up abruptly and left. Her cackling laugh echoed down the hallway, and Betsy slammed the door to drown out its note of mocking triumph.

CHAPTER 24

ETSY looked about her at the sparsely furnished narrow room. There was only one chair, crudely made from soft pine and without even the minor luxury of a rush-bottom seat. She lay down on the slender cot, with its mattress of dried cornhusks, and stared vacantly at the fly-specked ceiling.

The unfamiliar noises of Olney Lane came to her on the breeze that ruffled the ragged muslin curtains at the window. She had grown used to the quiet of her room at the rear of Sally's house next door. The clattering of horses' hooves and wagons groaning and creaking through the mud of early spring gave her a feeling of exposure to a workaday world she had almost forgotten.

She grew apprehensive at the thought of approaching nightfall, when she would again become part of the noisy streets beyond the window. She had known that world, even as a child, and it held no unfamiliar terrors. But now, she would be alone in it. There would be no Sam, no Jacques or Matt to protect her, and she would have to sell herself, not to one man, but again and again to many men. The thought of giving her body to strangers, men who might be not only unattractive but physically repellent, made her flesh shrink instinctively in loathing.

There was a knock at the door. She opened it to find Polly Clarke standing there, gay and smiling in a perky hat adorned with bright ribbons and carrying a large gunny sack, which she deposited on the floor with a thud.

Betsy threw her arms around Polly. There was nobody she would rather have seen at this bleak moment, and the mere sight of Polly's cheerful face, with its large features and warm brown eyes, was reassuring.

It had been a long time since Betsy had seen her, and there was a moment of awkward silence. Polly had the good taste not to comment on Betsy's transfer from Sally's relatively respectable house next door, a move geographically small but socially enormous. And although she was genuinely sorry that Betsy had lost her lover, she did not indulge in words of feminine commiseration. But silences oppressed her, and so she embarked on an account of how her father and Phebe had left Providence for North Brookfield.

"They was both so drunk, lovey, they could hardly stand. The day before they left they could hardly git on with their packin', they was so busy fightin' about what to take and what to leave behind. Papa was the drunker so he was the loser in the end."

She pointed her finger to the gunny sack she had dumped on the floor. "He left behind all his books."

"His books!" said Betsy. "Oh, he must have been very drunk. He loved his books better than anything in this world!"

"He told me I was to give the books to you. He wrote a note to you. Here it is."

Although the handwriting was shaky and many words had been crossed out and rewritten, Betsy was able to read it. "To Miss Eliza Bowen," it began, "I bequeath these immortal treasures of the mind: the pearls of philosophy, the rubies of history, the diamonds of poesy. But they be greater riches than precious stones. In the certitude of her appreciation of their perpetuity midst the fugaciousness of life's transitory joys and sorrows, I give them in tenderest regard. *Chère élève*, dear girl, *adieu*."

Betsy's eyes filled with tears. She saw again the blotchy red face with the sharp, intelligent blue eyes, heard again the pompous voice loudly adjuring her to use the intellect the Almighty God had given her.

"You liked my Pa, didn't you?" said Polly. As Betsy nodded, Polly looked away and added, "People wouldn't think it, but even with the drink, he was a good father to me, and a mother, too, come to think of it. Pity I wasn't a bright, bookish girl like you."

"With a warm heart like yours," said Betsy, "there's no need for reading books."

"Do you reckon you will read *all* them books?"

"Someday, I hope. But right now, Polly, I'll be too busy earning my way to have much time for the pearls of philosophy, and I'm scared."

"A girl as pretty as you will do right well in the business."

Betsy frowned, then sighed. Polly quickly moved to a place on the bed and took Betsy's hand in her own. "Now, what's the matter, lovey? You're not still thinkin' of *him*, are you?"

"Him?" Her voice went cold. "No, he's gone. I want never to see him again. I hate him! I'll hate him till the day I die! And the child he left inside me!"

Polly was shocked by the violence of Betsy's feelings. "Oh, you mustn't hate the child, Betsy. 'Twouldn't be fair."

"But it's the way I feel."

"Then best you git rid of it quick as you can. I'll take you to Freelove Ballou."

"It may be too late for that. It's been a couple of months now."

"Then there's no time to be lost," said Polly with authority. "We should go to Freelove tomorrow."

"If you say so, Polly. Tomorrow seems a long way off. It's tonight I'm worried about."

"What's to fear about tonight?"

Betsy's hands moved in a gesture of helplessness. "Polly, I don't know how to—to do it. How do you get them?"

"Get them?" Polly asked with a giggle of amusement. "All you'll have to do is look up at them and smile."

"Should I blink my eyes at them like this?"

Polly laughed. "Oh, lovey, only a tired old whore would do that! You mustn't be too anxious. The more anxious you be, the lower the price."

"You mean I should act like a lady?"

"Oh, no. That way they'll think your price is too high, and that you're cold mutton into the bargain."

"Then what *should* I do?"

Polly settled down, smoothing her skirt over her knee with the prim air of a schoolmistress about to begin the day's lesson. "You always got to think of *them*," she began. "A man gits feelin' horny some night, and he ain't got a girl or maybe his wife is cold as a gaffed haddock, or maybe he's fresh off a ship after a long spell at sea, and so he goes out lookin' for some whore to take care of him."

"But I know all that," said Betsy.

"But," Polly went on, "he's not lookin' for just any old knothole

271

in a fence. If that's all it was, he'd just bugger the cabin boy. No, he's out huntin' for the best-lookin' wench he can track down.

"But bein' a man, he's as proud as any struttin' peacock. He wants a wench that will take him for the hottest and handsomest thing she ever set eyes on. So you lets him know, by the way you look at him, by the way you talk, that he's right to your taste and the others don't stand a chance. You play him along like a hooked trout. You ain't anxious for *it*. But he is. And so, when he starts mentioning what he'll give, you right away got the upper hand in the bargaining."

"And when does he pay me, before or after?"

"Before! Before! Afterward, when a man's balls git cold, like as not he wants to run, and he'll pay the least he can. That way trouble starts. Always make 'em pay when they're pantin' to git started."

"Do I take the money right there on the street?" asked Betsy.

"That'd never do. They'd be a-feared you'd skip off with it, and just maybe a constable might see you and hustle you off to gaol. Wait till you're right to the door here. Then turn to 'em and say, 'I know you be a man of your word, sir, but my mistress orders that I get paid in advance.' So you takes the money or barter, and as you passes Black Tom at the door, you gives it to him for safe-keeping and writes it down in his little book with your name next to it. And that's all there is to it."

"I don't like any of it," said Betsy. "How long must I stay with him?"

"Only long enough for him to pleasure himself *once*," said Polly sternly. "Git him through as quick as may be, usin' every little trick you ever learned. But don't try to pleasure yourself, my girl, or you'll be all wore out before the night's half through."

"But supposing he's handsome and knows how to make love. What could I do to stop myself?"

"Think of a man you hate. Think of Matt, and how you hate him. Then start hatin' this man too, with all the hate you got in you, hate him for buyin' you and usin' you like a snot rag! Hate him hard enough and you'll be of no mind to let yourself go with him."

Betsy frowned. "But afterward, how do I make them leave?"

"Most men is ready to go quick as they've shot the rabbit. But if they hangs on, then you gits up and starts dressin'.''

Betsy, remembering Matt's prowess as a lover, asked, "And supposing they want it again?''

"Then they pays half what they paid the first time for every time after. And *that* money don't go to that slut Sally. It's yours. Sometimes, if you're smart, you can get more, anyway. Naturally, while they're at their work, you moans and groans like you was in heaven, even if you ain't. That gits 'em along with it faster and sets 'em in the right way of mind for something extra in silver. When they're leavin', you drops a compliment about what a lovely doodle they got and how much it pleasured you. A man is mighty proud of his doodle, you know. If it's small, say it's better than the big ones that won't git properly stiff. It it's big, tell him it's the biggest one you ever did see and gave such pleasure as you never had before.''

Betsy remembered her experiences with Jacques whenever he had drunk too much. "And supposing it won't stiffen up at all?''

"Well, no matter what, don't give 'em their money back! But be patient for a while, try little tricks with your tongue if you've a mind to. But if it's hopeless, then say you're sorry, maybe you'll see them another time.''

There was a silence, and Betsy looked thoughtful. At last, with a weary sigh, she said, "It's harder work than I counted on.''

"It's better than slavin' twelve hours over to the weavin' mill for next to nothin'.''

Betsy nodded agreement and stared at the floor in silence. Polly's instruction in the business of whoredom had brought to vivid life the cold-blooded details of her calling. For a moment, she even considered accepting Matt's offer of money. She knew that in this, at least, he would not fail her. But her pride swept aside all her feelings of repugnance.

And it was not entirely a matter of pride. Although she had been aware that Matt might act exactly as he had done, she had not really believed he would. Her love for him had been built on a heroic image, and in a few short sentences he had demolished that image forever. He had stood before her suddenly as just another imperfect, somehow squalid human being, a coward compromised by the demands of comfort and convention.

273

This thought lay at the core of her bitterness: the weakness of a love that went scampering for cover at the first cold wind of reality; a love so frail that even the prospect of hardship could make it wither like a blossom touched by frost. She knew that in his place she would have defied the world of practicality, would even have accepted the challenge with relish, taking pleasure in the battle and in the winning, however great the odds.

She hated him not so much for what he had done as for what he had failed to do. Her disillusionment had turned him into a strangely shrunken figure, a man who had deceived her into believing he was stronger and more admirable than he was. It did not occur to her that it was her own romantic imagination that had endowed Matt with qualities of courage that he did not possess and indeed had never possessed. She was aware only of her own contempt for him, and she hated him for his betrayal of her dream.

Although Matt might be weak, she was still strong, and she knew it. She was not beaten now, nor would she ever be. Somehow, some way, she would get what she wanted. She would become what she had never been in all her nineteen years, a woman who would be accepted, wanted, and loved.

It would be a battle, maybe long, maybe bloody, but it was a battle she intended to win. The ramparts of convention might be hard as granite, but somehow she would scale them. She would use the only weapons she had, her beauty and her intelligence. The prize was the same as it had always been, the silver and gold that could buy what she wanted.

When at last she looked up at Polly, her eyes had lost their anxious look. They had become alive and lustrous again. She smiled and said, "What time do we go to work, Polly?"

Polly reacted to Betsy's changed mood with conspirational delight. "Soon as it begins to git dark, lovey. Dress up good and warm, not too fancy, not too much paint. I'll come for you, and we'll head for Cheapside. We'll make believe we be sisters, out for a stroll in the evenin' air."

Betsy did not smile but looked at Polly with serious eyes. "Funny. My own sister's name was Polly too. But you be my real sister."

She pulled Polly up from the bed and hugged her in an impulsive embrace.

"It's good to know I'll have company on my first night as a whore," she said with a smile.

But Betsy went to Cheapside alone. Just as they had been leaving the house on Olney Lane, one of Polly's regular customers had arrived and demanded the immediate comfort of her services. And so, Polly had reluctantly returned to the house and Betsy had set forth alone.

She moved down the street in the gathering dusk toward the part of town known as Cheapside. By day it was a respectable area of small shops, but with the coming of nightfall it became a dark thoroughfare frequented by men in search of pleasure and by the women who were prepared to give it, for silver or often in barter for food, cloth, wine, or whatever might be offered.

As Betsy drew near the port, a light breeze from the river ruffled her hair. The March chill was still in the air, but its freshness carried a suggestion of spring. Her spirits rose and she found herself humming the old sea chantey that her mother had taught her.

As she walked in time with the tune, her imagination took flight. Magically, she was no longer Betsy Bowen walking down a dark, muddy street in Providence in 1794. It was 1767, and the place was Paris, and she was Marie Jeanne Bécu on her way to an assignation with Louis XV. Shortly, she would become Comtesse Du Barry, mistress to the King—in effect, Queen of France, adored for her kindness by her humble subjects, and by the King himself until the day he died.

There were no kings in Rhode Island, or, indeed, anywhere in America. But there were great men, men of wealth and power. Had not President Washington himself come to Providence only four years ago to attend the celebration when Rhode Island had finally ratified the new Constitution? She remembered standing on a footstool in the yard of the Allen house as the President's carriage rolled by, and how she and Sam had followed it until it came to a halt before the Golden Ball. She had so longed to enter the inn with all those men in brilliant military dress and their beautifully gowned women, to become part of that almost royal reception, instead of a mere onlooker, a girl of fifteen clad in homespun.

275

There might be no kings in America, but there was still an aristocracy of wealth, position, and authority. Why should not Betsy Bowen become part of it? Was it not possible that at this very moment, in the darkened doorway of a closed shop in Cheapside, there might be standing a great man, an Adams, a Lafayette, or even President Washington himself? For even great men, from Julius Caesar to Louis XV, had never been immune to the charm of a trim ankle, a full bodice, and a pair of tempting eyes. It was the perennial weakness in their armor, the unguarded opening through which a beautiful woman, however lowly in origin, could gain entrance to a whole glittering and radiant world of excitement and affluence.

Betsy, still lost in her dream, inclined her head graciously toward the sailor who was watching her from the shadowed doorway of a dry-goods shop. His lounging figure stiffened to attention; he gave a hitch to his trousers and moved toward her. Blocking her path effectively, he looked down at her with an assured smile on his tanned face.

"Be you lookin' for company, ma'am?" he drawled in the soft accents of the South.

Betsy, abruptly snatched from her dream of kings, stood stock-still before him, speechless. "Why—why—I don't know," she finally stammered. And then she remembered that she had come to Cheapside with a purpose, and she added, "Maybe—and good evening, sir." On impulse, still not completely free of her dream, she dropped a curtsy.

The sailor stared at her in wonderment. He scratched his head. "Beggin' your pardon, ma'am, I thought—"

She realized that he had taken her for a lady and said quickly, "No need to beg my pardon." She gave him a warm smile. "You done nothing to offend me."

He seemed relieved but still uncertain. "I was only askin' if you'd like my company—"

"And I said maybe." Betsy raised her eyes to his.

It was all the encouragement he needed, and he took a step toward her. His face came so close that she felt his rum-scented breath warm on her cheek. She turned her face to his and their lips met briefly.

As she moved away, she noticed that he carried a parcel under his arm. By its shape she knew that it was a bolt of cloth. It might be silk.

"Were you long in China?" she asked.

"Almost two years I been gone. How did you know?"

She smiled mysteriously and moved back toward him, this time lightly brushing the side of his face with her hand. It would be silk, all right, she thought to herself, and as his lips closed hotly on hers, she saw herself at a fashionable ball resplendent in a lovely gown of China silk trimmed with ruffles and bits of Belgian lace.

CHAPTER 25

I T was almost three weeks before Betsy got the Belgian lace, from the first mate on a ship just in from Bordeaux. By that time she had met many men of all ages, nationalities, and trades. But mostly, they were men of the sea from the American, English, and French ships that docked in Providence Harbor.

Her early distaste at the idea of making love with strangers soon wore off, and the ways of professional whoredom came to her easily. This was hardly remarkable because, except with Matt, the act of love had always been rewarded by gifts of money, clothing, or jewelry. But now, instead of one benefactor, she had many. Since Continental paper currency was almost worthless and silver was scarce, the gifts she received in barter were of an astonishing variety: a baker could provide a week's supply of bread; a butcher might offer meat or game; a farmer could supply butter, cheese, or eggs. Wealthier patrons might, of course, pay in the newly minted coins that the government had begun issuing two years before.

But it was the sailors' gifts that Betsy liked most, because they had come from faraway places. For her, they had an exotic magic about them: silk from China, calico prints from India, gloves and lace from Europe, Madeira from that tropical island, and red and white wines from France or Spain.

And she preferred the sailors themselves as lovers. The long days at sea made them set high value on a commodity that had not merely been scarce but sometimes nonexistent. They were more appreciative of feminine company and more generous in paying for it. Their camaraderie did not stop abruptly once their lust had been appeased. Often they would invite her, if the hour was not too late, to join them in a meal at a tavern. She liked, too, the fresh pine-tar smell of their bodies with its aroma of wood smoke, so unlike the rutting tomcat reek of landmen who worked indoors.

There were times when sailors were scarce, when the port would be almost empty of ships, and then, in order to meet Sally's demands for a share in profits, whether barter or silver, it was necessary for her to entertain local customers almost exclusively: the tightfisted tradesmen, the poor workers from the shipyards, the well-to-do young men from the hill and often their fathers as well.

With these men, she was at her most coldly professional. Her love-making was perfunctory, and she sent them on their way as quickly as possible. This was not difficult because usually they were eager to leave, anxious to return home before a waiting wife or wondering parents might become suspicious. They jumped into bed with dispatch and, like roosters in a hen yard, satisfied themselves all of a squawk and lay back panting. Then, almost immediately, pangs of conscience would set in, along with sudden fear of disease, and they would grab hastily for their pants, if, indeed, they had even bothered to take them off. Their contrition made them stingy and mean, in striking contrast to their earlier mood of generosity.

Betsy quickly learned from these men that she could expect little in the way of anything extra. Instead, she sometimes became a convenient target for their self-loathing. It was as though she, a sinful and wanton temptress, had lured them against their wills into the situation in which they now so uncomfortably found themselves.

On such occasions, she would tolerate little of their abuse, but learned to turn their own guilt-ridden vituperation back on themselves. If they called her a dirty whore and a Jezebel, she returned the compliment by making equally Biblical references to adulterers and profaners of the marriage bed, lechers who befouled the purity of their wives and children. Such reminders, delivered sternly in a highly moral tone, silenced them, and they left stealthily and quickly.

As for Betsy, the immorality of her new profession did not concern her at all. She remembered Sam's lectures about sin and regarded any concern about morals as the sheerest hypocrisy. But she did worry sometimes about disease. The pox was not uncommon, and the disease called "the clap" was fairly widespread.

Polly had given her detailed and lurid descriptions of the symptoms and the more horrible later effects of such love-born maladies. These included insanity, crippling, and a lingering death. Not the least of the consequences, and those which impressed Betsy the most, were a bad complexion and the loss of teeth or even of a nose. In comparison with these calamities, which could so effectually destroy beauty, death and insanity seemed infinitely preferable.

And so, Betsy was cautious. She memorized Polly's colorful but mostly accurate descriptions of symptoms. If she found that a customer might possibly be what Polly called "unclean," she amiably returned his fee and excused herself on the grounds of weariness. For those men who objected to being sent on their way, she kept an old and broken blunderbuss under the bed. Pointed at a man's naked belly, it was highly persuasive, and Betsy did not hesitate to wield it menacingly when necessary.

On one of these occasions the customer was Bobby Brown, the town sergeant. He was drunk and more unfriendly than usual.

"Well, my high and mighty little baggage, you've turned whore at last, just like your mother. This time I won't have to rape you; I'll just take you and pay for it and you can be sure Sally won't interfere."

Betsy looked at him with loathing. His face, covered by a red rash, was even uglier than usual. But she knew that Sally would not come to her rescue. Bobby, as town sergeant, was one of the people with whom Sally had to stay friends.

Bobby undressed quickly. Just as he was about to lurch into bed with her, she noticed that the rash on his face also covered his chest and shoulders. She pushed him away and got out of bed quickly.

"You be sick, Bobby Brown. You got the pox."

He laughed. "Ain't nothing. Come on to bed."

Betsy reached under the bed and produced the blunderbuss. She aimed it at his head, and he got up in sudden fear.

"Put on your clothes and get out of here!" she ordered.

"Just wait till Sally hears about this! You won't be working here, I promise you."

Betsy, still with the blunderbuss aimed at him, moved to the door and called down the stairs. "Black Tom! Black Tom! Come quick!"

There were loud footsteps on the stairs, and Tom appeared in the doorway. "Whatsa matter, Miz Betsy?"

"This man has the pox," said Betsy. She pointed to the rash on Bobby's shoulders, and Tom scrutinized it closely.

Bobby Brown had started pulling on his pants. "Look here, nigger, I'm the town sergeant."

Black Tom's voice became menacing. "I knows who you are. But iffen you got the pox, you can't have one of Miz Sally's girls. Them is orders from Miz Sally herself in person."

"I ain't got the pox," said Bobby. "You ain't a doctor. How would you know?"

"Maybe you ain't got it, but it sure look like it. All I know is you gotta leave. Right now!"

As Bobby hastily finished dressing, he said, "I'll talk to Sally about this tomorrow, and you'll both be out lookin' for new jobs."

"Mebbe so," said Tom. "You talk to Miz Sally, and if she say it's all right, you can come back. But right now, Mr. Bobby Brown, you moves your arse outa this house."

As Bobby slammed the door behind him, Betsy put down the blunderbuss and smiled at Tom gratefully. "Thank you, Tom."

Tom shrugged. "You was right, Miz Betsy. Sure looks to me like he got the pox, and I got my orders from Miz Sally."

The next day, when Bobby Brown protested to Sally about the treatment he had received, Sally asked him to take off his shirt.

Sally took one look and said, "Bobby, you better see the doctor. I can't run a business with sick girls."

"But I been a friend to you, Sally."

"I know that, and I appreciate it. But you must have been foolin' around with some other dirty whore. All my girls is clean, and I aim to keep 'em that way. Goodbye, sergeant."

Bobby shrugged his shoulders and left. As he walked down Olney Lane, he tried to regain his dignity by assuming an erect posture, with his rump stuck out. Angrily, under his breath, he said, "I'll get even with you, Miss Betsy Bowen, you stinkin' whore-bitch!"

Betsy's concern about the possibility of disease was not nearly so great as it was about the slow changes in her figure caused by her pregnancy. Although it was not yet obvious, she knew that she was putting on weight and was growing larger in the area around her hips.

At Polly's insistence she finally went to see Mother Ballou about an abortion. When they arrived at the weather-beaten, dilapidated house on Charles Street, its very appearance filled Betsy with fear and foreboding. Its gambrel roof sagged in disrepair, and the house sprawled ominously in the shadow of the dye works next door.

Inside, the air was hazy with smoke from damp logs that smoldered in the fireplace, before which sat an obese woman in a rocking chair. Although the room was large, a clutter of furniture and odds and ends of junk made it seem small and cramped.

As Betsy and Polly entered, a swarm of mongrel dogs and alley cats moved toward the door in a swirling tide of greeting. Polly pushed the friendly leaping dogs away and with her foot dissuaded the cats that encircled her legs in a frenzy of back-rubbing.

"Mother! Mother Ballou!" Polly shouted.

The woman in the rocking chair removed a corncob pipe from her mouth and looked up amiably. Her round pink face seemed constructed of bland planes of uneventful flesh designed only to emphasize the eyes that peered out from craggy brows. They were eyes of a startling blue, as unblinking, searching, and impersonal as those of an enormous owl. The straight black brows above them served only to enhance their look of blank scrutiny. The whole face was haphazardly framed by a tangled mass of frizzly gray hair that seemed never to have known a comb.

Freelove Ballou turned her face to her visitors and, in a voice so low-pitched that it might have been a man's, said, "I am not Mother Ballou. I am no one's mother. I am Freelove Ballou, formerly Freelove Whipple, the belle of Newport. My late father was a physician." Her eyes moved to Betsy. "And who is the pretty but pregnant young miss you've got in tow, Polly Clarke?"

Polly moved swiftly to the rocking chair and ruffled the mass of gray hair affectionately. "Oh, Freelove, 'tis my stepsister, Betsy Bowen. She's in a condition."

Freelove's eyes flickered in recognition as they continued to stare at Betsy. "One of Phebe Bowen's sea-borne waifs, no doubt. Tell me, child, was your father John Bowen, the sailor?"

Betsy moved forward, followed by an eddy of cats and dogs. She was trembling with apprehension as she said in a faint voice, "Yes, ma'am."

Freelove picked up a hickory walking stick and swung it at the assorted animal life. "Avast!" she roared at them, and they retreated to the other side of the room, seeking cover in the junk that was piled there.

"I knew your father, my child," she said in a reminiscent tone. "He was a no-good sailor and came to a no-good end that befitted him." She paused for dramatic effect and then added, "He was drownded in a storm sent by the righteous Almighty." With this matter settled, she looked acutely at Betsy again. "You're prettier than your mother, and not skin and bones like your father. Are you sure John Bowen *was* your father?"

"Mama says it might have been President Washington, when he was a general, that is."

A shout went up from the bulk of Freelove. Then, like a deflating balloon, she collapsed in a wave of small chucklings.

When the paroxysm had passed, Betsy said meekly, "I'm not sure it's true, of course."

Freelove looked at her in astonishment. "Why not? To look the way you do, my lass, there's got to be good blood in you somewhere. Now, with me, it came from my grandfather on my mother's side, a Bradford from Massachusetts. You've heard the name?"

"Oh, yes," said Betsy. "William Bradford was a governor of the Massachusetts Bay Colony. I can read and write, you see."

Freelove nodded her approval to Polly. "A scholar. And where did you learn to read and write, Miss Washington? From the General, no doubt."

"Oh, no, ma'am. From my—my uncle."

Freelove was momentarily thoughtful. Then she slapped the arm of her rocking chair in anger. "You're a very bright girl, but not bright enough to stay away from the baby-making implements of men! How long have you been this way?"

283

"Which way?" asked Betsy, not sure whether Freelove was referring to her moral or physical condition.

"*This* way!" said Freelove, with a crude gesture at her belly. "When did you first miss your flux?"

"I—I think it was January."

"Think? Don't you *know*, for Jesus' sake?"

"Yes, it was January."

" 'Tis almost April now. Well, you can still rid yourself of it, if you've a mind to," said Freelove.

Betsy was silent. She looked nervously toward the window at the back of the room. Through it she could see the sluggish canal that flowed through the backyard, its waters blood-red with color from the dye works. She shuddered inwardly and turned her eyes back to Freelove.

"Will it hurt much?" she asked. "Will I—will I die?"

Freelove's voice became unexpectedly gentle. "Hurt? Yes, it will hurt." She picked up her knitting from the table at her side. The bone needles glowed white against the black yarn. "I'll have to go into you with needles like these to break it up. And then you'll have to void it. Yes, it will hurt."

Betsy covered her face with her hands, holding back a scream of pure terror. Freelove waited until Betsy had gained control of herself and then continued in a soft voice, "Yes, you could die. But if all the girls I took care of had died, I wouldn't hardly still be in business, would I? You could die in labor, for the matter of that."

"How long would I be sick?"

"Two or three days, all depends. You can stay here till you're well. It all comes under the ten dollars you pay me. Well, what do you want to do?"

Betsy struggled to make up her mind. The image of the blood-red canal beyond the window kept coming back to her. Then her eyes moved again to the needles in Freelove's knitting.

"Far be it from me to push you," said Freelove. "But you ain't got much time. You're almost three months on the way, and the longer you wait, the more dangerous it gets." She paused. "Of course, you could always *have* the baby. I wouldn't charge for delivering it."

Betsy looked at her in surprise. "You wouldn't charge *anything?* Why not?"

284

Freelove rocked her chair back and forth. She seemed embarrassed. With averted face, she said, "I like babies."

Betsy felt a sudden warmth for this strange woman. Without quite knowing why, she found herself saying, "You can deliver mine, then."

Polly's head jerked to attention, like an animal scenting danger. "But, Betsy," she said, "you don't *want* the baby! It will only stand in the way of your workin'. You said yourself as how you hated it."

"I hate its father," said Betsy. "But it's hard to hate something—someone I've never seen. How can I ask for it to be killed? I won't do it, Polly—have the poor thing stabbed with a knitting needle."

Her face expressed a horror that she had no words for. Freelove's chair had stopped rocking. She stood up, shaking herself like one of her dogs roused from sleep. Then, with slow, ponderous steps, she moved toward Betsy.

She turned her unblinking gaze to Betsy's troubled face, and with a brusque pat on the arm, she said, "There'll be no stabbing, child. We'll whelp you of your cub with no trouble at all." Her eyes screwed up in a grotesquely humorous expression. "We'll present the President with a fine grandson, bastard though he be." She roared at her own joke and then seized Betsy by the hips. "Now, let's see how you're made."

Freelove began a methodical pushing and pressing of Betsy's slightly distended belly and womb, all the while carrying on a mumbling monologue of observations. "Hips and bones are good, you'll carry low probably. Three months—that'll make it October, a healthy month for childbearing." Her explorations at an end, Freelove stood up. She was still breathing hard from the efforts. "You're eating too much, child."

"I'm always hungry," said Betsy.

"Well, the more you eat, the bigger it'll get. And the more trouble we'll have bringing it out of you when the time comes. Reef sail on your appetite, Miss Washington, or it's sorry you'll be."

"Yes, ma'am. I'll try."

CHAPTER 26

I N the weeks that followed, Betsy waged a losing fight with her appetite. A gnawing hunger was with her night and day, a hunger she was unable to appease. In addition to three of the largest meals she could manage, she was always nibbling: sweets, buns, apples, whatever came to hand.

By the middle of June, her pregnancy was becoming obvious. She tried to disguise it in the folds of voluminous dresses. She bound herself in with wide swaths of linen. And then one night on a street in Cheapside she fainted dead away. Polly found her, took her back to the house, and put her to bed.

Her earnings fell, not only because her figure was losing its appeal, but because increasingly she felt too weak and ill to walk the streets and then go through with the gymnastics of love. Some nights she managed to entertain only one customer, other nights none. When the weather was cool and the spring rains fell in torrents on the street, she stayed in her room.

One morning Sally, all briskness and bustle, arrived for one of what she termed her "business talks." Betsy had known it was coming and dreaded it.

"You been one of my best girls, Betsy," Sally began, gently enough, "and I hate to tell you what I'm goin' to. But there's no help for it. What with your condition, you ain't turnin' enough profit even to pay the rent of your room. You'll have to go."

"But I'll try harder," said Betsy. "I'm feeling much better now, and I've made me a new dress, a dark-blue—"

"There ain't the dress made that can hide what *you're* carryin', and it's due to get bigger instead of smaller." She raised her eyes sanctimoniously to an imagined heaven and added, " 'Tis the workings of God and nothin' to be done about it."

"But I have no place to go, Sally," pleaded Betsy.

"Then you better find one." Sally rose, her business transacted. "Surely you didn't reckon to have the baby *here*, did you? I ain't a midwife, and I ain't keepin' a home for girls who get themselves in a condition. I got my business to think of. So I'll thank you to leave by the week's end, or Black Tom will see to it that you do."

The door closed sharply, and Betsy turned her face to the wall, drawing the bedclothes about her as though to assure herself that for the moment at least she was warm and secure in a bed of her own. If only her mother were still in Providence, she thought. The mud hut on the Old Warren Road had never seemed so inviting and comfortable.

There was always Matt, of course, but even now she would not consider asking him for help. Even Sam Allen would be preferable. At the thought of Sam, she sat up suddenly in bed. Surely he must have returned from China by this time, and even more surely he would take pity on her. He might even enjoy rescuing a fallen woman for the greater glory of God. There was always Mary Magdalene.

The thought of herself as a repentant Mary Magdalene made her smile, but she knew that she could play the role convincingly enough to renew Sam's interest, and even to arouse his guilty passions.

Getting out of bed quickly, she reached for the new dress that would show her at her most fetching and least pregnant. Fortunately, it was dark blue in color, with only small yellow ribbons for adornment. It was a dress made to order for Mary Magdalene.

Shortly after noon Betsy arrived at the Allen house on Benefit Street. The windows were shuttered, and the house had clearly been closed up for some time. Evidently Sam had not yet returned from his long voyage. But perhaps he had moved because the house had become too lonely for him without her. He might have taken a room near the waterfront. There was one man in Providence who would know, Nate Mason, at the Bulldog Tavern.

As she moved through the streets that led to the port, she had a sense of reliving the past, of retracing her steps on the night she had fled from Sam and had found herself at last, shivering and hungry, at the door of the tavern. She remembered how Jacques had suddenly appeared, rescued her from Bobby Brown and then taken her to his captain's cabin, where he revived her with bread, salt cod, wine, and his passionate love-making.

During the afternoon lull in business, Nate was behind the bar, polishing glasses and cleaning pewter tankards. He looked up as Betsy approached. His eyes showed surprise and pleasure, and then concern, as he noticed her slightly swollen contours.

"Mistress Betsy, 'tis good to see you after so long. You look—" and then, after a discreet pause, "well."

"I am well enough, Nate," she said, and then added with a smile, "in fact, *both* of us are well."

Nate blushed and looked fixedly at the bar. "Captain Jacques no longer comes here. They say he finds better trading in the port of New York. But I've my own opinion on that."

"How d'you mean, Nate?"

Nate reached for a bottle and two glasses. "Will you have a drop of Madeira with me, lass? 'Tis your favorite, I remember."

She nodded, and he poured the wine. "To you, ma'am, and good fortune," he said.

She inclined her head in thanks and they drank. Nate set his glass down and leaned forward on his elbows. " 'Tis a pity you broke off with the Captain," he said. "He was a good man, and he loved you true. After you went off, he never so much as had eyes for another girl."

Betsy found herself unexpectedly moved, and she turned her head away to avoid the possibility of tears. "I was a fool, Nate. A woman is a fool to fall in love."

Nate shrugged. "Maybe so. But that's what makes her a woman. And a man, well, sometimes he steers his ship to another port to forget a face."

Betsy avoided his eyes and took a sip of the wine. Then she said, "Nate, I didn't come here to ask about Jacques."

"No?"

"Where is Sam Allen?"

Nate looked at her in surprise. "Sam Allen? Why, surely you must have heard, Sam's dead."

She winced, as though the words had struck her physically. "Sam is dead? But when? How?"

"The *Lydia A.* docked—oh, it must be a couple of weeks ago, back from China. But Sam wasn't on her. He just disappeared on the voyage home. Leastways, that's what Eph Perkins says. Eph was first mate. Eph says 'twas a strange business altogether. But you got enough troubles, my lass, without me tellin' you sad tales."

Betsy was silent for a moment. Nate's news had shocked and saddened her. At last she said, "Tell me what happened, Nate."

"Well, Eph says there t'want no reason for it. He believes Sam just went out of his head. For weeks he'd been goin' around like a man walkin' in his sleep. Just stood on deck, lookin' at the sea all day long and never movin' his eyes away from it. And then the drinkin' began, always rum on his breath and his eyes all red and watery. When they laid over in the Sandwich Islands, he was gone for two days and came back drunker'n ever with a young native girl in tow. Eph wouldn't have believed it 'less he saw it with his own eyes. Well, he kept the girl in his cabin all night, and when she left the next mornin', she was cryin' and had marks all over her body like she'd been whupped." Nate paused and savored the drama of the scene.

Betsy shivered, feeling again the sting of the birch rod across her buttocks, remembering Sam's wild and tortured eyes, the flood of his angry passion as it exploded into violence and then subsided into tenderness and guilt.

"Well," Nate continued, "they sailed that night, on a calm sea with the moonlight as bright as could be. Sam was back on deck, still staring at the sea. Eph saw him there, and then, all of a sudden, he wasn't there. Just disappeared. They looked everywhere for him and laid over that night, waiting for daylight. They never found the body."

"And he left no note of farewell?" asked Betsy.

"Only his will, spread out on the ship's log. Left most everything to the Baptist Church, with a bequest for Nellie somebody-or-other."

"That was his servant woman," said Betsy, a note of resentment in her voice.

Nate nodded and then went on, "But there was another peculiar thing. You know what they found in his bunk? A girl's nightdress, all soiled and twisted up. It couldn't ha' belonged to the native girl. Eph says they don't wear no night clothes."

Betsy sighed. Nate's story had disturbed her deeply. The shock of learning that Sam was dead had been succeeded by feelings so confused that she could hardly have named them. She felt like crying but could not. She knew only that she wanted to leave, to walk, to run, to get outside where the sun still shone and the air was fresh from the sea. She thanked Nate and said goodbye. Nate, in a burst of friendliness, told her to stop by if she were ever hungry and low in funds.

Outside, the spring afternoon seemed strangely unreal. It was as though she had somehow lost her connection with these familiar streets and the people who hurried about them on their errands of business or pleasure.

In imagination, she was standing on the deck of a ship that moved out of a tropical harbor by moonlight, and she watched in horror while the tall, gaunt figure of a man with a stricken face disappeared quietly over the side. And in the bunk belowdecks, she saw the bunched-up lump of a girl's nightgown, the mute repository of a lonely passion that could never bear the light of day.

That it was one of her own nightgowns she never doubted, and the knowledge stirred feelings of guilt and complicity in her, as though she herself had been aboard the ship to goad him to his final despairing act. She brushed these feelings away as a slow anger began to rise in her. In those moments before he had destroyed himself he had remembered his church and Nellie, with never a thought for her, whom he had said he would always love. In a curious way, she felt that he, too, had betrayed her. Now, in her time of great need, he had chosen, like Matt, to run away.

She was alone now, more alone than she had ever been. Her mother, Jacques, Matt, and now even Sam, had gone their ways without her. By the end of the week she would be homeless and without money for food.

She could still sell herself, she knew, though perhaps not so easily or so often as before, but she would need a place to live. She thought of going back to Nate and asking him to rent her a room over the tavern. But she knew that would be impossible. Nate's wife would never countenance such an arrangement, and Nate himself would hesitate to embroil himself with the custodians of public morals by turning his tavern into a brothel.

And then, quite suddenly, she remembered Mother Ballou, who, according to Polly, was not above adding a discreet amount of pimping to her other clandestine services to the girls of the town.

The house on Charles Street was quiet and seemingly deserted when Betsy knocked on the door. Dogs barked and yelped, but there were no other signs of life within. She opened the door and entered the twilight of the huge downstairs room. She called Freelove's name, but there was no answer.

The dogs and cats were frantic in their greeting, and she realized that they were hungry. Mewing and whining, they followed her up the staircase at the rear of the house.

The second floor had been divided into three bedrooms and a small hallway. The bedroom at the rear was crammed full of odds and ends of castoff furniture and bedding. One of the two rooms at the front seemed to be a combined bedroom and workshop. In addition to a narrow cot and a chest, it contained a sturdy oak table on which were spread out a number of carving tools and knives, a small bucket of paint, brushes, and some turpentine in an old wine bottle. A half-finished wooden decoy representing a mallard duck lay on its side in a pile of wood shavings and chips. The bed was rumpled and gave forth a pungent odor of rum, turpentine, and human sweat.

In the other bedroom Betsy found Freelove, her mountainous bulk, fully clothed, sprawled in a four-poster bed that had a dingy canopy of faded red brocade. Her face was bluish-white, shining with perspiration, and as masklike as that of a corpse. But the noisy, labored breathing told Betsy that Freelove, though comatose, was certainly not dead. For a moment she watched the slow rise and fall of the enormous bosom as the lungs struggled for air.

"Freelove!" she called softly. "Are you all right?"

The figure stirred slightly but did not wake up. Betsy grasped a huge shoulder and shook it gently. The dogs yelped and jumped onto the bed in an ecstasy of tail wagging and whining.

At last Freelove's eyes opened and stared unseeingly at the ceiling. The dogs began a frenzied licking of her face and hands, and she slowly stretched out an arm to quiet them. She sighed and made groaning noises.

"Freelove, be you sick?" asked Betsy.

Freelove moved her head to the side, and her eyes stared at Betsy without recognition. Then, with an effort, they focused themselves and came alive.

"Miss Washington," she muttered and closed her eyes again. "Help me, child."

"Yes, Freelove. What's the matter? Do you have pain?"

The eyes opened again, and Freelove smiled faintly. "No. I have taken too much of the balm for all pain." She pointed to two empty rum bottles on the table near her bed. "I stand in need of reviving, much reviving. My no-account husband, Reuben, went off to the taverns, leaving me alone and abandoned."

Betsy took Freelove's hand in hers. "What can I do?"

"Brew me some tea, just as hot and strong as you can make it. Not a cup, a whole potful. While it's makin', take that coverlet there out to the well. Sop it with ice-cold water, put it in a bucket, and bring it back." As Betsy picked up the coverlet and turned to go, Freelove added, "And bring a broom with you."

"A broom? What for?"

"To whack me across the arse with. Gets the blood to moving." She smiled suddenly. "A fit punishment for a glutton overfond of the bottle."

Betsy went about the chores that Freelove had set her. She started a fire on the cold hearth, set a kettle on the hook to boil, went out to the well and plunged the coverlet into its cold water.

When she returned to the bedroom, Freelove still lay on the bed, but nude now and shivering. She instructed Betsy to throw the wet coverlet over her, and this done, the shivering became a veritable ague that shook the bed like a minor earthquake. Free-love, gasping and screaming as the icy water hit her skin, began to swear great rolling oaths, hurling them at the air like thunderbolts.

Betsy stared at her in wonderment. Her eyes fixed themselves on the grotesque hills of quaking flesh on the bed: the rolls of belly fat that shimmied like jelly, the gigantic sagging breasts that flapped about feebly like the wings of some great wounded bird.

"Now take the broom to me," Freelove commanded. And at

that moment the whole sodden mass rolled over, exposing a wide back larded with folds of flesh and a pair of gargantuan buttocks that rose up like twin hillocks on a plain.

Betsy picked up the broom and held it before her uncertainly.

"Well, what are you waiting for, slut? Whack me across the arse. Hard!"

Betsy wielded the broom with as much vigor as she could and brought it down on Freelove's buttocks with a whoosh.

"Harder! Harder!" screamed Freelove. "Get the blood to moving! Whup the hell out of me!"

And so Betsy flogged away until, breathless and red-faced, she collapsed in a chair. Freelove did indeed seem to be reviving. Her face, as well as her back and buttocks, began to take on a rosy hue, and though the sweating did not stop, the chills did.

An hour later, Freelove, with nine cups of black tea inside her, seemed almost herself again. When she learned that Betsy was to be evicted from Sally's whorehouse, she immediately invited her to take over the cluttered but unoccupied bedroom at the rear of the house.

"After all," she said, "you'll be coming here pretty soon to birth the baby, anyway. No reason we can't take you in sooner, especially when we're to have the honor of delivering the President's very own grandchild."

"I'll pay," said Betsy. "I can still get a few customers. But maybe your husband wouldn't want me here as a burden on you."

"Oh, him!" snorted Freelove. "He's just got home from his spring drunk with the hunters, sellin' his bird decoys for rum. Night after night all winter long, that man sits by the fire a-carvin' his birds. Then, soon as the ducks and geese start flyin' in the spring, he's up and off. His butcher business goes to hang, and nothing's to be seen of him for a couple of months. Well, he's home now, meek and remorseful as a Baptist sinner. He'll give you no trouble."

Pausing, she began clucking softly to herself like a happy hen. Her head nodded, her chin slowly lowering itself into the folds of flesh around her neck.

"Reuben's a good man. He likes his rum, and so do I. We be two of a—" Her voice faded, her head sagged abruptly, and she was suddenly asleep.

Betsy spread a clean, dry blanket over her and then went downstairs in search of food for the hungry cats and dogs, who still followed her with imploring eyes. She found some scraps that Freelove had evidently been saving for them, and there was some souring milk in a large earthenware pitcher.

After the animals had been fed, she sat down on a stool near the fireplace. She was tired and sighed deeply. But it was a happy and satisfied sigh. She had found a home.

CHAPTER 27

B Y the end of July Betsy had become so much a part of the
Ballou household that it seemed to her that she had always
lived there. Not since the days on the Old Warren Road with
Phebe and Jonathan had she felt so comfortable and secure. In
many ways, life with the Ballous was more tranquil, for Freelove
and Reuben seldom quarreled. They had arrived over the years at a
kind of truce, accepting each other with tolerant good grace and
never fussing about trifles.

The household itself was in a state of perpetual disorder, and at
first Betsy found this disturbing. She busied herself with cleaning
and mopping and tried to persuade Freelove to get rid of some of
the useless junk that was stacked about the large downstairs room.
But Freelove, who had watched Betsy's labors with quiet amusement, said, "Sure as I throw something away, there'll come a time
when I'll need it, and it won't be there."

And so, nothing was moved, and Betsy reduced her activities to
an occasional sweeping up. But she kept her own room at the end
of the second floor of the house in an immaculate condition. She
had salvaged a large bed, a chest of drawers, and a washstand from
the piles of junk that littered the house, and her room, though not
large, was cheerful and pleasant. A window looked out on the
canal, discolored and murky from the dye works. But she had
learned to look beyond it to the sloping hill where the houses of
the well-to-do shone prim and neat in the sun. The pot of red
button chrysanthemums that she had brought from Sally's had
been set on the window sill and had already formed small buds for
fall blooming.

As Freelove had predicted, Reuben Ballou gave Betsy no
trouble. He was a large man of amiable disposition, quiet to the

point of taciturnity when not made jovial and boisterous by alcohol. His drinking bouts were periodic, coinciding more or less with the game-hunting seasons in spring and fall.

In the times between, he went soberly and conscientiously about his business as butcher and sternly denied himself even an occasional drink of wine. In this, he was unlike his wife, for whom alcohol in some form was a staple of daily diet, although she seldom got as drunk as she had been on the day when Betsy had found her comatose on the bed.

Reuben accepted Betsy's presence in the house much as he accepted the cats and dogs. They were there, a part of his natural home environment. And just as he would occasionally stoop and pet one of them in absent-minded affection, so he would now and then pass the time of day with Betsy, asking about her health and the progress of her pregnancy. Then he would stare unabashedly at her belly with his watery blue eyes, rubbing his balding head in a satisfied way when she told him that things went well.

His only enthusiasm was for what he called his "birds," the wooden decoys that he carved with the care and concentration of an artist. One rainy Sunday afternoon, he showed Betsy his collection, a box of his favorite birds that he kept under his bed. These were birds that he could not bring himself to sell, not even for rum.

"They're mine, you see," he explained, like a small boy displaying his most valued marbles. Then, shy and embarrassed, he added, "They were so pretty and nice, I just couldn't part with 'em, not even for silver."

They were more than just pretty, and Betsy realized it. Reuben had somehow captured in his carvings the essential lines, the innate characteristics of individual game birds, be it a wild goose or plover or mallard duck. The faded blue eyes that seemed so faraway and listless evidently could become sharply observant when they lighted on the birds of water and shore, and his hands could make their figures come almost magically to life from the rough-hewn blocks of pine.

Betsy was charmed by Reuben's birds. She picked them up, one by one, pleasurably feeling their smooth forms with her fingertips, her eyes lighting in appreciation of their lifelike lines and characteristic attitudes.

Reuben beamed at her with shy pride. Impulsively, he gave her one of his duck decoys. Later, when he saw that she had displayed it on her window sill next to her beloved chrysanthemum plant, he swelled with the pride of an artist whose sculpture has been chosen to decorate a room in a king's palace. He said nothing, but from that time on his approval of Betsy became complete.

He began to go out of his way to do small things for her. Sometimes he would bring her special tidbits from his butcher shop, a small chicken or a pair of fancy chops. He would deliver these delicacies to her with the air of a conspirator, slipping her a neat package wrapped in newspaper when Freelove was not looking.

It was not that Freelove was jealous of these little attentions. But she had become uncharacteristically stern with Betsy on the subject of eating too much. She snatched buns from her hands at mealtimes, refused to give her any butter, and held forth at length on how enormous the baby would become and how much pain it would cause to birth it.

Betsy listened and promised to heed Freelove's warnings, and she did indeed try. But too often she secretly gave in to the demands of appetite. Her belly became larger and larger, and Freelove shook her head hopelessly.

In her sixth month of pregnancy now, Betsy hated to be seen on the street during daylight hours. Small boys jeered at her and called her "barrel belly." Women stared at her in self-righteous contempt, and men's eyes followed her with open leers. She did not feel guilty about being illegitimately pregnant, but it humiliated her to see herself so misshapen and ugly, a target for scorn instead of admiration.

But at night, under cover of darkness, she could almost forget her appearance. And yet, her altered figure was hardly stimulating to men in search of love. She was forced to sell herself cheaply, and even then her customers were few.

On a warm night in late July, as she waited wearily in the shadowed doorway of a linen shop, a young man paused before her. On his left shoulder rested a small monkey, its scrawny right arm clutched about the man's neck for support. Both man and monkey stared at her with bland, wide-open eyes, and then the man's gaze moved slowly from her face to the bulge between her hips.

Betsy stared back at him without embarrassment. She had already made the odd discovery that there were some men who found her condition not only unobjectionable but actually attractive. The swelling curve of her womb seemed to awaken in them a tender and gentle lustfulness.

"It is not good that you are here," the man said in a low voice. He spoke in the unaccented rhythm that English assumes when spoken by a Frenchman.

"I'm here to earn a living," she said. "Where did you get the monkey?"

"I bought him from Peter Daspré, the barber, when he was selling them two years ago January. His name is Danton. You know who is Danton?" When she shook her head, he said, "He was a noble leader of *la révolution* in France. They took off his head last April."

She shuddered. "The *guillotine?*" she asked, using the French pronunciation.

"You speak French, mademoiselle?"

"*Un peu,*" she said, "*très peu.* Can I pet Citoyen Danton?"

He nodded, and she extended her hand toward the monkey. He blinked his eyes at her questioningly and then grasped her forefinger, enclosing it tightly in his small bony hand. She laughed and looked into the young man's eyes.

He was even younger than she had thought. His thin beard had not yet toughened into stubble, and his skin was as clear as that of a girl. The dark curling hair that tumbled lightly down on his forehead emphasized the fairness of his complexion and the deep blue of his large eyes.

She did not move away when he touched his lips lightly to hers in a caress more friendly than passionate. The monkey had relinquished her forefinger and now began to tug angrily at her hair. He chattered his teeth at her, and his squeaky voice scolded her in a staccato treble.

"He's jealous," said Betsy.

The man nodded, stroking the animal in a soothing way. He turned his face to her and smiled with the spontaneous happiness of a small boy.

298

"How old are you?" she asked.

He drew up his smallish figure and swelled out his chest like a soldier coming to attention. This amused her, but she did not smile.

"I am twenty," he said. "I am a man."

"Of course you are a man," she said and then added, "and a very handsome man."

The compliment made him flush with embarrassment, and he turned away. She stretched out her hand toward his head and touched the crisp curliness of his hair in a reassuring way. He moved to her quickly, his arms encircling her. Now his lips were more insistent and pressed against hers hungrily. The monkey scrambled to the top of his head, where it took up a new and more advantageous position of attack. Then, burrowing both hands in Betsy's hair, it pulled hard, like a rider reining in his horse.

She cried out and broke away, then laughed and said, "We'll have to tie him up outside the bedroom door if you come home with me." She paused and asked, "Would you like that?"

For a moment she thought that he might bow from the waist and kiss her hand, but he merely took her arm in his with a courtly gesture and nodded vigorously. His eyes were as proud as those of a man who finally, after much maneuvering and seductive skill, had conquered a protesting lady of virtue.

But when they arrived at the Ballou house and had entered her bedroom, the sight of the bed, dimly lighted by a candle in Betsy's hand, seemed to paralyze him. She set the candle in a holder and then turned to face him, receptive and waiting. Abruptly he sat down on the end of the bed and stared at the floor. The monkey jumped up to his lap and clung to his chest. It stretched out its matchstick arms across him and turned its beady brown eyes on Betsy in an angry stare.

At last the man said, forcing out the words, "I have not—great knowledge—of woman."

She laughed. "A good-looking lad of twenty like you? I don't believe you."

"Oh, I am not—virgin. But I am not—not a good lover."

"And who told you that?"

"I do not need to be told. It is that I do not give pleasure to a woman." He fell silent and patted the monkey's back in a me-

299

chanical way and with averted eyes. At last he looked at her directly and said, his voice too loud, almost angry, "I arrive too quick. *Vous comprenez?* It is *tout fini* before I begin."

"You can always start all over again," said Betsy.

"I would, but always the lady is angry with me."

"Then the lady's a fool! And she don't really want you," she said, sitting down on the bed beside him. Once again she touched his hair lightly with her hand and then smoothed it back from his brow in a maternal gesture. But this time he did not respond.

"It is worse than that," he said. "I am very—small." With the innocence but not the enthusiasm of a boy inviting someone to feel his muscle, he took her hand and pressed it against his crotch. "You see?" he asked.

Betsy's gentle laughter filled the small room with warmth. She gave him a playful pat between his legs and said, "It's as good as can be. Why 'tis better than the ones carried by men who come here a-boasting and a-bragging how mighty they are!"

"Truly?"

"Truly. Now, leave off all the fretting. I'll tell you tomorrow whether you be a good lover or not."

The effect of her words was magical. With a frantic movement that sent Danton whirling to the floor, he rolled over toward her, his trembling hands seeking her breasts, his thighs pressed against her desperately.

As his mouth reached hers, she murmured, "Have a little regard for the small monsieur who sleeps inside me."

But her words were unnecessary. His body had already gone taut, his breath came fast, and his heart pounded against her. She knew that for the time being, at least, his love-making was over. She was quiet for several moments and held him against her protectively. Danton, who felt it was now safe to get back on the bed, tried to interpose himself between them and resumed his plaintive noises. Betsy patted him and then rose quietly from the bed.

The young man watched her as she slowly began to undress. Naked at last, she stood before the small mirror and began brushing her hair, which had been mussed by Danton. Her hair glinted red and gold in the wavering light of the taper.

The young man sat up. "You want me to go?" The question sounded like a statement.

She paused in her brushing and turned to look at him. He was sitting on the edge of the bed now, knees apart, his head lowered in humiliation. With his hands he tried to comfort the still-whimpering monkey.

"Do you want to go?" she whispered.

"No," he said. "But I—it was just as I told you."

"But you enjoyed yourself, didn't you?"

"Oh, yes," he said and then added hastily, "and I will pay, *bien entendu.* I am an honest man."

Her voice roughened in annoyance. "We'll talk about that tomorrow. Take off your clothes then. And for God's sake, tie that monkey to the foot of the bed. I'll not sleep with two for the price of one!"

This sent him into a burst of laughter, and with it his uneasiness disappeared. As he lay back on the bed, his hands clasped behind his neck, he began to talk, slowly at first and then with confidence and speed, like a mute who has been granted an unexpected miracle of speech.

His name was Michel Villeroi. He had come to Providence three years ago from Santo Domingo, where his father had been a captain in the French garrison at Cap-Haitien until the Haitian Revolution. Had she ever heard of Toussaint L'Ouverture? The garrison was sacked and burned. Both his parents had been murdered, and he had barely escaped with his own life.

For five weeks he hid in the jungle with three French soldiers who had fled with him. He survived. Maybe he did not look very strong, but he had great endurance. He was tough and wiry, like his monkey. And he was born under a star of good fortune. He was finally rescued by an American ship that was carrying a cargo of molasses to Providence. He liked Providence, and so he stayed, securing a job at the Wyatt shipyard.

Betsy raised her head, her hairbrush stopped in mid-air. "Did you know Matt Wyatt?"

"Oh, yes," said Michel. "He was my *chef,* my foreman. He is the son of the owner. A *beau garçon* who has gone away to Boston. Do you know him?"

"No," said Betsy. She put down the brush and turned to him. "You haven't taken off your clothes, and the monkey—"

"I talk too much. I am *bavard.*"

He picked up Danton and knotted his chain to the end of the bed. Then, with slow deliberation, he removed his breeches. Betsy, who meanwhile had turned down the coarse linen sheet and slipped beneath it, watched him with amusement as he kicked his clothes across the floor into the corner.

Shyness overcame him again as he stood naked before her, and then the sight of her figure outlined beneath the sheet stirred desire in him, and he forgot himself and his fears.

She smiled. "From the looks of things, I'd say you were all ready again, my lad. What are you waiting for?"

He waited no longer. Assured and confident, he took her, and this time his passion prolonged itself so that no apologies were necessary.

Afterward, as they clung to each other, perspiring and breathless in the warm July night, he began talking again, expansively, gratefully. In an impassioned mixture of French and English, he told her that she had made a man of him. Never had he been able to please a woman before, never had he reached such heights of ecstasy. He loved her. He would do anything she wished. He would marry her. It made no difference that she was carrying another man's child. He would love it as he loved her, would bring it up as his own.

Betsy found herself moved and touched by his flow of words. It was the first spontaneous proposal of marriage she had ever had. Although she knew that it sprang from gratitude, she valued it as something offered freely, without any demand on her part. And it was sincere. She knew that he would not retract his offer with the coming of daylight.

She felt guilty, as though she had duped him. It had taken so little effort on her part to restore to him the male confidence that he had lost, perhaps never had. A moan of pleasure that she did not feel, ecstatic murmurs and cries—they were pure play-acting.

It was not that she had been entirely without feeling, but since Matt had left her, it was as though the gates of pleasure had been locked and barred. If she had not needed money, she would not have sought the company of men at all. She did not perform the act of love so much as endure it, sometimes with boredom, often with active distaste.

With Michel, there had been a difference. Although he had not awakened her sensuality as Matt had been able to do, she had felt a tenderness toward him, not unlike the feeling she supposed she should have for the child within her. And did not have. For she still regarded the child with impatience, as a burden to be gotten rid of, so that her figure could return to its once lovely lines, so that she could attract admiring glances again. There were times when this impatience turned into active resentment, especially when the weather was hot and the baby's weight became intolerable. She became annoyed, too, when it chose the middle of the night as a suitable time for exercise, and its kicking woke her abruptly from sleep.

Michel's proposal had given Betsy an assurance that she needed. The mere fact of being wanted at a time when she felt so alone and undesirable tempted her to accept it. But instead, she thanked him seriously, gave him a light kiss on the cheek and said, "We'll talk about it tomorrow."

He sat up in bed and said firmly, "No. We will talk about it now. I want you for my wife."

"Things will look different in the daylight."

"In the daylight you will only be more beautiful." He tried to kiss her, but she pushed him away.

"Please, no more love tonight, Michel. I am tired, and I want to get to sleep before the child begins to kick."

His eyes opened wide in wonder. "He kicks?"

"Of course he kicks. All babies do, especially boys, they say."

"Oh, how I would like to feel him kick!" he said. "Will you let me the next time he does?"

She laughed. "Maybe. But why—"

"Because he is going to be my son," he said solemnly, "and I would like to feel him kick."

She smiled and pulled his head down toward her breast. He nestled there in silence, his cheek lying lightly against her shoulder. Soon he was asleep.

Betsy looked at the tousled darkness of his hair, listened to the slow rhythm of his breathing, and felt content. She did not even try to understand why this stripling of a man, so inexperienced, so lacking in confidence and assurance himself, should by his mere presence restore those very qualities to her.

CHAPTER 28

B ETSY did not accept Michel's proposal of marriage, not the next morning when it was renewed, nor in the days that followed. But she agreed to become his mistress and took with gratitude the generous share of his weekly earnings that he gave her. For the first time since Matt had gone away she was happy. She told herself that it was merely because she no longer needed to walk the streets in order to help Freelove with her household expenses, but it was more than that. Once again she felt needed.

As for Freelove, she was delighted with Betsy's "new French gentleman," as she called him, and even more delighted with his monkey, whom she added to her menagerie. At first the dogs looked at him with curiosity and the cats with fear, but eventually Danton achieved, if not exactly general acceptance, at least toleration.

Freelove pampered and fussed over him, even though her efforts to housebreak him met with total failure. This threw her into a daily rage.

"You're a dirty, filthy little beast!" she would scream whenever she discovered the droppings and puddles he left so casually about the house. While she cleaned up these messes, he would regard her in mock sorrow and penitence, sometimes even going so far as to make thoroughly inefficient attempts to assist her.

One day, when she found him in her rocking chair masturbating gleefully as he rocked, she let loose a more violent flood of vituperation, but her anger melted before the soft gaze of his eyes, and his utter hypocrisy moved her to laughter. Danton, well aware that he had made a conquest, thought up new mischiefs to provoke these exciting displays of emotion.

Freelove was not Danton's only conquest. In time, he completely captivated Betsy, too. During the day, when Michel was at the shipyard, he became her constant companion, riding about on her shoulder or prancing before her as she walked. He would lope and scramble ahead, then pause to look back, gibbering wildly and chattering his teeth. Then, in a surprise attack, he would leap to her shoulder with a graceful bound and plunge his tiny hands into the soft masses of her hair. Sometimes, with intense concentration, he would painstakingly part the strands in a constantly frustrated search for lice.

Michel's return in the evening was a signal for unrestrained joy. Then Danton's ecstasy knew no bounds. He cavorted and showed off, played with himself wantonly, danced a mad jig, and devoured anything remotely edible. Sometimes he nipped these people he loved with his little sharp teeth.

Michel was as delighted as Danton with his new way of life, and in his shy way he became almost as demonstrative. The adoration he felt for Betsy shone in his eyes whenever he looked at her. He needed to be close to her, to touch her lightly with his hand, with his shoulder, with his head, with some part of his body. Betsy, who had conceived a distaste for the pawings of men, did not seem to mind these casual intimacies. They were like the affectionate rubbings of a dog who wishes merely to make his presence known, as though to say, "I am here, remember?"

Slowly, in the days that followed their meeting, Michel took on the role of Betsy's protector. The strength that was in him had been suddenly released to be used freely and without restraint. He no longer needed to throw out his chest or flex his muscles to tell others, as well as himself, that he was a man. He was sure of it.

And yet his boyishness did not disappear, and it still charmed and amused Betsy. She found herself wishing that she could respond to him amorously, but she could not. It was one of the reasons why she did not accept his daily proposal of marriage.

This was the only source of disharmony between them. He argued, he cajoled, he begged, but persistently and gently she put him off. Only once did she lose her temper with him.

"You won't marry me," he said, "because you hope to marry the child's father, *n'est-ce pas?*"

She reacted with anger. "That's a lie!"

"It's true. Look how angry you are! It is proof!"

305

"It's proof of how I hate him! I wouldn't marry him if he—if he—" She broke off and began to cry.

"I am sorry," said Michel.

"And don't feel sorry for me!"

There was a silence, and then softly he said, "You must have loved him very much."

She lifted her head in a defiant way. "No, I made up a dream. I woke up, and there was nothing there." She laughed ironically and pointed to her womb. "Only *this* was there." Then, with venom, she added, "And I hate *it*, too!"

Michel seized her and clapped his hand over her mouth. "You must not say that!"

She was startled by the violence of his action. "But what do you care? It is not yours."

"I will make it mine," he said. "It will be my son, my first son. There will be more. I intend it." He smiled at her.

"But I haven't agreed to marry you!"

"You will, *ma chère*. I will wait, and one day you will say yes."

There were times when she wondered if he might not be right. Their life together had already taken on the habitual rhythms of a conventional marriage. She rose with him at dawn and prepared breakfast, like any housewife in any respectable home in town. They ate together, sometimes happy and affectionate, sometimes disgruntled and quarrelsome. At night, his return from work was the occasion for a small reunion, as though they had not seen each other for weeks, and it was celebrated by immediate love-making. After supper, they often took a stroll, arm in arm, to Market Square, with a stop at the Bulldog Tavern for a tankard of ale.

A shared existence was something new for Betsy. In her life with Matt, she had been for the most part alone. Alone, she had waited in her room for the uncertain hour of his arrival, and after he had left, she had slept alone. She had eaten her meals alone and walked alone on the street. Now she was aware that the disappearance of loneliness that she had accepted as a normal part of life lay at the root of her present feeling of happiness. And yet she could not bring herself to accept Michel's offer of marriage. When she finally told Freelove about her feelings, Michel gained a powerful and vociferous ally.

306

"You must be daft!" Freelove said. "He's a sweet-tempered man, he don't drink too much, and he ain't afraid of work. More than that, it looks to me like he loves your unborn bastard more'n you do. And all you got to say is 'But, Freelove, I don't *love* him!' Love! What's love?" She spat a stream of tobacco juice toward the hearth.

"But I *don't* love him," said Betsy.

"You mean he don't pleasure you?"

"Yes. That's part of it."

Freelove nodded her head so that her resemblance to an owl became more marked than ever. "When a woman's got a belly as big as yours, there's no room for pleasure in it, anyway. Even your Matt wouldn't be no good to you now, even if his prick was as big as a mule's."

"That's what I was wondering—" Betsy's voice trailed off in embarrassment.

"Well, what is it, girl? Surely you ain't a-feared of raising a maiden's blush to these old cheeks?"

"Well, you see, Michel is, well, he's a small man—"

"So that's what's bothering you?" Freelove extended an arm toward her with the awkwardness of a sea lion directing a protective flipper to one of its young. "Now, you listen to me, lovey. Bigness ain't got a thing to do with it. Hell's fire, my Reuben's scarcely got much of anything. Like anything else, they come in all sizes and shapes, just like hands and ears and feet. And it's rare for the Almighty to make 'em too small for propagating the earth. Of course, sometimes, they don't work proper, like my Reuben's when the drink is in him." She paused, as though stopped by a new thought. "Michel's is in good working order, ain't it?"

Betsy nodded, still too embarrassed for speech. It was not so much the nature of the discussion that made her blush but Freelove's bald reference to her husband's anatomy. Somehow, it had never occurred to Betsy that Freelove herself, so huge and grotesque in body, so lacking in feminine allure, might ever engage in love-making with Reuben, or with anyone else, for that matter. Her imagination faltered as she tried to envision it, and she had an almost uncontrollable desire to laugh.

"Seems to me," Freelove continued, "that a girl with as much acquaintance of men as you would know about this. Why is it that all women are the same, be they whores or housewives. Some-where they got the idea that the bigger it is the bigger the satis-faction. But it's only an idea in their heads. It just ain't true. It's how a woman feels about a man that makes the satisfaction, not the tool he's using."

"But that's just it," said Betsy. "I don't feel anything with Michel. I like him, of course, and he's so young and he needs somebody to love him." She paused and added, "But not me. Be-cause my heart ain't in it, and I want a man I can look up to."

Freelove snorted her contempt. "Oh, God save us, she wants a knight on a white horse to carry her off to a castle!"

Betsy's eyes lighted with interest. "A castle? Yes."

Freelove slapped her thigh and said, "So that's it! Why didn't you say so right out? You want a *rich* man!"

"Not just rich. Somebody important and powerful."

"Oh, a king maybe? Well, there ain't no kings in America, lovey."

"There are Presidents."

"So it's the President's lady you'd be! Damned if I don't believe you *are* Washington's bastard daughter!" Freelove laughed up-roariously.

Oblivious to Freelove's laughter, Betsy continued, "But a king would be better, and there are still some in Europe."

"And they're getting their heads chopped off," said Freelove.

"There'll be new ones. There will always be kings."

Freelove shrugged and reached for her chewing tobacco. "Well," she said as she bit off a huge wad, "I can see Michel don't stand a chance."

"No," said Betsy, "he doesn't, and I feel sorry for him."

Freelove spat into the fireplace. "Nice of you," she said.

CHAPTER 29

B Y the middle of September, the days had turned cool, and frost had already blackened the marigolds in Freelove's small garden. A fire burned on the hearth day and night, and darkness was beginning to come early.

Betsy, who usually enjoyed the coming of autumn and the renewed energies it brought with it, found herself feeling constantly cold and chilled. Even sitting before the hearth, with one of Freelove's large moth-eaten sweaters around her swollen body, she shivered.

"It means your time is coming closer," observed Freelove. "It ain't the cold so much as the fear of what's a-comin'."

"But I'm not afraid," said Betsy. "The sooner it happens the better. I want it over and done with."

"It'll come when it will come. Nature knows when it's time."

Betsy looked down at her distended belly with disgust. "Well, nature ain't had a look at me lately then. If I get any bigger, I'll bust."

And then, early in October, the weather turned warm and dry, and Betsy's chills disappeared. Indian summer spread its warm haze on the horizon, and the sky over Providence became a deep and cloudless blue. Betsy basked in the golden warmth and became as lazy and docile as a cow in a meadow. She gave up sitting at the fireside and moved happily about the house.

Michel's doglike devotion had become now almost reverence. He waited upon her, ran errands at any hour to satisfy her cravings for unusual foods, and regarded her with a kind of awe. As the time of her confinement approached, he even avoided touching her, as though she were a fragile object that would somehow be damaged by the slightest physical contact. He had long since given up love-making with her, and his only gesture of affection was a chaste kiss planted on her forehead when he returned from work.

Betsy knew that she should be appreciative of his solicitude, but as the long days of waiting went by, she became increasingly irritable. It was not in her nature to enjoy being pampered and treated like a china doll. She longed to be up and doing, to be part of the comings and goings of people again.

One night at supper, she stared with distaste at the roast chicken on the plate before her. The very sight of it made her feel ill. She got up quickly and left the table for a chair at the fireside.

Michel went over to her immediately. *"Qu'as-tu, ma chérie?"* he asked softly.

"Nothing," she said. "I'm not hungry, that's all. Go eat and leave me be." As he stood hesitantly before her, she said, "Oh, go eat, for God's sake! I'm all right. Just let me alone! Don't hang over me like a mother hen!"

Michel looked uncertainly toward Freelove, who motioned him to come back to the table. Without saying anything he returned to his place at the table, but his eyes kept looking toward Betsy in concern.

Betsy stared at the fire, and then, as boredom and weariness came over her, she fell asleep. Two hours later she awoke, thirsty and ravenously hungry. The fire had burned low, and a wool shawl had been placed over her. Michel dozed in a chair opposite her.

Her thirst was intolerable, and suddenly she had a vision of hundreds of raw oysters—cool, luscious, dripping with sea brine. She could see Sam Thurber at his oyster bench in front of *The Old Hooker*, the dilapidated hull of an old sloop that served as his shop at the water's edge. She could almost hear Sam's singsong voice hawking his wares as he pried open the oysters with unbelievable speed and set them down on the bench.

Betsy sat up in her chair and tossed the shawl aside. "Michel!" she said. "I want oysters—cold raw oysters from *The Old Hooker!*"

Michel awoke with a start, like a sentry caught napping on duty. "I will get them right away," he said.

"No! I'm coming with you. I'm tired of being cooped up in this place!"

She brushed aside his protests with a wave of her hand, placed the shawl over her head, and took his arm. As they neared the door, Danton appeared out of the shadows and in a long, frantic leap took up his position on Michel's shoulder, chattering in excitement at the prospect of an outing.

The Old Hooker was doing a lively business that night. A line of young men and their girls stood in the flickering light of a pitch torch that had been stuck in the sand near the oyster bench. Sam Thurber's hands manipulated the knife expertly, plumping down the opened oysters on the bench, from which they were snatched up by the customers as soon as they had deposited their coppers in a large pewter bowl.

Betsy stood aside and waited until it would be Michel's turn in the line. She was so engrossed in watching Sam at his work that she was not aware of the figure that had moved stealthily to her side. It was not until she felt the pressure of a thigh being pushed against hers that she turned around and found herself staring into the rum-swollen face of Bobby Brown. His bloodshot eyes looked at her in blearily lustful concentration. The corners of his mouth were turned down in a derisive smile. Startled, she moved quickly away from him and turned her eyes back to the oyster bench as though she had not recognized him.

"Hey, there, Bouncing Bet!" said Bobby in a loud voice. "You got a pretty big belly to be so high and mighty! Whose bastard is it? Matt Wyatt's?"

He staggered toward her again, now leaning his drunken weight against her so that his crotch pressed against her hip. His arm went around her shoulders and he pulled her close.

"Leave me be, Bobby Brown!" she said. She gave him a shove that sent him off balance so that he almost fell, but he recovered himself and advanced on her again menacingly.

"Too good for me, huh?" he snarled. "A whore that's been poked by every pizzle in town except mine—"

"Hold your dirty tongue before my husband hears you!"

People had begun to watch them now, and Betsy caught sight of Michel's tense face looking at them.

"Husband!" roared Bobby. "That little French pip-squeak is your *husband*?" He pointed his finger in scorn at Michel.

Betsy shook her head at Michel and implored him with her eyes not to intervene. Michel disregarded her, abruptly stepping out of line and striding to her side. His hand was on the small Haitian dagger he always carried in his belt. He moved threateningly toward Bobby, while Danton, perched on his shoulder, bared his teeth and screamed.

The crowd sensed that a fight was in the making and slowly edged around in a semicircle. There was fury in Michel's face. He stood before the town sergeant like a lithe animal ready to spring.

Through clenched teeth he said, "You are drunk, monsieur. Go away and do not insult my wife or I will kill you!"

Bobby laughed. "Kill me? You'd kill me to protect the honor of a slut, a whore with a bastard in her that's not even your own?"

The crowd was silent, and the words echoed in the frosty air. And then Michel flung himself on Bobby, and the two men fell to the ground, where they grappled with each other. Danton fled to Betsy in panic, and she picked him up in her arms. She watched in horror as the dagger in Michel's upraised hand flashed briefly in the torchlight. A woman in the crowd screamed.

In drunken desperation Bobby seized Michel's arm and twisted it savagely. The dagger fell to the ground, and Bobby pressed his momentary advantage. With a sudden powerful movement he rolled Michel aside and then under him, so that he was able to pin him down with all his weight. Michel struggled to free himself, and his hands sought frantically for the dagger in the sand. But Bobby, from his superior position, spotted it and seized it in his right hand. With all his strength he plunged it deep into Michel's chest.

The crowd gasped and began moving toward the two men. Someone grabbed Bobby by the arms and pulled him away from Michel's prostrate form. Michel groaned and, as though still fighting, turned on his side. He tried to rise but fell back and lost consciousness.

Several men moved forward to go to Michel's aid. One knelt and propped Michel's head against his thighs. Another loosened the jacket that still covered his chest. On the shirt beneath there was a small spot of crimson where the dagger had entered. Michel's breathing had become labored and he struggled for air. Suddenly he gagged and vomited forth a quantity of bright blood. The man who was cradling Michel's head looked up.

"I'm a-feared he's done for," he said. "It went right to his heart."

The silent crowd parted as Betsy moved into the semicircle of space at the center of which lay Michel's unconscious form. She looked at him in disbelief. It had all happened so quickly. Even the sound of his gurgling efforts to breathe seemed to come to her from faraway, only half heard.

It was when Danton leaped from her arms and loped over to Michel's body that she seemed to become aware of what had happened, and she moaned, "Oh, God, he ain't dead, is he?" No one answered her.

Her eyes moved to Danton, who had begun a frantic, chattering dance that took him back and forth the length of Michel's body, his hands clasped before him in desperation. Once he paused and reached out to touch the wound, which was now bleeding more profusely. He withdrew his small hand in panic as he felt the warm blood on his skin. Then he became quiet and huddled himself by Michel's head, moaning piteously.

Betsy had begun to cry now, uncontrollably and hysterically. She flung herself to the ground beside Michel and placed her hand gently on his bloodstained cheek.

"Michel! Michel!" she sobbed. "Don't die! Please don't die, *mon cher!* I'll marry you, I promise. But please don't die!"

For a moment, it seemed as though he had heard her and recognized her voice. He tried once more to raise himself, as though to speak. But he coughed up more blood and then fell back with a long-drawn, rattling exhalation of air. She waited for his breath, but it did not come.

She began to scream, shrill, agonizing cries that came from the depths of her being. The stunned crowd came suddenly to life. There was a babble of voices as people surrounded Betsy, who sat awkwardly on the ground, her legs apart to accommodate the bulk of her womb that protruded itself before her. Danton, frightened and desolate, was clinging desperately to her breasts, and she clutched his brown warmth to her in a convulsion of grief. The gabble of voices seemed to come to her from some place far away.

"He's dead all right. Murdered by the town sergeant, that's what!"

" 'T'ain't murder to kill a man in self-defense! The Frenchy attacked him with a foreign dagger."

"Too many damned Frenchies around anyway."

"Bobby Brown'll go scot-free, mark my words!"

"He's a no-good son of a bitch, mean and drunken and loud-mouthed, and he oughta swing for it, only he won't!"

"Look at the poor bitch. I swear she looks like she's gonna give birth right here at *The Old Hooker!*"

Betsy was aware that her belly and thighs had become sopping wet, and she wondered if someone had thrown water on her to revive her. And then she noticed that her belly was oddly tight and hard. She seemed to hear Freelove's voice saying, "If the water breaks early, you'll have a dry labor."

The realization that her labor was about to begin swept even the horror of Michel's death from her mind. To a woman who was leaning over her, she whispered, "Please, it's beginning—the baby. Take me to Freelove Ballou. Please."

A sharp pain shot through her, and she cried out in surprise. And then, as the spasm dissipated itself, she slipped into unconsciousness, falling back to the earth with Danton still clasped in her arms.

CHAPTER 30

THE large downstairs room of the Ballou house was almost brilliant with light. Candles glowed from branched candlesticks. A freshly built fire blazed on the hearth. Before it an improvised mattress of clean straw covered with worn sheets and blankets had been spread on the bare boards of the floor.

In the center of this lay Betsy, stretched out full length on her back with a small pillow beneath her head. She had been stripped naked, and her white, immobile face with its closed, unseeing eyes gave her the look of a toppled statue, an abandoned and very pregnant Venus.

Nearby, there was a small pine table on which were a pair of scissors, a length of string, a bowl of hot water, and an assortment of small bottles containing homemade medicines. Another table, much larger and of sturdy oak, was partly covered with a clean wool blanket, and on it a large washbowl had been placed.

Freelove came waddling down the stairs with the deliberate movements of a fat woman in a hurry. Behind her came Reuben, blinking and yawning as he fumbled with the buttons of his trousers. He paused for a moment and regarded Betsy's naked figure with wide eyes.

Freelove turned to him impatiently. "Ain't you never seen a naked female before? Stop gawking and do like I told you."

He watched Freelove as she shook out a clean blanket and covered Betsy with it. Then he said, "But I don't know where to look for her."

"Oh, for God's sake, Reuben!" said Freelove. "Try Sally Marshall's first. If she ain't there pleasuring a customer, she'll be down at Cheapside looking for one."

"But it's almost midnight," protested Reuben.

"And what time do you think whores go to work, anyway? Now get out of here and find her! I'm going to need help, and Polly's the only friend Betsy's got. Hurry!"

As Freelove raised her arm threateningly, Reuben ducked and made quickly for the door. Freelove returned to the hearth and looked down at Betsy, her brow wrinkled with concern. Then she rocked back and forth like a goose getting ready to sit and finally managed to squat down near Betsy's head.

"Betsy!" she shouted. "You got to wake up, hear me? You got work to do!"

Betsy stirred and moved her head away from the bellow of Freelove's voice, but her eyes did not open. Then, as a new contraction shook her, her body suddenly went taut, and she gave a sharp cry and moved her head back and forth in pain. When the paroxysm had passed, she opened her eyes and stared blankly at Freelove. Then, as memory returned, she began to cry. "Oh, God, oh, God," she moaned.

Freelove moved laboriously to a position behind Betsy and pulled Betsy toward her. When Betsy's head rested at last against her heaving bosom, she whispered, "There now, lovey. Rest easy and don't cry. You got to save your strength."

Betsy nuzzled her tear-streaked face against Freelove's breast, whimpering like a child seeking comfort from its mother. After her sobs had quieted, she said in a small voice, "Oh, Freelove. Michel—is he really dead?"

"Yes, lovey," said Freelove, and tears started to her own eyes. "But you mustn't think about it now. We can't change it. We can't bring him back." She tried to inject a note of cheerfulness into her voice as she said, "Little Georgie Washington wants to get himself born, and the stubborn little bastid won't wait, no matter what's happened."

Betsy raised her head in anger. "Oh, to hell with Georgie! I don't care if he dies a-borning."

"And well he might, and you along with him, if you don't start to work."

"Work?"

"You didn't think he was just going to pop out of you like a grasshopper, did you? Why d'you think they call it labor?"

"All right. Let's get it done with. What do I do?"

"When the next pain comes, bear down on it hard!"

"And when will that be?" asked Betsy.

"Maybe in half an hour. Do you feel strong enough to stand up?"

"I don't know. My back hurts."

"Good. That means it's on the move. Now try to raise up, but easy now."

Freelove's hands clasped Betsy's and pulled her forward. Slowly and with great effort, Betsy got to her feet. Dizziness overcame her and she swayed. Freelove's arms went around her.

"Don't faint, lovey," she commanded. "Hold on!"

Betsy's teeth locked together in determination. "I won't faint, goddamned if I will."

Freelove led her to the heavy oak table that had been placed nearby. "Now, missy, you just grab the edge of this table, lean forward and hold on hard!"

Betsy sighed with relief as she felt the smooth edge of the table beneath her hands. Meanwhile, Freelove had moved to a position behind her and was massaging the small of her back. She pushed against it with a steady pressure.

As the pain eased, Betsy began to talk. "Oh, Freelove, I'll never forgive myself. If only I hadn't gone with him, if only—"

Freelove stopped her massaging, seized Betsy roughly by the shoulder, and swung her around so that she faced her. "Now you listen to me, Betsy Bowen! There ain't no sense saying 'if only' every time life kicks you in the arse, blaming yourself instead of the Almighty. He knows what's going to happen and you don't."

"You mean it's His fault?"

"Sure it is. And most of the time He ain't even got the common decency to warn you so you can watch out."

"You really think there is a God, Freelove?"

"Yep. But He's a bastid."

Betsy smiled, and Freelove went back to massaging. In between grunts, Freelove added, "Maybe He knows what He's doing, and maybe He don't. But He ain't giving anybody any explanations."

Betsy fell silent. She saw again the still body of Michel stretched on the ground, his face so white and without expression, with the smear of drying blood across his cheek. Again, she watched the forlorn figure of Danton as he moved back and forth in desperation.

"Where's Danton?" asked Betsy.

"Locked in your bedroom, out of the way."

"Let him out."

"Now look, lovey, we can't have a monkey traipsin' around during a childbirth."

"I said let him out! And be quick about it!"

Freelove paused, ready for argument, but then she sighed and moved toward the stairs. Suddenly, there were footsteps outside the door and then voices. Polly came quickly into the room, followed by Reuben. She had dressed hastily, and her dark hair fell in confusion about her shoulders. Without even a word of greeting, she went over to Betsy and put her arms around her.

"Reuben!" said Freelove. "Go upstairs and let that dratted monkey out of Betsy's bedroom, will you?"

"What for?" asked Reuben.

"How do I know what for? She wants him down here, that's all." Freelove turned to Polly and said in a businesslike voice, "Did you ever help with birthing a baby?" Polly nodded. "Good! Well you better take off that fancy dress then and start being helpful."

"What do you want me to do?" asked Polly.

"Make us lots of strong tea. We won't be doing much sleeping tonight, my girl. That baby's a big one, and I got a feeling he's going to make trouble."

Betsy cried out as another pain went through her.

Freelove looked up and began rubbing her hands together in an anticipatory way. "They're coming closer together. With luck maybe we'll see the head in another twelve hours, what with this dry labor."

"Twelve hours!" shrieked Betsy. "Twelve hours of *this?*"

"I said with luck. It could go on for a day or so."

"Oh, my God," Betsy moaned.

Freelove plunged her right hand into a bowl of fresh unsalted butter on the table and then faced Betsy. "Turn around so I can get at you," she commanded. "Got to grease up the alleyway, y'know." She administered the butter with casual efficiency.

"Oh, it hurts, Freelove, it hurts!" Betsy wailed.

Freelove paused in her ministrations and looked up with a grin. "Sure, it hurts. The pain comes out where the pleasure went in, lovey! Now grab the edge of that table, begin pushing, and save your breath."

Five hours later, Betsy lay on the floor in a reclining position. A straight-backed chair had been placed upside down behind her, with a bag of barley as a cushion. She leaned back against it, weak and exhausted, her face pale and wet with sweat. Dark circles had begun to appear beneath her eyes. The pains were coming at ten-minute intervals now, and the contractions lasted longer and were more violent than before. Between times Betsy dozed, only half-conscious of what was happening. The real world had faded away, and she felt that she was living in some nightmare land, where a monster had seized hold of her and would not let her go. Relentlessly, he ravished her at regular intervals, but instead of pleasure, she felt only intolerable pain. When she cried out, her voice sounded far away.

Polly, clothed in her shift, sat on the floor near Betsy's head. She mopped the sweat from Betsy's brow and murmured consoling, encouraging words. But Freelove's voice had turned strangely harsh and unsympathetic. Her tone was that of a sergeant on a drill field as she bellowed out orders. "Bear down! Bear down! Push the bastid out!"

As the sound of her voice echoed through the room, Danton, perched precariously on the chair against which Betsy rested, would cover his ears with his hands and cringe. Frightened at first, he now seemed calm and was watching the proceedings with fascinated, beady eyes. Like Betsy, he sometimes dozed between the pains and would awaken again at the sound of Freelove's thundering commands.

Like all good midwives, Freelove possessed a variety of medicines calculated to ease the pains of childbirth. There were fresh dogwood berries, red and poisonous-looking, and a kind of tea made by pouring hot water over crumbled basil leaves. Betsy dutifully chewed the berries that Polly put into her mouth. They were so intensely bitter that they made her gag, and she washed them down with the basil tea. But her pain, instead of easing, became more violent.

As a final resort, Freelove herself administered two teaspoons of a special syrup that she kept on hand for such occasions. It had a musty, vinegary smell, and Polly asked what it was. Freelove became mysterious in the superior way of all medical practitioners and refused to tell. She did not feel it would be helpful for Betsy to know that it consisted of thirteen fat, juicy sow bugs drowned in white wine, with some loaf sugar added for greater palatability.

And so she merely said, "It's a secret recipe and it almost always works."

Betsy swallowed the two teaspoonsful of this elixir and grimaced. The next contraction did, indeed, seem less painful, and Polly looked at Freelove with new respect.

"Where did you learn to make such good medicines, Freelove?" she asked.

"Well," said Freelove loftily, "my father was a physician, y'know." She did not add that he had also been so perennially drunk that he practiced medicine only in his rare intervals of sobriety. "He had," Freelove continued, "many old books of recipes and simples, some of them more'n a hundred years old." In a hushed voice, she added, "Some were used by witches for all manner of wicked purposes, like love potions that would keep an old man hard as a rock all night long!"

Polly's eyes widened. "Oh, Freelove, please don't use witchcraft on poor Betsy. She's in enough trouble already."

Freelove disregarded her and said, "Now there was one recipe for childbirth pain that I've always wanted to try. It's made of powdered virgin hair and twelve dried ants' eggs mixed with a pint of milk from a red cow. Only trouble was I could never find a virgin to get the hair from."

"D'you think it would help Betsy?" asked Polly hopefully.

"Maybe." She turned her eyes full on Polly in an insolent stare. "Surely you ain't offering me some of *your* hair, are you?" Freelove paused and looked thoughtful. "It might help if we had his hat."

"Whose hat?"

"The father's. Matt Wyatt's."

The sound of Matt's name wakened Betsy from her dozing. She opened her eyes and looked at them. "What about Matt Wyatt?"

"D'you have a hat that belonged to him?" asked Freelove.

"I've got nothing that belongs to him except this varmint I'm trying to get out of my belly. What would I do with his hat, even if I had it?"

"You'd put it on," Freelove explained. "And when a pain comes, you'd reach up with both hands and pull the blazes on the brim to ease yourself."

Polly stood up. "I'll go up to the Wyatts' house right now and get one of his hats."

Betsy said, "You'll do no such thing! I'll die with this cursed pain before you ask Matt Wyatt for anything!" Another pain seized her, and she screamed. The anger she felt made her bear down all the harder.

The day that followed seemed to Betsy the longest she had ever lived through. The pains continued, and the intervals of respite between them became gradually shorter. She ate dogwood berries and drank basil tea. She finished the bottle of Freelove's mysterious syrup and, not so mysteriously, vomited. And still the baby's head had not appeared.

Freelove, her arms greased with butter past her elbows, made explorations into Betsy. These were painful and unrewarding. In intervals of lucidity, Betsy pleaded with her to do something, anything that would put an end to the nightmare process that continued so relentlessly.

At one point, she screamed, "Kill him! Drag him out of me! Cut me open with the bread knife and take him away! I've had enough of this, d'you hear?"

"Now, Betsy, you listen to me! He's big. It's because you ate so much. So now it's going to take longer for him to move out into the canal. Once he gets there, it'll be smooth sailing."

Betsy ground her teeth. "Oh, I hate him! I hate him! The fat little bastard! Kill him! Do it!" She reached for the knife that lay on the table. Polly seized her hands and pushed her back against the bag of barley.

Freelove bent over her and without saying a word struck the

palm of her hand hard on Betsy's jaw. "Behave yourself, slut! I'm not going to risk your life or the baby's either, not unless I have to. And then I'll call Dr. Bentham."

Betsy whimpered, "Oh, Freelove, call him now, call him now."

"Not yet. Maybe after twenty-four hours—"

Betsy began to cry again. "Twenty-four hours! But surely it's been that already."

"Not until midnight tonight. Now stop crying and get back to work. When the pain comes, push! Bear down!"

"What the hell d'you think I've been doing? I've pushed until everything in me has come out. I'm filthy!"

"Never mind that now," said Freelove. "Everything's come out except the baby. I want to see its head. So work!"

Betsy closed her eyes and with resignation did as she was told.

It was after sunset and the early darkness of autumn had turned the windows into rectangles of black. Polly slept in a chair near the hearth, with Danton curled up in her lap. Betsy writhed and moaned on the floor, barely conscious of her surroundings. The pains were coming at intervals of only a few minutes, so that she had no spells of quiet at all. She had barely recovered from one paroxysm before another shook her.

Freelove was seated on the birthstool, facing Betsy. Her figure sagged with weariness; her eyes were swollen and red-ringed from lack of sleep. A frown of deepening concern furrowed her usually smooth brow, and she clenched and unclenched her hands anxiously. At last, she raised her great bulk from the stool and got down on her hands and knees before Betsy to make another examination. A few moments later, she withdrew her arm jubilantly and smiled.

"It's there!" she announced in triumph. "The head's coming out. I was scared he was coming out arse-end first, but hes' sticking out his head like a regular little gentleman! Betsy, did you hear me?"

Betsy opened her eyes, which were expressionless, only half alive. In a faraway voice, she whispered, "What?"

"Take heart, girl!" said Freelove. " 'Twon't be long now!"

"How long?"

"Maybe two hours."

"Two hours more? God, isn't there any end to this?"

"You can't stop working now, lovey, so don't rest back. Every time the pain comes, you just take a deep breath and bear down some more."

The pains had become more frequent now and more violent. Betsy collected her strength for a renewed battle, and angrily she bore down with all the force that was in her. After every deep breath, she swore at the child with the fury of someone cursing a mule that refused to move. "Get out of me, you bastard, get out! I hate you!"

Polly now lay sprawled on the floor near Betsy's head, stroking her hair and placing wet cloths on her forehead. "Oh, Betsy, you mustn't say things like that to your own little baby! A mother's curse might cripple him for life!"

"Leave her be," said Freelove. "If it makes her feel better to cuss him, let her cuss him."

And so, for the next two hours Betsy strained, sweated, cursed, and breathed deep. But now, instead of moaning in despair, she was fighting. And the enemy was the tiny creature that was inching its way into the world through her sore and ravaged body.

At long last, George made his formal appearance, and Freelove was ready for him. With infinite care she moved her greased hands about his head, manipulating him, supporting his head with one hand, coaxing his shoulders out with the other, until finally he lay, in a mess of blood and filth, on the blanket beneath Betsy's widespread thighs. Then he let forth an angry, squalling cry.

"Quick, Polly! The scissors and string!" bellowed Freelove. With steady and expert hands, she cut the umbilical cord and tied it. Betsy lay back exhausted, but now she wore a half smile of relief, the muscles of her face no longer contorted with strain.

On her knees, Freelove picked up the baby and, with her left hand supporting his back, held him up before her. Her eyes studied him appraisingly. "It's a boy, all right, and damned if he don't look like George Washington!" The infant gave vent to another loud squall, and Freelove turned to Polly. "You know how to bathe a baby?" Polly nodded. "Wash him down with the white wine in the jug there, and be careful with his head."

Polly took the child from Freelove and looked at him in wonder. Her large brown eyes took on a glow of warmth and pleasure, and for a moment she held him lovingly against her. Then she moved to the other side of the room, where the table had been placed. On it was a large earthenware washbowl, a jug of white wine, a towel, and a small blanket. She set the baby down in the washbowl and with many cooing noises began to give him his first bath.

Meanwhile, Freelove had again turned her attention to Betsy. "You ain't through yet, me love. You got to keep on working until we get that afterbirth or you'll be in trouble for fair!"

Betsy had raised herself and was looking down at her body in disgust. "Oh, Freelove, clean me up! I'm covered with filth!"

"Time enough for that later. Birthing a baby ain't a dainty business, missy. Now you just keep bearing down till we get that afterbirth."

For the next half hour Betsy worked and strained as the contractions continued to shake her. But the afterbirth did not appear. She began to bleed, slightly at first and then copiously. Freelove was alarmed, but her face, as impassive as that of a Buddha, gave no indication of her mounting concern.

She got to her feet and moved to the table where she had spread out her midwife's paraphernalia. Picking up a blue bottle, a length of black string, and a small bowl that contained a matted mass of dirty cobwebs, she returned to Betsy, who had lapsed into unconsciousness. She knelt and deposited the stuff on the floor, then began slapping Betsy's cheeks with the open palm of her hand. "Wake up, you slut!" she shouted. "Don't let yourself go! You still got work to do!"

But Betsy's head lolled to the side loosely, and she did not even hear Freelove, whose voice had risen to a shrill note of panic. Her hands trembled now and her breath came fast. With nervous fingers she tied the black string around Betsy's belly and pulled it tight. Then she cut off a short length of it and wrapped this several times around the little toe of Betsy's left foot. She scooped up a handful of cobwebs from the bowl and thrust them into Betsy to stanch the flow of blood.

Once again she attempted to revive Betsy, slapping her hard on the thighs and pinching one of her nipples between her thumb and forefinger. Betsy twitched in pain, lifted a hand in protest, and then opened her eyes.

Freelove shouted into her ear, "Listen to me, Betsy, and listen

324

sharp! You're bleeding bad and you're a-gonna die unless you do what I tell you!"

Betsy's eyes widened, and in their depths there was naked fear. "No! No! I don't want to die! Freelove, please!"

Freelove extended the neck of the blue bottle toward Betsy's mouth. "Then blow into this bottle to stop the bleeding. Blow as hard as you can!"

With what breath there was in her, Betsy blew into the bottle again and again. But the bleeding did not stop. It was then that Freelove, in her desperation, remembered a Biblical quotation that some midwives believed to be effective in stopping hemorrhage during childbirth. The verses were from Ezekiel, and Freelove had committed them to memory.

She bowed her head and solemnly intoned, " 'Thus saith the Lord God unto Jerusalem; Thy birth and thy nativity is of the land of Canaan; . . . And when I passed by thee, and saw thee polluted in thine own blood, I said unto thee when thou wast in thy blood, Live; yea, I said unto thee when thou wast in thy blood, Live.' "

But the verses had fallen on deaf ears, for Betsy had slipped into unconsciousness again, the blue bottle fallen to the floor at her side. Freelove, her face sweating now with fear, looked at Betsy with deep concern. Then, coming to a sudden decision, she greased her right hand and arm with butter and knelt down low, her enormous rear end in mid-air. With a swift, determined, and yet gentle movement, she plunged her arm into Betsy halfway to the elbow. Her eyes narrowed in intense concentration as her fingers searched and probed.

Betsy stirred into half-consciousness, and Freelove screamed at her, "Bear down, Betsy! For the love of the sweet Christ, bear down, or you're a-gonna die!"

The words came to Betsy from far away, but she sensed their meaning and made an effort to respond. She roused herself, and soon Freelove could feel the muscles moving once more against her hand.

For the next half hour Freelove worked like a woman possessed by the Devil. She exhorted, she cajoled, she prayed, she scolded, and somehow she kept Betsy from slipping back into unconsciousness. Finally, her efforts were rewarded. The afterbirth, which had been retained so long, was expelled, and not long afterward, the bleeding stopped.

Freelove, breathing hard and perspiring from every pore, shouted in triumph. She called loudly for Reuben. "Get the spade, Reuben!" she said. "The afterbirth's out and needs burying!"

Reuben, who had performed this chore more times than he could remember, got up from the chair where he had been sleeping and came dutifully forward. As Freelove handed him the sodden mess wrapped in a cloth, Reuben asked sleepily, "Is she all right, Freelove?"

"I hope so. Leastways, the bleeding is stopped. Now get on with the burying. And remember, *three* feet deep! We don't want no evil effects coming out on the grandson of the President of the United States!"

As Reuben reached the door with his unsavory parcel, he turned and with a grin said, "I s'pose you'll be writing the President letting him know."

Freelove smiled. "You get out of here, mister!" she said. She waddled over to her chair near the fireplace and sank her enormous bulk into it with a long-drawn sigh.

"Polly!" she shouted. "Leave that little bastard and put a couple of logs on the fire. We been working for twenty-four hours, and it's time for a midnight tea. And while you're up, bring me a bottle of rum, there's a good girl."

She looked over toward Betsy and her face softened. "Well, my lass, we done it," she said proudly.

But Betsy was asleep. He face, still white and with the dark smudges beneath her eyes even darker, wore a tranquil expression from which all traces of pain and struggle had disappeared. Instead, there was a look of utter relief and the shadow of a smile that somehow suggested conquest.

FREELOVE celebrated the birth of George Washington Bowen by becoming first gloriously and then soddenly drunk, and so Polly stayed in the household for the duration of Betsy's slow convalescence. She cooked, she washed, and she fussed over the new baby with a maternal delight that was altogether lacking in Betsy, who at first had even refused to nurse the infant. Polly's arguments only made her more obdurate.

"I'll not do it, and that's an end on it!" she said. "I carried him around for nine months and let him turn my figure into a sack of potatoes. Then he almost killed me getting himself born. And now he wants to suck my breasts out of shape! Well, he's not going to do it!"

"But, Betsy, it's not *his* fault, lovey," said Polly. "He didn't ask to be born, and now all he wants is to live. Babies have to suckle or they die." Polly's eyes filled with tears.

"Get him a wet nurse, then!"

With a flash of temper Polly said, "Betsy Bowen, you're an unnatural mother!"

"That's as may be, but I'll not have the little wretch bothering me any further."

In the end, it was nature and not Polly who won the argument. Betsy's breasts, heavy with milk, became swollen and painful, and finally she put the child to nurse. But she took no pleasure in it. At necessary intervals, she allowed the infant to relieve her of discomfort, holding him stiffly against her and looking down at him without feeling.

As the days went by, her indifference did not give way to affection. Whatever love was in her seemed to center itself on Danton. She was unhappy when she realized that the monkey was jealous of any attention paid to the child. He would come close to her, snuggle against her shoulder, and look into her face with imploring eyes. Once, when he made a move to suckle at her other breast, she laughed at his boldness and gently cuffed him away. Then in mock sorrow he placed one hand dolefully over his eyes and peered at her from the slits between his fingers. Finally he disappeared entirely during the periods of nursing. Polly, sent in search of him, would find him hiding in a closet.

Although Danton's antics were a source of amusement to Betsy, his very presence made her painfully aware of the absence of Michel. The horror of his death had become less vivid to her as time went by and had assumed the unreal dimensions of a nightmare, but she missed the warmth of his companionship, the gaiety of his laughter, the touch of his hand on her shoulder, the quick brush of his lips across her cheek that told her she was loved and wanted.

Sometimes, looking at Danton, she would burst into tears, and the monkey seemed to sense her sorrow. He would spring lightly into her arms and nuzzle his velvety face against hers. Then she would hug the small furry body against her and kiss the top of his head.

On these occasions Polly watched with curious eyes, and one day she said, "I declare, Betsy, I believe you love that damned monkey more'n you do your own baby."

Betsy returned her stare with honest eyes. "I do," she said. "He loves me."

"But the baby loves you, too," said Polly, "and he's a human being."

"Loves me?" Betsy laughed. "All he wants is my tit in his mouth when he's hungry. Is that love?"

To Betsy, Polly protested that the child was scarcely a week old and could hardly be expected to be very loving, but to herself she had to admit that young George was oddly unresponsive. His eyes were solemn and impassive, and he never smiled. When he was placed at Betsy's breast to nurse, he wriggled like a crab plucked from the sea until his hands closed on a breast and he voraciously put his tiny mouth to the nipple. When his appetite had been satisfied, he showed no desire to stay at her breast and sleep. Abruptly, as though in revulsion, he would turn his head away and begin squirming and kicking again until Polly picked him up and placed him back in the wooden cradle that Reuben had made for him.

Then Betsy would look at him in a detached way, with a faintly ironic smile playing about the corners of her mouth. She felt used, as though she were a wet nurse for someone else's baby. And yet she did not actively hate him. She even grew tolerant of his wailing and screaming when he became irritable. Eventually, she was even able to soothe him, and would rock him in her arms with a brusque, mechanical motion.

As soon as Freelove had recovered from her celebration of George's birth, Polly returned to Sally Marshall's house on Olney Lane. As she said goodbye to the baby, who reached out for her hand and enclosed her forefinger in his tiny fist, tears welled up in her big sentimental eyes.

"See that?" she said. "He *is* a lovin' baby, Betsy."

Betsy shrugged. "Oh, he's bright enough to know who's been changing his diapers and bathing him. Naturally, he don't want you to go."

"Oh, Betsy, you just won't see any good in him, will you?"

"Why should I?" asked Betsy.

Polly shook her head hopelessly and prepared to leave. Betsy put down the baby, who immediately set up a loud wail. Betsy ignored him and went over to Polly. She put her arms around her and kissed her.

"You're a sweet, loving girl, Polly. I shan't forget how good you've been to me. And some day, I don't know how, I'll repay you. I swear I will."

Polly drew away in embarrassment. At the door she paused and said, "You can repay me a little, Betsy, by being good to George. Promise that you will."

Betsy smiled and looked hopelessly toward her squalling baby. "I'll do my best, Polly, but 'twon't be easy."

It wasn't easy. Her patience with the infant was quickly exhausted. During the long months of pregnancy she had found herself thinking only of the happy moment when she could get the child out of her body, and now that he was born, she looked upon him as an unwelcome burden, and somehow, some way, she wanted to be free of him.

Freelove was even more critical of Betsy's lack of maternal affection than Polly had been. From experience she knew that mothers who had undergone a long and painful labor sometimes disliked their babies at first, but then they eventually became warm and affectionate as the memory of pain blurred and finally was forgotten entirely. But Betsy was different. She remembered every detail of her ordeal and almost willfully refused to allow herself to forget the pain her child had caused her.

Betsy's attitude made Freelove furious. "What's the matter with you?" she would scream. "Have you no heart? You don't act like a mother at all!"

"What do I do wrong? I nurse it. I change its filthy diapers. What else am I supposed to do?"

"You're s'posed to love it! Why, you never fondle it or play with it or talk to it—"

"Talk to it? Why it wouldn't understand what I was saying if I did!"

"Maybe not. But just your voice—why a *real* mother sings to her child!"

Betsy shrugged. "All right. I'll sing to it."

She sang some of the bawdy sea chanteys her mother had taught her, and Freelove stopped her ears in horror. Though her own language was hardly pure, the thought of singing lewd songs to a mere infant filled her with superstitious fears.

"You'll corrupt the child," said Freelove. "Don't you know any lullabies?"

"No. These are the only songs I know. My own mother sang 'em to *me*."

"Well, it's no wonder you turned out a whore and a slut! Do you want your son to be a no-good pimpin' son of a bitch? Here, give me that child!"

Betsy handed the baby over, and Freelove pressed it against the vast expanse of her bosom. She made gurgling sounds and cooing noises, tickled the baby's ears and nose with her forefinger. In sudden ecstasy, George grinned toothlessly. Then Freelove, in her rum-cracked voice, began to croon a lullaby, so wildly off-key as to be scarcely recognizable as music. But George responded with rapt attention, and then, as the tuneless croaking continued, he fell into a gentle slumber.

"There!" said Freelove triumphantly. "Now why can't *you* do that?"

Betsy looked thoughtful. "I don't know. But I don't feel anything for him. It's like he wasn't my baby at all."

"Well, he ain't my baby either," said Freelove, "but I love him, and so does Reuben. Why, he struts around like he was its father!"

Freelove did not exaggerate. The arrival of young George had had a remarkable effect on Reuben. Whenever he looked at the baby, his eyes lost their spiritless, faraway expression and came alive with pleasure. He waited upon Betsy like an attentive husband and even learned, under Freelove's amused tutelage, how to bathe the infant and change its diapers. He was so absorbed by these new duties that his "birds" lay forgotten in his bedroom, a half-finished plover decoy gathering dust on the workbench. From the very first he had insisted that there was a striking resemblance between George Washington Bowen and his namesake. There was no doubt in his mind that the child was, in truth, the President's very own, if illegitimate, grandson.

He felt that the date of so notable a birth should be set down for posterity. He searched the house for a Bible in which the event could be properly recorded, but there was no Bible in the Ballou household. In fact, there were no books at all except those that had been bequeathed to Betsy by Jonathan Clarke. And so, with Betsy's permission, he searched among these for a volume that would be suitable for the registry of George's arrival. The books that luridly described the more dissolute royal courts of France and England and the lives of mistresses to kings seemed altogether inappropriate, and Reuben was horrified at the thought of entering the Washington name on the flyleaves of those volumes that recorded the confessions of famous highwaymen and prostitutes. He rejected, too, the more sedate editions of Plutarch, Plato, and Aristotle as being too pagan to be associated with a child born in Christian times. He had almost decided on a crumbling edition of Shakespeare's tragedies when an old and dog-eared volume caught his eye.

With approving nods and tongue-cluckings he read the title aloud: "*First Part of the Life and Raigne of King Henry the IIII extended to the end of the First Year of his Raigne.* Written by J. Howard. Imprinted at London by John Wolfe and am to be sold at his shop in Pope's Head Alley near to the Exchange. 1599."

Grasping the book triumphantly in his hand, he hurried to his bedroom with it. It seemed highly satisfactory to him that young George's name should be inscribed in a volume that possessed such a long, impressive, and thoroughly respectable title. Seated before his workbench, he searched for the special quill pen that he reserved for the signing of formal documents. For the next half hour he wrote, laboriously and with many flourishes and ornamental curlicues, an elaborate inscription on the flyleaf of King Henry IV's royal history.

> George Washington Bowen, born of Eliza Bowen, at
> my house in town, Providence, R.I., on the 9th day
> of October, 1794.
>
> (Signed) Reuben Ballou

He surveyed his handiwork with pride and then hastened downstairs to show it to Betsy.

"But why did you write 'Eliza'?" asked Betsy. "I've always been called Betsy."

"Betsy is only a nickname," said Reuben. "It wouldn't hardly be fittin' to set down the name of the mother of the President's own grandson in common language."

Betsy repressed a smile. "No. Of course not, Reuben. Eliza is really my name, and it's better than Elizabeth, which is too hoity-toity."

"That's what I thought," Reuben agreed.

Betsy looked thoughtful. "Eliza is what Captain Clarke always called me. Maybe I'll just use it as my very own name from now on. Betsy *is* a vulgar name, I suppose."

"It ain't got," said Reuben, "no dignity. And now that you're a mother, dignity is what you should have."

"Even if I be a mother to a bastard?" Betsy asked with a smile.

Reuben became indignant, and his voice rose in anger. "Eliza! You will never again use that word about George as long as you stay in this house!"

Betsy looked at him in surprise. In all the time she had known

332

him, she had never seen his easygoing nature ruffled by temper. It was clear to her, and a matter of wonder, that her fat, solemn, and unwanted baby had found a champion. She felt comforted by the thought that someone might love this child, softening somehow the faint but persistent sense of guilt caused by her own lack of maternal feeling.

The depth of Reuben's interest in the baby set her to thinking about the future. She wished she could just give George to Reuben and Freelove since they seemed so fond of him, but it seemed unlikely that they would be willing to adopt it as their own. It was one thing to admire and even love a newborn infant, but it was something else again to assume complete responsibility for its care and upbringing.

She was aware, too, that something inside her rebelled at the thought. However immoral she might have been in the eyes of the world, she had never shrunk from assuming whatever duties circumstances had thrust upon her. Phebe herself would be highly disapproving of such an action, and most especially by her own daughter. And so Betsy dismissed the idea, attractive though it might be. With resignation she made up her mind to assume her duties as gracefully as she could and even to make an effort to love the child as a mother should.

But it was still Danton, and not her child, who was a matter of most concern to her. The monkey's jealousy had taken a new turn. He no longer accepted his situation sorrowfully, hiding in the closet and avoiding the sight of George at her breast as something too painful to be borne. He had become actively hostile not only to his rival but to the human race in general—to everyone except Betsy. Even Freelove no longer dared to pet him. If anyone approached him, he bared his teeth and screamed. He would bite an outstretched hand that came too close.

At nursing times, he openly and aggressively tried to attack the baby. Only Betsy seemed able to control him, but the effect of her scolding was only momentary. He resorted to new tactics, attacking suddenly and without warning from ambush. Finally, Betsy had to lock him in the closet before she dared feed the baby.

Danton did not accept this discipline supinely. When Betsy scooped him up in her arms to imprison him, he chattered in protest and struggled to get free. And one afternoon he did get free. Before Betsy could catch him, he had leaped into the cradle and had sunk his sharp yellow teeth into George's outstretched hand. The child screamed in pain, and the sight of its bloodied hand sent Betsy into a rage against the animal. She seized him roughly by the tail and whacked him across the rump as hard as she could.

Danton backed away from her and shrieked in hysterical terror, his eyes wide with the hurt of betrayal. Then he clamped his small hands around his head and ran from the room. Through the open back door he loped out into the garden and disappeared.

Betsy felt instant remorse for the violence of her blow, but George's continued screaming demanded her attention, and she went quickly over to him, mopping the blood from his hand and examining the wound. It was not as deep as she had feared. While she was cleaning it with some of Freelove's rum, for the first time she felt a tenderness for the child. She had never seen him in real pain before, and his tears moved her to pick him up in her arms and soothe him. He cried for a long time, and finally, she sat down in a chair by the fireplace and rocked him in her arms. She even tried singing to him to quiet his sobs.

When Freelove came home from the market, the picture that greeted her made her stare in disbelief. Betsy was dozing in the chair by the fire with young George asleep in her arms. Freelove approached curiously, and then she saw the child's hand bound up in its bloodstained bandage.

She shook Betsy by the shoulder. "Wake up, Betsy! What happened?"

Betsy opened her eyes. "Oh, Freelove, thank God you're home."

"How did he hurt his hand?"

"It was Danton. He bit him."

Freelove set down her bag of provisions with a thud and bellowed, "That goddamn monkey! I'll kill him! Where is he?"

"I don't know," said Betsy. "I hit him and he ran away. Oh, Freelove, I hit him terrible hard—"

"Well, I should hope so!" said Freelove. "That beast is getting out of hand, Betsy. You'll have to get rid of him. It just ain't safe to have him around anymore. Why, just the other day, he bit little Danny Woodhull when he brought the bread."

"I told Danny not to pet him, but he did anyway."

"Don't defend the dirty little varmint. He's turned vicious."

"He's not vicious, Freelove. He's only jealous. He don't know any better."

Freelove exploded again. "Now you listen to me, Betsy Bowen. Know better or not, you can't keep an animal that bites your own child, and if you don't get rid of him, I will! I'll have Reuben shoot him."

Betsy stiffened in her chair. "Oh, no! I'll not let you do that. Maybe—maybe we could give him to someone."

"And who'd have a biting bastard of a monkey around the house?"

Suddenly, Betsy remembered the January afternoon when she and Matt had gone to Peter Daspré's to view the "Natural Curiosity" that he had advertised in the *Providence Gazette*. For ninepence each, they had been allowed to see Peter's newly arrived collection of monkeys. She recalled now that it was from the old barber that Michel had bought Danton.

"I'll take him back to Peter Daspré, that's what I'll do!" said Betsy.

"Well, take him somewhere. Because I'll not have him in this house a minute longer, biting our poor baby's hand." Freelove leaned over and gently inspected George's hand. "Did you put a poultice on it to draw out the poisons?" she asked.

Betsy shook her head. "I don't know how to make a poultice. But I put some rum on it to keep it from festering."

Freelove nodded her head approvingly. "I'll tend to it," she said.

Preparations for supper were suspended while Freelove set about ministering to the baby. It was growing dark now, and still Danton had not come back. Betsy searched upstairs and downstairs for him. She hoped that he had returned stealthily without her being aware of it, but he was nowhere in the house.

In spite of Freelove's derisive comments, Betsy lighted a lantern and went into the back garden, calling his name softly. She felt no anger toward him now, only remorse for the temper that had made her strike him harder than she intended.

335

It had begun to rain, and a cold wind blew from the northeast, rustling through the dry, dead vegetation of the garden and roughening the dirty, leaf-strewn water in the canal. Betsy shivered and drew her cloak more tightly about her. She raised the lantern and peered into the bushes, but there was no sign of the monkey anywhere.

A sense of desolation filled her, and the memory of Michel became all at once sharp and intense, no longer blurred by time, but immediate and painfully vivid. In the moaning of the wind she seemed to hear his voice calling her name, and the whirling dead leaves that brushed her face were his hands stroking her cheek. She began to cry softly and bitterly, and then, in rising desperation, she called the monkey's name louder, again and again.

From the garden she went out into the street before the house. The hard rain hit her in angry gusts, and her cloak was soon drenched. As she walked farther along Charles Street, the wind became a gale, a northeaster that she knew would rage all night long. The thought of Danton, lost, cold, and helpless in the storm, sent her into a frenzy of searching and calling his name.

By the time she had battled her way as far as the grist mill, she was exhausted. She turned around in defeat and headed toward home. The roar of the wind had become so loud that it drowned out her voice, and she gave up calling. In the hope that the storm might have driven the monkey home in her absence, she quickened her steps, and with the wind at her back now, she soon reached home.

But Danton had not returned, and that night Betsy refused to go to bed. She sat alone by the fire, her ears alert for the sound of the monkey scratching at the door. A dozen times, above the whistling of the wind and the spattering of rain, she thought she heard him and ran to the door with a lantern. But each time emptiness greeted her.

Along toward midnight the storm became ominously quiet, as though to catch its breath for a new attack. In the sudden stillness, she heard him. It was a long-drawn whimpering cry of misery, and it cut through her heart as George's wails had never done. She ran to the back door and flung it open.

The small, rain-drenched figure lay on the doorsill. Sagging and immobile, he was hunched forward, head between his updrawn legs. She lifted him tenderly, her hands under his armpits, as though he were a baby. His body dangled limply against her, and the cold, wet fur against her breast made her shiver. She set him down on the warm bricks near the fire and went in search of a towel.

After she had finished drying him, she put her ear against his chest and listened for his heartbeat. At last she heard it, faint, slow, and irregular. She got Freelove's bottle of rum and tried to force some of it into his mouth. But his jaws were tightly shut and the liquid dribbled onto the floor. Then his lips drew back in distaste and he made a swallowing movement. Immediately, she forced more rum into his mouth. He choked, raised his hand weakly, and opened his eyes.

He regarded her steadily, without blinking. As she reached out her hand toward him, he made a slight cringing movement. Tears welled up in her eyes. She sat down on the floor and took him in her arms. She cradled him against her breast and talked softly. "Danton, my baby. I'll never hurt you again. You're the one I love," she crooned.

The soothing sound of her voice seemed to reassure him, and he closed his eyes again. Then, slowly and with great effort, he moved a hand until it rested lightly against her breast. She looked down at him in compassion, and impulsively she pulled at her bodice and pushed a bare breast toward his mouth. He opened his eyes and looked at her in wonder. She thrust the nipple between his lips, and he began to nurse.

There was a look of satisfaction on her face as she watched him. As in a mirror she saw herself—a woman nursing a monkey. She laughed as she imagined Freelove's shocked reaction to this scene, a picture as profane as that of a madonna suckling a monkey instead of the infant Jesus.

But her laughter dissolved into an all-pervading tenderness, a deep wish that this small creature should take nourishment from her and live. All the emotions that she knew she should have felt toward her own child she now experienced for the first time, emotions focused on a creature that had not come from her womb at all. And yet Danton was somehow a part of her and of the affection she had felt for Michel.

Betsy did not go to bed that night but dozed in the chair by the fire, with the monkey clasped closely to her. As morning approached, his body was hot with fever, and she knew that he was seriously ill. He had begun to cough with hacking spasms that racked his body, and he brought up blood. He refused her breast when she offered it to him again and twitched his eyes in pain. Chills seized him, and his body shook against hers violently. She gave him more rum, but it did not help. The alcohol began to make him drunk, and he became so weak and limp that he could not even hold his arm about her neck.

At daylight, the baby set up a wail of hunger, and so she set Danton on the towel before the fire and went to the cradle. The sight of George's bandaged hand with the poultice on it saddened her, and she picked the child up in her arms to soothe him. She gave him her other breast to suckle and turned her back to the fireplace so that Danton would not be able to watch her.

But Danton's eyes had closed as he lost consciousness, and when Betsy finally returned to tend to him, she found him grotesquely stretched out full length, one arm extended in space as though clutching to bring air into his congested lungs. He had stopped breathing.

Betsy knelt down and tried to revive him, but he was as limp and lifeless as a rag doll. She rubbed him briskly, shook him in desperation, talked to him. She listened for his heartbeat, but there was none. At last, she placed him hopelessly back on the bricks of the fireplace and stood up.

She did not cry. A strange numbness had come over her and she sat down in the chair by the fireside. Her eyes stared fixedly at the dying embers of the fire, and soon her eyelids began to droop in exhaustion. Finally, she slept.

By noon of the next day the storm had spent itself. The wind died down, the rain stopped, and though the sun did not shine, the sky lightened to a leaden, cold brightness that gave trees and buildings starkly clear outlines that lacked warmth and color.

Inside the house, there was that unnatural hush that descends on a household where a death has occurred. The only sound was Freelove's heavy breathing as she moved about the hearth preparing a noonday meal of tea and johnnycake. Betsy followed her movements with her eyes.

"Where did you put him?" she asked.

Without turning her attention from the kettle of water, Freelove said, "I wrapped him in a towel and put him over there. Reuben will bury him."

Betsy tried to hold back her tears but could not. As she stifled a sob, Freelove turned her face toward her. Her eyes were sympathetic, but her voice was matter-of-fact. "You'll feel better when you eat something. Sitting there all night with that sick monkey— well, it's a mercy he's out of the way."

"It's not a mercy," Betsy said tearfully. "He's gone, and he was all I had."

"All you had! If you'd stop your sniveling over a dead monkey, you might remember you've got a son!"

Betsy said nothing, but got up from her chair and went over to where Danton lay. As she picked up the stiffening body, the towel fell away from his head, and she looked down at him. She heard a sudden cooing sound and looked over to the cradle. George's round and vacant eyes were fixed on her. Then his mouth curved in a one-sided, crooked grin. It was as though Matt himself had come into the room and now lay there smiling at her in smug triumph.

In an uncontrollable rage, she screamed, "Bastard!" She ran over to the cradle and spat full in the infant's face. George's smile puckered into a grimace of anger, and as he began to wail, Betsy clutched the monkey fiercely against her and ran out into the garden.

Deaf to Freelove's commands to come into the house and eat, she got a spade and began digging a grave in the soggy, rain-drenched earth. All her sadness dissolved into a savage fury of work, of jabbing and pounding the spade into the earth, as though she were hacking and killing a mortal enemy.

When at last the hole was dug, she lifted Danton in her arms, wrapped the towel tightly about his body as though to protect him, and then tenderly placed him in the shallow pit. She scattered clods of wet earth over him until he was quite covered, then looked around for a stone with which she could mark his grave.

339

Finding one, she knelt down to set it in place. Tearless now, she stared down at the ground in silence for several moments, remembering the monkey's clownish antics, his irrepressible glee at the mere fact of being alive.

But this was the way it was, she thought to herself. This was how it ended. All the joy and excitement, the sorrow, boredom, and ecstasy—they all stopped here in the silent, uncaring earth. Lydia Allen was here, that mad, unloving woman who had hated life and whose life had therefore been no life at all, only a succession of days and years strung together in a chain of tormenting and unfulfilled desires.

And Michel, he was here, too, in a fresh and nameless grave in a place not even known to her. And it did not matter. For the boyish laugh was forever gone, and with it his desperate need to prove that he was a man, even at the risk of death. And now, Danton, simple beast though he was, had been a victim of his jealous passion and had found peace at last, locked in a shroud of mud.

It was a peace she did not want, now or ever. But she knew now, as she knelt on the cold earth, that it would come to her, too. It would happen. But not yet. Before that instant of utter stillness struck, there were things to be done, to be enjoyed. The inevitable ending was something to be postponed for as long as possible, and if passions made it come early, then she would do without passions.

Again, the vision of Danton rose up before her, the gaily cavorting figure he had been before love and jealousy destroyed him. She saw the monkey prancing and leaping in an endless dance of joy. Suddenly, a peal of laughter rose in her throat, and she threw back her head, letting the laughter surge through her without restraint.

She flung down the spade, and then, with her eyes turned to the sky, she thumbed her nose at heaven.

That night, Betsy could not sleep. The lethargy that had possessed her since the baby's birth had disappeared in a rush of overflowing energy. It was as though after weeks of wandering in the shadows of a dense forest she saw suddenly before her an open path made radiant by a shaft of sunlight. It offered escape. And life.

It would be a new life, and George and even the city of Providence would not be part of it. There was nothing here that she wanted, not the memories of Sam, Matt, and Michel, and most of all, not this child whom she knew she could never love.

Her only friends were the Ballous and Polly, but her love for them was not strong enough to hold her in a place that she had grown to hate, a place that she would hate more if she stayed. Here in Providence, she would always be Bouncing Bet, a town whore like her mother, her station in life forever fixed by the presence of a bastard son.

For the first time, she seriously considered Matt's offer to care for the child. The pride that had made her dismiss the idea out of hand months ago seemed somehow ridiculous to her now. In the urgency of her need to escape the past and begin again, she found herself not really caring what he might think of her. Even her anger toward him seemed to have lost its fire and changed into indifference. If he would assume the burden of the child, she would let him.

She doubted whether the Wyatt sense of responsibility would extend so far as to include the introduction of a bastard child into the eminently respectable mansion on Angell Street. Though it might be an act of Christian charity to adopt a grown child like her sister, Polly, the precipitate arrival of a newborn infant was something else again, an event that would be cause for town gossip and hotly debated conjectures as to which of the Wyatt males was its father.

The solution was clear to her. Reuben and Freelove liked the child and would welcome it even more enthusiastically if it were to offer them a source of income. All that was needed was money, and Betsy intended to get it.

She was sure the Wyatts would be delighted to see her leave Providence, delighted enough to pay the cost of her passage to a place sufficiently far away to eliminate all possibility of future embarrassment. The fact that her plans depended on a kind of blackmail did not even occur to her. They would be effective. The only question in her mind was where she wanted to go.

Betsy's imagination leaped lightly over the globe, like that of a prospective traveler planning a holiday. There were really only two places that beckoned—Paris and New York. When she thought of Paris, she had an immediate picture of herself at a royal ball in Versailles. In a resplendent gown that glittered with gold thread and sparkled with precious stones, she danced the mincing, graceful steps of a minuet with King Louis himself, while Marie Antoinette watched in jealous fury, her small ivory fan fluttering with annoyance.

This lustrous vision disappeared abruptly as Betsy remembered that Louis and his queen had been beheaded last year and that all France lay bleeding in the convulsions of its revolution. Paris could wait.

It would be New York, then, a city neither as far away nor as romantic as Paris, but certainly the most exciting place in America. The island city had already displaced Philadelphia as the nation's capital, even though plans were afoot to build a new one somewhere in the swamps of Virginia. But new capital or not, New York was the center of fashion, of politics, of everything important, and an altogether fitting place to begin a new life.

Even George Washington was there. She saw no reason why she should not present herself to him—as respectably and fetchingly as possible, of course—and make known to him their probable, though unproved, relationship. Quite carried away by her fantasies, she felt sure that he would be proud and pleased to claim her as his daughter, even if he had never so much as set eyes on her mother.

More and more, Betsy had come to believe Phebe's oft-repeated tale of that night in 1774, when she had patriotically comforted a chilly general with the warmth of her once-lovely body. He had, after all, slept in so many places during the years of the Revolution, and it was well known that he had visited Providence at some time during 1774, the year before her own birth. He could certainly have spent one night in Phebe's highly hospitable bed. And that night, she was sure, he had slept only fitfully, and she, Betsy Bowen, was the lovely and admirable, if illegitimate, result.

She saw herself at long last as the person she had never been—accepted, admired, loved, and in very truth, the daughter of the President of the United States. But her child was not part of that picture. He would not take his place as a royal grandson. She would see to it that he remained what he in fact was, a Wyatt bastard, to be brought up by Reuben and Freelove Ballou, and no part of her, now or ever. Whatever connection there had been between them had been severed along with the umbilical cord. He would be such a well-kept secret that for her, at least, he would no longer even exist.

CHAPTER 3 2

BETSY and Freelove paused in the waning autumn sunlight that slanted through the bare trees on Angell Street. They looked hesitantly at the imposing lines of the Wyatt house that lifted itself proudly behind its wrought-iron fence. Freelove, with young George clutched to her bosom, batted her big eyes nervously. She was awed by the sight of a house that represented the wealth and respectability of Providence.

Now that the moment of facing Henry Wyatt had arrived, she had misgivings. In imagination, she saw herself and Betsy being forcibly ejected from the premises at gunpoint, or, worse still, of being arrested by Bobby Brown as blackmailers and carted off to the town gaol. And she knew only too well what treatment they could expect at the hands of Bobby Brown, who still flourished as a pillar of law enforcement. He had pleaded guilty of killing in self-defense and had not even been charged with Michel's murder.

In a voice that trembled in fearful anticipation, Freelove said, "Oh, Betsy, I don't dast go in. I'll wait for you."

"You'll do nothing of the sort," said Betsy. "You're to be part of any agreement we make. What are you scared of? The child is their grandson, and it ain't my fault he's a bastard."

"You and I know he's Matt's son. But do *they?*"

"Matt asked his father's consent to marry me. The old man knows, right enough. He'll be glad to pay."

But Freelove still hesitated. "If only you'd written a letter asking leave to see him. Why, you don't even know if he's to home."

"Ask his leave? Who is he that I should ask his leave? He'll be home, and he'll see me. Come along, Freelove."

Betsy pushed open the gate resolutely, and with anger. Then she paused, took a deep breath, and drew herself up to her full height.

344

She was wearing the cream-colored gown adorned with black ribbons, the gown that had been her favorite in the days before pregnancy had made it unwearable. Now it fitted her once again, and its snug feeling gave her the confidence of a well-armored soldier entering battle.

She had groomed herself carefully. The red-gold masses of her hair were piled high upon her head, capped with a bit of delicate Belgian lace. Her face, with its fair, smooth skin, had a serene and chiseled look, and her dark-violet eyes seemed more than usually lustrous and shining. Even her uptilted nose seemed to have achieved a kind of dignity. She had never been more beautiful, and she knew it.

Moving gracefully up the red-brick walk, she mounted the double-flighted steps to the ornate, pedimented doorway. She waited until Freelove had lumbered up the steps and stood breathless at her side. Then she lifted the well-polished brass door knocker in her gloved hand and rapped it smartly three times. After a few moments, a servant girl opened the door.

Betsy's voice was crisp and businesslike. "I would like to see Mr. Henry Wyatt. Tell him that Miss Eliza Bowen is here."

The girl, impressed by Betsy's appearance and her imperious tone, ushered them in, motioning to two Queen Anne chairs that flanked the doorway.

"I'll tell him," said the girl. She moved up the side stairway with its curved mahogany banister.

As the stillness of the house was broken by the sound of footsteps above, Betsy felt her heart begin to beat fast. To calm herself, she fastened her eyes on the small marble statue that graced the newel post of the stairway. It was a naked, but not too naked, Juno, who looked blankly at heaven, her gracefully outstretched arms ready, no doubt, for a connubial visit from Jove.

Freelove, nervous and uncomfortable on the narrow chair, followed Betsy's eyes to the statue. "Heathenish," she said to no one in particular.

The servant's footsteps had stopped on the floor above, and now there was the sound of someone moving about. With the silent swiftness of a ghost making an unannounced appearance, the form of Polly Bowen stood framed in the doorway.

Betsy rose to her feet and smiled in greeting. It was reassuring to see a familiar face in these strange and elegant surroundings. But there was nothing reassuring about the aloof and disdainful expression on her sister's face.

"What are you doing here?" asked Polly. Her voice was as cold as the china-blue of her small round eyes.

Betsy drew back. "That's none of your business, Polly." She paused and gave her sister an appraising glance. She noted the simple elegance of her dress, which still could not conceal the awkward boniness of her undeveloped and childlike figure. But it was the face that held her attention. It was still plain, but even more unattractive now. There were lines of discontent about her mouth, and her lips seemed permanently pursed in a pout of ill temper. At the moment, all her features seemed to have frozen into a jealous mask of envy.

When she spoke, her voice was monotonous and low. "If you've come to bother Matt about your bastard child, you may as well go home." She paused, and then with malicious pointedness, she added, "He's to be married, you know."

With an effort of will, Betsy kept her face expressionless. "Oh?" she said casually. "Then he's come back from Boston?"

"I didn't say that," said Polly.

"Oh, Polly, you might be a bit friendly. We be sisters. At least we have the same mama."

"I have no mama." Polly accented the last syllable of the word and the emphasis became a comment on Betsy's diction and upbringing.

"*Mama!*" Betsy laughed in genuine amusement. "Well, my lady, mama or ma*ma*, you were brought into this world by Phebe Bowen, same as I was."

"Phebe Bowen," said Polly in measured tones, "abandoned me when I was twelve. She was a drunken harlot."

Betsy slapped Polly's cheek as hard as she could. Polly burst into tears and drew back in fright.

"Bitch!" said Betsy. "You'll not talk about Phebe that way to me! Give yourself all the ladylike airs you please, but don't set yourself above your own mother! Especially as seeing how you're not exactly a virgin yourself!"

Polly, with her hand at her stinging cheek, whimpered, "I'm not a harlot! I'm not!"

"No? Why, ever since you was fifteen, Dick Wyatt's been riding you like you was his pet pony. That body of yours must be as well used as any in Cheapside, my girl!"

Polly's pale face flushed to a hot redness of shame. Sobbing and furious, she ran from the room.

Freelove, who had watched the reunion of the two sisters with mild amusement, turned her owlish eyes on Betsy. "Damme," she said, "if you didn't have such a foul tongue, you'd be more of a lady than she is."

Betsy regained her poise quickly. "For all her grand airs," she said, "I feel sorry for the little slut. One of these days she'll be finding herself in a condition. The Wyatt men be very manly, as I have reason to know."

Betsy moved quietly back to her chair, and then, pensively, her gaze rested once again on the statue of Juno with outstretched arms. A vision of Matt rose before her, naked, beautiful, and tender, the man she had loved so much and now hated. She wanted to cry out to him, to have him back in her arms again, to let him fill the aching emptiness that had remained somewhere deep inside her ever since he had gone. It was a hollowness that no one had been able to fill, not even Michel, loving and kind as he had been.

Abruptly, she shook herself free of the warming, engulfing memory, telling herself that it was not Matt whom she wanted to recapture. It was the dream of loving and being loved, something as unreal as the imaginings of a child at play. The world, she had learned, was a cold place of hard, unbending lines, with little concern for the romantic yearnings of people foolish enough to indulge in them.

As she looked at the statue of Juno again, a smile, both contemptuous and good-natured, lifted the corners of her mouth. Under her breath, she said, "Foolish slut. You'll get what you ask for—no more, no less."

Freelove was looking at her oddly. "Talking to yourself is a sign of madness, they say."

"Then I'm mad," she said.

"I expect you're upset to hear that your bully-boy's going to get married."

"Upset? Why, it couldn't come at a better time. A wedding on

347

the way makes an extra-good reason for sweeping bastards under the rug. Mr. Henry Wyatt will be of a mind to talk money!"

Freelove shrugged. "I hope you're right, lovey. This whole affair is making me jumpy as a flea in July, and I wish it was over and done with."

There were footsteps abovestairs again, and soon the servant girl glided quietly down the staircase and came to an awkward stop before them. "Mr. Wyatt will see you now, ma'am," she said.

Henry Wyatt stood quietly near the west window of his upstairs sitting room. He looked down the hill toward the harbor, and beyond that to the marshes of Cowpen Point and his shipyard. But the view, which ordinarily filled him with pride and pleasure, held no interest for him at this moment. He did not even see it. His eyes were withdrawn and concentrated inwardly, and the skin on his forehead was wrinkled in a frown that suggested displeasure rather than deep thought.

In March, when he had first learned of Matt's involvement with the Bowen girl, he had momentarily expected a visit from her. He had made plans for a swift financial settlement, as meager as possible, and a subsequent and equally meager monthly allowance for fifteen years, to be terminated sooner if the slut by some chance should find a man foolish enough to marry her.

Proper legal papers absolving him of further claims had been drawn up. All was in readiness. And then he had heard nothing from her. As the days passed into weeks, he had begun to hope that a timely abortion had solved the whole situation. By summer, he had almost forgotten the episode completely. And Matthew seemed to have forgotten it, too, for he had applied himself to his studies at Harvard College with more industry than he had ever shown before. Henry was pleased, and he was even more pleased when Matthew, during the summer holidays, had become engaged to Patience Ashton. The Ashtons had money, but more important, they were an old and respected family of the town.

And now, out of the blue, the Bowen woman had appeared, belatedly, perhaps, but bringing with her, according to the maid, very tangible evidence of his son's lapse from virtue. And so, while

Betsy waited downstairs, Henry had searched for and found the papers that had already been prepared. He reread them and made a note to lower the stipulated amounts substantially. It might even be possible, he reflected, to frighten her off without payment of any kind. The woman was evidently resourceful or she could not have maintained herself thus far without help.

Henry believed in encouraging individual initiative and industry. From a strictly business standpoint, free enterprise might certainly include the profits derived from prostitution. As for his own conscience, he did not see how he could hold himself responsible for encouraging immorality. After all, he did not really know how she had supported herself, and he had no intention of asking. The less he knew about her the better. She was disreputable, and therefore someone to be gotten rid of as quickly, painlessly, and inexpensively as possible.

And so Henry was not at all prepared for his reaction to the sight of Betsy when she appeared in the doorway of his upstairs sitting room. At the sound of her approach, he had turned from the window, and his eyes were startled at her appearance. The woman who stood there did not look in the least disreputable. Indeed, if he had not known who she was, he might have assumed that she came from one of the families on the hill. And her voice, when she spoke, had none of the vulgar overtones of the common speech of Providence.

"Mr. Wyatt?" she said softly. "I am sorry to intrude on you, but I have come on a matter of urgent business. I am Miss Eliza Bowen."

Henry moistened his dry lips, swallowed, took a step toward her, and suddenly halted. "I know," he said awkwardly, and then added with a nervously polite wave of his hand, "Won't you come in?"

"Thank you," Betsy murmured. She advanced gracefully into the room, followed by Freelove, who minced after her on tiptoe with tiny, ladylike steps. The sleeping baby jiggled against her heaving bosom but did not awaken.

With a polite gesture of her hand, Betsy called attention to Freelove's presence. She looked directly at Henry and said, "This is Mrs. Reuben Ballou, my son's nurse."

349

Henry acknowledged the introduction curtly and waved them both toward the handsome yellow camel-back sofa with its highly polished stop-fluted legs. "Do be seated," he said.

Betsy sat down on the edge of the sofa and then helped Freelove arrange her bulk next to her. She raised her eyes so that their gaze fell full on Henry's stocky, fashionably appareled figure.

"I thought, sir," she began, "that you might like to see your grandson."

Henry averted his eyes and smoothed the brocade of his waistcoat with moist palms. Then he sat down behind his desk and looked at her with the practiced coolness of a man used to dominating others in business transactions.

"There is no proof, madame, that the child be any kin of mine," he said.

Betsy regarded him with surprised eyes. "But I thought Matthew had told you. At least that is what he gave me to understand."

"He mentioned it. He was not sure that the child was his, and neither, I'd wager, are *you!*"

Betsy's eyes flashed cold disdain. She rose silently and quickly. "Come, Mrs. Ballou. We have no business here, after all." She paused and then inclined her head regally in the direction of Henry. Her voice was quietly sharp and cutting. "I did not come here to be insulted, Mr. Wyatt, or to do business with a liar. And lawful or not, the child will be known in the town as George Wyatt, for a Wyatt he is! Good day to you, sir." She turned and moved at an unhurried pace toward the door.

"Wait!" said Henry. "I spoke in haste. Please, Miss Bowen—"

At the sound of the formal address, she turned her head. "Yes?"

His tone was apologetic. "I—I find this a matter of distaste. It is very upsetting to me—"

"It has been upsetting to me, too, Mr. Wyatt," said Betsy with an irony that was lost on him.

"It is true," said Henry, stumbling over his words, "that I—that I told Matthew that I would perhaps assume responsibility for— for the care of the child. That is, I would be willing—after all, the child must be supported."

"And so must I, sir," Betsy said, again taking her seat on the sofa.

"Yes, yes, of course," said Henry hastily, cowed into momentary submission by the direct look in her eyes. "Now, do let us sit down and talk about this quietly—just the two of us. Cannot Mrs.—er—Ballou wait outside?"

"No," said Betsy. "It will be Mrs. Ballou who will bring up the child. I have other plans."

"Other plans?" Surprised, he looked at her in fearful speculation. "What other plans?"

"I intend to leave Providence as soon as may be."

"Oh. And where will you go?"

"To New York. I do not wish to stay in Providence."

"But surely you will take your child with you?"

Her eyes looked into his boldly as she said, "No. I will not take him with me. I don't want him."

Henry was not accustomed to hearing women say such things. In moments of anger, they were capable, of course, of saying almost anything, of making the most outrageous assertions, but they were not supposed to make statements like this in a calmly logical tone of voice. It violated not only morality and ordinary decency but nature itself. Even wild animals loved and protected their young.

His voice took on the tone of a judge addressing a guilty prisoner. "You are a most unnatural mother, madame," he said.

"And your son," said Betsy, "is a most unnatural father! For the matter of that, sir, it would seem that you are a most unnatural grandfather, since you evidently do not care what happens to the child at all! I, at least, am here to make provisions for his care and future!"

Henry's face reddened, and for the moment he could think of nothing to say. Standing abruptly, he plunged his hands into the pockets of his satin breeches and walked to the fireplace.

Betsy shifted her position on the sofa, gave her hair a reassuring pat, and waited while Henry silently stared into the fire. Freelove looked out of the corner of her eye at Betsy and nodded her head in a jerk of approval. At last, Henry turned to face them again.

With a nod toward Freelove, he said, "And who is this woman who will have the care of—of—"

"Your grandson will be in good hands," said Betsy. "Mrs. Ballou already loves the child. Her husband is Major Ballou, a butcher by

351

trade." Betsy's voice took on a sentimental quality. "It is a most respectable family, sir, though unfortunately childless, until now, that is. Young George will greatly add to their happiness."

"I'm sure," said Henry, looking at Betsy with an ironic smile. "In fact, Miss Bowen, it seems that the plans have already been made, and all that is needed is my approval—my financial approval, that is."

Betsy gave him one of her most dazzling smiles. "That is true, sir." She got up quickly and went over to him, taking one of his roughened stubby hands between her own.

The feel of her soft flesh made him start, and the sudden closeness of her body made him catch his breath. He withdrew his hand quickly. He hardly heard her voice as she said, "Oh, Mr. Wyatt, I was sure you would be a man of feeling—and of honor."

Hastily, Henry moved away from her toward the cherry secretary at the end of the room and planted himself firmly behind it, as though it were a fortification. Although he had regained some of his calm, he was now so physically aware of Betsy that he had difficulty in concentrating on the business at hand.

He found himself in sudden sympathy with Matthew and his fall from grace. Whore though she might be, she was irresistible. On the fringes of his imagination, he saw the two of them, young, naked, and beautiful, lying together, making love with abandon. He closed his eyes as though to blot out the obscene image. Then he sat down abruptly and, with trembling hands, picked up the documents from his desk. As his eyes moved through the jungle of legal mumbo-jumbo, he waited for his violently beating heart to calm itself.

Betsy stood watching him, a confident half smile on her lips. She was well aware of her effect on him. Indeed, it had been calculated and altogether deliberate, and she had no intention of losing her advantage now. She moved toward the desk and stood looking down at him. As she leaned forward, her breasts were only slightly and tantalizingly above the level of his eyes.

Henry looked up from the papers, blushed, and hurriedly turned his gaze to the fireplace. He cleared his throat and forced himself to stand up. He cleared his throat again and said, too loudly, "Miss Bowen—I have here—the necessary papers. Perhaps you will be good enough to read them and see if they meet with your approval."

He dared not hand the documents to her for fear that she might touch him again, and so he slid them across the polished surface of the desk toward her. He hoped that she would return to the sofa to read them, but she did not. She stood there before him, and though he turned his back so that he would not have to look at her, the scent of her young body, mingled with clove and nutmeg, came to him and set his heart to pounding again. To distract himself, he rummaged in a pocket, brought forth a silver snuffbox, took a pinch, sneezed, and then honked his nose loudly into a fine linen handkerchief.

Betsy finished reading the papers and placed them back on the desk without comment. She looked at him with eyes that were luminous and sad, as though she might be on the verge of tears.

"Well?" asked Henry at last. "Is it agreeable to you?"

"I had hoped," said Betsy, "that you would find it in your heart to be more generous."

"You don't find these terms generous?"

"Sufficient, yes. But hardly generous. After all, the boy is a Wyatt, and I would think—" She let the unfinished thought dangle in the air and looked away, as though embarrassed by this mundane discussion.

"Very well, then," said Henry recklessly. "Shall we add a pound a month to it?"

Betsy turned her face to him quickly, radiant and smiling. "Oh, sir, bless your kind heart." She made the trite phrase sound almost sincere. Again, she moved her hand toward his in a gesture of gratitude, but Henry, on guard now, stepped back swiftly. He seemed to have regained control of himself and became brusquely businesslike.

"What assurance do I have that Mrs. Ballou and her husband will not gossip about the child's—ah—origins?"

Freelove looked up at the mention of her name. "Me? I'm the most closemouthed woman in Providence, Rhode Island. Why, if I was to tell one-half of the things I know about people in this town—"

Betsy interrupted quickly. "Mrs. Ballou is a woman of her word."

"She had better be," said Henry. "Because if any gossip comes to my ears, I'll know where it came from. And the monthly allowance will stop at once!" He turned to Freelove, and raising his voice, he added, "Do you understand that, my woman?"

"I ain't deaf," said Freelove tartly, "and I ain't your woman, so stop yelling at me! My lips be sealed, now and forever. And I speak for my husband, too."

Henry nodded and then turned to Betsy. "And you, Miss Bowen, I must have your assurance, too." He pointed to the documents on the desk. "In these papers, you will renounce all claims upon the Wyatt family in consideration for the generous allowance to be made for the child's care. But I must have your word that you will not talk about this arrangement to anyone."

"Talk about it? I want to forget the whole thing. Why else do you think I am leaving Providence? In fact, sir, when you have arranged for my transportation to New York, it is unlikely that you will ever see me again."

Henry stared at her. "I am to pay for your transportation, too?"

"Yes. By packet. Captain Curry's sloop sails on Thursday. The trip to New York by stage would be too bumpy for a woman so recently delivered of a child. Don't you agree?" She smiled at him winningly.

Henry snorted. "I'm damned if you haven't thought of everything! Very well, have it your own way. I'll pay the fare. Now, if you will just sign the paper, our business will be at an end."

Henry picked up the quill pen, dipped it in the inkpot, and handed it to her. She took the pen and leaned toward the desk to sign. Henry's eyes moved irresistibly to her bosom, which was now close enough to touch. The bursting roundness of her breasts as they pushed against her bodice filled him with a feverish lust that he had not felt since he was a young man. It was all he could do to keep from seizing her and ravishing her right there on the floor of his richly appointed upstairs sitting room.

Sighing with relief when she moved away, he was able to say, "Mrs. Ballou, will you sign as witness to our signatures?"

Freelove handed the still-sleeping baby to Betsy and waddled over to the desk, Henry handed her the pen, and she signed her name in the places he directed her to. Then she returned to the sofa and took the baby from Betsy into her arms again.

Betsy went to the desk and looked at Henry gratefully. "Thank you," she said. "May I have my copy of the agreement, if it please you?"

Henry gave it to her and watched her as she read it. Even the sight of Betsy's face was disquieting to him. Her skin, at close range, had a clean and glowing quality, and her eyes, when they looked at him again, shone warmly into his, as though they found him attractive and desirable.

"Before I go," said Betsy softly, "perhaps you would like to look at your grandson? He does resemble Matt—and you."

He had no wish to see the child now or ever, but the invitation offered a possible distraction to dissipate the lust that still burned in him. Unable to speak, he nodded his head.

"Freelove!" called Betsy. "Bring the baby here."

Freelove started the elaborate preparations that always preceded her rising from a chair. She planted her feet far apart, and then, with a series of wagglings and waddlings, managed to rise slowly, like a mammoth goose. She approached them with the mincing steps she reserved for occasions when she must play the lady and came to a halt before the desk.

Henry moved boldly out from behind his fortification and stood awkwardly at her side while she lifted the baby up so that he could see its face. As he peered down at it studiously, the child's eyes opened and gave him a blank blue-eyed stare. Then it began to frown, and Freelove hastily tickled it under the chin with a forefinger to forestall the threatened wail. It turned its eyes to Freelove and smiled Matt's crooked, one-sided smile.

Henry stepped back and looked at Betsy apologetically. "I must ask your forgiveness, Miss Bowen. There is little doubt that the child is a Wyatt. But God willing, none but the three of us will ever know it."

"And Matt," said Betsy.

"And Reuben, of course," added Freelove.

At the mention of Matt's name, the vision of Matt and Betsy together came back to taunt Henry, its young lustiness jeering at his dreary, dried-up middle age, with feelings that lived mostly in the gleaming but lifeless hulls of his ships.

"Well, ladies," he blurted out, "I'll say good evening to you

355

then." For the sake of good manners, he added, "And a calm voyage to you, Miss Bowen."

But Betsy seemed hesitant to leave. "About the packet—I promised to pay Captain Curry the nine dollars tonight."

Henry went swiftly to his desk, opened the drawer where he kept his money box, and took out nine of the newly minted American silver dollars.

As he handed the shining coins to Betsy, she could not help exclaiming, "Oh, real silver coins! How handsome they are!"

Henry nodded and started to move away from her, but she seized him by both arms and in a rush of relief and happiness pulled him to her.

"Oh, thank you, thank you, sir! You are such a kind and generous man, I would be proud to call you father!"

This effusion embarrassed Henry to the point of speechlessness, and the vibrant closeness of her young body was so heady that his senses whirled. He found himself pressing toward her and heard his voice, suddenly that of a stranger, saying, "It is a great pity, lass, that you must go to New York."

Laughing, she drew away from him gently. "Perhaps it is," she said softly. And then, without warning, he felt the moistness of her fresh lips brush the lobe of his ear and heard her voice, low and slightly mocking, say, "Goodbye, my almost-father."

They were gone, and Henry stood dazedly in the middle of the room. As the sound of their departing footsteps came to him from the stair well, he took an impulsive step forward as though to follow them. The feel of Betsy's lips on his ear still lingered. Lust spread through him like a hot acid that dissolved reason and prudence alike, leaving only an imperious need for satisfaction. He would have her, if not now, later. She liked silver. He would give her more, quite a lot more. He ran to the door to call her back, and then stopped in his tracks.

"No! No! No!" he muttered fiercely.

He turned and with frantic, hurrying steps went into his bedroom. He opened the door of a large closet, entered it, and locked himself in. And there, in the stuffy darkness, he tore open his breeches of fine satin, ripping and tearing at the confinement of underclothes. Then with trembling, violent hands he seized himself.

The faint perfume of Betsy's young flesh, the spice of her scent, of the freshly laundered dress she wore, seemed to fill his nostrils like an intoxicating incense. His whole body flamed up in passion, and as the spasm shook him, he whispered hoarsely, "Hussy! Whore-bitch!"

His body sagged against the doorjamb, and he stared down at himself in loathing. He cursed her again. The feel of his wet hand sent a fresh wave of disgust through him.

In a rush of penitence and guilt, he fell to his knees, and with sweat rolling from his brow and down into his eyes, he asked God to forgive him for committing the sin of Onan and to remove all such temptation from his path in the future and ever more, amen.

CHAPTER 33

T HE day Betsy sailed from Providence was one of those late
autumn days when November gives up its gray skies for
a burst of sunlight and chill breezes. The packet *Roger
Williams* had tied up at Hacker's Wharf and was waiting on the
tide for sailing. A brisk wind from the northwest promised fair
weather and a quick voyage to the port of New York.

Betsy had gone aboard early, having already given Captain
Curry the nine shining silver dollars that she had received from
Henry Wyatt for her passage. She had only three dollars and some
change in her purse, barely enough to buy her food and lodging
for a few days in New York. But she was not worried. New York
was, after all, a port, and there would be sailors there who would
be happy to pay for her services.

Freelove and Reuben Ballou had come to say goodbye, and so
had Polly Clarke. Against Betsy's wishes Freelove had insisted on
bringing the baby along. She did not feel that it was proper for
Betsy to leave Providence without kissing George goodbye at the
dock.

George slept contentedly in Freelove's arms. He had been
weaned from Betsy's breast to a bottle containing cow's milk, and
Freelove had already persuaded him to eat soft cornmeal mush
mixed with milk once a day. Freelove objected to weaning a baby
only seven weeks old, but in view of Betsy's precipitate departure
she saw no alternative. And George, who adored Freelove and
responded to her as though she were his real mother, would do
almost anything she wanted him to do.

Betsy was in high spirits now that the sailing day had at last
arrived. She had dressed for the occasion in the green silk dress
that she loved so much, and around her neck was the jade pendant

that Jacques had given her. Because of the chilliness of the weather, she had put on her best winter coat. By wearing it she had not had to pack it.

Her luggage consisted of only one battered but sturdy traveling bag that contained clothing. She had given most of her dresses to Polly, and these, which she had used during her pregnancy, fit Polly's larger figure very well. Reuben had found an old sea bag in the junk that littered the living room. It was large enough to hold all of Jonathan's books, which Betsy insisted on taking with her. Reuben was pleased when he learned that she was also taking the duck decoy he had given her.

Polly came close to tears as the time of sailing drew near. To divert herself, she chattered nervously, regaling Betsy with all the latest town gossip. She detailed the idiosyncrasies of her latest and more genteel customers who lived in fine houses on the hill. Suddenly, in the midst of this recital, she stopped abruptly.

"Oh, Betsy!" she said. "I've gone and forgotten to tell you the most important thing I was going to. It's about Bobby Brown."

Betsy, who had been listening to Polly's ramblings with only half an ear, came to full attention. "What about him?" she asked.

"It looks like he's done for. The pox has caught up with him faster than it usually does. He's got the shakin' palsy, and sometimes he takes fits right there on the street, falls down and foams at the mouth. And his head is always twisted to one side like he's got a stiff neck."

"How can he do his work in a condition like that?"

"He can't. They got a new town sergeant last week. And Nate Mason told me Bobby's eyesight is so bad that he can't hardly find where his drink is at the bar—when he's got the money to pay for one, that is."

Betsy was silent, a grim look about her mouth, and her eyes were hard. At last she said, "I suppose I ought to feel sorry for the poor creature, but I don't. I'm glad. He had it coming." She paused again and added, "Maybe it's like Sam used to say. Thy God is a just God. Michel's death has been avenged." Tears filled her eyes. "But all the vengeance in the world won't bring the sweet lad back to life."

Captain Curry approached them. He touched his hand to his cap in a gesture of apology. "I'm sorry to interrupt you ladies and your goodbyes, but the tide is running full now and we'll be leaving soon. So it's best that visitors go ashore."

He gave Betsy a long and appreciative look that moved from her face to the lines of her body. She intercepted his glance and smiled. Captain Curry became flustered and looked down at his feet in embarrassment.

"Sorry," he said apologetically and walked away quickly.

Now that the moment of parting had come, Polly could no longer hold back her tears and flung her arms around Betsy. "I can't bear to see you go. You're my only real friend."

Freelove said, "And what am I, Polly Clarke? Your mortal enemy?"

Polly smiled. "Oh, no, Freelove. I don't know what I'd do without you and Reuben."

At the mention of his name Reuben shuffled his feet nervously. "There's no sense in long goodbyes, Freelove. Let's be going now."

Betsy had succeeded in consoling Polly. Polly's fit of weeping had begun to subside, but she still clung to Betsy's hand.

Freelove, with the sleeping baby in her arms, went over to Betsy. "It's time to kiss your son goodbye," she said in a stern voice.

Betsy leaned over the infant and kissed him on the mouth. He woke up and looked at her. Then he began to scream. This upset Freelove so much that tears came to her eyes.

Betsy put her arms around Freelove tenderly. "Dear Freelove, how do you thank somebody who has saved your life—and given you your freedom, too?"

"You don't," said Freelove gruffly. "You don't because you don't need to. I know how you feel, dear girl, and words ain't needed."

While the baby continued to wail, Betsy clasped Freelove closer and kissed her full on her nearly toothless mouth.

Reuben had started toward the gangplank, drawing Polly after him. "Come along, now!" His own eyes had misted with tears, much to his embarrassment. "Enough's enough!" he shouted. "Let's get off this blasted boat before we all find ourselves in New York!"

Betsy watched them as they descended the gangplank. Polly was now carrying the baby because she knew that Freelove's weight would make the descent precarious. When they had arrived at the dockside, they all waved, and Betsy waved back. Polly was reluctant to leave, but Reuben took command and marched them all down the street and away.

As their figures, still waving, grew smaller in the distance, Betsy now found herself overwhelmed by tears and stood at the deck rail sobbing. But she was soon distracted by the sounds of departure. The shouts of the captain to the crew as the sails went up to catch the wind made the leave-taking suddenly real to her. A chill ran the length of her spine, and she shivered in anticipation. And when at last the sailors began to push the boat away from the dock with long poles and the *Roger Williams* moved out into the Providence River and headed south toward Narragansett Bay, Betsy gave a sigh of relief. At last she was on her way.

She ignored the presence of the dozen or so other passengers. She stood alone in the bow of the boat, her eyes fastened on the outline of the town. She felt only joy as she watched it grow smaller and smaller on the horizon. By the time the packet passed Fox Point the only thing that she could distinguish was the spire on the Baptist Church, and soon even that was gone. There was no more Providence, Rhode Island.

When the small ship entered Narragansett Bay, Betsy had the feeling that she was surrounded by endless miles of water, even though she could still see land on both sides. She was filled with a sense of freedom such as she had not felt since the night she ran away from Sam in search of her mother. But then, she had felt fear, too. Now she felt only the exultation that she imagined a prisoner must feel when he is released after years in jail.

For the first time in her life complete aloneness did not frighten her. She was dependent on no one except herself. First, she had been tied to her mother, then to Sam, and to Jacques and Matt. Even with Michel, she had never felt free, because his love for her carried with it a sense of responsibility that she did not want. And now, even the last and least tolerable of her bonds had been broken—the child she had so unwillingly borne was no longer hers.

She stood alone at the ship's bow until the light began to fail. The cold of the northwest wind made her button up her coat. The other passengers had long since disappeared from deck. When she heard the sound of a bell and a voice announcing that supper was being served in the galley, she turned and headed for the steps that led to the quarters below.

The supper was a simple one, but the food was plentiful, and Betsy was hungry. She ate a great deal. The other passengers did not interest her. There were five women, two young children, and three men. Ordinarily, she would have been curious about them and would have wanted to know who they were and why they were going to New York. Although she was pleasant and friendly with them all, she said little and remained preoccupied with her thoughts.

There was a sleeping cabin divided into two sections by a curtain separating the men from the women and children. There were no beds, only pallets stuffed with clean straw placed on the floor. Each side had three chamber pots, not only for normal use but for passengers who might become seasick if the voyage turned rough.

Betsy was far too excited to sleep, and by midnight the cabin had become stuffy and foul smelling. Putting on her winter coat, she went up the gangway to the deck. The wind was cold but refreshing, and she again took up her position at the ship's bow. She could still see land on both sides and occasionally a faint glow from a town on the shore.

She was so absorbed by her thoughts that she was not aware that someone was at her side until she felt the touch of an arm against hers. Captain Curry was standing next to her.

"I am sorry," he said. "I didn't mean to startle you. Do you feel seasick?"

"Oh, no. The water is calm. I came on deck because the quarters are a little stuffy. People were snoring and I couldn't sleep."

"Our accommodations," said the Captain, "are not luxurious, but they are warm. It is chilly up here. Aren't you afraid of catching cold?"

"No. I dressed warmly for the voyage. When will we arrive in New York, Captain?"

"If this wind and good weather keeps on, we ought to be there in about eighteen hours. We've already left Narragansett Bay and are heading into Rhode Island Sound."

"I'll be glad when we get there. I'm too excited to sleep."

Captain Curry looked at her in an apologetic but curious way. "May I ask you a question, a sort of personal question?"

"Yes," she said, "but I don't promise to answer it."

"I know that you are Betsy Bowen. Why did you sign on my packet as Miss Eliza Capet?"

She looked at him in the light that came from a starboard lantern. "Because from now on, Captain, I shall *be* Eliza Capet. Betsy Bowen is gone and forgotten, along with all her miseries. I'm starting a new life with a new name."

"Were you so unhappy in Providence?" the Captain asked. "I have heard stories about you, I'll admit, but you always seemed to be so happy, so gay—"

"Those were stories, Captain, and only stories."

He paused, and then, looking her full in the face, he said, "It is very chilly here on deck. Won't you join me in my cabin for a mug of rum?"

"I would like that," said Betsy.

The cabin was warm and comfortable. Betsy was reminded of that night, which seemed so long ago, when she had gone to Jacques' cabin after running away from the Allen house.

Captain Curry poured her a generous portion of rum in a mug and an even more generous portion for himself. He raised his drink in a toast. "I hope that you will find happiness in New York, Miss Bowen—Capet, that is. But I must warn you that it is a wicked city."

"More wicked than Providence?" she asked with a smile.

"Yes, I believe so. But very different. It is not a small town."

"Good!" said Betsy. "I hate small towns."

There was a silence, during which Betsy looked at the Captain more closely. He was a man of perhaps fifty, rather thin and small in stature, but his healthy complexion and brisk movements gave the impression of a man still in his forties. He was not unattractive. She was surprised to note a look of sadness, a pensive expression, in his clear gray eyes. The silence began to be oppressive, and to break it, Betsy said, "And you—you are happy in Providence?"

He did not answer immediately. "I could be, but I am not. I am growing old."

"How old are you, Captain?"

"Fifty-two."

"That's not old. There's something else, surely."

"Yes. Since I'll probably never see you again, I can be honest with you. It is my wife—"

"She does not love you?"

"Oh, yes. She loves me in her way. But she does not want to—to make love with me. She has never liked it, and of late she will not permit it."

"But there are girls in Providence who would welcome your attention—for a small price."

"I know." The Captain became unexpectedly vehement. "But I don't like whores. They're cold. I've tried them, and I—I could not perform the act of love with them."

"I can understand that," said Betsy. "Cold mutton."

He laughed at her phrase, and she joined him.

Then, suddenly quiet, he said, "And so I have become entirely without the ability to—to make love. I am a man old before his time."

"Nonsense!" said Betsy. "The love muscle is like any other. It withers unless it's used."

"You speak God's truth," he said. "You are wise in these matters, I see."

"Let's say that I've had experience—something I'm sure you've heard from the gossips."

"'Tis true," said the Captain, "and when I saw you come aboard, I will admit that my hopes rose that perhaps— Well, to be honest, it's why I looked for you out on deck and why I asked you to come here to my cabin."

His frankness pleased Betsy. "Then you would like to see if you could make love with me?" she asked.

He looked away in embarrassment. When he raised his eyes to hers at last, he said, "You are warm and friendly, not like a whore. With you—"

"Yes, with me, Captain Curry, I think you might be able to make love very well. I must also tell you that at one time I was a whore and made love only for money. At the moment, I am arriving in a strange city with only three dollars in my possession."

He looked at her questioningly. "You are suggesting that you would expect—"

"I would expect, under the circumstances, that if we made love, you would return my passage money to me."

"All of it? The nine dollars?"

"Yes."

He laughed and then said, "That's a very high price. But if you could restore to me the manhood I fear that I've lost, it would be worth many times that."

Betsy said, "I can make no guarantees, Captain, but I'd like to try. I feel confident that I could give you what you are so sadly in need of."

The Captain could restrain himself no longer. He moved quickly to her and took her in his arms. He kissed her with passion, and she did not find it difficult to respond. She felt sorry for this little man who had so frankly and sadly confessed his need of love. She had not lain with a man since Michel's death, and when they began making love, there was an urgency in her response that surprised her.

Captain Curry restored faith in what he called his manhood not once but three times. When at last Betsy began to get dressed, he sat on the edge of his bunk and watched her in admiration.

"You are very beautiful," he said.

She turned to him and smiled. "Thank you, Captain."

"I wish you would call me Bill. And are you sure that you cannot spend the night here?"

"No—Bill. I must get some rest even if I can't sleep."

He got up then and drew on his breeches. When she had finished dressing and had put on her coat, she turned at the door and looked back at him expectantly.

Captain Curry moved quickly to his desk. "I was forgetting," he said. "I promised to return your fare." He opened a drawer and fumbled in his money box. He counted out nine silver dollars and went over to her.

As he placed the coins in her outstretched hand, he said, "What you have done for me, Eliza, is worth much more than nine dollars."

"You are a fine man and a good lover, you may be sure." She was staring at the nine silver dollars in her hand. "You may think it daft of me, Bill, but could you give me the nine shiny new dollars I paid you in place of these?"

He laughed, took the coins from her, and returned to his money box. He searched until he had found the nine newly minted dollars. He went back to her and dropped the coins, one by one, into her hand.

"Thank you," she said. "They're so pretty when they're new and shining, don't you think so?"

"I suppose so, but money is money, after all."

As she placed her hand on the knob of the door, he said, "Eliza, tell me, shall I ever see you again—in New York, I mean? I make the trip at least once a week, sometimes twice when the weather is fine."

"I would like that," said Betsy. "But meanwhile, why don't you go to Sally Marshall's place on Olney Lane and ask for Polly Clarke? She's a good friend of mine and a warmhearted girl."

"Like you?"

"More warmhearted than me, I think."

"But not as beautiful. I've never met anyone as beautiful as you. But if I tried to find you in New York, I wouldn't know where to look."

As Betsy opened the door, she said, "Go to whatever place the whores go to—near the ships probably. You'll find me there, at least for the time being. Good night, Bill, and thank you."

She opened the door quickly and left. But she did not return to the sleeping quarters below. She went up the gangway to the deck. But now, she did not go to the bow of the ship. She placed herself as near to the prow as passengers were allowed and looked straight ahead. She knew it was impossible, but she was looking for the lights of New York on the southern horizon.

"New York!" she whispered, and the sound of the words quickened the beating of her heart. And there, standing at the rail and looking out at the sea and the stars, she began once more to spin her dreams of glory.

EPILOGUE

O N an evening in May 1808, Madame Stephen Jumel had given one of her sumptuous dinner parties in her large house on fashionable Whitehall Street in New York City. The dinner had been, as usual, beautifully prepared by Jean, her *chef de cuisine*, and it had been elegantly served on a gold-encrusted set of china that Madame herself had bought during her last visit to Paris.

Because the guest of honor was the Comtesse de la Pagerie, the evening had been more festive than usual. The Comtesse had entertained everyone with the exciting and often humorous story of her escape from France just before the Revolution.

Sixteen guests had been seated at the large dining table, over which hung a magnificent crystal chandelier with a myriad of glass pendants sparkling prismatically in the glow of the many candles in the silver candelabra lining the walls.

But now, the party was coming to an end, and Stephen and Eliza Jumel stood at the door bidding farewell to their departing guests. Eliza, regally gowned in a dress of dark-green satin trimmed with Belgian lace, was so youthfully beautiful that she would scarcely have been taken for a woman of thirty-two. Her lithe and voluptuous figure moved with grace, and the gestures of her small bejeweled hands expressed natural refinement and good breeding.

One by one, the coaches that lined Whitehall Street drew up before the entrance to the handsome house of yellow brick, while a footman in livery announced the name of the coach's owner.

The Comtesse de la Pagerie had been one of the first guests to arrive and was now one of the last to leave. A little the worse for too much champagne, she embraced Eliza effusively and a bit unsteadily. Then, with an impish grin on her lined face, she stepped back and regarded her hostess. "*Dites-moi,*" she said, "tell me, *ma chérie,* where is your so charming *friend* Mr. Burr?"

The politely social smile on Eliza's face disappeared instantly, her figure straightening in quick tension. The question had taken her by surprise, and momentarily she was at a loss for words.

"Mr. Burr?" she repeated, as though she had never heard the name. "Oh, you mean Aaron Burr, I suppose." She paused and then, shrugging her shoulders, added, "Why, he is still somewhere in the South, I imagine."

The Comtesse was persistent. "But you receive a letter from him sometimes, yes?"

"No. Why should I?"

The Comtesse smiled sadly. "But then, *bien entendu.* He is so many times in jail for treason that *peut-être* he has not the time for writing. But I am happy that he is always—how do you say—"

"Acquitted," said Eliza and quickly added in a coldly critical voice, "Really, Comtesse, you must study harder at your English lessons. I wish you a pleasant good evening."

She abruptly turned her back on the Comtesse to say good night to the last of the guests. Then she walked slowly toward the silk-curtained doorway of the front sitting room. She heard the front door close and the sound of its being bolted for the night by one of the footmen.

When Stephen appeared in the doorway, she was sitting wearily in the newly acquired Empire chair upholstered in blue damask. There was a look of concern on his face as he went over to her.

"You are very tired, *ma chère* Eliza," he said softly. When she nodded, he said, "Is it *vraiment* necessary that you go to Providence tomorrow? Why not rest for a day and go on Thursday?"

"That's not possible, dear Stephen. As it is, I will barely arrive in time for the funeral. The letter did not come until today."

"This Captain Carpenter, who has died, he must have been a very good friend."

Eliza looked thoughtful. "He was more a friend of my family's and came often to our house on Benefit Street. Now that my mother and father are both gone, I feel it is my duty to be there."

Stephen smiled at her tenderly. "You are a good woman, and more than that, you are a woman very *têtue.*"

"*Têtue?*"

"What you call—stubborn. But I do not mind."

He had learned in their eight years together that when Eliza made up her mind to do something, she did it, with or without his help or assent. But he admired this quality in her. Clinging and fragile women had never had any appeal for him.

"I will take the coach," said Eliza, yawning, "and the four black horses. That will make the journey faster."

"See how tired you are? If you are leaving at dawn, you had best go to bed *tout de suite*."

Eliza smiled, rising from the chair. "*D'accord*, my sweet husband."

Arm in arm, they went up the ornate staircase together. When they had kissed each other good night and Eliza had reached her bedroom, she went to the side table near her large, silk-curtained four-poster bed. Opening the drawer, she took the letter from where she had concealed it.

With a slight frown on her face, she reread it. The letter was signed "Freelove Ballou," and there was no mention in it of a Captain Carpenter or his death.

In Providence four days later, Eliza Jumel, exquisite in a dress of cobalt blue, imported from Paris, descended the grand staircase at the Golden Ball. She passed the liveried footman who stood in attendance at the newel post. As he bowed, she inclined her head graciously.

"I beg pardon, Madame," said the footman, "but I am not sure you will wish to see the woman who is waiting in the sitting room. She is poorly dressed and—"

"I sent for her to come, monsieur," said Madame quietly, "and I would like the curtain drawn so that we may converse in private."

"Yes, Madame," said the footman, as he ushered her toward the small sitting room at the right of the stairs. Then he announced, "Madame Stephen Jumel will see you now, miss." He left quickly, pulling the curtain that closed off the entrance to the room.

Polly Clarke stared in disbelief at the resplendent and beautiful woman who stood before her. She opened her mouth to speak but could not.

Eliza laughed gaily. "Polly, whatever be the matter with you?

You're still my dearest friend, though my name is no longer Betsy Bowen."

With that, Eliza threw her elegant manners to the winds, pulled Polly to her, and encircled her with her arms in a hug that expressed more than just recognition of an old friend.

When Polly drew herself away and stood looking at Eliza, her face was wet with tears. At last, fumbling for words, she said, "Madame—I—"

"Enough of the Madame nonsense. To you I shall always be Betsy Bowen, whose bastard child you helped to birth fourteen years ago."

"But you've become such a lady—and even more beautiful now than you were at nineteen. How did you ever get to be so—so—But it's none of my business."

Eliza laughed. "Why not? It's very simple. In 1800 I met a Frenchman named Stephen Jumel, a rich wine merchant, and the most sought after bachelor in New York."

"And you got him!"

"Truth to tell, Polly, it wasn't that easy. I lived with him as his mistress for four years and then—" Eliza paused and chuckled as though at a secret joke. "Well, I persuaded him to marry me."

"And now you are happy and rich!"

"Rich," said Eliza pensively, "and almost happy."

Eliza's face turned toward the little girl who was standing at Polly's side. The child was pretty and about seven years old. She stared at Eliza in wonderment.

"But tell me, Polly, who is this lovely little girl?"

" 'Tis me daughter, Mary Bownes."

"So you are married, then?" asked Eliza.

Polly bowed her head. "No. David Bownes left me a month after Mary was born." Polly choked back a sob of shame.

This sent her into a fit of coughing that continued for several moments. At the end of it, she spat into her kerchief, and Eliza noticed that the sputum was streaked with blood.

"Polly! You are sick! Have you seen Dr. Bentham?" She had suddenly remembered Lydia's fatal illness, the coughing and the blood.

"No. I ain't got the money," said Polly, still struggling to regain her breath. "Anyway, 'tis nothing. When the warm weather comes—"

"Come, lie down on the sofa for a while, and we can talk." Eliza turned to the child. "And you, Mary Bownes, would you like to sit on my lap?"

Mary nodded her head eagerly and climbed onto Eliza's lap. Eliza hugged the child to her and then turned once more to Polly.

"You've lost a lot of weight," she said.

Polly smiled. "The men find me more attractive now that I am thin. But let's talk about you and the fine lady you've become. Why would you ever want to come back to Providence?"

"For two reasons. One was you. Freelove wrote me that you were sickly and in need. The other reason—" She paused and clasped Mary more tightly to her bosom. "The other reason has to do with my son. Freelove wrote that since Reuben died six years ago, the boy has had to give up school and go to work."

"Yes," said Polly. "He went to Deacon John Dexter's school until he was eight, and then, after Reuben died, he tried working for two or three farmers, but the boy never did take to farm work. It seems like he's happier now. He has Danny Woodhull's old job, peddling water crackers from a wheelbarrow for Mr. Weeden, the baker. He's still living with Freelove."

"I know." Eliza cradled Mary still more closely in her arms and added, "I would like to take him home with me."

Eliza's last words had a strange effect on Polly. She got up from the couch abruptly and said, "Well, Betsy love, I'd best be goin' now." She reached out to take Mary from Eliza's lap, but Mary seemed reluctant to leave.

"Mama, I like this pretty lady," she said.

"But you like your own mama better, don't you?" asked Eliza. As the child nodded her head vigorously, Eliza's eyes filled with tears.

Polly moved tentatively toward the door, with Mary's hand in her own. When Eliza went over to her to say goodbye, she pressed several gold coins into Polly's hand.

"Betsy! I did not come to see you for money!" Polly's voice rose in anger as she said, "Take it back!"

"I am not a fool, Polly Clarke!" said Eliza in annoyance. "I well know that you didn't come here for money. But you are going to take it because you need it and I can well afford it."

"But I am your friend, and I cannot—"

Eliza's voice became imperious. "You will take it, and that's an end on it!" It was a voice that Polly scarcely recognized, the voice of a woman who was used to giving commands and having them obeyed. "And furthermore, dearest Polly, you will give me your promise that you will go see Dr. Bentham this very afternoon! You must become well again!"

Polly, still awed by the tone of Eliza's voice, was silent.

"Long ago, I told you I would repay you for your kindness to me, for the loving friendship you gave to me when I was sorely in need of it. And the debt is not yet fully paid."

Polly, so overcome by emotion that she could not even say thank you, fled from the room in tears. Eliza, lost in thought and memories, stood looking after her. She was suddenly aware that Mary was still there, tugging at her skirt.

"Why did you make my mama cry?" she asked.

Eliza knelt down and placed her hand on the child's cheek. "Because—because she is my oldest friend and I gave her some money. Can you understand that?"

Mary pondered this. "I don't know why Mama should cry about that. We are very poor, and we need money."

"You're a bright little girl, Mary Bownes." On impulse she hugged the child to her and kissed her.

At last, Mary moved to the door. "Well, goodbye. I must go to Mama now." She paused before leaving. "You are a very nice lady, I think. Especially because you smell so good."

Eliza smiled, but as soon as the child had left, her own eyes again filled with tears.

Later that afternoon, Eliza walked along Benefit Street on her way to see Freelove Ballou. The street had changed very little in fourteen years. As she passed the Allen house, a wave of melancholy nostalgia swept over her, but she shrugged it off with impatience. She had learned not to dwell on past unhappiness and to turn her mind to the day before her. And today, she told herself, an old dream was becoming a reality. She was walking down Benefit Street as a rich and renowned woman.

The townspeople who passed looked at her in astonishment. Some of them recognized her. If they smiled at her in a friendly way, she smiled back. If they averted their eyes, she raised her head and walked on proudly.

The Ballou house on Charles Street seemed even more dilapidated than Eliza remembered it. As she walked up the path to the door, she found herself hoping that Freelove would not be lying comatose in her bedroom the way she had once found her.

She knocked loudly on the door, and soon there was a sound of footsteps inside. The door opened, and Freelove stood before her. She stared at Eliza for a moment. Then her mouth dropped open in a toothless grin and she stepped forward to embrace her.

"My God, it's Betsy! Damned if you don't look like you *are* George Washington's daughter!"

Eliza smiled. "Now that's a fine way to greet me! Aren't you even going to give me a kiss?"

"No. My face is all dirty."

Eliza seized Freelove by the arms and planted a firm kiss on her dust-begrimed face. They hugged each other then and finally went into the big cluttered downstairs room to the hearth. Freelove set about brewing some tea and stirred up the fire to toast some johnnycake. Meanwhile, she chattered away, enumerating the deaths of people Eliza had known.

Bobby Brown had died of the pox in 1796. A year later, her sister, Polly, had gotten pregnant by Richard Wyatt and had died of an abortion. Not long after that, the news came to Providence that Phebe and Jonathan had perished during a plague of yellow fever in Williamston, North Carolina.

"North Carolina!" said Eliza. "How did they get there?"

"Walked, I s'pose. They was always wanderers, you know, always figgerin' their luck would change if they moved someplace else. And then my Reuben—the Lord took him to his bosom on April 3, 1802. He died easy and no pain. He was drunk, of course, God bless him."

Eliza's eyes were full of tears, and she blew her nose gently on her perfumed silk handkerchief. At last she said, "I hope they all died easy and no pain—even my poor sister."

After Freelove had served the tea and johnnycake, she sat down wearily in a chair opposite Eliza. "Well, anyway, I still keep a-goin', God knows why. I lost a lot of weight. That's because Dr. Bentham told me if I kept at the rum like I was doin' I'd join Reuben in the graveyard in less than a year. He said my liver was swoll up like a millstone. So I gave it up."

"Entirely?" asked Eliza incredulously.

"Well, I take a little nip now and then when the rheumatism hurts bad."

There was a brief silence, and then Eliza leaned forward tensely in her chair. "I came because I got your letter about Polly and George. Why didn't you write me before now?"

"How was I to know you was the great Madame Jumel? Nobody ever told me until just two weeks ago. I was talkin' to Captain Curry and he said you was the talk of New York, and your name was Madame Jumel and you lived on Whitehall Street. Is it true that Mr. Burr and Mr. Hamilton fought that duel over you?"

Eliza, ignoring the question, said, "I saw Polly this morning and she told me that George had to leave school and go to work right after Reuben died. Didn't Mr. Wyatt hold to our agreement?"

"Oh, he would have, if he'd lived. But he died right after my Reuben did."

"But surely Matt would have—"

"Maybe. But Matt and the old man quarreled, and the old man cut him off without a cent. Matt's a lawyer in town now. He's had a hard time gettin' ahead, and he couldn't keep up the payments, that's all."

Eliza said nothing. How strange, she thought to herself, that Matt had been disinherited after all. She might have been pleased by this news, except that it had caused George to leave school and go to work.

"And George? How is he?" she asked at last.

Freelove turned her head away and for a moment did not answer. "He lives here, and he's working for Mr. Weeden," she said briefly. Then she added, after a pause, "He hates you, Betsy—

says you deserted him. I didn't even tell him you'd be here because he wouldn't have come home if he knew. He ought to be here any minute now." She paused. "Maybe you better leave, Betsy."

"No," said Eliza. "I'll wait."

About half an hour later, George Washington Bowen stood before Eliza, staring at her coldly and appraisingly. A good-looking, stockily built boy of fourteen, he had scarcely acknowledged Freelove's nervous introduction. He had Matt's thoughtful gray eyes and her own red-gold hair, which framed his freckled face.

Eliza was aware of the cold insolence with which he regarded her, and she was nervous. Her voice, when she spoke, quavered. "George," she said at last, "I would like to take you home with me to New York and right the wrong I have done you."

The boy still stared at her but said nothing.

"I know how you must feel," she said. "But I'd like to explain to you why I left you—"

The boy interrupted her. "There ain't nothin' to explain," he said tonelessly.

"But I'm your mother."

"Freelove is my mother."

She played what she hoped would be her trump card. "I am rich now, George. I can offer you advantages, education, a lovely home—" She paused, and then, drawing herself up, she added, "I am now Madame Stephen Jumel."

A corner of George's mouth turned up in Matt's one-sided smile. "You're nothin' but a stinkin' whore! And I don't want to see you again—not ever!" He cleared his throat and spat at her feet. Then he turned and ran out of the house.

Eliza sat down quietly in her chair.

Freelove, her face streaming with tears, went over to her. "Oh, Betsy, my poor darling, I knew this would happen." She put her arms around Eliza in an effort to console her, as she had done so many times before.

Eliza did not cry. At first she was too stunned even to speak, but when she did, her voice was steady and calm. "It is only what I deserve," she said. "The only mother's love he has known came

375

from you, dear Freelove. The boy spoke truly. You *are* his mother. I'm leaving now." Eliza got up and moved toward the door.

Freelove followed her, a pleading look on her face. "But, Betsy, where are you going?"

"To see Matt. If he cannot afford to support our child, then I will. It's the least I can do. Where does Matt live?"

"It's a small house on Powder House Lane, just where it bends to go into Old Gaol Lane."

Eliza smiled at the mention of Old Gaol Lane. "Not a very fancy part of town, is it?"

"Well, it's not Benefit Street. But like I told you, he's had a hard time. They say he's too fond of the bottle. But I could hardly blame him. That wife of his is a shrew. The house is painted white." Freelove grinned. "For purity, no doubt."

Eliza paused at the door. "I want you to listen to me carefully now, Freelove. There will be a monthly allotment for you and George. And Polly Clarke—she's not well. Make sure that she sees the doctor, and if she is ever in need, write to me. You know my name and address now."

Freelove threw her arms around Eliza and began crying again. "God bless you, my girl. Even if you're not Washington's daughter—and maybe you are—you got a noble and generous heart. And George—"

"You are not to scold him, Freelove." Eliza's voice again took on the commanding, imperious tone. "I want you to promise not to tell him that I am helping him and you."

"I promise," said Freelove tearfully. Eliza gently disentangled herself from Freelove's embrace. She said goodbye and then started up the path to the street.

As she turned her steps once again toward Benefit Street, she took a deep breath and walked quickly, in a quietly determined fashion.

Eliza turned off Benefit Street and into Powder House Lane. When she knocked on the door of Matt Wyatt's house, a servant girl appeared. She looked at Eliza in awe. Then she curtsied and said, "Oh, yes, ma'am."

"Will you kindly tell Mr. Wyatt that Madame Stephen Jumel is here to see him on urgent business?"

Eliza entered the small hall, while the girl disappeared upstairs. From somewhere in the rear of the house there came the sound of a baby's wailing.

Matt descended the stairs slowly, a puzzled frown on his face. As he reached the entrance hallway, Eliza rose to greet him. He stared at her, and it was a few seconds before he recognized her.

"Betsy! What are you doing here? The girl said a fine lady, a Madame Somebody-or-other—"

"I am Madame Stephen Jumel now, Matt."

Matt was still recovering from the shock of seeing her. He said nervously, "Won't you please come into the sitting room so that we can talk?"

Eliza, thoroughly at ease, sat down in the chair Matt offered her. She folded her skirt gracefully about her and then looked at him in a curious way as he moved to a chair opposite her. For a man of thirty-seven he was still very attractive and easily recognizable as the man she once had loved, although he had put on some weight, his hair was thinning, and the boyish look had all but disappeared except when he smiled. His face was tired and careworn, but at this moment it wore an expression of animation and interest.

He leaned toward her and studied her intently. "You were always beautiful, Betsy, but now—now you are more beautiful than ever."

"Thank you, Matt." She looked about the room, which was comfortably but not expensively furnished. "I was sorry to learn that things hadn't been going too well for you."

"Not as well as I had hoped. I quarreled with my father two years before he died. I was a fool. It began with an argument about nothing really. I was hotheaded, said some daft and thoughtless things. And then I was too proud to apologize."

"And so you ended by being disinherited"—she paused for emphasis—"anyway."

"Yes." He was silent. There was a thoughtful look on his face. "As things turned out, I could have married you, as I wanted to—"

"But you didn't want to enough," said Eliza. The tone of her voice was not critical, merely factual.

"I suppose so. But I still wish—well, I wish I had."

"Your marriage is not a happy one?"

"I am married to a women who thinks of nothing but her house, her clothes, and her children. She is a nagger and a shrew."

Eliza smiled faintly. "At least she is a good mother."

Matt shrugged his shoulders. "Yes. But to me—well, she is not a loving, affectionate woman." He leaned forward in his chair and his gray eyes looked straight into hers. "I am still a passionate man, Betsy."

There was no mistaking the look in his eyes. It stirred unexpected and unwanted memories in her, and she looked away quickly.

"I came here, Matt," she said hastily, "to talk about our son, George."

The remark had its intended dampening effect on him. He sat back in his chair and said, "Yes. I expected that you had. My father left no provision for the boy in his will, and my brothers flatly refused to continue the payments for his support."

"And you?" asked Eliza.

"I was finding it difficult to support myself and my family. I had only begun to practice law. Times were hard, and my wife doesn't know about our child."

"And I suppose it is she who manages the finances?" asked Eliza with a suggestion of mockery in her voice.

"Well, as a matter of fact, she does. And if she doesn't get her way about things, she flies into a tantrum."

Eliza smiled ironically. "Somehow, Matt, I'd never have thought of you as a henpecked husband." She paused, and her voice took on a businesslike tone. "But now I gather that your income is much better. Will you be able to take over the responsibility for George?"

Matt was silent. He stared at the floor in embarrassment. "It would be extremely—difficult. Anyway, I believe the boy is working now for Mr. Weeden, the baker. After all, he is fourteen."

"And his education?" asked Eliza.

"I'm afraid I cannot help there, either. It's not just the money. It's the gossip—"

Eliza rose quickly. "Well, have no fear, Matt. I am very well-to-do now, and I will take over the whole responsibility." She moved toward the door, and Matt followed her.

"I am sorry, Betsy. I am truly sorry."

"Never mind," she said softly. "It is not the first time that you've disappointed me, Matt."

He reached out to her, almost in desperation. "Betsy, please don't go. Wait a moment. I still love you—I —"

He moved to her quickly, seized her in his arms and kissed her with passion. Eliza, against her will, found herself responding. The memory of their old love became suddenly alive and vivid. But she pulled herself away from him.

"Betsy," he said, "you cannot leave like this. Say that you will see me again."

"I'm leaving for New York tomorrow—in my coach."

"Then tonight," he implored. "We can at least have dinner together."

As Eliza reached the door, she turned toward him. "Very well, Matt. I am stopping at the Golden Ball. Meet me there at nine."

As he opened the door for her to leave, he seized her hand again and kissed it. "Oh, Betsy, thank God you've come back! This is a stroke of good fortune that I don't deserve!"

"No," said Eliza slowly, "you don't."

As she walked down the steps to the street, Matt still stood in the doorway, his eyes following her every movement. When she reached the gate, she turned, waved, and gave him one of her most dazzling smiles.

That night, at ten minutes before nine, Matt went to the Golden Ball. He was dressed in his finest clothes—a plum-colored waistcoat and a shirt with ruffles down the front. His hair was neatly combed and shone with imported French pomade.

He approached the liveried head footman confidently, and there was a note of condescension in his voice. "I should like to see Madame Jumel," he said.

"Madame Jumel is not here," said the footman.

"But of course she is here. She is stopping here while in Providence."

"Yes, sir. But she left in her coach at six o'clock to return to New York."

Matt stared at the footman in stunned disbelief. At last he stammered, "But she was going to have dinner with me. Perhaps she left a note?"

"No, sir. Nothing. She just went. She seemed to be in a great hurry."

Turning, Matt went through the doorway to the street. He suddenly remembered her words of that afternoon when he had said that this was a stroke of good fortune that he did not deserve. "No, you don't," she had answered. And she had meant it.

He laughed ironically and said softly, "The bitch!"

He wanted to get drunk, and quickly. He comforted himself with the thought that there would be women at the Bulldog Tavern, available women to ease the consuming disappointment that filled him.

Yes, there would always be women. But none of them would be Betsy, the only woman he had ever loved.

AUTHOR'S NOTE

The main outlines of the early life of Betsy Bowen, or Eliza Jumel, as I have recounted them, are true. There are only two invented characters—even the monkey, Danton, existed.

My own interpretation of Eliza herself is fiction. Many parts of her life remain a mystery. Only a handful of her letters survive and they reveal only that she was literate, though hardly literary. If she kept a journal or diary, it has never been found. Even the Mémin miniature portrait of her, labeled "Madame de la Croix," may not be she, although in all probability it is.

I have read far too many books about the social life and customs of Providence (1785–1794) for individual mention here. For help in my research I am greatly indebted to: The Rhode Island Historical Society in Providence; The Library of the New York Academy of Medicine; W. H. Shelton's "Clues to the Enigma of Madame Jumel's Life," New York *Times*, May 13, 1928, and *The Jumel Mansion;* and Edwin D. Mead's "Historic Towns of New England."

But most of all, I am grateful to William Cary Duncan, whose biography *The Amazing Madame Jumel* is the definitive work on her life, especially in its separation of the facts from the many fictions that have clustered about this astonishing woman. Many of the fictions, it should be noted, were invented by Eliza herself to enhance the already romantic legend that she became in her lifetime.

Last of all, I wish to thank Mrs. Betty Gibbons for her invaluable assistance in preparing the manuscript.